RECTIFY INJUSTICE

RECTIFY INJUSTICE

EXCEPTIONAL S. BEAUFONT™ BOOK 6

SARAH NOFFKE

MICHAEL ANDERLE

DISRUPTIVE IMAGINATION

Copyright © 2020 LMBPN Publishing
Cover by Mihaela Voicu http://www.mihaelavoicu.com/
Cover copyright © LMBPN Publishing
A Michael Anderle Production

LMBPN Publishing
PMB 196, 2540 South Maryland Pkwy
Las Vegas, NV 89109

First US Edition, June 2020
Version 1.03, June 2021
eBook ISBN: 978-1-64202-952-9
Print ISBN: 978-1-64202-953-6

THE RECTIFY INJUSTICE TEAM

Thanks to the JIT Readers

Angel LaVey
Dave Hicks
Deb Mader
Debi Sateren
Diane L. Smith
Dorothy Lloyd
Jackey Hankard-Brodie
Jeff Eaton
Kelly O'Donnell
Kerry Mortimer
Larry Omans
Paul Westman
Peter Manis
Veronica Stephan-Miller

If we've missed anyone, please let us know!

Editor
The Skyhunter Editing Team

For Diane H, whose support has meant so much. And for all the stickers!

— Sarah

To Family, Friends and
Those Who Love
to Read.
May We All Enjoy Grace
to Live the Life We Are
Called.

— Michael

CHAPTER ONE

Death by a thousand cuts would be a kinder death than what Trin Currante had planned for the man who had "recreated" her.

As blood trickled down the face of the scientist currently bound in the chair before her, she smiled outwardly. The sight of blood had never bothered her. Staring down at her arms, which were covered in bolts and wires, she grimaced. No, blood didn't bother her. She had a lot less of it than she should. Her body was made of metal, which grossed her out. It was unnatural and wrong, and the means by which it happened was far from ethical. Now Trin Currante was that much closer to finding the man behind what had been done to her.

Mika Lenna.

The light overhead created shadows on the prisoner's face. The scientist Trin Currante had abducted spit out blood and a broken tooth that landed on the floor at her feet. She eyed it casually before bringing her chin up, the movement always marked by a motorized sound.

This was the man who had done this to her. She remembered looking up from the operating table and seeing his cold gray eyes over the mask after being abducted. On Mika Lenna's orders, he'd taken out her perfectly functioning organs and replaced them with magitech, turning her into the cyborg that she was.

Alexander Drake, one of the scientists Trin Currante had captured from the Saverus Corporation, for as worthless as he was had finally proven helpful. He had been the only scientist who didn't get away when she stormed the place, looking for Mika Lenna and answers.

The other scientists, along with Mika Lenna, had taken underground tunnels to flee, their plan if they were ever invaded by one of their "creations." Unluckily for him, Drake had been in the bathroom when the sirens sounded, marking Trin Currante's invasion.

If she had known those sirens cued a protocol that erased all research data and procedures, Trin Currante wouldn't have come into Saverus with guns blazing. Someone hit the alarm, and no one stayed to fight her. They all fled. All but Drake.

He hadn't been on the cyborg projects entirely, only assisting, and therefore, he couldn't help to fix her, although reluctantly, he had advised. It was easy to encourage him since she had broken most of the bones in his hand during their initial conversation. Now he worked for her, maybe out of fear, but she wanted to believe also out of guilt. It was because of him she knew when the dragon eggs hatched that she'd need the blood of a young good and evil dragon. Those were gone now, and she needed a new strategy.

Drake had come through, informing her after her hundredth time asking him to remember anything of use, that Samuel Jacobs ate a specific hot sauce manufactured and sold at a boutique store in Los Angeles. Samuel Jacobs was the man who had performed the surgery that ruined her life.

The cyborg knew she should do a stakeout at the hot sauce shop until she saw Samuel Jacobs, and follow him until he led her back to the new headquarters for the Saverus Corporation. Since the change, she hadn't been good at controlling her temper.

When she saw the soulless gray-haired man enter the store to get his favorite hot sauce, her rage got the best of her. On his way out of the shop, she attacked him and abducted him the same way they'd taken her, gagged and bound.

Trin Currante had been so patient, biding her time as the librarian for the Great Library, waiting to secure the information she needed to reverse what had been done to her. She'd practiced delayed gratification every step of the way toward her recovery and retribution. When she saw the man who remade her, something took over. Something she couldn't resist.

Now Samuel Jacobs was sitting in front of her, covered in his own blood, more dead than alive in a darkened room that often bobbed up and down, since they were on a ship.

Trin Currante knew how it felt. That was every day for her. The Saverus Corporation had made her into a machine when she had once been a perfectly functioning magician. And why?

According to Alexander Drake, Mika Lenna had an obsession with making monsters. The Finnish billionaire had a company before the Saverus Corporation that made genetically altered werewolves. The place, Olento Research, had abducted men and turned them into monsters, all because Mika Lenna wanted to see if he could do it, and because he had investors who wanted deadly assassins.

The project had gone to hell when the subjects escaped and rebelled. Mika Lenna, in an effort to become the alpha wolf and get his "projects" back, had dosed himself with the most powerful drug meant to make him a werewolf. It took him over and killed him. Or so they thought.

According to Alexander Drake, Mika Lenna wasn't even close to dead, but since his heart wasn't beating, he was issued a death certificate and buried. Bad men have a way of coming back from the dead. In Mika Lenna's case, he clawed up from his grave and returned to the world he wasn't happy in unless he was mutilating something.

Trin Currante had to give it to him. Mika Lenna was a survivor. He'd been able to come back from nothing and start the Saverus Corporation, again abducting innocent people, magicians this time, and turn them into cyborgs. He did it to hundreds of them.

SARAH NOFFKE & MICHAEL ANDERLE

Why wasn't even the question for Trin Currante. She just wanted to know where this diabolical mad man was so she could destroy him and everything he valued. There was no way she was stopping until she brought Mika Lenna down.

The man had survived for this long because he knew how to hide, and was great at running. However, she had the one person who could lead her to him—his head scientist—Samuel Jacobs.

Lowering her face and pressing it into his, she narrowed her eyes, looking into his rimmed with blood. "Tell me where the new Saverus headquarters is."

Samuel Jacobs shook his head, his face swelling from the beating he's endured.

She grabbed his chin with her metal hand, gripping it so tightly she could feel the bones ready to give way. He didn't even moan, although she knew the pain had to be excruciating. "You realize I'll kill you if you don't tell me, right?" she asked through gritted teeth.

Again, he shook his head but tried to move his jaw. She released him, but only so he could talk.

"There are things worse than death," he said, bubbles of blood spilling from his mouth.

She laughed. "Like living your life looking like a freak no one can understand." Trin Currante motioned to her body. She used to be beautiful, with high cheekbones and voluptuous hips. Now her black hair was mostly live wires that danced around her head and bits of metal peeking out from the skin on her face.

Samuel Jacobs narrowed his swollen eyes at her. "No, like your entire family being punished if you so much as breathe a word about where the Saverus Corporation or Mika Lenna is located."

Trin Currante blew out a breath. So that's how Mika Lenna was maintaining secrecy. Of course.

If threatened, most would talk. Life was the most precious thing in the world. Family for many trumped that. Hostages would talk if afraid their lives hung in the balance. The one thing that ensured compliance if they were captured by the enemy was not to kill them but threaten their families if they talked.

4

Trin Currante considered threatening to find Samuel Jacobs' family. She'd beat Mika Lenna to it. Jacobs would have to pick Trin Currante if she was the one making the bold threats.

She couldn't do it.

Innocent people shouldn't have to die for her to take down an evil corporation. That's the way she wanted it, anyway. She'd already had to do despicable things to the Dragon Elite, and they hadn't even worked. Which was one reason she was here interrogating the man who'd made her. Alexander Drake had figured out that even if they had the freshly hatched dragon's blood, he didn't know the formula to fix her. Only Mika Lenna would know that, and the one person who could tell her where to find him wasn't talking.

They'd been at this for hours, and Samuel Jacobs wasn't any closer to telling her than he was in the beginning. Now Trin Currante realized why. He was going to take the beating, knowing it would probably result in his death.

Looking at his face covered in blood didn't bring her satisfaction anymore. Deforming him with assaults hadn't been as rewarding as she thought. Trin Currante reasoned that was because whatever they'd done to her at Saverus, she still had her soul.

Lowering her face, she looked into Samuel Jacobs' eyes.

"You won't tell me where Mika Lenna is or why he did what he did," she began, turning off her olfactory senses, not wanting to smell his stink. "Tell me why you did it. Those might be the last words you ever speak, so make them good."

He looked at her, a sadistic smile on his face. "That's where you're wrong. I will tell you why Mika did it. Simple. He's sick like that. Me? Well, I did it for the money."

The rage took over her. Trin Currante's metal hand reached out without her permission. It wrapped around his neck, and with a force no human could survive, her hand jerked swiftly, breaking his neck with a horrible popping sound.

Samuel Jacobs' chin fell forward as the scientist died instantly.

Trin Currante backed for the door, horrified by what she'd done and also surprised she hadn't done it earlier.

She shook her head at the dead man before her. "You are sick too," Trin Currante said, motioning to her body. "No amount of money would make a sane person do this to another."

CHAPTER TWO

"I think he knows," Sophia said to Wilder, who sat close to her at the dining table.

Ainsley laughed as she came through the swinging door from the kitchen. "You think? Of course, that dumb Viking knows you two are an item. Hiker totally saw you guys snogging on the Expanse."

Quiet, who was trotting behind the housekeeper carrying a tray of pastries, mumbled something.

Another laugh popped out of Ainsley's mouth. "Oh, good one. That's my new favorite nickname for Angry Beard."

"What is it?" Wilder asked, an amused expression on his face.

Ainsley set a platter of sautéed spinach onto the table, looking at it proudly. "You'll just have to wait until I unveil it." The housekeeper was obviously still pissed at Hiker for breaking her heart centuries ago and lying to her about who she was, making her the housekeeper for the Castle when she lost her memories and nearly died.

"Spinach for breakfast?" Sophia questioned. "That's a bit unusual."

The elf took the tray from Quiet and laid it on the table next to a bowl of cream of wheat and a plate of pickled beets.

Wilder leaned back, a grin on his face. "I see what you're doing here."

"Ensuring we starve?" Sophia asked.

He shook his head, pointing to the various dishes. "These are all foods Hiker can't stand."

Ainsley nodded triumphantly. "Don't worry, S. Beaufont. I've got a thing or two I know you'll enjoy, but that barbarian doesn't like."

Wilder peeked at the pastries Quiet had brought from the kitchen. "Pistachio scones and poppy seed muffins. Very clever."

The gnome slid into his normal seat, muttering as Evan and Mahkah filed into the dining area.

"Dumbface knows about you two," Ainsley said, indicating Sophia and Wilder. "It's made him madder than hell." She smiled sweetly. "Keep it up. Maybe you could sit in his lap during breakfast, S. How does that sound?"

"I approve," Wilder answered at once.

Sophia rolled her eyes and shook her head. "I think we shouldn't push things until Hiker has his new powers under control."

"As well as his anger management problems." Evan ran his gaze over the spread, not appearing excited about the options. "Oh, man, why can't Hiker despise bacon and eggs?"

"Don't worry," Ainsley called, heading back to the kitchen. "I've got turkey bacon and vegan eggs coming up."

Evan laughed. "He's going to be pissed. I can't wait to see this."

"See what?" Hiker Wallace asked, thundering into the dining hall, Mama Jamba waltzing in behind him, a pad of paper in her hands as she added up numbers.

"See these two love birds canoodling," Evan stated, grabbing a muffin and giving Quiet a look. "Do you want this one?"

The groundskeeper nodded.

With a wicked grin, Evan lobbed it across the room, making it stick to the far wall.

"That was rude," Sophia scolded.

Evan nodded proudly. "The little guy doesn't like it when I'm nice to him. He made everything in my room black, so now I feel like I'm living in a cave. My shower only has cold water, and my sink only has scorching hot water. Why did the short jerk do this, you ask? Because last night when I passed him in the hallway, I said, 'Have a good night.'"

"Seems like if you shower in the sink, you might be okay," Wilder offered.

"The way I figure it," Evan continued, grabbing a muffin as Quiet went for it and snatching it from his grasp, "I might as well be mean to the naughty gnome if he's going to punish me for being nice."

"Or you could try being nice just for the sake of being nice," Sophia interjected.

Evan seemed to consider this before tossing the muffin over his shoulder, where it landed on the floor with a splat. "I could, but that's not really my style."

"Your style is costing me work, you little twit," Ainsley scolded, trotting back into the dining room carrying a tray of turkey bacon.

"Quiet punished me before for teasing him," Evan argued. "Now, he's ten times worse to me for being nice. So, I'm just going to be ten times meaner."

Sophia grabbed a scone and bit into it. "Seems like a flawless plan. I can see no way this will backfire."

Hiker, who had stood looking down at the table with an angry stare, glanced up at Ainsley. "What's the meaning of this?" He threw his arm wide, indicating the table of breakfast foods.

She shrugged. "I wanted to ensure you started your day off right."

"How am I supposed to do that when you've served all foods I hate?" Hiker asked, his face blossoming into a shade of red.

"Oh," she said, clasping her hand to his chest. "You misunderstand me. When I say I want you to start your day off right, I mean 'how you deserve.' So really, I'd like you to have a stomachache first thing, followed by a sour mood and something worth complaining about. That's all I really want for you."

"Would you stop this and bring out something I'll actually eat?" Hiker demanded.

She batted her eyelashes at him. "I do so love your little nickname for me. Would-You is such a thoughtful pet name. I hope you'll like the one Quiet came up with for you."

Mama Jamba took a seat across from Sophia, her attention still on the pad of paper in her hands. "I don't think he'll like it."

"Oh, I don't know," Ainsley countered. "He calls me Would-You, and I call him Drop Dead. It really is the sweetest romance."

"Ainsley," Hiker growled, a warning in his voice.

She curtsied. "I'll go and get the hash browns, sir."

He sighed. "Finally, something I will eat."

Ainsley nodded mischievously as she headed for the kitchen. At the door, she paused. "Speaking of romances, remember Sophia and Wilder have made things official."

A seething expression covered Hiker's face. "Don't think I've forgotten."

Tilting her head to the side, Ainsley gave Hiker a dreamy look. "Your annoyance really does bring joy to my heart."

"You two," Hiker said, indicating Sophia and Wilder. "You know I don't approve of this. I made that abundantly clear."

"Was that before or after you made me think my entire life was a lie?" Ainsley asked, bustling back into the dining hall, carrying a plate of steaming hash browns. She laid them down in front of Hiker and backed away at once with a rebellious smile.

"It was after," he declared, answering the question like that was at all necessary. Hiker kept his light-colored eyes trained on Sophia and Wilder as he shoveled hash browns onto his plate.

"This really isn't appropriate for dragonriders," Hiker continued.

"There aren't any rules against it," Mama Jamba argued, her attention on the pad as she counted on her hands.

"I make the rules!" Hiker boomed.

Mama Jamba shot him a look over her paper and pursed her lips. "Really, son?"

He stuck his fork into the hash browns, nearly breaking the plate. He was doing that a lot lately when trying to eat due to this enhanced strength. "Well, you might be in charge of this planet, but you put me in charge of the Dragon Elite. We don't fraternize with each other."

"You said fraternize," Evan stated with a chuckle.

"That's because there's never been a girl among us, though," Mahkah supplied, daring to enter the conversation.

"It doesn't matter," Hiker argued. "Relationships are a distraction. We have too many priorities right now and this…" He waved his hand at the couple. "Well, it distracts from our missions."

"Some would say love only makes everything better," Mama Jamba observed, scribbling on her pad.

"This isn't love," Hiker grumbled. "It's two people losing sight of what's important."

Ainsley stuck her hands on her hips, a defiant expression on her face. "How dare you try and define their relationship! Love is important. It's what's most important. It's why people fight and defend. Dare I say, it's why people make sacrifices, and why someone would risk their life for another."

Hiker lowered his chin and gave the housekeeper a murderous expression. "Don't make this about us. I don't want to talk to you right now."

"Oh, I wouldn't dream of it," she sang, heading for the kitchen again. "Once I am cured and I can leave this place, I'll be sure never to speak to you again. Call it my farewell gift for all these years of serving you while you kept secrets from me."

"Quiet did too!" Hiker exclaimed.

Ainsley shot the gnome an affectionate look. "Yes, and he said he was sorry. Is that something you can do?"

Hiker's mouth formed a hard line as he remained speechless.

"That's what I thought," Ainsley stated. "Stubborn and also cowardly. What a perfect combination."

He shook his head and stuck the bite of hash browns into his mouth. In mid-chew, he spat them out into his napkin. "Did you put tarragon in these? You know I can't stand that herb."

"Why, yes, I did," she told him proudly, pushing through the kitchen door. "Drop Dead."

"Oh, tarragon," Mama Jamba marveled. "That's a great idea!" She turned the pad sideways and wrote along the edge of the paper.

"What are you doing?" Evan inquired, peering over to see what she was writing.

She edged away, preventing him from spying. "Carry the two and then divide by din."

"Din isn't a number," Evan challenged.

Mama Jamba glanced at him. "It isn't anymore. Papa Creola had it erased eons ago because he felt it wasn't necessary, but I think it's useful in this case."

"Cool, numbers that don't exist anymore because Father Time didn't like them," Evan said, still trying to get a glimpse of her paper. "As you were saying, what are you working on?"

"I wasn't," she chimed in her Southern accent, flashing him the pad. "But since you must know, I'm working on a new species of plant."

"That you're sketching out on..." Evan squinted at the paper. "Is that hotel stationary?"

She nodded. "It's how I craft my best ideas."

"This plant," Evan continued. "Will you name it after me?"

"There's already a plant named stinkweed," Wilder teased.

Mama Jamba smiled good naturally. "I haven't named it yet. I won't until Sophia plants the seeds."

"Me?" Sophia asked, surprised.

"Sophia?" Hiker questioned, also surprised. "She has training with me and missions to attend to."

"And hopefully a hot date when you give her a second off work," Mama Jamba argued. "I want Sophia to plant the seeds, but not yet. I have to get the formula just right first."

"The Dragon Elite don't get time off," Hiker said, turning his attention to the guys. "I have adjudication missions for you all. Mahkah, you already have the details on yours."

Mahkah nodded in reply.

"Evan, I have a dispute you need to resolve in Asia," Hiker went on. "Wilder, there's a case that requires you to take a leave of absence for a while."

Mama Jamba's chair scraping against the floor when she rose

made a screeching noise. She narrowed her eyes at Hiker. "That's very transparent, son."

He held up his hands. "Call it what you will, but I have missions to complete and will assign them as I see fit."

Mama Jamba nodded. "I won't object, but if you think for one second I'm going to allow you to make rules against people falling in love, you've got another think coming, Hiker Wallace. Now since you've thoroughly upset the housekeeper and it doesn't appear she'll be bringing my pancakes, I'm going to go sulk in your office."

"I would eat pancakes," Hiker muttered, looking at the breakfast options with annoyance.

"Sort things out with Ainsley," Mama Jamba ordered, making for the exit. "I want pancakes."

"There's no reasoning with a madwoman," Hiker replied, standing as well. He cast his eyes down on Sophia. "Well, shall we start training?"

She grabbed a piece of bacon and took a nervous bite. There was something in the heated expression he was giving her that made her think he needed time to cool down before they trained together. She didn't even know how she was supposed to help him control his powers. He thought that because she was a twin-like him, she'd have some strategy to help him.

"I will as soon as I'm done eating, sir," she replied between bites.

He continued to stare down at her, a warning on his face.

With a sigh, Sophia pushed out her chair, realizing he wasn't going to let up until she complied. "Oh, look, I'm all done. Let's train, sir."

He marched for the door, his shoulders pinned up high.

Sophia took off reluctantly after him, giving the guys a pleading expression over her shoulder. "Wish me luck."

"You don't need luck," Evan teased with a chuckle. "You need thick armor."

CHAPTER THREE

The man known as Hiker Wallace had never known such a challenging time in his very long life. Even when his twin brother was hunting him down, trying to kill him for his power, things hadn't felt this bad. Presently, Hiker felt he couldn't control his own riders, his housekeeper was furious at him for something he could do nothing about and worst of all, his powers were so overwhelming they were out of control. He felt ready to explode at any moment. He had embraced the power he had inherited from Thad, but that was only the beginning. Now he had to discover how to control it before it destroyed him.

Sophia marched behind Hiker as he led them out to the combat area on the Expanse. She almost ran into him when he pivoted abruptly. All the dragonriders moved swifter than most, even magicians and elves, who were quite stealthy in their own right. Hiker Wallace moved with a unique grace that made it nearly impossible to predict his movements.

Sophia sucked in a breath and looked up at the man before her, peering into his nostrils.

"Hey," she said, taking a step back and loosening her throat with a cough.

"Hey," he replied, his voice gruff.

"So, what did you have in mind for training?" she dared to ask.

He returned her question with a question. "What have you learned?"

"Well…" she began, thinking of what she'd discovered reading *The Complete History of Dragonriders* the night before. Bermuda Laurens had taught her how to use the book by thinking of specifically what she needed to find and then seemingly randomly flipping the book open. The intention acted as a sort of table of contents, bringing her to exactly what she was looking for.

She could have just given the book to Hiker to read—it was his book after all, but for whatever reason, Quiet wasn't allowing the leader of the Dragon Elite to have access to it. Every time Sophia gave it to him, it ended back up in her room on her desk. Once again, Quiet had reasons for the strange things he did, and no one but he knew why.

She had learned something she thought would be of help for Hiker.

"I think you're out of balance," she continued. "According to what I found, when a twin inherits another's powers, there are a couple of factors that impact it." She held up a finger, listing what she remembered from the book. "The first is guilt, which I think was your initial obstacle. You didn't want to have to kill Thad, because you were the good twin. The book says this is common with good twins. So you were reluctant to embrace the power, which created a concentration of it, like when something gets bottlenecked."

Hiker nodded, chewing on the inside of his cheek. "Go on then."

"Well, because of that, when you did embrace the power," Sophia explained, "the levels were out of whack, overwhelming you."

He nodded. "You're telling me. I've broken most things in my study, just going about my usual business."

Sophia had to stop herself from laughing, having witnessed the Viking put his coffee mug on his desk and breaking the cup to pieces while also putting a dent in the solid wood desk. She swallowed to cover her laughter.

"In cases like this, it's a balancing issue," Sophia went on, motioning to the Expanse where the grounds were littered with bowling ball-sized dragon eggs of various colors. "Just like half the dragon eggs from this batch are going to turn out good and the other half evil, there has to be balance within you. Yin and yang. The power within you is sourced from both good and evil, so I think you need a way to equalize the forces."

"Like how?" he asked at once, his temper flaring.

Sophia shrugged. "I'm sorry, but the book didn't elaborate. It simply said that in cases such as these, the dragonrider needed balancing forces."

"Why don't you have this problem?" Hiker asked, his eyes narrowed.

"Well, I think at times, I do struggle, but I inherited Jamison's powers at birth, and therefore, this is my normal," she explained. "You're having to deal with it after five hundred years, and that can't be easy."

"Don't give me your sympathy," he spat.

Sophia shook this off. "More than anything, I think you have to get control over your emotions. The bad ones are creating more of an imbalance, making it harder for you to control your powers. This is just a guess, but I think it makes the most sense."

Hiker scowled at Sophia. "I'm perfectly in control of my emotions."

Again, Sophia had to resist the urge to laugh. "Really? So, this Ainsley situation doesn't have you upset?"

The scowl deepened on his face. "That topic is off-limits."

"That's why you'll continue to smash teacups," Sophia fired back, folding her arms and giving him a defiant expression.

"That has nothing to do with this!" Hiker picked up a sword from the weapon's area and swung it, testing the balance.

Sophia tensed but worked to hide it. "It seems like it might be affecting you more than you're willing to admit."

He held the sword out, not at her, but it would take minimal effort for him to switch directions and slice her in half. It was risky business having this conversation with an out-of-control Hiker Wallace, and yet, Sophia had somehow, out of everyone, been nominated for this task. She would have rather signed up to teach Evan how to use recording software, a thing he'd been begging for her to do after listening to electronic music and learning about disc jockeying.

He dropped the sword to his side and spun to face her. "You defied me."

It took everything she had not to roll her eyes at him. "You overstepped your bounds. You can assign me cases. You can tell me how to conduct myself as a dragonrider. However..." She dared to take a step forward, keeping her chin up and her face deadly serious. "You don't control me as a woman. If I want to be with Wilder, then that's what I'll do."

"I told you not to," he said through gritted teeth.

She shook her head. "That wasn't your call to make. Maybe part of your problem controlling your powers is that you're trying so hard to control things you have no business managing. Focus on you. Attend to the problems you have and then—"

"How dare you," he interrupted, menace making his face red.

Sophia wanted to fire back with, "I dared." Instead, she took a calming breath. "Emotions directly affect magical powers. I get things are complicated for you. I think resolving some of these issues would help you to balance things."

What Sophia wasn't saying was that Hiker needed good old fashioned counseling. She'd slowly hint around at that one when he wasn't holding a sword. "For instance," she continued. "You could attempt to smooth things over with Ainsley. She's mad and—"

"I know she's mad," he cut her off. "But there is no fixing things with her. There wasn't then and there isn't now. She's always been a fiery redhead who doesn't listen to reason."

"If what Saint Valentine said is correct, then Ainsley can't be cured and recover her memories as long as she's heartbroken," Sophia reasoned. "You don't have to mend things, but you can apologize."

He shook his head. "It wouldn't matter."

"So that's it?" Sophia argued. "You've just decided you can't do anything to help the situation, and you're not even going to try?"

He yanked the sword up to his chest, the weapon shaking slightly in his hand. "Mind your place."

Sophia didn't back down but instead continued to hold his angry glare.

After a moment, he sighed. "Even if her heart was mended, I don't know the cure."

"Well, what have you tried?" Sophia asked.

He threw the sword like a spear, making it land in a bale of hay. "I don't know. I haven't really."

"You what?" Sophia couldn't believe it. "You never looked for a cure for Ainsley?"

"The Gullington brought her back from near death," Hiker explained quickly. "I realized it was keeping her alive. She had lost her memories and couldn't leave the Barrier for long, and then the world shut down when mortals couldn't see magic, making the Dragon Elite useless. There wasn't really any way for me to look and then…well, time just got away from me."

"Yeah, a few centuries," Sophia stated. It was then she realized that maybe without knowing it, Hiker didn't want to cure Ainsley back then. She had forgotten she once loved him or that he broke her heart. If she was cured, she would have left the Gullington, and he would never see her again. She would have returned to the elves and moved on with her life. Maybe because he couldn't move on with his, he didn't want her to.

This man was a real piece of work, Sophia thought. He didn't want to fix the heart he'd broken or cure the woman who had risked her life to save his. She was about to be furious about the realization when something else occurred to her.

Hiker still loved Ainsley.

CHAPTER FOUR

Cruel summer. Cruel, cruel summer, what are you doing to us? Lunis asked with a sigh, shaking his head.

Sophia looked at her dragon, rolling her eyes. "It's not all that bad."

Steam issued from his nostrils when he growled, *They are ruining everything.*

The blue dragon was referring to the evil baby dragons who had recently hatched. They weren't literally ruining everything, but they were definitely making a mess on the Expanse. Between the three of them, they'd found some of Quiet's equipment and were tearing it into pieces, breaking the machinery until it was unusable.

Just wait until the little devils have fire, Lunis complained. *I say we drop them in the middle of the North Sea before that happens.*

Sophia shook her head. "We have to find a way to embrace this. Or find a solution that doesn't involve murdering a rare species that's near extinction."

Okay, we don't drown them, he offered. *We put them on a deserted island.*

"They will be able to fly soon," Sophia argued.

You didn't let me finish, Lunis said, glaring at her. *The island is sinking...*

"So they drown."

Exactly, Lunis said triumphantly.

"You know, we don't *know* they are evil," she observed. "One could be evil and influencing the others. We can't make judgments too early. They are young and will mature, showing their true personalities."

In the meantime, Lunis said, watching as the three fearless dragons bounded toward a shed next to the Castle, probably full of more tools, *we'll just watch this place get run into the ground.*

Sophia shook her head. "Quit being so melodramatic. It doesn't suit you."

I'll tell you what doesn't suit me. It's that you haven't bought the stuff on my wish list from Amazon yet, he complained.

Sophia laughed. "What are you going to do with a Tardis sleeping bag?"

He giggled, which was a strange thing for a dragon to do, but here they were. *I'm going to sleep on it, obviously.*

"It's like a quarter of the size of you," she stated.

Lunis' eyes widened with offense. *Are you calling me fat?*

"Oh, for the love of the angels. Is this really happening?"

Hey, do you want to hear a knock-knock joke? he asked, his tone shifting. *Of course you do. Here you go. Knock knock.*

Sophia lowered her chin, getting ready for the ridiculousness. "Who. Is. There?" She enunciated each word, as she often did when answering her dragon's knock-knock jokes. Another thing most dragons—scratch that—no other dragons did. Sophia swept her eyes over the Expanse full of eggs. This new generation would be different, she suspected, but none of them would be quite like Lunis.

Doctor, he answered.

Sophia smiled. "Doctor Who?"

Exterminate. Exterminate. Exterminate. Lunis erupted with laughter, rolling over on his back and kicking his legs like a dog.

"Yes, that was about as bad as I would have expected," Sophia mused.

Best. Joke. Ever, he said, continuing to roll around.

"When you're done," Sophia began. "I'd like to discuss real matters that affect the world."

Lunis' laughter halted abruptly as he rolled to his feet. He gave her an annoyed expression. *Doctor Who affects the world. Did you know that because of him, the—*

"It's a fictional show," Sophia interrupted.

What did Plato tell us about fiction? Much of it was nonfiction that was put in the wrong section, Lunis explained. *I have every reason to believe this happened to Doctor Who. Out there is a lone Time Lord traveling the universe, looking for a companion.* He gazed longingly at the sky. Then like he had a sudden idea, he whipped around to face Sophia. *Do you think I could become the Doctor's companion?*

"First of all," Sophia began, mock irritation heavy in her tone. "You are my dragon and we work for the Dragon Elite, serving as world adjudicators."

Boring, he said, blowing out his lips.

"We are literally the most powerful governing body on Earth," she argued. "What we say goes on all mortal matters on this entire planet."

Why you always trying to hold me down and fit me into a little cookie cutter? Lunis complained.

"Okay, and speaking of which," Sophia continued, "you are a dragon. How are you going to fit inside the Tardis?"

Duh! he exclaimed, rolling his head, along with his eyes. *It's bigger on the inside.*

Sophia shook her head. "I can't even believe you went there. And you say my jokes are bad."

The worst, he agreed.

"If you're done, I wanted to discuss a real person who really does affect this world," Sophia said.

Go on, but if this is about a cyborg you sympathize with, then I'm going back to the Nest to binge-watch Nailed It *on Netflix,* Lunis imparted.

"On second thought," Sophia told him, "I don't think I need a dragon anymore."

You're a dragonrider, he corrected.

"Yeah," she sang. "But I do things differently as the first and only female rider. So maybe I don't have a dragon, and you go off with the Doctor to ride around in a little blue box."

He sighed. *Okay, all kidding aside. I agree Trin Currante isn't all bad. We have to figure out her story. What did you have in mind? Use government surveillance to determine where she could be? Metal detecting tech to scan the population to find all the cyborgs? See if we can find a smart man or woman with a sonic screwdriver who can find Trin Currante?*

Sophia couldn't help but laugh. "I thought I'd go ask my fairy godmother."

He deflated. *Yeah, I guess that could work. The boring approach.*

"Because so many people have fairy godmothers, they can just pop over to and ask about their projects."

I know a few, he argued.

"Who?" she challenged.

Look, can we continue this later? Lunis asked. *I've got to go.* Nailed It *is about to come on, and I don't want to miss it.*

"It's on Netflix, which means you can see it whenever you want," she stated.

He stretched out his wings. *I knew you'd understand. Thanks, Soph.*

She shook her head at the strange dragon as he took off, launching into the air as he unfolded his wings and soared to the Nest in the distance.

Oh, Lunis said, looking over his shoulder at her from the air. *Since you're not busy with commitments like me—*

You're buzzing off to watch prerecorded cooking shows, she interrupted.

As I was saying, your Amazon wish list, he insisted. *Get on it. I also need a potato peeler.*

What for?

He turned his head back for the Nest. *I can't say. But get a couple. I'm bound to break the first one.*

CHAPTER FIVE

Only the young were required for Mika Lenna's newest project. Young magicians weren't easy to find, but that hadn't stopped the CEO of the Saverus Corporation.

There just weren't as many magicians as the other magical races, but they were the only ones that worked for creating cyborgs. Elves, giants, and gnome's DNA rejected magitech, whereas magicians embraced it. It made sense because they were the inventors. Where the other races preferred the natural elements, magicians had always been more cutting edge.

Identifying magicians wasn't the issue. Mika had learned how to do that long ago. It was finding them. They didn't usually congregate in mortal areas, and since he wasn't of any of the magical races, he couldn't portal onto Roya Lane, which they frequented.

Mika Lenna was a Dream Traveler, one of the rare race of mortals who could travel anywhere with his dreams. It offered him a few psychic abilities like telepathy and telekinesis but not the ability to portal through time and space.

To make things worse, since magicians had started going missing again, the House of Fourteen had issued a warning, telling its members to stay inside. The magical community hadn't liked the self-imposed isolation but had agreed to do it to preserve their lives.

The first time Mika had worked to create his "projects," the House of Fourteen had been under different leadership and hadn't acted fast enough. Now with hundreds of magicians having gone mysteriously missing, they weren't taking chances.

That was before one woman had nearly destroyed the Saverus Corporation.

Trin Currante.

She'd sabotaged many of Mika Lenna's efforts, but he'd still gotten away. Just like when he had to rebuild his first company, Olento Research, he had weathered the storm and rebuilt yet again.

Mika Lenna flexed his fingers, feeling the incredible power he wielded flowing through his veins. He had used his own technology to genetically alter his DNA, blending it with a wolf. Now he was the stuff of legends. He didn't shift into a werewolf on a full moon or howl, but he had superhuman speed, strength, and a lust for blood.

Mika Lenna wasn't just a werewolf. He was the strongest one he had made. The organization, the Lucidites, thought they'd brought him down. They had no idea he'd come back to life and dug himself out of a grave.

The worst thing anyone ever did was doubt Mika Lenna.

He watched as the magician stumbled out of the bar, late at night and mostly drunk.

It didn't matter. Even with their magic, magicians were no match for Mika Lenna. This one was dumb enough not to heed the House of Fourteen's warning about staying inside, especially at night.

He watched the man cross the street not at an intersection and nearly get hit by a car as he stepped out in front of it. The magician shouted profanities, shaking his fist at the motorist.

Mika Lenna shook his head. It was always someone else's fault. That was the problem with society. No one ever took responsibility. That was flawed thinking because when everything is someone else's fault then it's impossible to fix.

Mika Lenna's problems were his own, and he sought solutions.

Like when he created a few hundred cyborgs who rebelled, he figured out his mistake. It was the same error he made with the werewolf project.

The subjects still had emotions—fears and desires. Those created problems. They created rebels. Subjects such as that escape their confines and then return, freeing hundreds and destroying a multi-million dollar facility, looking for answers. Trin Currante may have been successful at ruining the Saverus building and freeing the prisoners, but she hadn't gotten the one thing she desperately needed answered. A solution to how to fix her.

She wasn't going to get it. Mika Lenna would see to it personally after all the trouble that rejected project had caused.

However, there had been a valuable lesson to it all. Before, the subjects had rebelled because they still had their emotions. There was one very easy way to fix everything.

Death.

Kill the subject and bring them back as a cyborg, and they were robots without any desires. Of course, the magitech that had to be innovated to bring a magician back to life defied all sorts of laws.

That's what Mika Lenna was best at. Breaking the confines of science.

Necromancy wasn't something he ever thought he'd dabble in, but having reliable products was the key objective.

"Why?" his head scientist Scott Jacobs had asked.

"Why not," Mika replied firmly. He had created the genetically altered werewolves to become assassins. That had been the idea with the first batch of cyborgs. Now he wanted an army who would do his bidding. Actually, he thought they'd make the perfect soldiers to go after the werewolves and cyborgs who had escaped.

Hiding in the shadows of a dark alleyway, Mika watched the magician turn down the street, headed in the opposite direction. Many might be worried he'd get away, but that wasn't a concern for Mika Lenna. This one wasn't getting away.

He looked up at the sky, black save for a crescent moon, as the shift took over. To say it hurt to morph into his werewolf form was an understatement. Mika Lenna had known many pains in his life full of suffering and experiments. However, when his bones broke and shifted to make his form larger, it was utter agony.

The claws slipping out of his fingers felt like knives slicing through his skin ten times over. The fangs that dropped out of the top of his mouth were the worst part. They felt like a double extraction done by the lousiest dentist in the world.

The change was always worth the pain, though. Mika Lenna glanced at the empty store window directly across from him and took in his appearance.

The stuff of legends. That's what he had become.

His hulking form was reminiscent of a werewolf with the claws and fangs and rippling muscles, but he wasn't some science fiction horror monster covered in hair, with wolf ears. Mika Lenna's intention was to make classic werewolves, and he had succeeded.

His red eyes flashed, glowing brightly before he took off, darting out of his hiding spot.

The road was empty, save for the drunk magician singing loudly to himself at the end of the block. It took Mika Lenna less than a second to cross the distance.

The magician didn't even have a chance to react before the werewolf arrived behind him, his massive hands on either side of the man's head. With force no normal magician could resist, he yanked the man into him, his mouth opening wide.

Horror registered in the magician's eyes just before fangs sunk into the side of his neck and tore through flesh and veins. The hunger was the best part of being a werewolf and satisfying that hunger never got old.

The magician screamed, but that didn't stop Mika from feasting on the man's body, unconcerned about the damage he was doing. He would fix him and make him anew.

CHAPTER SIX

"You need to calm down," Mama Jamba warned, her eyes narrowed in Hiker's direction.

The temperature seemed to rise ten degrees when Sophia stepped over the threshold into his office.

"That's what this one said in so many words." Hiker pointed an accusatory finger at Sophia, making her pause, an uncertain expression on her face.

She held up her hands as if in surrender. "I simply pointed out magical powers are connected to emotions."

Hiker banged his fist on the surface of his desk, making papers and various objects hiccup and clatter around. "I already know that!"

"Okay, I was simply reminding you." Sophia peeled back slightly. "You did ask for my help."

"She said you were part of figuring out this power balancing issue." He shot his accusatory finger at Mama Jamba.

Mama Jamba wasn't lounging across the leather sofa as usual. Instead, like a little child, she was sitting on the floor, leaning over the coffee table and coloring in one of those adult coloring books. This one was full of fairies and woodland creatures created by Selena

Fenech. The drawings were quite detailed and full of whimsy even before they were filled with bright colors.

"She can help you," Mama Jamba sang, trading out a lime green pencil for a yellow one.

"How?" he growled, obviously not happy with how their first training session had gone. If anything, Hiker seemed more flustered. Perhaps from something Sophia had said about Ainsley or something Mama Jamba hadn't said—dangling secrets in front of his face.

Right on cue, Mother Nature shrugged, coloring stars in a night sky over a centaur's head. "I can't really tell you. We're not there yet."

He threw up his hands, rolling his eyes. "How didn't I expect that answer?"

She shook her head of short gray curls. "I really don't know, son. You should have. Now try taking some deep breaths." She indicated the teacup on his desk that was vibrating. "You're going to make that thing explode."

He closed his eyes for a half-beat. "It would be the third teacup today. Ainsley will be livid."

Mama Jamba suppressed a laugh. "Yes, that's why Ainsley would be cross with you and not for the more personal reasons—"

"Not you too," he interrupted, cutting his eyes at Sophia. He was obviously going to hold grudges for her telling Ainsley the truth and then encouraging him to make amends with her.

So be it, Sophia thought. *As long as he doesn't make my head explode like a teacup.*

"Try breathing, son," Mama Jamba encouraged as the cup continued to vibrate on the saucer.

"Oh, is that the big secret you're keeping from me?" he asked sarcastically.

"No, that's just general advice for all living creatures," Mama Jamba explained, giving Sophia a proud look. "I require it for a good reason."

"Because it connects us to the Earth?" Sophia guessed.

Mama Jamba gave her a polite smile. "Good guess. Because I lost a bet with Papa Creola. He loved the idea of something so simple being the difference between life and death. You all are just minutes away from fatality at any given moment, depending on the circumstances."

"That seems like Papa Creola," Sophia said with a laugh. "Totally morbid."

"It connects the Earth to you, ironically. Not the other way around," Mama Jamba went on. "In the most poetic sense, the Earth is breathing you. I know how much you enjoy your poetry, dear Sophia."

She nodded. "That's a nice sentiment."

"But yes," Mama Jamba continued, returning her attention to Hiker. "No matter how powerful you are, son, you are as vulnerable as the weakest human when deprived of air. Your breath can give you strength, or it can take it away. It can calm you, or if you keep holding it, it will bottle up the anger in you more. The options are easy, but the practice not so much so."

"I'm not holding my breath!" Hiker exclaimed, his face beet red.

She nodded, returning to coloring her picture. "Sure, son. Sure."

Hiker cleared his throat and narrowed his eyes at the teacup, giving it a threatening expression, as though trying to force it into compliance. Apparently, it worked because it settled slightly, making less of a vibrating sound on the saucer.

"Anyway," he said with a sigh, returning his attention to Sophia. "I have a mission for you."

Hiker picked up a newspaper and handed it to Sophia. "It involves the House of Fourteen, which is why you were picked."

She nodded. Her relationship, growing up at the House of Fourteen and being related to two of their members, made her the obvious choice when picking delegates to deal with the magicians' governing body. Sophia also knew Hiker wasn't in a position to talk directly with strangers. He liked them a whole lot less than his riders, and currently, they were making him livid.

Peering at the paper, she read the headline: "Hundreds of Magicians Continue to Go Missing, House of Fourteen Loses Credibility."

"What?" Sophia gasped. "This sounds serious."

Hiker nodded. "It very well could be. Right now, the fallout between mortal governments and the House of Fourteen falls under our immediate jurisdiction. The current political climate is making mortals untrusting of magicians."

"Which after just learning they were the reason they were blind to magic for a few centuries, isn't good for trust-building," Sophia finished.

"Exactly," Hiker affirmed. "There've been all sorts of disputes as a result. I need you to visit the House of Fourteen and meet with the council. Find out what's going on with magicians. This will inevitably result in us having to preside over matters, but we need more information."

Sophia skimmed the newspaper article, which didn't have much on the mysterious disappearances. "This is unsettling."

Hiker glanced up absentmindedly as though he had momentarily forgotten she was there. "What? Oh, the magicians? Yes, that's concerning but might be nothing."

"How can hundreds of magicians going missing be nothing?" Sophia asked.

"Well, it's not like they are in danger of going into extinction like some," Hiker said bitterly.

Sophia's eyes fluttered with annoyance. "I thought only magicians could be dragonriders. If the population dries up, then even when our eggs hatch, who will be left to magnetize to them?"

Hiker's expression changed. "Good point. See what you can find out. Maybe they all are just at some retreat."

"What like Burning Man or Coachella?" Sophia asked with a laugh. "They are magicians, not elves."

Hiker shivered with disgust. "Elves are the absolute worst, always doing eccentric stuff like that."

Sophia didn't think it was a good time to remind him he was once in love with an elf. However, that did make her wonder how Ainsley and Hiker got together. She guessed the elf made Hiker cut loose and he reminded her of the more practical side of life. Or they bickered at each other all the time—like they did in their present roles.

"My point is magicians don't just disappear," Sophia argued. "They aren't prone to going off the grid or escaping the confines of modern society like the other magical races."

Hiker agreed with a nod. "Go find out more information."

"Yes, sir," Sophia answered, making for the door.

"Oh, and Sophia," Hiker said, pausing her at the threshold.

"Yes?" she asked, turning back.

"Subtly," he began slowly, his voice careful, "remind the House of Fourteen we are in charge and not the other way around."

CHAPTER SEVEN

Bad blood had always existed between the House of Fourteen and the Dragon Elite, according to Lunis. It went back to when the House was run by corrupt magicians who wanted absolute control. The Dragon Elite was the supreme ruling body on the planet. What they said was law. It just so happened they disappeared for a few centuries, and reestablishing dominance was taking some effort.

The House of Fourteen had come back even stronger than before magic had disappeared, but the Dragon Elite was still struggling to rebuild. They had their thousand dragon eggs...well, 997...but still, eggs were just the beginning. The dragons had to hatch and magnetize to riders for the Elite to grow back to what it had been. In the meantime, Sophia, under Hiker's direction, had to exert dominance over the House of Fourteen. As a very young magician, working for the Dragon Elite, which was near extinction, this was about like a lanky kid telling a group of cardigan-wearing soccer moms what to do. Sophia reasoned the kids really ran the show with their activities and preferences and whatnot.

"Just act the part," Sophia encouraged, giving herself a pep talk as she stepped through the portal between the Castle and the House of Fourteen. "Don't let them get the upper hand."

"I think the phrase is, don't let them see your hand," King Rudolf Sweetwater corrected at Sophia's back.

She spun around, not used to anyone being in the corridor when she stepped through. She was very surprised to find the fae there since the other magical races weren't allowed in the residential section of the House, just the Chamber of the Tree. Then Sophia noticed Liv beside Rudolf and realized she must have taken him on an excursion.

"Yes, Soph," Liv said, giving her sister a hug when she was closer. "If I've taught you anything, it's that you can't let them see your hand. You got to know when to hold them and know when to fold them."

Sophia shook her head at her sister's ridiculousness. "Right and know when to walk away and know when to run."

Rudolf gave them both a disappointed expression. "There's no running in poker. You should be seated the entire time and have snacks."

Liv pursed her lips at the very attractive fae.

"What are you all doing?" Sophia asked, trying to figure out where they had come from. "Did you take Rudolf to the library?"

Liv laughed. "Whatever would he do there?"

He huffed. "You know, I have to nap just as much as the next fae."

"Right," Liv said, drawing out the word. "That's what a library is for."

He shook his head. "No, a library is the place to go if you want to seduce wallflower mortals. When one is bored with that, the places which contain portal stories are fantastic for naps."

"Books," Liv corrected. "Those little rectangular things are known as books. Not portal stories."

He shrugged. "I say French fries and you say chips."

Liv's brow scrunched. "Why would I call them chips? I'm not British."

"Then why do you always talk about the queen and what a dimwit she is?" Rudolf challenged. "More than once, you've said we speak different languages."

"I'm talking about *your* queen," Liv answered. "What language do you think the British speak?"

He sighed as though explaining this to her was costing him greatly. "They speak Great Britain, and we speak American."

"I didn't expect this of you, which speaks poorly of me," Liv stated, glancing at Sophia. "House business?"

She nodded. "What were you two doing?"

"Oh, I needed to find some family stuff, and this one followed me because that's what lost puppies do." She pointed over her shoulder at Rudolf, who was smiling delightedly like a happy-go-lucky dog.

"Were you looking for stuff for the wedding?" Sophia asked and immediately regretted it.

The shock that jumped to Liv's eyes told her something very important.

King Rudolf Sweetwater didn't know.

"Sophia, you're getting married?" Rudolf asked, surprise making his face light up.

She froze, her eyes shifting between Liv's tense face and Rudolf's excited one. "Um, actually, it's not me."

"Oh, good," Rudolf said with a relieved sigh. "I mean, if it was, I'd pretend to be happy for you and not think that you were ruining your life."

She gawked at him. "What are you talking about? You're married."

"Yes, and it took me over five hundred years to make that decision." He leaned in and gave her a stern expression. "I hope you don't jump into anything until you're at least half a century old. You need time to know yourself. You and Liv are mere babies in your first century." He nodded with sage confidence. "No, only a complete moron who notoriously made bad decisions would get married young. So..." He rubbed his hands together excitedly. "Who is getting married? Is it Rory and Maddy? John and Alicia? Clark and Gordon Ramsey?"

Liv blinked at him in confusion. "Clark is straight, and I'm fairly sure he doesn't even know Gordon Ramsey."

Rudolf shrugged. "Yeah, but he's always watching the guy's shows."

"It's none of those couples," Liv told him, hesitation covering her face.

"Oh, well, I can't think of any other couples then." Rudolf screwed up his face, racking his brain for the answer.

"It's Stefan and me," she muttered, running her hand over her mouth to drown out the words.

"Oh, you and Stefan." Rudolf at once nodded. Then it registered, and his mouth dropped open. "No, Liv, no. You can't marry the demon hunter because you're going to get fat and only want to hang out with him. You'll ignore me. It will ruin your life. Haven't you been listening?"

"I can't get fat as a magician," Liv reasoned. "Not if I'm using my magic. I don't hang out with you anyway."

He rolled his eyes. "Exactly. But really, you're too young. Give it another four or five hundred years. Take the time to get to know yourself. Take time to get to know Stefan. Do you even know his last name?"

"Ludwig," she answered immediately.

"Yeah, but is that his *real* last name?" Rudolf challenged.

"Well, it's written on the magical wall of the Chamber of the Tree that's spelled to only present Royals," she answered.

He sighed, shaking his head. "That's such faulty reasoning. I bet you're one of those people who believes everything they see with their own eyes."

"Versus?" Liv asked, tilting her head to the side.

"Believing what you see with your eyes shut, of course," Rudolf explained.

"Yeah, you got me there, bud," Liv said, shaking her head. She looked at Sophia, giving her a commiserate expression. "I was looking for our father's wedding band. Clark had said that he thought it was in their stuff since he wasn't wearing it when he went to the Matterhorn."

The expression on Liv's face was telling.

"You didn't find it, though?" Sophia asked.

Liv shook her head. "No, but I'm not giving up."

"Well, maybe it's with mom's," Sophia suggested. "Then you can use both."

Her sister laughed. "Like me, Mom didn't wear a wedding or engagement ring. Warriors are always battling something, and rings would be a hazard. I don't really need to lose a finger because my wedding band gets caught on some ogre's dewclaw."

"Good point," Sophia stated.

"Wait, ogres have dewclaws?" Rudolf asked in surprise.

"So, what did Stefan give you when he proposed?" Sophia asked.

Liv held up her arm, showing a small rope fastened around her wrist.

"Is that a friendship bracelet?" Sophia asked.

"It's a 'lock you down' bracelet," Liv answered with a laugh.

Sophia laughed. "That's more your style."

"Wait, but Stefan is a Warrior," Sophia said after a moment of realization. "Can he wear a wedding ring?"

"Yeah, because he has fast healing, and I want to put a ring on that," Liv joked.

Sophia nodded. "Good idea. I see the way mortals look at him."

Stefan Ludwig was attractive by any standard, with his jet-black hair and piercing blue eyes. Add to that the swords strapped to his back and his billowing black cloak, and he was most women's fantasy.

Both sisters' attention slid to Rudolf, who was busy scrolling through his phone, shaking his head like he was having trouble finding something. "That won't do at all. No. That's absurd." He rejected options as he swiped through.

"What's absurd?" Liv asked.

"All these options for your bachelorette party," Rudolf told her, glancing up suddenly, his expression shifting. "I mean, unless you *want* a gnome stripper? Is that your thing? You *are* short."

Liv shook her head. "No to strippers. No to gnomes and to gnome strippers. Why are you even looking at bachelorette party stuff?"

"Well," he said, clasping his hand to his chest. "As your maid of honor, I feel that it's my duty to throw the best bachelorette party. I mean, it's only your first wedding. I'm sure, when I marry you off to your second or third husband, we'll have real blowouts, but I still want to do right by you."

A pained expression crossed Liv's face. This was why she hadn't told Rudolf yet. She'd probably been looking for the right way to break the news to him, and Sophia had revealed the information unknowingly.

"The thing is Rudolf, you're not my maid of honor," Liv said, her tone careful. Sympathetic.

"What?" Rudolf exclaimed. "I'm not. B-b-bu…"

"It's just that—"

"I'm your best friend, though," he cut in. "I've saved your life on many occasions. I'm always there for you. If you ever needed anything, I'd drop everything, including the fate of my people, to help you."

Liv appeared crushed. Her shoulders drooped. "For once, Ru, I can't argue with a word you've said. The thing is, I didn't make you my maid of honor because—"

"You're giving her away," Sophia interrupted, the idea suddenly occurring to her.

Liv's eyes widened slightly before filling with relief. "Yes! I needed you for the more important job of giving me away."

Rudolf's mouth fell open as joy took over his face. "Are you serious? I get to pretend to be your father for a day?" His features shifted, making him look strict. "You be home by nine, missy. Have you washed behind your ears? Where are the boots I loaned you?"

Liv gave him a reluctant expression. "You have a very strange father-daughter relationship with your girls. You're not going to pretend to be my father. I just want you to walk me down the aisle and give me away."

The king of the fae took Liv's hand and brought it to his mouth—charm overflowing his every movement. "Liv, I would be honored to give you away." He thought for a moment, a genuine smile on his face. "Actually, I'm glad you didn't choose me to be your maid of honor. I can't imagine who you did choose but talk about pressure. All I have to do is walk, which we all know isn't rocket science."

"It depends on the day for you." Liv laughed and flashed a wink at Sophia. "I don't know. I think the person I chose for my maid of honor will handle the pressure flawlessly."

CHAPTER EIGHT

"Call it what you want," Lorenzo Rosario began, his tone terse, "but we don't need the support of the United States government to do our jobs—or that of any other entity."

The Councilor narrowed his eyes at Sophia as she stepped into the Chamber of the Tree.

Many of the members of the House of the Fourteen were present. The Councilors sat on the high bench, looking down at the Warriors, who stood in a half-circle. Flanking them were Jude and Diabolos, the regulators, a white tiger and a black crow. They upheld truth during the council meetings. Overhead, the dome ceiling sparkled with the lights representing magicians all over the world. There weren't as many as Sophia remembered from her last visit.

Rudolf and Liv stalked past Sophia, taking their usual spots in the chamber. Many of the Mortal Seven and their chimeras were present, but they often remained quiet, only letting their voices be heard during voting. The Warriors were to remain quiet during the proceedings unless they were Liv Beaufont. She was rarely quiet, regardless of what was going on.

Sophia strode forward, not pausing until she was standing in front of the Councilors, glaring up at them as they conversed.

"I think discounting having the support of foreign governments is a mistake this Councilor has made before," Hester DeVries stated, her tone matching Lorenzo's.

Bianca Mantovani scoffed. "I contend that once again, the members of this council are putting too much stock in other governing bodies. We are the House of Fourteen, the oldest governing agency on the planet."

A forced cough shot out of Sophia's mouth.

Clark shot her a curt expression, but everyone else seemed absorbed in the heated debate brewing hotter.

"I agree," Lorenzo stated, nodding in Bianca's direction. "Looking for approval from other organizations undermines our authority, which should be absolute."

Another cough rocketed from Sophia's mouth this time louder.

This earned her a few looks, but Bianca ensured that it didn't last.

"Councilor Lorenzo has been around long enough that he speaks from experience," she said smugly. "Bowing down and asking for support is as good as leveling ourselves with others when we really need to position ourselves as superior."

The next cough didn't come from Sophia. She suspected it was Liv behind her, but it did the job of getting all eyes on the council to revolve in their direction.

"Is everything all right?" Hara Takahashi asked.

"It appears the Beaufonts have some sort of bug," Bianca observed, wiggling her nose.

"You want to hug?" Liv asked her, a smile in her voice.

The woman looked at her with a pinched glare and shook her head before glaring down at Sophia. "We don't have you on the schedule, Sophia. What are you doing here?"

"Apparently, coming to correct a bunch of misconceptions." Sophia sighed. "And not a moment too soon."

"Excuse me?" Bianca remarked, offense in her voice.

"It's weird," Sophia began, "but the last time I was here, I seem to remember having to explain the hierarchy of the Dragon Elite over the House of Fourteen, yet it seems I'll need to give a refresher lesson."

"Bianca is getting old and losing her mental faculties if you know what I mean," Liv remarked.

Bianca gasped. "I'm not getting old."

"We're all getting old," Raina Ludwig remarked. "That's inevitable."

"Well, unless you're breaking one of Father Time's laws," Liv stated, warning in her voice.

"My point," Bianca fussed, "is that I'm not losing my memory."

"Yet you don't seem to remember the Dragon Elite is the oldest governing organization or that we're the supreme ruling force over all organizations," Sophia explained.

Lorenzo leaned forward. "If that's the case, then we call on you to help." There was a condescending quality in his voice that challenged Sophia. "Mortal governments worldwide have refused compliance with us, stating that the trivial matter of a few magicians going missing is cause to question our authority."

"A few?" Clark objected. "There have been a few *hundred*."

Hester nodded. "It's almost as bad as the last time this happened."

"The last time?" Sophia questioned.

"Yes," Clark answered. "It was several years ago."

"Who was behind it?" she asked.

The council members glanced at each other, obvious nervousness on their faces.

"We never determined that," Raina answered after a long pause when no one else seemed willing to respond to the question.

"Were the events surrounding the disappearances similar to now?" Sophia continued to speculate.

"That's not your concern," Bianca told her. She wasn't satisfied unless she was making enemies, Sophia thought.

The dragonrider sighed, wondering if she'd get in trouble for stunning the snob who had memory issues, or more likely, tolerance issues. "Hiker Wallace, the leader of the Dragon Elite, sent me here because the House of Fourteen is losing credibility with governments, causing disputes worldwide since you're unable to come to any consensus on matters pertaining to mortals and magicians."

"That is more a reflection of their unwillingness to accept our scope of power." Lorenzo's voice sounded tired like the conversation was boring him.

"I would argue it's more a product of governments already having their doubts about us based on past events," Clark stated confidently. "Now we can't account for the disappearance of hundreds of magicians and our own aren't heeding our warnings about safety. We've lost respect and authority. The other organizations are losing confidence in our governing, so why would they want to work with us directly on matters?"

"Because we are the House of Fourteen!" Bianca objected.

Clark lowered his chin, a disappointed expression on his face. "That doesn't hold the same weight it once did. Our mismanagement of this situation will only continue to affect other's perceptions of us."

Hester nodded. "For instance, thinking of the disappearance of our race as trivial is exactly why we are losing our reputation. If that was to get out."

Lorenzo narrowed his eyes at the healer. "We've given recommendations to our community about safety measures. We've assigned a Warrior to the investigation." He indicated Trudy DeVries on the far side of the chamber. "What else are we to do?"

"Maintain a working relationship with foreign governments," Clark offered. "We are no island, and turning our backs on them now will only make things harder to repair when we need their help."

"I was actually thinking," Trudy began, her voice small at first but growing in strength as she spoke. "For my investigative efforts, it would be helpful to employ the use of mortal police resources. Cameras, crime reports and other—"

"And make us look like we need them!" Lorenzo exclaimed, shaking his head.

"Well, it's just that I haven't had any luck with—"

"Then you'll just have to find other methods," he interrupted Trudy again. Turning his pointy chin to Sophia, he narrowed his eyes at her. "If the Dragon Elite truly wants to show their worth, then how about you as adjudicators rule over this dispute and require the other governments to bow to our authority?"

Sophia wanted to laugh. Instead, she said, "I don't object to the caution you're being shown. As world adjudicators, I'm going to hold off on ruling on this matter. That will come after you find out who is behind it. Your first priority—everyone's—needs to be stopping the disappearance of magicians. I think all governments will conclude that's most important. Then we can resolve issues related to the perception and reputation of the House."

A frustrated sound spilled from Lorenzo's mouth. "As you have already heard, we are trying to stop the disappearance of magicians."

"Then it sounds like you need help," Sophia observed confidently.

"We don't ask for hel—"

Sophia held up her hand, pausing Bianca. "I'm not offering it. I'm demanding that you take it. Things have gone too far."

Bianca's face flushed red. "You can't do—"

"Actually," Sophia cut in, a smile on her face. "If you remember correctly, as the supreme ruling force, the Dragon Elite can do what we like."

She turned to face Trudy, a pleasant, non-threatening expression on her face. "I will be adding our investigative and protective efforts to yours."

An expression of relief sprang to Trudy's face. "That would be welcome. Thank you."

Sophia nodded and turned her attention back to the council. "There you have it. First, we are going to find out who is behind this. Protecting magicians is of the upmost importance. Then the Dragon Elite will preside over the disputes that resulted from this and review the practices the House put into motion as a result of this. If we find that the council didn't take decisive action to protect—"

"How dare you?" Bianca's voice was shrill when she accused, but it didn't fluster Sophia in the least.

Instead, a tiny smile tugged on the side of her mouth. "Oh, I dare. Please note, any council members who are judged as not taking matters of this sort seriously will have to answer to the authority of the Dragon Elite, potentially facing punishment or termination."

Bianca's eyes popped open, almost as wide as her gaping mouth. "You can't do that."

Clark leaned back and crossed his arms over his chest, a proud expression on his face. "She, as a Dragon Elite, absolutely can."

CHAPTER NINE

All too well, Sophia knew the interior of the House of Fourteen. She'd grown up hunting around the corridors. Well, really hiding in them avoiding other Royals.

Unlike the Castle that changed based on whatever weird mythology used by Quiet, the House remained mostly the same. The library was a bit different, though, and it was ruled by the many books inside of it. One could easily become lost inside the space. Finding a book there was more of a safari than it was a research project, and getting out was like navigating a maze.

The rest of the House of Fourteen was mostly predictable. That's why Sophia was surprised when the portal door that led to the Castle was locked. She glanced around, trying to decide if she was in the right place. It was where she'd come through earlier.

"Why isn't it opening?" she asked out loud.

"Because you're not supposed to go through yet," a seemingly disembodied voice said.

Sophia spun around, expecting to find someone hiding in the shadows. There were no ghosts in the House of Fourteen that she knew of. The place, much like the Castle, could only have its members present inside of it.

Then her gaze fell to the ground, and she remembered the one entity who defied that rule. She sighed. "Hey, Plato."

The lynx flicked his tail, prancing by her, a nonchalant expression on his face as he continued down the hallway. His eyes seemed to say, "Follow me, if you dare."

"Why am I not supposed to go through the portal, back to the Castle?" she asked, stalking after the magical creature.

"Because…" he said, a hint of mischief in his tone.

Catching up with him, she glared down at him. "You must be exhausted after offering such a lengthy explanation."

Without warning, he sat down and began licking his paw. "I could use a nap."

"So, what do you have on the agenda for me?" She watched as his white-tipped tail patted the floor slightly.

"I thought we'd discuss your future plans, ways you can help to save the world, and something I need you to fetch."

"Only if this all involves a ton of riddles that leave me mostly confused and irritated with you," she bargained, more amused than frustrated by this uninvited diversion.

"How you feel on matters will really be up to you," he said matter-of-factly.

"Did you shut the portal to the Castle?" she asked, glancing over her shoulder. "I didn't think you could do that, although since no place is off-limits to you, I guess I should have."

"You really should have," he agreed, continuing to bathe himself. "I only closed the portal so I could reopen the one that connects the Castle and the Great Library. It's like a reboot of sorts. All portals were down during the reset."

"Right," Sophia said, drawing out the word. "We can get to the Great Library once more? It's not locked on the other side?"

He shook his head. "No, the lock Trin Currante put on it has been removed."

"Good." Sophia was glad to have access to the largest library in the world once more.

"Soon, I'll have to start interviews for the new librarian," he continued. "Which reminds me, have you cured Ainsley yet so she can leave the Gullington?"

She gave him an annoyed expression. "I'm certain you know I haven't. Is that your way of telling me to get on it?"

"Maybe," he sang coyly.

Shrugging, she told him, "Well, I'll get right on that when time allows."

"Haven't you heard, time is a servant that works for you," he explained. "Ask for more, and you shall have it. Need less, and it will shrink. You really should know how to make this element bend in your favor. I mean, your sister is the one and only diplomat of Father Time, after all."

"Does Liv know this? It is a radical idea."

He gave a noncommittal expression. "Another thing I've told her a dozen times, but she probably didn't hear me."

Sophia sighed. "Let me guess. Was she asleep on these occasions?"

He gawked at her with mock surprise. "How did you know?"

"I would say I'm grateful my sidekick isn't as sneaky as you, but…"

Plato snickered. "I can take many pages out of Lunis' book and I have. The dragon and I are two of the same."

She nodded. "Tell me about it. What is it about the Beaufonts that we get the most helpful slash unhelpful magical creatures?"

"Luck?" he asked.

"Yeah, I don't think that's it." Sophia finally allowed herself the chance to glance around and realized she knew where they were. Behind her was a door she'd entered many times, more than any other at the House of Fourteen. "Plato, why are we standing in front of the Beaufonts' old family residence?"

"Oh, look at that." He sounded surprised. "We do happen to be here. What are the chances?"

She swung back to face the lynx. "Not as small as one might think, I'm guessing."

"I was just thinking that Liv couldn't find the object she was looking for because it doesn't exist," Plato explained.

"What?" Sophia asked. "Our father's ring is gone?"

He nodded. "It was on him at the time of his death and…you don't want to go after that."

She grimaced, pushing the idea of her father's dead body out of her mind. "No, I don't."

"However, I think there's something which belonged to your mother I think Liv would like, although she may not have even thought about it."

Sophia batted her eyelashes at the lynx. "Let me guess, you didn't bother to tell her about it, did you?"

"Why do that when you can go hunt it down and surprise her?"

Letting out a long breath, she shook her head. "Are you planning to tell me what I'm looking for?"

He gave her a sly grin. "And take the fun out of it?"

CHAPTER TEN

Haunted. That's how the old Beaufont family residence felt when Sophia entered. The space was dark and smelled of dust.

Clark had moved in with Liv a while ago, and Sophia well before that. They'd covered the furniture with sheets and gone back infrequently since then. The place would always be theirs, as long as they had positions in the House of Fourteen. That was for the best because neither Liv nor Clark wanted many of the possessions inside of the residence, but they didn't want to get rid of them either—so it became a storage facility.

Sophia halted inside the main room, the words she'd seen every day since she could remember etched across the main wall, just as they graced her bedroom at the Castle and Liv's house with Clark and Stefan.

Familia est sempiternum.

It didn't matter how many times she saw the Beaufont family motto or said those words, their meaning never diminished.

Family was forever. They were the most important part of her life. They were why she fought for a better world. It was why Liv had come back to the House of Fourteen and taken her magic back. There were few things worth risking it all for, but when it came to family, there was no question at all.

Sophia had no idea what she was looking for in the old family residence. She'd shared the space with Clark, Ian, and Reese for most all her life. Before, when her parents were alive, and Liv was with them, they'd lived in a bigger unit. After their mother and father died, they moved—probably also to help the Beaufont children to grieve. Still, Sophia still felt the ghosts of her dead family in this space. Maybe that was because all their possessions were still everywhere.

She studied the pictures on the wall and the many shelves filled with trinkets, wondering what she was looking for. Her parent's things were everywhere. Sophia could tell Liv had recently been scavenging through the space since things were moved, showing the outline of dust where they had sat prior.

It appeared that in an effort to find their father's ring, Liv had searched through various decorative boxes from different places in the world. They were souvenirs Guinevere Beaufont had brought back from her travels when on Warrior expeditions for the House of Fourteen. Clark had told her fondly about how their mother's return was always marked by two things. First was a flood of relief on Theodore, their father's face. The other was usually a gift for her children. Their mother apparently loved boxes because "there was always a reason to hide things."

Sophia didn't dig through any of the boxes on the shelves in the living room. If Liv had been through them, then Sophia didn't expect to find what she was looking for.

That was just the thing. Sophia didn't know what she was actually looking for. Of course, Plato wasn't going to tell her. He didn't even share with Liv that her father's ring wasn't here. It was the way of the lynx, and there was hardly any reason to question it.

"What am I looking for?" Sophia asked the lonely space, the sound of her voice strangely making her feel better.

Purpose, Lunis offered in her head. *A sense of direction, maybe? Or possibly the meaning of life?*

Sophia snickered, grateful to have his presence reassuring her in his own strange way. *I was thinking more along the lines of an object,* she told him. *Something Liv would want for her wedding.*

I've heard that one needs a veil to get married, Lunis supplied. *Well, and also a dress. Maybe you can find your mother's old one.*

That's a great idea, Sophia remarked, excitement erupting in her chest. *Although I don't think Liv would be caught dead in a veil, she'd probably wear our mother's dress.*

Sophia turned to face a room she hadn't entered for a long time. It was the study, but no one had ever gone in there to read or do work. Ian had just moved all their parent's most personal artifacts in there after their death and closed it up.

Sometimes, when Sophia was younger, she would go in there and play, but Clark usually gently persuaded her to find another area for her spells and such.

Holding her breath, Sophia tried to open the door and found it stuck, probably from disuse. If she thought the Beaufonts' living area smelled of dust, she was sorely mistaken. This place had such a pungent mustiness in the air, it made Sophia sneeze three times in quick succession.

How long has it been since someone's been in here? she asked Lunis.

It's hard to go back to places that remind you of the people you can't go back to, he offered sensitively.

Sophia loved that dragon more than air.

He knew how to be funny when she needed it, and he saved her butt when she was in peril. More important than anything, he knew how to give her comfort when her heart was fracturing. Lunis had the knack of giving Sophia what she needed when she needed it.

There was an old writing desk in the corner. It wasn't her father's, she knew. Sophia had found the desk in a plantation house in Louisiana when searching for his journal. She'd gotten the journal but left the desk.

From hearing Reese's stories, she knew the writing desk had belonged to their mother, who played with the idea of writing down her many adventures. Apparently, she'd taken a page out of Stephen King's book who had said, *"It starts with this: put your desk in the corner, and every time you sit down there to write, remind yourself why it isn't in the middle of the room. Life isn't a support system for art. It's the other way around."*

Sophia's mother had always looked for ways to humble herself. She'd told her children often it was the sign of a good Warrior. "As soon as you inflate your ego, the villain strikes you down. Stay modest and they'll never see you coming."

Smiling to herself, Sophia vaulted the words in her memory, knowing they'd save her more than once in her lifetime.

Beside the desk were rows of books that belonged to her parents. There were also various pieces of furniture: armchairs, coffee tables, old rugs, and an armoire.

For a moment, Sophia wished it was the wardrobe that took one to Narnia and she could be off on another adventure.

You really picked the right calling, didn't you, Lunis observed.

Sophia grinned. *I guess so. I'm my mother's child.*

And your sister's sister, Lunis stated, referring to Liv.

Although I didn't so much pick being a dragonrider, she argued. *It sort of picked me.*

Any regrets? he asked.

She shook her head, a grin on her face. *Not a one,* Sophia replied.

Good, he said. *Because you're stuck with me.*

I'm okay with that, she assured him.

Forever, he added for good measure.

Sophia's smile widened as she approached the wardrobe. She pulled at the door and of course, found it locked. Sighing, Sophia deflated.

It had to go like this, she grumbled to her dragon.

He laughed. *Would you have it any other way?*

She shook her head. *Really, for once could the mysterious lynx just tell me what I'm looking for and how to get it?*

As he would say, where would the fun in that be?

Sophia grimaced at Lunis' reply and looked around the room. "Where is the key?"

How do you know what you're looking for is in there? he questioned.

It's in there, she declared. *It's always in the locked cabinet.*

He chuckled. *Yeah, I know. Just testing you.*

It was weird to find something locked in the Beaufont home. Sophia thought back and realized nothing was ever locked. All doors were always open and there were no keys around. Even their family home was not locked since for the most part, one could not enter unless they were a Beaufont. Adler Sinclair, the corrupt magician who had nearly destroyed the House of Fourteen, had found a way to break that law when he stole Lunis' egg.

Maybe you don't need a key to open it, Lunis offered.

Sophia slumped. *How about a riddle? I really prefer those over obvious solutions.*

Good to know, he teased humorously. *Now I know what to get you for your birthday.*

Yes, please ensure my gift is wrapped in a riddle I have to work out before I can open it, she said.

Remember your family cottage on the coast, Lunis reminded her.

Sophia thought back, remembering her dragon had access to her memories. That usually made things convenient. Sometimes it made things embarrassing depending on the memory. However, she'd given up trying to feel separate from her dragon. They were two of the same, and feeling embarrassment from him about her feelings or memories was like feeling that way about herself.

Yes, she said, recalling the place where Ian and Reese were murdered by the same man who had stolen Lunis' egg—Adler Sinclair. The lock was undone by an incantation.

Now that Sophia was studying the wardrobe, she realized there actually wasn't a lock.

So, it is an incantation, she stated, appreciating that Lunis probably already noticed this.

You can try an unlocking spell, he offered.

She shook her head but tried one anyway.

The wardrobe didn't open.

As I suspected, she said. *It can't be that easy.*

You just need the magic password, he said with a laugh.

"Please open," she said, jerking on the handle. Again, it didn't open.

Try "Open sesame," he commented. *That one always works.*

By always do you mean, never?

He laughed again. *Of course I do. You could also try abracadabra.*

Sophia shook her head. *It's something obvious.*

Like a family motto everyone in the Beaufonts knows by heart, Lunis supplied.

Sophia's eyes widened. It can't be that easy. It's never that easy. She reached out again and tugged hopefully on the wardrobe door as she muttered, *"Familia est sempiternum."*

Right on cue, the wardrobe opened, showing her a whole new world she never would have expected to find inside it.

CHAPTER ELEVEN

Enchanted by what she saw, it took Sophia a moment to understand what she was looking at.

This wardrobe didn't lead to another world like Narnia. However, it wasn't a typical armoire either.

Wow, Lunis said, awe in his tone. *It's bigger on the inside.*

A laugh fell from Sophia's mouth. She should have expected it. Much like the Tardis, the inside of the wardrobe was much larger than it should have been on the inside. It was another room exactly like the one where she was standing.

Turning, she checked to ensure she was right. For a moment, she thought she was looking into a mirror, but there were a few items in the wardrobe room that weren't in the room where she was.

For instance, there was a double bass sitting in the corner. There was also a large chest in the middle of the room.

Sophia paused before stepping into the wardrobe, finding the space chillier than she'd expected.

What do you make of this? she asked Lunis.

It's storage, he answered.

Why does it look exactly like the room where the armoire is? she questioned.

I think it's a safety measure, he mused. *It isn't really the same as the room where you are. That's just camouflage.*

How do you know?

Try to pick up one of those books on the shelf, he ordered.

Sophia did as he instructed, and the book wasn't in her hand for more than a second before it turned to dust and slipped through her fingers.

She spun to survey the room. *I don't get it,* she said to Lunis.

It's a security box of sorts, he observed. *Only the things that aren't in the room where it resides are in it.*

Sophia ran her hand over the double bass, remembering Clark had said their father once played the instrument. Unlike the book, it didn't turn to dust under her fingers.

Her eyes skipped to the large chest in the center of the room. Excitement built in her as she approached it. It dissipated when she opened it to find the chest was completely empty.

Well, that's disappointing, she said with a sigh.

That's where I left that, Lunis exclaimed.

Left what, she asked.

My whole lot of nothing.

Sophia laughed. Again her dragon was making her feel better in his own weird and wonderful way.

I guess if we ever need to hide something, we know where to put it, he offered thoughtfully.

Sophia nodded. *Good point.*

She glanced out the door of the wardrobe at the almost identical room. The musical instrument and the chest appeared to be the only things different between the two spaces.

Not so fast, Lunis stated, sounding victorious.

What, Sophia asked, searching the other room for what he was referring to.

On the shelf, he told her.

Sophia glanced at the shelf in the real room and then the one in the wardrobe space. It appeared identical, but then she saw it.

Sitting next to the books on the far end was an antique jewelry box. It was large and made of mahogany. Inlaid on the front was an intricate carving made out of ivory.

It's beautiful, Sophia observed, approaching it carefully afraid to touch it, thinking it would turn to dust.

The jewelry box had to be another gift her mother brought back from her travels. Asia, she thought, studying the design.

To Sophia's relief, the jewelry box didn't evaporate into thin air when she opened it. The inside was somehow even more beautiful than the outside. It was lined with emerald green silk with more intricate designs done in embroidery. It was definitely from Asia, Sophia thought.

Even more beautiful than the jewelry box were the items within. For a moment, Sophia thought she'd find their father's ring, but then she remembered Plato had said he'd had it on him when he died.

There was a large pendant that was no doubt full of magic. There were also a few diamond rings, various mismatched earrings, and a broken watch. Sophia combed through the jewelry, wondering what she was looking for. The jewelry was all nice, but nothing jumped out at her as something Liv would "need" for her wedding.

"You sneaky lynx," Sophia muttered to herself. "What did you have in mind for me to find?"

Yeah, none of that stuff looks like Liv's style, Lunis observed.

He was right, Sophia realized. Liv wouldn't wear rings or a pendant. She wasn't a jewelry kind of person, but for her wedding, she needed something.

Combing her fingers through the various earrings, she looked for pearls or something simple and understated, like the Warrior for the House of Fourteen. Her finger found a rip in the seam of the jewelry box.

At first, Sophia didn't think anything of it, but as she pulled it back, she once again found something she wasn't expecting.

Exactly like the wardrobe, she was looking into another jewelry box.

Well, I didn't see that coming, Lunis said. *It's a security box inside a security box.*

Sophia laughed, feeling exhilarated by the experience. In this hidden jewelry box, there was only one item, and it was what Plato had intended her to find. She knew it without a doubt.

Sophia was certain as she reached for the sapphire necklace, not just because it was extraordinarily beautiful and reminded her of Liv. The gems lining the necklace were the color of the Beaufonts' eyes. The whole family had those trademark blue eyes. It was the tag attached to the necklace that confirmed what Sophia knew already. She turned it over and read the words neatly printed on it aloud.

"For my daughters on their wedding days."

CHAPTER TWELVE

"You belong with me."
Those were the words engraved on the back of the necklace. Next to them was a single initial: T.

Sophia knew it stood for Theodore Beaufont, her father.

He gave this to my mother, I bet, she thought, running her fingers over the sapphires.

She probably wore it on her wedding day, Lunis added.

Something blue, Sophia said, a giggle popping out of her mouth from elation.

It's something old, too, Lunis stated.

Now I just have to get Liv something new for her wedding day.

Well, her dress will be new, Lunis commented.

Sophia laughed. *I highly doubt I can get her to wear a dress, even on her wedding day.*

She'll wear a dress, he told her. *You just have to find one that's her style.*

One with a sheath for her sword, Sophia replied.

Something she can throw a roundhouse kick in, he joked.

Sophia held the necklace close to her chest, feeling a strange warmth radiating from the object. She looked forward to giving it to her sister on her wedding day. However, it would have to wait.

She had more pressing issues. Most important was getting to the bottom of the disappearance of the magicians. She needed to track down Trin Currante. When all that was resolved, there was the Ainsley and Hiker business.

Since Sophia had no clue where to begin to look to unravel these mysteries, she knew there was only one place to go.

With a fondness in her chest, she left the wardrobe and made her way out of the old Beaufont family residence, hoping to return soon and explore some more. For now, she needed to pay her fairy godmother a visit.

CHAPTER THIRTEEN

B lank space stretched between where Sophia stood and Happily Ever After College.

She had started for the pink door at the front of the building when a group in the distance caught her attention. Among the students in uniforms, she recognized Mae Ling, her fairy godmother bobbing around the crowd, pointing wildly.

For being under five-foot-tall, Mae Ling had a presence that made her appear larger than most.

Many of the students had their mouths covered when Sophia approached. She thought this might be cause for concern, but when she was closer, she heard many excited gasps.

Mae Ling snapped her fingers in the air and shook her head, a stern expression on her face. "They aren't cute cuddly creatures...well, they are, but more importantly, for your purposes, they are tools."

On the grass in front of the group were little baby bunnies, mice, chicks, and sparrows. The birds hopped around, not taking flight, which was surprising to Sophia. All the young animals seemed to be paying attention to Mae Ling, the instructor, as if they were the students in the class.

"Now," Mae Ling began, her hands behind her back as she charged one way and then the other. "You have a Cinderella, and she needs an entourage to attract the attention of a Prince Charming. Which of these tools would you employ?"

Multiple hands shot up into the air, waving excitedly.

"Go ahead, Jaz." Mae Ling pointed to a girl with short curly brown hair.

"It would depend on the Cinderella," Jaz began. "If she's a bit shy, I'd use the bunny. A more outgoing type would be matched well with a squirrel."

All heads swiveled to Mae Ling, looking for approval from their instructor. "Although that's a logical answer, it's not correct," she began, continuing to pace. "A fairy godmother has to work with what she has available to her. You will need to learn to adapt your magic to the situation. Not the other way around."

Mae Ling waved Sophia over to her. "Look, we have a wonderful model right here. Now let's pretend this Cinderella needs to go to a party, but she can't like this obviously."

Peering down at her armored top and black pants, Sophia shrugged. It wasn't really party attire. Mae Ling pointed to one of the girls standing nearby. "Torrie, put our Cinderella into an appropriate outfit using what you have available to you."

A very tall girl with long blonde hair stepped forward, furrowing her brow. "What I have available..." Her eyes scanned the area. She did a double-take when they ran across a bed of roses nearby. A spark of excitement filled her face before she swiped her hand in the direction of the roses.

They disappeared, and a weird constriction took over Sophia's body. Her head jerked down as her clothes were replaced with a tight dress covered in a rose pattern. It was elegant and yet fashionable.

"Bravo," Mae Ling approved, clapping her hands. "Sophia would definitely attract attention in that. Roses last much longer for clothes than other types of flowers, although time restrictions would still apply." She turned, centering her attention on another girl—this one with a ponytail and a nervous expression. "Now, Nicole, our

Cinderella is going to need some help to attend this party. I'll leave it up to you to figure that out."

Nicole stepped forward, tapping her finger to her chin as she thought. "First she'll need transportation."

Mae Ling nodded. "That's right."

Nicole glanced around before pointing at a nearby log. It morphed into a car with a wooden panel on the side.

"Very good," Mae Ling commented.

Nicole stayed focused as she pointed to one of the mice. It shot up at once, transforming into a short man with a round belly and a mouse-like face. He looked at the car and smiled before turning to face Sophia.

"You ordered an Uber?"

She grinned in reply.

"Lastly, no party is complete without a wingwoman," Nicole stated, pointing to the squirrel. The animal shifted until it took the form of a young woman with brown hair and a mischievous glint in her eyes.

"Who wants to party?" the lady asked.

No one answered, but the applause from the class confirmed Nicole had done what she was supposed to.

"Good work," Mae Ling declared. "You will break into groups and practice shifting animals into little helpers. I'll be back shortly to monitor your progress. For now, it appears my charge requires my assistance."

CHAPTER FOURTEEN

Daylight streamed through the branches and leaves overhead, creating dancing shadows on the ground as the wind swept through the trees.

Sophia ambled beside Mae Ling, enjoying the grounds of Happily Ever After College. Things weren't overly manicured. The flowers grew tall in the beds around the trees, and woodland creatures hopped around, not at all nervous about the two magicians strolling by.

"So is a fairy godmother's job mostly as a matchmaker?" Sophia asked, enjoying the fresh breeze on her cheeks.

"For the most part," Mae Ling answered. "Our jobs are to assist. There's no better way to do that than with love. However, with Cinderellas like you, I offer a lot more than just help with romance, so it depends. A fairy godmother's job is diverse and always changing, depending on our charge or the world around us or the future."

Sophia nodded. "Well, I don't need any help with romance at the moment."

Mae Ling gave her a knowing expression. "I realize that. You're in a good place there, but you have many other areas where you could use help."

"Yes," Sophia affirmed. Knowing how things worked with her fairy godmother, she told her about the disappearance of the magicians, Trin Currante, and Ainsley and Hiker. Even if Mae Ling knew her problems, she could only help Sophia if she was asked for help.

The small woman was quiet for a long moment after Sophia had run through everything. The expression she gave her made her worry.

Sophia sighed. "You can't help me, can you?"

"I can't help you with everything," Mae Ling answered finally. "The thing about life is we rarely have all the answers at once. Usually, we get them one at a time. One answer leads to another and then another. That's why solving our problems is important. It leads to more information."

"Okay, so do you have anything you can help me with?"

"I can't tell you how to solve your mystery with the disappearing magicians," Mae Ling explained, disappointment in her voice.

Sophia nodded, deflating slightly. "I understand. I think I have it too easy having people like you who can offer me insights into my problems."

"Oh, I wouldn't say there's anything easy about your predicament. Please remember you have a fairy godmother for help because of the scope of your problems and how far-reaching they tend to be."

That made Sophia feel marginally better.

"What I can tell you is the only person who can help you find the disappearing magicians is Trin Currante," Mae Ling continued.

Sophia halted suddenly, not having expected that. "Say what?"

"I realize it must be frustrating to you that I can tell you some answers but not others," Mae Ling said sympathetically. "You are exposed to others who can 'see' things, so I'm sure you realize sometimes we can see some things and not others."

Sophia nodded, remembering a recent conversation with Liv. Apparently, Father Time could see future events, but not entirely. They changed so frequently that as soon as he saw something, it began to shift, making his vision not entirely accurate. "I get that things aren't straightforward in this world."

"You are quite mature for your age," Mae Ling observed.

"So, I was right to go after Trin Currante, then?" Sophia asked, grateful to have the affirmation.

Mae Ling nodded. "Yes, your instincts are very good on this matter. She isn't what she seems."

Sophia watched as two hummingbirds spiraled in the air, playing or fighting she couldn't really tell. After a long pause, she pulled her attention away. "How do I find Trin Currante?"

"I can't tell you that, but I can tell you that you have other resources who will know better than me."

Sophia thought for a moment before the answer occurred to her. "Mortimer," she guessed.

Mae Ling nodded in reply. "I can help you with the Ainsley situation since heartache is part of my specialty, but I can't help you yet."

"I heard heartbreak can't really be fixed. Is that true?" Sophia inquired.

"Yes and no," Mae Ling told her. "There is no magic cure for heartbreak, just like there's no spell that can cause it. Heartbreak is a result of real interactions, failed expectations, and actions that hurt others. To fix it takes the same efforts that caused it. People have to talk, fall back in love and work for it. There are no shortcuts to mending the heart."

"That makes sense," Sophia said. "So, I have to help Ainsley and Hiker genuinely deal with their problems?"

"It's the only way," Mae Ling agreed. "Although once they are past that point, I will try and have solutions for you to continue to fix things. Mending hearts is just the first part."

Sophia nodded. She knew what Mae Ling meant. After that huge obstacle, then she'd have to find the cure to actually fix Ainsley and restore her memories. One thing at a time, though, she decided.

Mae Ling turned back to the group of students in the distance turning bunny rabbits into supportive colleagues and thoughtful friends and sighed. "I must get back to my class. I fear they aren't thinking outside the box."

Sophia didn't know what she meant since the students seemed to be turning various animals into different types of people. "I think you've done very well with them."

Mae Ling shook her head. "I've taught them what to do, and they are using old protocols to solve things. Remember, dear, sometimes we have to break out of how we used to do things to find the right solution."

Sophia nodded, not really knowing what her fairy godmother was referring to. "Okay, well, thanks for your help."

"On this occasion," Mae Ling began. "I don't think I was much help. I can offer you some advice about the trip you take next."

Sophia only offered her a confused expression.

"We all like gifts," Mae Ling hinted. "The one you're visiting next for answers likes things that are named after his race."

CHAPTER FIFTEEN

I t was nice to have a friend who was privy to so much, Sophia thought as she stepped through the portal onto Roya Lane, intent on visiting Mortimer. First, she had to make a stop, though.

She didn't have to think too hard to know who Mae Ling was referring to when she offered her last bit of advice, so she didn't have to think long about where to get him a gift.

Brownies apparently liked brownies and the treats named for them. She suspected the Crying Cat Bakery would have suitable options she could get for Mortimer. At the very least, the experience at the magical bakery would offer a laugh, a scare, and possibly a headache.

Sophia headed for the bakery straight away, keeping her head down as she strode through the busy lane. When she entered the bakery, she expected to find Lee leaning against the counter, sharpening a blade or licking blood off it. To her surprise, the assassin-baker was sitting at one of the tables along the windows, her face screwed up with confusion as she leaned over a mound of paperwork.

"Are you doing your taxes?" Sophia joked, expecting Lee to look up when she entered.

Instead, the assassin's gaze stayed trained on the papers in front of her. "No," she groaned.

"Oh, is it an assassin contract?" she joked.

Lee did look up then, a frustrated expression on her face. "What kind of assassin has a contract? Like I need a paper trail linking me to murders." She shook her head. "It's weird you know nothing about assassins."

"Not as weird as you'd think since the whole idea goes against pretty much everything I believe in," Sophia argued.

"You do agree some people need to die?" Lee asked.

Sophia shook her head. "I believe that's you putting words in my mouth."

Lee sighed. "Okay, so you have killed before, right?"

Sophia nodded.

"It was kill or be killed, right?" Lee questioned.

"Yeah, but I don't think your job and mine are the same," Sophia stated.

Lee nodded and picked up a pen. She wrote on a piece of paper that seemed to be a list of names. Under the last one, she wrote *Sophia Beaufont.*

"Why did you just put my name there?"

Lee waved this off. "Just reminding myself who I need to get Christmas gifts for."

"It's June," Sophia argued.

"Never can start too early," Lee told her.

Sophia dismissed this and pointed to the pile of paperwork. "What is all this?"

"Oh, it's one thing or another," Lee muttered. "Insurance stuff. Citizen BS. Then there are bank forms. I went to go get help, but I'd apparently already been helped once that day, so the teller told me I had to come back tomorrow."

Sophia couldn't help but laugh. "You can only be helped once a day?"

"Apparently," Lee answered. "So now I'm stuck having to fill out a Form 129, which to the best of my knowledge isn't in English."

Sophia glanced at the top form. The first line read, *Did your nonreturnable outgoings for the first half of the year exceed your deductions for the quarterly VAT return?*

"Oh, dear, that's like rocket science there."

Lee nodded, pushing the papers away. "Is it any wonder I want to kill people for a living?"

Sophia pressed her eyes shut for a half-beat. "It really is better for us if you don't tell me what you do for a living repeatedly."

"I'm a baker," Lee agreed. "I feed people sugar and lard laced with MSG. That's how I kill people. Duh."

Deciding it was better to move on, Sophia turned her attention to the case of pastries and baked goods. "I need a brownie. Do you have any?"

"Of course I do," Lee said matter-of-factly. "You can have it for a tiny little price."

Sophia almost laughed. "Do you need me to recover a katana from the depths of hell?"

Lee's eyes widened. "That's right. You haven't delivered on the last thing. Man, this brownie is going to cost you."

"How much?" Sophia asked, realizing she didn't have any money.

Pointing to the paperwork, Lee said, "You have to fill out and file my Section 49 form and then renew my registration for the assassin association."

Sophia shook her head. "I'm not doing any of that."

"It was worth a shot." Lee trudged to the other side of the bakery counter and began grabbing various pastries and putting them into a paper bag. "I did learn some information that will help you to get my katana. Have you figured out how to get Zac Efron, a magic compass, or the magical chewing gum?"

"Strangely," Sophia began, "I have solutions to everything but kidnapping Zac Efron."

"Do you need to borrow my ski mask?" Lee wanted to know.

Sophia shook her head. "I don't believe in sharing such things, but don't worry about it. I'll make good on my end of the bargain."

"I know, because you like your kneecaps."

Sophia realized she'd made the strangest friends, and she was okay with this. "You have a lead for me on the katana?"

"Yeah, but since you don't have Zac yet, I'll wait," Lee stated. "That gives me time to firm up the location since I need to check the word of a drunken gnome who might have just been telling me what I wanted to hear."

"Why would he do that?"

Lee shrugged. "That's what people do sometimes when being held at knifepoint."

"Imagine that," Sophia said as she took the small white bag of brownies from Lee. "What do I owe you for this?"

"A lifetime of servitude," she answered.

Sophia halted, obvious hesitation in her movements.

Lee shook her head. "I mean, nothing. Just return when you have everything in place for the katana mission. Then I'll have more information. I feel that you and I have entered into a beautiful partnership. I give you poisoned goods, and in return, you do illegal things for me."

"What?" Sophia questioned at once, looking down at the bag of pastries.

"Huh?" Lee replied. "Nothing. I was just saying how great it is to work with someone who owes me big favors."

Sophia shook her head. She had better keep her enemies close and her friends closer—because they scared the hell out of her.

CHAPTER SIXTEEN

Red bricks stretched the length of the block in front of Sophia. She didn't know how she knew the exact spot where the magical door to the brownie official office was located, but somehow she did.

When she spoke her name and title, the small door appeared in front of her, welcoming her to the office.

After crawling through the small door, she found herself in the usual reception area. This time Mortimer's wife and children weren't hanging out in the space. It was strangely quiet, which gave Sophia pause.

"Mortimer?" she called quietly.

The head of the brownies slipped out of the back office, looking over his shoulder nervously. When he affirmed everything was okay, he turned his attention forward and tiptoed down the hallway in Sophia's direction.

She gave him an uncertain expression when he stopped in front of her. "Everything okay?"

Cautiously, he glanced back over his shoulder again. "Everything is...stressful. When I'm stressed, then the family is. Pricilla hasn't been sleeping well at all lately, which means the children haven't. I finally got them all to take a nap."

"Oh," Sophia whispered. "What's going on that everyone is so stressed?"

He sighed. "Well, the upset between mortals and the House of Fourteen has put a strain on many households worldwide. You see, mortals do best when they work in conjunction with magicians. Before Warrior Beaufont fixed things, mortals weren't as happy, which made our job as brownies much more complicated. Then things got easier. Now they are back to how they were. Anyway, the family feels my stress and what can I say, that's the way it goes."

He combed his hands through his thinning hair on the top of his head.

"Are you okay?" Sophia asked, feeling bad for coming to him with her problems. If she could fix the problems with the House of Four-teen, she hoped it would make life easier for him.

"I'll be fine," he answered. "I don't need to sleep. A bit of some-thing..." He sniffed the air, his eyes widening as his gaze fell to the white bag in her hand. "That isn't..."

Holding the bag of brownies out, Sophia said, "It is."

The little guy looked overwhelmed with sudden emotion. His bottom lip quivered, and tears welled in his eyes. He shook his head, his long ears nearly hitting him in the face. "How did you know, Sophia Beaufont, dragonrider for the Dragon Elite? The one thing I really needed was a brownie. That's the best way to recharge us when we're down."

Sophia smiled inwardly. Of course, Mae Ling knew this and sent Sophia with exactly what she needed to endear herself more to the brownie.

A groan rolled out of his mouth as he grabbed for the brownie. "It's still warm. How is it still warm?"

Sophia didn't know since she'd watched Lee take it out of the case. "I'm guessing magic is in play."

He smiled wide as he took a bite. "Cryin' 'at 'akery makes da bessssst."

"Yes, they do," Sophia affirmed, having gotten the gist of what he was trying to say.

Mortimer licked his fingers, his eyes closed like he was having a religious experience. "That. Was. Perfect."

Sophia could hardly believe it, but the brownie had downed the entire brownie in record time. He rolled up the bag, tucking it under his arm.

"The rest will come in handy later," he said, waving her over to the seating area next to the receptionist's desk.

"Mortimer, are you going to be okay?" She was worried about the little fella.

"It's lovely of you to be concerned about me, S. Beaufont." The color was returning to his face, and his eyes were shining brightly once more. "I've weathered many storms with the mortal world, and I have every hope I'll get through this one, especially because you're on the case."

"I guess you know that's why I'm here, then?" Sophia asked.

He nodded. "I figured one of the Beaufont sisters would be by for information on the disappearance of the magicians."

"Liv wasn't assigned this case," Sophia explained.

"I think one Beaufont sister will do the trick, but only with the right information." Mortimer's ear swiveled in the direction of his office like he heard something. After a moment, he relaxed. "Now, what can I help you with?"

"Well, my source," Sophia began, not wanting to disclose it was her fairy godmother. She figured Mortimer knew anyway, but she was keeping all her private inside contacts secret to be on the safe side. "They tell me that in order to get to the bottom of the missing magicians, I have to track down the cyborg Trin Currante. Can you help me with that?"

He nodded, twirling the long hair that sprouted from his large ears around his finger as he thought. "Yes, I figured you'd want information on Trin Currante, and I think I have a lead."

"Great news," Sophia exclaimed.

"Yes, I've heard rumor of a dog that might be connected to her."

Sophia peeled back, not having expected this piece of information. "A dog? Are you sure?"

He shook his head. "No, I'm not. That's why I'll need a little more time to firm up details." Rubbing his belly, he smiled. "Now I'm in the perfect position to get to work and find the information for you."

"Thank you, Mortimer. This is really great."

"Sophia Beaufont, I appreciate you think I'm helping you, but really, we all work for each other, don't we?"

Sophia nodded, liking the sentiment. "Yeah, I guess we do."

"I help you find what you're looking for, and you go and save the world bit by bit," he said proudly. "I can't think of a better arrangement."

She returned the thoughtful expression he gave her. "You're right. I can't either."

"Until we meet again." He bowed to her. "I'll be in touch as soon as I know something which I only hope gives you what you need to take decisive and swift action."

Sophia remembered the stressed expression on Mortimer's face when she'd entered the office. She wanted to get to the bottom of the missing magicians for the obvious reasons. She wanted to help Trin Currante because she felt oddly compelled. Now, she had a new motivation, knowing this situation was indirectly hurting the innocent and sweet brownies.

CHAPTER SEVENTEEN

"This is why we can't have nice things," Ainsley complained when Sophia entered the front door of the Castle.

The housekeeper was on the floor, arranging the pieces of a broken vase Sophia remembered seeing in the front area. Before it had been in one piece, not hundreds of them.

Evan stood nearby, leaning against the wall with his hands covering his face. "I told you, it wasn't my fault. I was being chased."

"By..." Ainsley chirped.

"I'd rather not say," Evan muttered through his fingers.

"Oh, no," Ainsley stated, pointing at the pieces of the vase. A few rose together, mending in midair before falling apart again and landing back on the floor. "It's going to take me forever to fix this. You're going to indulge me with what made you knock this ancient heirloom over."

"Just make the Castle fix it," Evan offered.

Ainsley shook her head. "Why didn't I think about that? Castle, why don't you repair the vase?"

They all waited.

A moment later, when nothing happened, Ainsley stuck her hands on her hips. "As I suspected, the Castle isn't going to fix it."

"Because Quiet wants me to be in trouble," Evan complained.

"Again, go ahead and tell me what was chasing you that made you knock this over," Ainsley ordered.

"It was a pterodactyl," Evan said, his hands still covering his mouth, partially obstructing his words.

A laugh popped out of Ainsley. "Did you say pterodactyl?"

He sighed, dropping his hands from his face. "I get that it's ridiculous since they are extinct."

She shook her head. "No, that's not why it's ridiculous. You do realize there are wards on the Castle to prevent other winged creatures from entering? Otherwise, I'd be shooing birds out from the rafters like I did a few centuries ago before putting measures into place."

"Oh, right," Evan said. "That didn't come to mind when a clawed creature was screaming at me and chasing me through the corridor."

"You are a dragonrider," Ainsley argued. "How come a little bird scared you?"

"Have I mentioned the claws and that it was very hungry?"

Ainsley shook this off, standing from the floor. "It was obviously the Castle messing with you."

Evan sighed. "Obviously. That is that short, round man's problem. I was just minding my own business getting ready for my next mission and then this beast descends on me from the ceiling. I didn't even have my sword or anything on me."

"And your magic was apparently broken." Ainsley brushed off her dress.

"I didn't have time to think," Evan argued. "I know you think you know what you'll do when faced with a threatening situation, but it's much more complicated than you'd think. You don't jump right to the option of using magic. Half the time, it doesn't even work right because fear messes it up."

The housekeeper narrowed her eyes, murder written in her gaze. "No, I wouldn't know how I'd react when faced with danger since for the last few centuries, I've been cleaning this Castle, trying to figure out what I was missing. Oh, that's right! My memory!"

Evan shot Sophia a look that said, "Oh, hell. What have I done?"

She backed up a step as the redhead's face blossomed into a shade the same color as her hair.

"I didn't mean it that way," Evan said, his voice trembling with fear.

"No, you never mean it that way until you've done your damage." Ainsley nearly yelled, her fists by her side, her chin low as she took a step forward. "The Dragon Elite members just do as they please with no concern for those who serve them and how they feel."

"Is that what Quiet's problem is?" Evan asked, blinking rapidly.

"Quiet's problem with you is very simple." Ainsley was shaking all over. "He just doesn't like you."

Evan actually relaxed a little. "Really? Well, that makes sense. I'm not that likable. When I was in school—"

"Would you be quiet?" Ainsley interrupted, seeming to grow more frustrated by the second.

"I can't because I'm not a little gnome," Evan joked. He obviously wanted to die, Sophia thought.

She was going to come to Evan's rescue when a hand grabbed her from behind and tugged her into the weapons room. When she saw who it was, she was surprised to feel their strength—although she shouldn't have been, she realized.

CHAPTER EIGHTEEN

"I know places where those two would turn extremely peaceful people into warmongers," Mama Jamba said, shaking her head and indicating the next room where Ainsley and Evan could still be heard arguing. Evan was mostly apologizing, usually followed by a backhanded compliment.

"I get why Ainsley is upset, though," Sophia offered.

"Of course, dear," Mama Jamba stated. "But fixing her doesn't happen yet. She's not ready. Hiker isn't ready, and you've got other things on your plate. Namely..." She held up a small pouch and swung it in the air.

"What's that?" Sophia asked, hesitation obvious in her voice.

"Magic beans," she answered.

Sophia laughed, waiting for the real answer. When it didn't come, she replaced her laughter with a serious expression. "You're not joking?"

Mama Jamba shook her head. "Of course not. I just completed creating them."

"These magic beans; what will they make?" Sophia was not sure if she wanted to know the answer.

"Something magical," Mother Nature sang, mischief bouncing around in her periwinkle blue eyes.

Sophia realized she should have expected this answer. This wasn't a person who volunteered much information or provided tons of details about things, ever.

"You want me to do something with those?" Sophia guessed.

Mama Jamba nodded proudly, handing the pouch over. "I knew you'd be up for the job."

Sophia hadn't really said she was, but she wasn't going to say otherwise to Mother Nature. The pouch was surprisingly heavy for its size and the fact it contained beans.

"Do you want them planted on the Expanse somewhere?" she asked, indicating to the window where the glowing green hills of Scotland could be seen sprawling in the distance.

Mama Jamba jerked her head back and forth. "Oh, no. I need you and Lunis to take these far, far away from here."

Sophia thought she'd covered up the expression on her face, but hiding anything from Mama Jamba was impossible.

"Oh, I know," Mama Jamba groaned, pretending to be annoyed. "It's never easy or convenient. Travel across the globe, Sophia. Follow my riddle-like instructions. Risk your life for a mission I refuse to explain fully." She stuck her hands on her hips and frowned. "The things you have to put up with."

Offering her a humorous smile, Sophia said, "I don't mind, really. Just tell me what I have to do."

The frown turned upside down. "Oh, you know better than to expect clear instructions."

Sophia nodded. "Right, riddle-like instructions. How did I so soon forget?"

"You have a lot on your mind," Mama Jamba offered. "I will tell you that you need to leave right away."

"Are the beans time sensitive?"

The old woman offered a sympathetic smile. "That they are, but also, it will take you a while to get to New York."

"Really?" Sophia questioned. "Can't we just travel through a portal?"

The expression on Mama Jamba's face was telling.

Sophia slumped with sudden understanding. "Let me guess, we can't portal, can we?"

"You can." Mama Jamba tossed her gray curls back and forth, but they didn't move. "It could possibly negate their effects."

"Right," Sophia said, drawing out the word. "So, we need to fly to New York."

That would take a whole day. Mama Jamba was right, they'd need to leave right away.

"Yes, and I can tell you the actual planting of the beans is relatively simple," Mama Jamba explained. "Just drop them in some dirt in the city and you'll be good."

"Oh, okay." Sophia sighed with relief. "Anywhere in New York?"

The sly smile on Mama Jamba's face made the relief evaporate. "No, I think you know it's got to be a bit more specific than that."

Sophia nodded. "Okay, where in New York? I'm ready for the riddle."

"It's nice to see you embracing this challenge," Mama Jamba approved. "It's going to be a part of something very important. Something the Dragon Elite desperately needs."

That made Sophia feel better, even if she didn't get to learn specifics about the mission.

"Now, my dear," Mama Jamba continued. "Once you're in New York, you need to find a very specific plot of land. It won't be large, but the beans will hopefully lead you to it. They will undoubtedly vibrate, light up, and possibly hum with music when you get to the place they should be planted."

"Well, that's something, at least," Sophia said, a bit more hopeful. "Anything else you can tell me about this small plot of land?"

Mama Jamba nodded. "Yes, it's holy ground."

CHAPTER NINETEEN

"Holy ground?" Sophia questioned, on top of Lunis and riding out of the Gullington. They hadn't wasted any time setting off, knowing they needed to start on the voyage right away.

Thankfully, Lunis was well-rested for the very long journey since he'd just been hanging around the Nest. This would be the farthest he had ever flown. He wouldn't get any breaks crossing the Atlantic Ocean, which meant Sophia would have to aid him with spells to keep him going.

Yeah, that part is perplexing, Lunis agreed, flying through the Barrier. *I mean, New York is not Jerusalem or the region of Palestine.*

"Wow, you sound so learned right now," Sophia said, not used to her dragon being serious.

Hey, what do you think I've been doing while you've been galivanting about without me?

"I have no doubt you're going to tell me," she told him with a laugh.

Watching CNN, of course, he answered.

Sophia laughed "Well, of course. I didn't realize you could get cable inside the Nest."

I stole it from the neighbors. He snickered.

"Wouldn't the neighbors be the other dragons in the Cave?"

He shook his head. *No, it's you in the Castle.*

"I don't have cable," she argued. "I just watch Netflix and Amazon."

And cable, he agreed. *Don't check your credit card bill if this is an issue.*

She shook her head. "I don't even know how you'd manage that at the Castle. It's not like we can get wired for cable."

No, but a certain gnome likes you, and someone might have told him you needed the sports package, Lunis admitted.

"You didn't!"

I did, he said, glee in his voice.

"You're so strange."

So did you bring something for the long trip? Lunis asked as they flew over the rolling hills of Scotland, the coast quickly approaching.

"Like what?"

Like Pictionary or Monopoly.

Sophia giggled. "Um, I'm on the back of a dragon."

There's room, and I can remain steady so that pieces don't move, he argued. *Well, unless you're winning. And then...*

Suddenly Lunis flipped to the side, causing Sophia to have to grab the reins to remain in the saddle. "Whoa!"

He simply laughed, amused as he straightened back out.

"You're evil," she fired, her chest vibrating from the sudden adrenaline.

I'm playful, Lunis disagreed. *Those newly hatched dragons are evil. There's a difference.*

Sophia sighed, wishing she'd had more time to investigate that problem. At some point, they were going to have to figure out how to deal with the new dragons and the others who hatched and were apparently corrupt. According to *The Complete History of Dragonriders,* half of the batch of eggs would be evil and the other half would be good. She kept telling herself the concept was relative and the bad dragons could be changed. There would be options.

Sometimes beings are evil and you can't fix them, Lunis argued, having heard her thoughts. *That's not really the point.*

"What is it, then?" Sophia asked, realizing her dragon was having one of his rare serious moments.

Sometimes our job is to keep the balance, he began. *Sometimes it's to combat evil. But most of the time, our job is to protect the good in a world where it's impossible to erase evil.*

Sophia nodded, taking that in. Yes, she'd like to erase the world's problems, but that really wasn't her job. Her role as an adjudicator was to resolve disputes around the globe—not to get rid of them. Maybe there was someone else who had that job, but she suspected there wasn't. In the real world, there weren't superheroes who ensured bad things didn't happen. No, she suspected that more likely, there were people like her who fixed things when they did.

She was still off in thought a long while later when they were nearly past Ireland. Sophia had been looking without seeing for so long, that for a moment she thought she was seeing things.

Straightening, she blinked, trying to clear her vision. They had only seen birds in the sky since they weren't on the routes planes took, mostly to keep mortal pilots from having heart attacks. Seeing a dragon flying through the sky hardly ever went over well.

Whatever was up in the distance most certainly wasn't a bird or a plane. It was mostly black and appeared to be a person flying, its long wings resembling those of a fairy. Unlike the fae Sophia was used to, this one wasn't colorful or cheerful. Even from a distance, Sophia could read the menace around the creature.

Its long black hair spiraled all around, and flowing ripped fabric waved in the wind as the creature quickly approached. Its mouth opened, and a scream like a siren shot out.

"What is that?" Sophia asked, leaning forward to get a better look at the figure streaking up and down, not making a direct path to them.

Trouble, Lunis answered. *Big freaking trouble.*

91

CHAPTER TWENTY

I *don't want to live forever,* Lunis began, breathless. *But I was hoping to live through this seemingly straightforward mission.*

"What is that?" Sophia asked again, watching as the creature dipped up and down as though riding the waves in the ocean.

It's an Unseelie fairy, Lunis explained.

Sophia, feeling her dragon's tension, pulled her sword, but that only seemed to anger the fairy, making it open its mouth wide to scream again. Her enhanced vision spied long dagger-like teeth in the creature's mouth.

"I don't understand," Sophia began. "Most of the fairies I know are harmless. I mean, the fae are no doubt annoying and could irritate someone to death, but they don't really have the brains to be vindictively harmful or dangerous."

This is a unique fairy native to these parts, Lunis imparted. *There are the Seelie and the Unseelie. We've managed to come across the latter, and they are very malicious.*

The Unseelie fairy was now only fifty yards away. From that distance, Sophia spied a weapon appear in its hands, a long ax.

"It wants to go toe to toe, I see," Sophia said, wondering if she should have pulled Inexorabilis. Maybe the creature could have been reasoned with or avoided altogether.

Few cross paths with an Unseelie fairy without confrontation and death, Lunis stated.

Sophia gulped. "What's the best way to fight the thing? Can you use fire?"

I can try, Lunis stated, opening his mouth as the Unseelie fairy shot forward, sensing what was coming next.

Sophia felt the heat below her as the fire pooled in her dragon. An eruption of flames shot from his mouth and across the air, hitting the Unseelie directly. When the blast stopped, Sophia expected to see the figure charred and falling.

Instead, the beast was upright as though standing on firm ground, two hands on the ax it held out in front of it. The fire had gone around the fairy, who had shielded itself efficiently from the attack.

That didn't work like I planned, Lunis offered.

"No, it appears the ax blocked it," Sophia agreed.

Well, let's just stay away from that ax, Lunis said, tension in his tone. *I don't have a good feeling about that weapon if we get close.*

The Unseelie lifted the ax over its head and threw it forward, still holding onto it. A moment later, a hot blast of wind shot at them, nearly knocking Sophia off Lunis and tangling his wings from the gale-like force.

They recovered by spinning to the side, allowing the majority of the gust to pass them. If the blast had hit them directly, they would have been split apart.

Sophia gulped, tightening one hand on the reins and the other one on her sword. "Looks like we don't have to be close to that ax for it to be dangerous."

No, but to kill that thing, we're definitely going to have to get closer for an attack, Lunis said.

Sophia nodded. She spun Inexorabilis in her fingers as she narrowed her eyes with determination. "Then let's get closer. I'm not allowing an ugly fairy to take us down."

CHAPTER TWENTY-ONE

Treacherous wasn't the right word for the Unseelie fairy spiraling at them. That word seemed mild compared to the beast swerving like a crazed mental patient, ready to murder the air and everything in its midst until it sliced through them.

"Thelma is going to be stealthier than us," Sophia observed, watching the way the monster danced.

Thelma? Lunis questioned.

"Yeah," Sophia answered. "Thelma's always seemed crazy."

My mom was a Thelma, he teased.

"You didn't have a mom," Sophia argued as Lunis slowed, catching the wind on his wings. "I just mean Thelmas have a wild side to them."

What do you mean, she'll be stealthier. He sounded offended. *I'm nimble.*

"Yes, you are," she agreed. "But you can't deny we're much larger than her. Thelma's smaller size will make it easier for her to maneuver."

Yeah, but she doesn't have a long spiky tail, Lunis argued, flicking his tail so it came into Sophia's peripheral vision.

"Is that the strategy then?" she asked as they nearly came to a halt in the air.

Lunis was letting the ugly fairy make up the rest of the distance. *I think our strategy needs to be you cut her and I'll keep her guessing on where we are,* he suggested.

"All right," Sophia said, standing in the saddle, Inexorabilis in her grasp, the sword pulsing in her hands and ready for a battle.

CHAPTER TWENTY-TWO

Fearless and obviously bent on murder, the Unseelie fairy shot in their direction, the ax in front of it and its fangs bared. Thelma's red eyes glowed with vengeance and a strange satisfaction as it neared.

Sophia was ready for it when Lunis dropped suddenly, spoiling the crazy fairy's plan to ambush them straight on. Throwing her sword up over her head, Sophia aimed to slice Thelma's midsection as she passed over them.

This apparently wasn't the Unseelie fairy's first air battle. It flipped to the side, a strange scream spilling from its mouth. As the monster rolled, its figure blurred, and for a moment, all Sophia could see was the ripped black fabric around them like dark clouds had cast them in shadow.

The fairy's head ducked and it flipped like a swimmer changing directions. It was strange to Sophia that Thelma seemed to move more like it was swimming than flying. There was a weird grace about the monster that wasn't exactly beautiful, but definitely alluring, like a hurricane.

Lunis reset their position, but not as fast as Thelma. The psychopath was screaming and barreling back in their direction before Sophia could bring her sword into position. She barely had it over her head before the ax struck at her, nearly catching her in the face.

Holding Inexorabilis with everything she had, she kept the ax at bay. Face to face with the monster, Sophia stared into its gaping black mouth and hollow red eyes, and a violent chill ran over every inch of her body.

She wasn't sure how much longer she could hold the ax off. The pressure Thelma was exerting was greater than Sophia's strength. Lunis, sensing Sophia was going to lose this round with the monster having the upper position, swerved to the side and raced away, trying to get some breathing room from the evil fairy.

Thelma wasn't going to have that, though. The monster, like a possessive girlfriend, raced after them, screaming the entire time.

To Sophia, the high-pitched wail seemed to say, "Get back here! You'll be mine or you'll be dead."

As fast as Lunis was, the fairy kept up with him.

Glancing over her shoulder, Sophia saw that he kept Thelma at bay by waving his spiked tail rapidly. As it swerved, he flicked his tail and nearly caught it in the face many times. This seemed to put a tiny bit of caution into the Unseelie and it slowed, but only slightly.

Thinking they had finally caught a break, Sophia let out a tense breath, hoping to reset. Then she realized things weren't about to get easier.

She's just started pulling out her bag of tricks, Lunis said as the fairy threw a round of sharp, deadly icicles in their direction.

CHAPTER TWENTY-THREE

*H**ow do you kill a fairy who has ice magic and an ax?* Lunis asked, a bit of humor in his voice despite the tense situation they'd found themselves in.

This time he shot straight up in the air to avoid the dagger-like icicles. They zoomed under him, nearly catching him in the belly.

"I should have seen the icicles coming," Sophia apologized. "She's a fairy, and ice is their strongest element."

And mine is fire, Lunis said, preparing to blast the fairy again as she lined up another shot at them from underneath.

"No," Sophia argued. "Not only did that not work the last time because of the strange ax she has to create a shield around her, but we can't have you burning through your reserves. We've got a long journey ahead of us."

Lunis rolled to the side to avoid a collision with another round of icicles. Sophia only had a split-second warning to hug her dragon, ensuring she stayed on his back rather than tumble to the ground hundreds of yards down.

Avoiding the ice attacks wasn't a sustainable strategy, and both Lunis and Sophia knew it. Moreover, it wasn't advisable for Sophia to use her magic to defend them. They had a long journey ahead, and if she used up her magic with combat spells, they might not make it across the Atlantic Ocean.

"Are you thinking what I'm thinking?" Sophia said to her dragon. She felt him smile. *Yeah, let's play hardball.*

CHAPTER TWENTY-FOUR

"Stay...stay...stay," Sophia encouraged her dragon as the crazy-ass Unseelie fairy drifted from side to side as though on a violent breeze.

Thelma kept its distance, but that was because its attacks could be made from afar, and it didn't want to risk the wrath of Lunis' tail.

When facing a deranged creature Sophia thought only existed in Scottish lore, it was difficult to stay unmoving in front of the monster.

It was like the opposing sides were having a stare-off.

Thelma narrowed its red eyes, seeming to try to decide why they weren't darting away from it to get distance like before. As soon as they faced off with the demon, it halted its attacks. Sophia assumed it sensed they had changed their strategy, but thankfully it hadn't seemed to have figured it out.

Should I give chase again? Lunis asked, sinking a few inches before beating his wings slightly to make up the distance. It was like breathing. He'd lower a bit and then regain the height. Sophia hoped it had a mesmerizing effect on Thelma, but guessed the creepy fairy was just planning its next attack.

"No, let's stay where we are," Sophia said, trusting her instincts.

"She's about to throw something at us again. She isn't sure why we don't have a panicked look about us like before."

Panicked. Lunis scoffed. *Speak for yourself, Soph. I'm not the least bit panicked. I mean, sure, I was a little concerned before about getting cut by that ax of hers, but something tells me it could filet me where most blades shouldn't be able to cut.*

"Yeah, there's definitely something about that ax," Sophia mused. If Wilder were there, he would know what was up with the weapon.

"The key is to stay put when she throws the next attack," Sophia encouraged.

The thing is, Lunis began, *she's not throwing any attacks anymore. Think she has telepathy and knows our plan?*

Sophia shook her head. "No, we're both too good at shielding. I think we're just not running, and that's giving us away."

Then we should run, he offered.

Again, Sophia shook her head. "I don't think the plan will work. I'm good at sports but not when on the back of a dragon, racing through the air."

That's funny, Lunis snickered.

"Doing sports on the back of a dragon?" she asked.

He shook his head. *No, that you're good at sports.*

"Ha-ha," she said. The only way to get the red-eyed beast to play was to give it a reason.

Using her magic sparingly, Sophia held out her hand and gathered up a bit of wind before launching it at the Unseelie like it was a baseball.

The monster reacted immediately, easily darting away. Then it played right into Sophia's hand and threw several deadly icicles in their direction.

That was the moment of truth.

"Don't move," Sophia demanded, holding her sword tight in her grasp.

Don't worry, I'm not moving, Lunis said tensely. *But those attacks aren't going to hit me. They are all aimed at you.*

CHAPTER TWENTY-FIVE

The last time Sophia played baseball had been on a video game Liv had. That was the only time, but she reasoned she was a quick learner and would figure it out quickly.

Or die, Lunis teased as the icicles raced at them in slow motion.

Sophia didn't back down from the challenge by encouraging Lunis to drop away from the attacks. Instead, she sucked in a breath and clutched her sword, knowing there was also an instinct held deep within Inexorabilis she could rely on to help her in battle. It wouldn't play ball for her, but it could help her with the precision of her attacks.

When the first icicle raced at Sophia's face, she pulled Inexorabilis around, hitting the sharp shard of ice and knocking it to the side. It shattered, raining cold down on them.

She didn't even notice since she yanked her sword two more times in quick succession but only connected with one of the icicles. The other raced by her face, grazing her cheek.

Sophia ducked, thinking she'd been hit hard. She lifted her hand to her face and found a scratch.

Just a scratch, she thought.

A magical attack, though, Lunis stated, obvious worry in his voice.

"Not enough to keep me down," Sophia said as the angry fairy threw another round of icicles at them.

This time Lunis did move, but only to put Sophia in the best position to volley the attack. The idea was to keep up a good defense, but as Sophia hit one icicle after another, another idea occurred to her.

"Can you get us a little closer?" she asked Lunis when she'd knocked down the last of that round.

You got it, boss, he told her in an upbeat voice, moving forward several yards.

This didn't deter Thelma. Instead, the fairy clenched one fist, the ax in the other and threw another round of icicles.

Sophia dodged the first two attacks. When the third raced at her, she set herself up in what she hoped was the perfect position. She knew she couldn't swing too early. What she needed was a home run, not a bunt. This was about winning now, not about defense.

At the last possible moment, Sophia swung Inexorabilis, waiting for a tug from the sword before yanking it.

The blade connected with the icicle that had been thrown with a precision to impress. It knocked it back, not breaking it this time. Instead, Sophia sent the icicle back the way it had come.

Thelma's red eyes widened in horror at the realization of what had happened. It began to react, but just as it turned to get away, its own attack stabbed it in the back, making both its arms shoot out as a wail that could be heard all over Ireland erupted from its mouth.

CHAPTER TWENTY-SIX

Better than revenge with her sword was for Sophia to end her enemy with her own attack.

She watched from high atop Lunis as the deadly fairy spiraled toward the green hills of Ireland below. Taking her first deep breath in what felt like forever, Sophia was caught by surprise when Lunis darted into a downward dive, headed straight for the falling Unseelie fairy.

"What are we doing?" Sophia asked in a rush, gripping the reins before she was yanked off the back of her dragon.

We are ensuring that a potential weapon isn't lost or falls into the wrong hands, Lunis said quickly. *Sorry, it just occurred to me, and there was no time to discuss it.*

"What aren't we discussing?" Sophia asked as the wind whistled past her ears. Her cheeks felt like they were darting behind her like flags in the wind because Lunis was speeding toward the ground so fast.

The ax, he said simply, as though that should be enough information.

A dip into his thoughts, and Sophia knew at once what he intended for her to do.

She nodded proudly. "Good idea," she approved, "but can we make it in time? She's falling fast."

We can sure try, he encouraged. *You didn't know how to play baseball and nailed her with her own ball.*

"Hey, I'm a great batter," she argued as they closed the distance to the Unseelie fairy, who was falling faster every second. Not only did they need to catch up with it, but they needed to somehow get to the ax before it fell from its grasp.

When Lunis arrived beside the fairy, Sophia realized there was no worry of the beast letting go of its ax. Her dragon continued to descend alongside the fairy as Sophia reached out for the ax. She nearly lost her balance.

Tightening her grip on her dragon, she reached out again, grabbing for the ax. It was pinned in the dead fairy's hands like it was cemented there. Sophia pulled on the handle, but it didn't budge.

Twice more, she tried to yank it free, but in life or death, Thelma wasn't letting its weapon go.

Sophia, Lunis called, grabbing her attention.

She gritted her teeth and dared to take both hands off the reins to try to pry the handle from the dead fairy's hands.

What? she nearly yelled in his mind.

Don't want to rush you, but the ground is quickly approaching, he informed her.

She pulled her gaze away from the fairy to find he was right. There was much less sky between them and the ground than seconds prior. They couldn't grab the Unseelie fairy since that could be a recipe for disaster. She might not be dead. She might be full of poison. Some fairies exploded into flames shortly after death. There were all sorts of potential dangers.

Sophia knew she had seconds to get the ax or otherwise give up on the mission.

One last chance, she thought as she drew in a breath and held it.

With everything she had, Sophia jerked on the handle to the ax. At first, she was certain it was the end and they'd have to veer up, abandoning the weapon. Then it jumped free of the fairy's bony fingers, nearly making Sophia topple off the other side of Lunis from the momentum.

Knowing she had the object of their desire, he pulled up at the last minute as a loud bang erupted from the earth below, followed by an explosion of fire that singed Sophia's boots and Lunis' belly as he took off for the sky, the ax held proudly in Sophia's hands.

CHAPTER TWENTY-SEVEN

If this was a movie, Lunis began, out of breath from the dive toward the earth, *this would be when the triumphant music played, and we took a victory lap.*

"No victory laps," Sophia said, eyeing the strange ax. There was something different about it and she wasn't sure if it could be trusted. She slipped the weapon into her belt, securing it as she focused on the path ahead. "We have enough of a distance to cross, so I say we just keep going and not add any more to our journey."

Copy that, Lunis agreed, flapping his wings. *So, Thelma...*

"Yeah, what do you think her problem was?" Sophia asked.

Anger management, he answered. *We should tell Hiker that's where he's headed if he's not careful. One day he'll be this crazy-ass fairy with a bad attitude and fiery eyes no one can reason with.*

Sophia giggled, her chest loosening. "You're in charge of telling him that."

Lunis shook his head. *Nah. I'm good. I don't know about the Unseelie fairies. They just turned out bad for some reason. Mama Jamba would know.*

Sophia sighed as they left Ireland behind and began crossing the Atlantic Ocean. "Yeah, but we both know she's not talking."

She's not talking to you, Lunis pointed out.

"Oh, you and Mother Nature chat?" she asked, amused.

Maybe, he lied. *You might want to replenish your reserves before the next monster jumps up and demands to be fought.*

Sophia shook her head. "No, I'm hoping for the most boring voyage across the Pond. No more impromptu villains." She did heed his advice and pulled a candy bar from her cloak pocket. For Lunis, it would be easy enough to refill his reserves on the long journey. He'd just go fishing with Sophia in tow.

She took a bite of the candy bar, enjoying the creamy chocolate.

You should also consider taking a nap for a bit, he offered.

Sophia shook her head. "And leave you all alone?"

He smiled. *I'm not alone. You're here.*

"I'll snore," she argued.

Yeah, but you're the one who is going to lend me your strength when I tire, he explained. *You can't do it unless you're rested. Don't worry, I've got this.*

"But Lun—"

Oh, would you look at that? he interrupted.

"What?" she asked, back on full alert. She jerked her head back and forth to search for whatever he was talking about.

The wave down there, he said.

She squinted at the blue water below them that went on for miles and miles and miles.

Oh, and look, there is another one, he joked. *And another. If you're not going to sleep, maybe we could count them. One, two, three—*

"I don't think that's necessary," she quipped.

Do you want to play the license plate alphabet game? Lunis asked her.

"I don't think that will work out here," she answered.

Looking for an A. Let me know when you see one. He swiveled his head back and forth, looking at the sea of blue that seemingly stretched on forever.

Have you found one yet? he asked after a long moment.

Sophia laughed. "No, not yet."

Oh, cool, he declared. *Look at that down there.*

"What?" she asked, finding herself yawning.

I found another wave, he answered. *Oh, and there's another one. And another. And another.*

Feeling the sleepiness tunneling into her head, Sophia smiled. "Okay, fine. I guess I can close my eyes for a bit, but wake me up if something happens."

Like if I find the letter A on a license plate? he asked.

"Yeah, that," she answered.

You got it, Soph, he said as she laid her chest onto him, enjoying the constant beat of his heart and wings as they soared over the Atlantic Ocean.

"Night, Lun."

CHAPTER TWENTY-EIGHT

H*ey, Stephen,* Sophia heard Lunis say in a distant corner of her mind as she hung between the confines of sleep and the waking world. *What's your spirit animal? Mine is a human.*

Feeling like she'd been asleep for a hundred years, Sophia tried to open her eyes. She could hear the wind racing by her. When she'd fallen asleep, that had been part of what had helped her to drift off. Lunis under her had been like a cradle, gently rocking her back and forth like she was a baby. Now it seemed to imprison her in this state of sleepiness.

Do you find when you need your spirit animal most, they magically show up? Lunis continued to speak as the wind rushed by her ears.

With more force than she would have thought necessary, she pushed up, finding her face cemented to her dragon via drool. She was pretty sure she didn't look pretty with her hair matted to her saliva-encrusted face. Her eyes struggled to regain focus.

Well, hey there, sleeping beauty, Lunis said, having heard her thoughts.

She wiped the grossness off her face. "Who are you talking to?"

You drooled on me, he stated matter-of-factly.

"Who is Stephen?" Sophia asked.

My imaginary friend, he replied.

Sophia blinked and found varying shades of blue. Dark ocean with a light blue sky on top was pretty much it as far as the spectrum of colors went.

"You have an imaginary friend?" She was strangely amused even though she was still combatting the grogginess of sleeping while in flight.

I have a lot of things, he told her, sounding offended. *A pet rock named Herman. A phobia of dark places that smell of cheese, and an imaginary friend named Stephen.*

Sophia was certain she was hallucinating and none of this was real. She must still be dreaming, she rationalized. The smell of the salty air and cool breeze on her face made her consider maybe this was real.

"I have so many questions based on what you've told me," she said and realized how dry her throat was. Grabbing her canteen from her cloak, she took a drink.

Well, I met Herman in the Cave, but he's since moved into the Nest with me, Lunis offered as an explanation. *The dark places thing started when I was in the Cave too. I blame Bell because she's got gas that smells like—*

"Please stop," Sophia urged, wiping her mouth with the back of her hand.

Okay, fine, he said, sounding hurt. *Share time is over. I get it.*

"I'm your spirit animal?" Sophia asked.

Lunis snickered. *No. I said my spirit animal was a human. Gosh, you don't have to think so highly of yourself that you assume it's you. It could be all humans. Or a few. Or maybe it's Evan.*

Sophia erupted in laughter. "Evan is your spirit animal?"

Maybe! Lunis exclaimed. *You really shouldn't eavesdrop on my conversations.*

"You were having it out loud while I was on your back," she argued.

While you were asleep, he stated. *I was bored. Who else was I supposed to talk to?*

"I'm not your spirit animal?" She was surprised to find that hurt her feelings. "Because all humans are your spirit animals?"

He sighed. *Of course it's you, Soph.*

She smiled, shaking off the sleepiness. "Where are we?"

Over the ocean, he answered at once.

"Thanks," Sophia replied dryly as a sudden wind blasted by them, nearly tearing her off Lunis.

"Whoa!" she yelled. "What was that?"

Wind, he answered at once, struggling in the air.

"Yeah, I got that much," Sophia said, gripping the reins tightly. "But why does it feel...so forceful?"

She could sense Lunis struggling to cut through the air. There was something wrong.

I think we're running into a storm, Soph, he said, all lightness evaporating from his voice.

CHAPTER TWENTY-NINE

Invisible wind streaked past them, throwing them off course. It was such a sudden change from the smooth ride they'd been having. Sophia bumped up and down, her butt landing hard on Lunis' back.

"What's going on?" she asked, wondering if they were about to encounter another villain.

Lunis indicated a huge storm ahead. *I think it's a regular old hurricane.*

"Oh, good." Sophia sighed. "Just a regular old hurricane."

He groaned. *Well, what do you want me to say? The good news is we can make it through it with only minimal damage.*

"I don't want any damage," she argued.

That's the bad news, he told her. *We have to go straight through it.*

Sophia groaned as well.

I don't have the energy and you don't have the reserves to go around it, Lunis explained. *That would take too long and take us too far off-course.*

"So we're willingly going to charge through a hurricane?" she questioned.

Just pretend you're from Florida and can't be inconvenienced to take shelter during a tropical storm, he said with a snicker.

She smiled and patted her dragon. "Okay, if you're up for the challenge, I'll be here to weather the storm with you."

Sophia felt him smile. *I'll weather all storms with you, dear Soph. But just so you know...*

He paused as the winds turned dramatically more violent.

"Yes?" Sophia asked, worried about what he was going to say next.

On the way home, he began. *I'm going to be your getaway car.*

CHAPTER THIRTY

"Getaway car?" Sophia questioned.

It seems only fair, Lunis argued, struggling to stay level as the winds grew stronger. They now carried debris that must have come from the ocean, neighboring islands, or ships.

Sophia watched as seaweed flew by and nearly hit her in the face. "You're my getaway car?" she remarked.

Well, if the getaway car streaked straight through the police barricades, Lunis said, never losing the humor in his voice even as they barreled straight at the storm, which was turning the blue waters black.

Sophia hadn't been in a hurricane, but something told her this wasn't a normal storm.

What makes you think that? Lunis asked curiously.

She ducked as a propeller from a plane nearly lopped off her head. The debris in the wind was increasing as they neared the storm.

"It just doesn't seem right," she insisted. "Something seems off about it."

What makes you think that, though? Lunis questioned.

A cow flew by them, mooing like it was annoyed by being tossed around in the storm.

Sophia tensed. "The flying cow is part of my reasoning."

SARAH NOFFKE & MICHAEL ANDERLE

Lunis sighed. *I get that I've been eating a lot of carbs lately, but you don't have to resort to name-calling.*

Although Sophia wanted to laugh, the severity of the moment was building in her. "Lunis, why do you think cows, plane parts, and…is that a frozen yogurt machine?"

A large object with a name brand for frozen yogurt flew by them before disappearing into the water.

Is it too late to go back? Lunis whined. *I could really use something sweet.*

"Focus, would you?" she implored.

I don't know the answer, Lunis told her. *We passed a cruise ship back there, and there were also freighters.*

"They've gotten caught up in this storm too, then," Sophia reasoned.

Well, it's their fault if they went straight into it. He scoffed. *I mean, who would do that?*

"We are doing that," she said as fish streaked by her face.

Oh, I always wanted to see flying fish, Lunis observed fondly.

"They aren't meant to fly," she declared, looking around. "Something isn't right, Lunis. There's no reason a cruise ship would sail into the path of a hurricane."

It could have turned quickly, he argued. *That happens.*

She nodded. "Something tells me it didn't, and innocent, unsuspecting people got caught in this storm, which doesn't feel natural."

I'll need more reasoning than that, he demanded.

"Well," she began, trying to work it out in her mind, "Mama Jamba sent us on this mission. She knew we had to cross the Atlantic right now on this course. I have a hard time believing she would have sent us straight through a hurricane, knowing we couldn't expend energy to avoid it."

You have a hard time, or you don't want to believe it? he questioned.

Sophia sighed. "I know she's not always forthcoming and all, but she wouldn't endanger us."

Oh, like when we had to battle a ton of men and snow and other torrential environmental elements to find her originally? he argued.

120

"This is different," Sophia insisted. "She didn't know if she wanted to be found then, and she wanted us to prove we were worthy."

Maybe this is a test, he pondered.

Something huge shot out of the water as they neared the eye of the hurricane, making it nearly impossible for Sophia to keep a grip on Lunis. She pretended her hands were cemented onto him and didn't allow herself to let go.

"I don't think this is a test." Her teeth began to chatter from the rain and wind assaulting her in the face.

Why? Lunis pressed, pushing all his energy into keeping them in the air.

Sophia indicated an object in the distance. "Because Mama Jamba wouldn't have sent us to face that."

A large purple octopus shot up out of the water from the eye of the hurricane, and suddenly both dragon and rider realized it wasn't a storm. Everything they were experiencing was a result of the giant angry creature in front of them.

CHAPTER THIRTY-ONE

This, love, is when we tuck tail and portal home, Lunis joked.

Sophia couldn't help but smile. It didn't matter what the circumstances. Her dragon would always find time in dire situations to kid. She loved that about him. She appreciated he knew they were far enough from the monster octopus to have time for banter.

"We aren't turning back," Sophia argued. "And not just because the magic beans will be ruined if we portal."

Because you want to do some shopping in New York? he asked.

"Because whatever that thing is," Sophia said, pointing to where the large monster was splashing, spinning, and all-around creating chaos in the waters of the Atlantic, "we have to stop it."

It seems to be minding its own business, Lunis observed as a palm tree hurtled passed them. *Who are we to judge him and make him act differently?*

Sophia rolled her eyes. "He's creating a hurricane-like storm in the ocean and has apparently attacked cruise ships and freighters and who knows what else. That has to be where all those objects are coming from."

Maybe he's like Thelma and misunderstood, Lunis reasoned.

Sophia lowered her chin. "Do you think I'm misjudging Hatch Two?"

Hatch Two? Lunis questioned.

"When I was a kid, I had an imaginary friend who was an octopus," Sophia explained, then shook her head, knowing Lunis had access to her memories.

Yeah, you pretended he lived in the fountain in the gardens of the House of Fourteen, Lunis finished, sounding impatient, like he'd heard the story a hundred times.

"Well, I liked that Hatch," Sophia reasoned. "Who was also a large purple octopus. Something tells me I won't like this one."

She ducked as a washing machine sailed over her head.

What makes you think that? Lunis sounded curious.

"Ha-ha," she replied. "Anyway, this is Hatch Two. Or—"

Evil Hatch, Lunis supplied. *Because for every good, there is bad. It's the way of the world. There are Seelie fairies and Unseelie fairies. There are good and evil dragons. And there's a good Hatch and a bad one.*

"Exactly," Sophia said triumphantly, the heat of the upcoming battle starting to pool in her chest.

A real quick thing before we charge ahead, Lunis mentioned with a coyness in his voice that should have made Sophia groan. The spiraling giant octopus thrashing its tentacles in the air and creating utter chaos made her cut the extra reaction.

"What?" she questioned.

It's sort of ridiculous that you had an imaginary friend. Just saying.

CHAPTER THIRTY-TWO

*N*ever grow up, Soph, Lunis told her in a rush as a blast of water nearly hit him in the face. *But right now, I need you to get out a large sword and kill that beast.*

Sophia would have laughed if a spray of water hadn't nearly sent her off her dragon. She tried twice to grab for her sword, but letting go with both hands proved difficult.

Evil Hatch rose into the air as they approached through the rain and wind, which splattered Sophia's face so hard it stung.

The monster was unlike anything Sophia had ever seen. It resembled an octopus in every way, with its eight tentacles with large suckers. However, it was easily the size of a two-story house.

Its black eyes were huge and shone with anger as it spun, propelled by the motion of its tentacles spiraling and creating a cyclone that threw water and wind in every direction for at least a square mile.

Whatever this thing was, it was angry and bent on destruction. That's when Sophia noticed planes flying in from the opposite direction.

They will never get close enough, Lunis stated, having seen the same thing.

"What are they going to do?" Sophia mused, watching as the

aircraft struggled to get in close. The tumultuous winds knocked them back, sending them in the wrong direction.

They are going to do what mortals do best when fearful, Lunis said, bitterness in his voice. *They are going to drop bombs.*

"Is that any better than what we'd do?" she questioned, still trying to pull her sword but unable to take her hands off the reins.

Yes, because when we take that thing out, we are only killing it, Lunis told her.

Right on cue, a jet shot a missile at Evil Hatch, but he easily deflected it, knocking it out of the sky like it was a pesky fly. It crashed into the water, where it detonated a moment later, sending fish and other sea life rising to the surface of the ocean—all dead.

See? Lunis asked, anger in his tone. *They didn't even injure Evil Hatch, and they've harmed a lot of creatures.*

"He's injuring a lot of wildlife," Sophia observed as a school of fish flew past her head.

Yeah, but they are making it worse, Lunis stated, getting charged up. *Let's end this before the mortals make it worse.*

Sophia agreed, finally pulling her sword and able to maintain balance as they rode in closer to the monstrous octopus.

CHAPTER THIRTY-THREE

Miss Americana and the Heartbreak Prince had found a way to cut through the wind. She felt a charge as they neared the east coast of her home country. She knew Lunis was more fired up than usual after witnessing the senseless deaths of the ocean creatures. He was ready to take names and take out an octopus.

It was surprising to Sophia that the closer they got to Evil Hatch, the less the winds affected them.

It's because he's the eye of the storm, Lunis offered.

"That makes sense," Sophia said, looking over her shoulder, and trying to get the attention of the fighter jets in the distance. It was probably hard for them to make out much around the chaos of the giant beast, but she hoped they realized the dragon and rider were on the job and they wouldn't fire any more missiles.

I can shoot fire at them to encourage them to retreat, Lunis remarked.

Sophia shook her head. "No, then they'd see us as enemies too. Any educated person on this planet will know the Dragon Elite is back and realize we're here to help."

Yeah, can you imagine the realities we're challenging right now. Lunis laughed. *Oh, there's a giant evil octopus, Bob,* he said, doing his best impression of a mortal. *Cool, we don't need to fight it anymore because the ancient dragon and its tiny rider are on the case.*

Sophia snickered as she spied the jets retreating. They had seen her and Lunis and appeared to be giving them a chance to fight the monster. They didn't retreat too far and seemed to be waiting to see what would unfold.

"If we don't take out Evil Hatch," Sophia began, "I think they are going to want a turn."

Lunis grinned. *Well, too bad for you, Bob, you're not getting one. Go get coffee because we've got this one.*

CHAPTER THIRTY-FOUR

*R*eady *for it?* Lunis asked as they approached the flying tentacles that sped through the water-soaked air.

"I don't think I could ever be ready for this," Sophia joked. "My training doesn't involve fighting a huge deranged octopus."

Well, we have fought giant sea creatures, Lunis reasoned, veering around more unknown debris. *Think of this like when you fought Hydra.*

"Please tell me the tentacles don't grow back like its heads," Sophia groaned.

Only one way to find out, Lunis teased, turning to the side, and diving over a tentacle before it swung up, nearly clipping his tail. *Get ready. I'm getting you into position.*

"Okay," Sophia said, sucking in a breath. "We'll take out the tentacles and then the beast itself."

I think once the tentacles are gone, so will the monster be, Lunis imparted.

She lifted Inexorabilis over her head, preparing to slice through the tentacle they were racing toward. Sophia stood up atop her dragon, her legs pressing against him tightly to keep her balanced and upright.

With both her hands tightly around the hilt she let out a guttural yell, yanking the sword as a purple tentacle soared straight in her direction. Evil Hatch was going to make this easier for her by bringing its wild limbs to her.

The blade hit the tentacle, but unlike when it had cut through giant worms or dragon's necks, it didn't slice through. It didn't even puncture the skin. Instead, the blade hit the tentacle like it was coated in reinforced steel and bounced back off, making every part of Sophia's body vibrate like she'd struck the inside of a large bell in a clock tower.

She thought she could recover from the assault, but the combination of the wind and Lunis swerving to avoid colliding with another mad tentacle headed straight in their direction sent her off the side of her dragon. She dropped her sword. It went one way and she went the other, ungracefully falling down Lunis' back and knocking into several spikes on his side and tail.

She was certain she'd fall to the churning water below, but at the last possible moment, she caught herself on his back leg.

Nice one, Lunis commented with relief. *Good save.*

"Thanks," Sophia said, her legs flying out behind her as they soared high and then low to avoid colliding with the impenetrable tentacles. Sophia felt remorse about her sword that had fallen into the ocean below. She was more concerned with her survival, so she centered her attention on getting back up onto her dragon.

I'll give you a boost, but you better be ready for it, Lunis told her.

"I don't think we have time for me to get ready," she disagreed, feeling her grip slipping. "Just do it."

Here goes, he said, flicking his back leg back and up high.

Sophia released when at the top and surprised herself by doing a flip in midair. She came out just as she was over the saddle and slid down onto it like an acrobat in a trapeze act.

Well, that was impressive, Lunis said, swerving to avoid several attacks.

"It was totally unplanned," Sophia said, leaning away as she came eye to eye with the angry octopus. It was like looking into a giant abyss full of death and destruction. She had no idea where this thing had come from or what had made it, but she'd figure that out after she stopped it from creating more upset in the Atlantic.

"What are we going to do now," Sophia mused, looking around, hoping her sword was somewhere she could see—maybe floating on the water, pushed up by Evil Hatch.

She knew it was a pipe dream. The sword would have sunk.

Survive, Lunis said, his word clipped as he dove around a large sucker inches from sucking off his face.

Sophia reached out, considering using her magic to summon the sword. Since she was bonded with Inexorabilis, she could draw the weapon to her.

No, don't, Lunis exclaimed. *Inexorabilis didn't work anyway. Don't waste your magic right now trying to summon it.*

"Do you have another idea of how we can stop this beast?" she asked, thinking maybe his fire would work.

I don't think fire will work, especially with the influx of rain. You do have another weapon that might work.

"I do?" Sophia questioned, chancing a glance down at her waist.

The ax. She'd forgotten about the ax they'd taken from the Unseelie fairy. There was a strange magical property about the weapon. Although the battle wasn't a good time to tap an unknown object, she could still use it like she would any blade.

Yanking the ax out of her belt, she remembered how heavy it was. Thankfully it had a long handle, which would hopefully mean they didn't have to get as close to the flying tentacles.

"Let's give it another go," Sophia stated, attempting to stand up again.

Okay, this is going to be a roller coaster ride, just so you know, Lunis said and then dipped into a ninety-degree dive toward the surface of the water.

A tentacle as big around as Sophia whipped up like a wall to stop their progress.

Sophia yelled, forcing all the air out of her lungs as she brought the ax down decisively. She half-expected to hit the tentacle and bounce off it like before. To her surprise, the ax sliced through cleanly, and the majority of the tentacle fell into the ocean.

Lunis used a burst of speed to avoid colliding with the broken-off tentacle as Evil Hatch screamed, its mouth opening wide, easily the size of a small vehicle.

Not wasting a moment, Lunis shot into the air, like climbing the hill of a roller coaster, giving Sophia perfect access to the neighboring tentacle. Fueled by her recent success, she swung the ax at the tentacle. She didn't use as much force as before. It sliced through easily, splashing the tentacle down into the waters, now filling with crimson.

Lunis then dove, making Sophia's stomach jump into her throat. Again and again, she swung the ax into the tentacles, nearly being hit in the head several times by the limbs. They were starting to slow down, making her job easier. The screams of the octopus were almost unbearable.

Thankfully, Sophia only had two more tentacles left, and they mostly flailed haphazardly, like a blind creature trying to feel its way forward. For a moment, Sophia felt sorry for the angry octopus. Maybe it had been confused, placed into a world where it didn't belong, or maybe it was misunderstood. She didn't know, but she had to think of others first, and the dangerous creature posed a risk to many and therefore had to go.

That was her last thought as she sliced through the final tentacle. It fell off the creature like a tree falling in the woods.

Timber, Lunis joked as the monster's black eyes closed slowly before opening again. It opened its large slit of a mouth and mouthed two words that took Sophia by surprise.

She thought she was hearing things as Evil Hatch sank into the red water and slid under the tumultuous waves.

In case she had any doubt about what the octopus was saying, it repeated it several times, and the last time before its face sank below the surface, she heard it plainly and knew without a doubt.

"Thank you," she heard Evil Hatch gurgle before it disappeared.

CHAPTER THIRTY-FIVE

S *hake it off,* Lunis encouraged as they took a victory lap around the spot, which was red with blood and bubbling up with debris from the chaos.

Things were starting to calm, although that seemed strange to Sophia after slaughtering a very magical creature.

Two, Lunis corrected. *If you count the Unseelie fairy. Those are pretty rare. That might have been the last of its kind. This Evil Hatch might have been the only one of its kind.*

"If you're trying to make me feel better, it's not working," she grumbled, rolling her shoulders, which were already sore from swinging the heavy ax.

Soph, you did what you had to. Sometimes we have to take out spiders in the Australian outback who are posing a risk to our lives, only to find out they were the last of an almost extinct species.

"Seriously, this isn't helping," she muttered.

My point is, you did what you had to do. Look at how many you've probably saved, Lunis remarked.

Sophia glanced over her shoulder at the jets in the distance. They circled for a moment before zooming in the other direction, having determined the creature was no longer a danger to anyone.

Sticking the ax into her belt, she reached out and summoned the sword that had once belonged to her mother, Guinevere Beaufont. When Inexorabilis shot out of the water and the hilt landed in her hand, Sophia smiled with relief. She would have moved on if she'd lost this last and very important part of her mother, but that wasn't a heartache she wanted to experience.

Thankfully, she didn't have to. She and Inexorabilis would go on to fight another battle and slay more monsters.

CHAPTER THIRTY-SIX

*W*elcome to New York, Lunis sang as they entered the sprawling
area of Manhattan.

"I've never been here," Sophia said, overwhelmed by how much
concrete there was. That was saying a lot, coming from a native Los
Angeles girl.

So, we're looking for holy ground, Lunis mused, looking around.

"Should we try a church?" Sophia questioned.

Well, sure, he said, mischief in his tone. *Do you want to narrow down
the hundreds of thousands of options?*

Sophia pursed her lips. "Yeah, good point."

She pulled the pouch of magic beans from her pocket. "Didn't
Mama Jamba say these would help us to find the right area?" she
asked.

Yeah, maybe they are little magic compasses, he teased.

Sophia emptied the contents of the pouch into the palm of her
hand. She was underwhelmed by how ordinary the beans looked.
They were...just beans. There was nothing special about their brown
color or hard texture. Sophia didn't know how something so normal
could help them to find the holy ground they were looking for.

Maybe any church will do, Lunis reasoned.

Sophia pulled her gaze away from the beans to the skyline of New York City. "Well, over there I see a cathedral. Take us in that direction."

You got it, Uber customer, Lunis said with a laugh.

"Hah-ha," Sophia stated, closing her fingers tight around the beans, not wanting to lose any as Lunis flew forward toward the church.

When they were over the grassy cemetery and grounds of the church, she dared to open her fingers again, expecting them to have changed.

They hadn't.

The beans simply rolled around in her palm like any old beans would do.

Well, any bright ideas? Lunis questioned.

"Nope," she said with defeat. "I guess we turn around and go back to the Gullington."

Very funny, he said, not sounding amused. *How about instead we continue to fly around New York City, and you tell me if the beans do something?*

"Like jump around?" she asked.

Or hum or glow or whatever Mama Jamba said they might do.

"I'll let you know," Sophia said, patting her dragon. "Don't you think you could use a break? Like, a pit stop to get some water or something?"

Yes, like a donut, maybe, Lunis agreed, inhaling deeply. *The smells of New York City are intoxicating.*

"I think that's the smell of sewage bubbling up from the underground." Sophia chuckled.

I don't know about you, but I smell curry, Lunis declared, gliding toward a busy street, glamouring himself as he neared pedestrians.

Mortals could see dragons, but it didn't mean they needed to.

CHAPTER THIRTY-SEVEN

"Cornelia Street," Sophia said when they touched down on the pavement of a narrow road lined with tall buildings full of shops and restaurants.

Lunis had covered himself in glamour, thankfully not attracting the attention of those enjoying meals on the patio of the nearest café.

It was better if they saw him as something less interesting, like a drone in the sky or a Volkswagen bug on the street.

So, you want a donut? Sophia asked, gauging the options available to them. There were many different venues with colorful fronts and awnings hanging over the outdoor areas.

This didn't seem like a place where they could plant the beans. For the most part, it was concrete. There were a few patches of ground, but they were tiny and usually filled with a stick-straight tree that looked to be struggling to grow among the smog and pavement.

Those are pee spots, Lunis offered, indicating the closest patch of dirt that had gotten Sophia's attention. She was so used to seeing the green rolling hills of the Gullington that to be surrounded by so much gray hurt her heart. It didn't feel natural and made her want to return to the Expanse, where the green was overwhelming.

How is that? Sophia asked him, glad they were talking telepathically so she didn't look like she was talking to her car.

That's where the people of New York City take their dogs to pee, Lunis explained.

As he did, Sophia noticed a man with a small poodle stopping off at a tree down the road. The dog hiked its leg and peed on the twig-like tree before they trotted on.

Oh, wow, she stated. *I guess that's what you have to do when you pave every part of Mother Nature in the name of industry and urban development.*

Yeah, it's definitely different than what we're used to, Lunis said as they strode down the road toward a bakery in the distance.

Lunis halted, looking down at Sophia. *Do you hear that?*

How could I not? she asked. *It's overwhelming.*

She, of course, was referring to the helicopters overhead, the sirens in the distance, and the honking. All the noises of the city competing for her attention.

Lunis shook his head. *That gentle buzzing.*

Sophia's eyes slid to the right as she concentrated. Over the orchestra of chaotic noise, she did hear the faintest sound. It was coming from her hand.

Opening her palm, she noticed to her utter surprise the magic beans were glowing.

Turning in a complete circle, she surveyed Cornelia Street.

Is there a church here? she asked, looking around.

It didn't appear so.

The holy spot they are supposed to be planted in must be close, Lunis offered.

She nodded. *We walk on?*

Absolutely, he answered.

The pair walked down Cornelia street, Lunis watching that Sophia didn't get hit by a pedestrian or traffic while she kept her eyes trained on the beans in her hands.

As they progressed, the beans began to hum louder and glow brightly, bouncing slightly in her hand.

After several yards, the beans glowed so brightly they hurt Sophia's eyes. They hummed so intensely she squinted.

The spot must be close, she said, halting and searching around. *There's no church, though, or anything else that could be considered holy ground. Just shops and bars and stuff.*

Lunis cleared his throat. *Oh, Soph. I get it.*

She glanced up at him. *What do you mean?*

It's hole-y ground, he explained. *Not holy ground.*

Furrowing her brow at him, she blinked, trying to understand what he meant.

He pointed his chin down, indicating with his eyes. *Hole-y ground. See.*

She followed his gaze and saw what he was talking about.

On the side of the pavement was a small patch of dirt. A tiny stick-like tree had been pulled up, probably because it had died. In the broken dirt were a bunch of holes where the roots had come out.

Oh, Sophia exclaimed, having to close her fingers to keep the magic beans from jumping loose. *It's hole-y ground, not holy ground.*

Exactly, Lunis stated with pride.

That tricky, tricky woman, Sophia said, kneeling by the patch of broken earth. She opened her hand and had no doubt this was where the magic beans should be planted. She wasn't sure what they'd produce or why, but she trusted the sneaky woman who was Mother Earth enough to do as she was told without question.

With a heart hopeful that the magic beans would bring goodness to this dead piece of earth, Sophia gently laid them in the soil. She was going to help cover them with dirt, but they sank into the ground, disappearing at once.

Looking up, she gave Lunis a surprised expression. *Well, I guess we're done.*

He nodded. *Now I think we deserve that donut...or twelve.*

CHAPTER THIRTY-EIGHT

*G*orgeous, Lunis remarked when they had flown through the Barrier over the Gullington. The grassy hills were a nice contrast to the gray streets of New York City.

Sophia too was grateful to be home. Her home reunion was short-lived because as soon as she landed, she got a message from Mortimer.

I have information. Please come to Roya Lane to see me.

Well, it looks like you won't be getting a nap and a bubble bath like you wanted, Lunis stated.

She gave him a curt look after dismounting. "I believe that's what *you* wanted."

I can't argue with that, he said, sauntering in the direction of the Nest. *I'm going to Netflix for ages. Do call on me once I've rested so we can adventure through peril and fight strange magical creatures.*

"Will do," Sophia said, realizing she wouldn't have a chance to change before heading off. Or see Wilder, not that she knew where he was or even if he was at the Castle.

Maybe he didn't want to see her, she told herself. They were still so new, and there was all this pressure and so many impulses to run. Well, she had those impulses, but they were real, and not giving into them was hard. Most days, she had the fleeting feeling to throw away her life and change her name, erase her identity, and become a barista at Starbucks. Her life wouldn't be easy, but it would be different. She would have fewer worries but more demands, since making coffee at breakneck speed seemed harder than riding a dragon, but it was all relative she reasoned.

Sophia shook off the insecurities, knowing that's what they were. She'd deal with them later. Or not at all. Right then, she was going to go collect information on Trin Currante. Then she'd get to the bottom of this magician disappearance business.

Putting her finger in her ear, Sophia found seaweed and something she thought had to be Evil Hatch guts. She wondered what had created that strange creature. It didn't seem natural, and its last words stuck with her. The creature had been grateful to be put out of his misery. Something had made it angry and go on a rampage. When afforded the time, she'd look into that. Right then, though, she had a date with Mortimer. After a quick whiff, she realized she couldn't disgrace him by showing up in her present state.

She had time for a shower, she reasoned, making for the Castle.

CHAPTER THIRTY-NINE

Tied together by a smile were Rudolf and Serena Sweetwater, standing with their triplets wiggling around in their strollers. Sophia grinned at the family when she stepped onto Roya Lane through the portal. She felt refreshed after a quick shower and a change of clothes. She'd dropped the ax in the weapons room, which was where she expected to find Wilder if he was at the Castle. He wasn't. She'd have him tell her about the strange weapon of the Unseelie fairy later.

The last time Sophia had seen the mortal Queen Serena Sweetwater, she had been reluctantly eating a magical cupcake that would extend her life so she could spend more years with her halfling children and fae husband. Almost as important was that it would make King Rudolf Sweetwater happy so he would be a better ruler to the fae.

Sophia's gaze fell on the squirming babies in the stroller, Captain, Captain, and Captain. She suspected, based on something Papa Creola said, they were a huge part of this equation with the fae. Father Time had hinted their wellbeing was important for the untold future.

"How are you?" Sophia asked, unaccustomed to seeing Serena

smiling…or during the day. Or dressed or upright, or sober, for that matter.

"Captain Morgan said her first word," Rudolf told her proudly, pointing to the first baby in the set of strollers.

Sophia blinked with disbelief. "She's an infant."

The king of the fae nodded like that wasn't to be questioned. "Yeah, a bit behind the pack, but I'm hoping she'll catch up with other fae children soon. Her sisters are sure to somersault with their progress right after they learn how to somersault."

Sophia gave him a sideways look, not knowing where to begin based on this information. "Wait, so the fae talk early?"

"Oh yeah," he said with confidence. "We're pretty much born talking and walking and doing math."

"Then what happens?" she asked, never having met a smart fae before. Most interactions with them robbed her of her brain cells.

"Lust, wonder, and lots and lots of drugs," he declared.

Sophia nodded. "That seems about right. It sounds like you are slated for great things."

"Yeah, but we spoil it with our impulsive nature and need for immediate gratification," Rudolf answered. He shrugged. "It's a part of the design. Could you imagine how we'd rule the world with our long lives and beauty if we held onto our intelligence? It would be devastating to the rest of the magical races."

"So, you dumb yourself down for the rest of us? How very altruistic of you," Sophia said dryly.

"Oh, she said it again!" Serena exclaimed when Captain Morgan made a noise.

Rudolf clapped. "Oh, and she's already so cultured. Maybe she'll become a culinary expert like her grandfather." He gave Sophia a proud look. "He invented marshmallows."

"Wow," she replied dryly. "You must be very proud."

"Not as much as I am of the cousin who had the idea for the hokey-pokey." Rudolf sighed. "He was working on the meaning of life and came up with the song and dance."

"You're more proud of that?" Sophia questioned.

"Well, what if the hokey-pokey *is* what it's all about?" Rudolf reasoned.

Sophia shook this off, remembering a conversation with a fae was about like going through a maze blindfolded. It was inevitable to get lost. "What is this first word you just heard Captain Morgan say?"

"Oh, her first word was ghee," Serena answered, smiling wide. "If you listen, she'll say it again." She looked at Rudolf, suddenly quite serious. "What if she's trying to tell us she doesn't want to be a vegan?"

He nodded like this made sense. "I was thinking the same thing. If clarified butter is what my baby wants, then that's what she gets."

Sophia's eyes simply widened with complete horror. "You realize those are baby noises she's making? That's what they do...I've heard."

Rudolf dismissed this at once. "That's what simpletons believe, but we know our children well enough to know she's saying real words." Turning his attention to his wife, he said, "I think we can get some organic ghee at the shop down the lane."

"You're going to give an infant butter?" Sophia didn't know why she was even going to argue with the Sweetwaters. It would only cost her more brain cells, but she felt it was her social responsibility to at least try.

He scoffed. "No. Not until she's had her hemp protein shake and vegan sausage puree. What kind of monsters do you take us for?"

"If she doesn't want to be vegan anymore, should we switch her over to regular milk?" Serena asked her husband.

He nodded. "Yeah, but let's go with a type of milk that's hard to get, and we have to buy on the black market."

"Like something from an endangered animal like a panda or a German shepherd?" Serena asked.

"Um, German shepherds aren't on the endangered animal list," Sophia argued.

"Well, the ones that actually speak the language are," Rudolf countered.

Serena nodded boldly, crossing her arms and giving Sophia a challenging look that said, "Yeah, take that."

Sophia shrugged off their insanity and forced a smile. "You two are strangely perfect for each other."

He cast a fond expression on his wife and nodded. "We really are, and thanks to your help, we are happier than we've ever been."

This made a genuine smile grace Sophia's face. "I'm really happy to hear that."

CHAPTER FORTY

Clean wasn't the word for it. The brownies' official headquarters was spotless. The smell of lemon was strong in the air when Sophia entered the reception area.

Sophia froze when Ticker ran a feather duster over her feet and legs.

"Dou yirty," the little brownie stated.

She smiled down at the little guy. "You should have seen me earlier. I was filthy and covered in octopus parts."

From seemingly nowhere, the little fairy pulled a squeegee and a spray bottle out of thin air. "Cwueaky slean."

"No thanks," Sophia said politely and stepped away from the enthusiastic brownie.

His mother Pricilla rushed from the back office, her youngest in her arms. "I'm sorry, Sophia Beaufont, if he's bothering you. Ticker has just gotten excited about his new upcoming assignment and is practicing."

Waving off her concern, Sophia told her, "He's not bothering me. Ticker is already starting his first assignment?"

Pricilla nodded. "Yes, a bit late, but I wanted to keep him with me for a little longer." She gave her son a fond expression. "I just didn't want to let him go yet because once they are off, it's hard to get them back."

"Wow, brownies start work early," Sophia observed, curious about how the different races evolved at different and seemingly faster rates than mortals and magicians.

"Yes, and I'm excited he's enthusiastic about the work we do out there in the world, cleaning noble mortal's homes." She gave her son a prideful expression.

"He's going to do the best job if this is any proof." Sophia indicated the spotless office.

"Yhank tou," Ticker said, batting his large eyes up at her.

"Well, Mortimer is expecting you in his office," Pricilla offered, holding her arm out to the door down the hallway. "We won't keep you any longer since you have important business to attend to."

The head of the brownies was spinning in his office chair when Sophia entered.

"Well, hello, S. Beaufont, rider for the Dragon Elite," the brownie squeaked, always formal. Liv had said it was a part of the fairies' culture, which respected hierarchy almost as much as cleanliness.

"Hi," she replied. "How are you?" Sophia remembered the last time she'd seen Mortimer; he'd been quite stressed about the current global unease.

He spun again in his swivel chair, leaning his head back as he stared at the ceiling. "I've had better centuries, but we will weather this storm with the mortals losing morale over the magician situation."

Sophia nodded, appreciating the brownie's optimism.

"Now, I've got a lead on how you can find Trin Currante," Mortimer began. "There's apparently a dog who should know the headquarters of where Trin and her cyborgs are hiding out."

Tilting her head to the side, Sophia gave him a hesitant expression.

"How is the dog supposed to tell us where that location is? Does it speak?"

Mortimer shook his head like this wasn't a weird question. "Not that I'm aware of. My brownies tell me the canine has super intelligence."

Sophia lowered her chin, putting it all together. "Let me guess, an enhanced creature then? Created by the same lab that made Trin Currante and the other cyborgs?"

"I'm thinking so," Mortimer replied. "Although I don't know how, I think the animal should be intelligent enough to help you find the location of the headquarters."

Dogs were great for search and rescue missions and sniffing out bombs and drugs. One could reason they could lead them to a specific place.

"Okay, so where do I find this super-smart dog?" Sophia asked.

"It's at the location Trin Currante was at and blew up," Mortimer explained.

"But it was blown up," Sophia argued, deflating slightly. "The dog probably was in the blast or maybe even got away on the plane with the cyborgs."

Mortimer shook his head. "I don't think so. My brownie tells me the animal is still hanging around the site, confused and lost."

Sophia's heart sank. They'd left the animal behind, so no wonder it was confused and lost. It was probably some experiment of the Saverus Corporation, and now it had been abandoned. They had to go get it.

"Is there anything else you can offer?" Sophia watched as Mortimer began spinning around again.

He paused and thought, then shook his head. "Not at the present moment. My brownies are always sneaking around behind the scenes, so if I hear of anything I think will be of use, I'll send you a message."

"Thank you."

Sophia was grateful to have such helpful friends—in all the right places.

CHAPTER FORTY-ONE

"I wish you would just admit you need my help," Evan said, sitting across from Sophia at the table in the dining hall at the Castle.

Sophia rolled her eyes. "I don't need your help specifically. I just need backup. Mortimer says there are traps left behind at Medford Research."

Evan stretched his arms over his head. "Sounds like you need my head."

"It really comes down to that you're the only one free," Sophia told him, taking a sip of her tea, her stomach grumbling. She was starving after all the long adventures. "Wilder has to leave on another mission. Mahkah is doing high-level stuff on adjudication missions. So that leaves you."

"You need me," he sang as Ainsley carried out a plate of grilled chicken with a Thai peanut butter sauce.

She laid it down with a smile, looking at the arrangement of food proudly.

Evan pointed to it. "Hiker is going to hate this."

"I know," she said with a smile.

"He doesn't like anything Asian," Evan told Sophia.

She'd been around the Viking long enough to know he liked meat, potatoes, whiskey, and that was about it.

"Oh, that reminds me," Ainsley exclaimed with excitement, hustling back for the kitchen.

Sophia gave Evan a knowing expression. They both understood that whatever she was hurrying to get would be something Hiker didn't like.

"Okay, I'm ready." Evan leaned back in his chair, tipping back on the hind legs.

"Ready for what?" she asked, giving him a reluctant expression.

"Go on and beg me for my help," he replied.

"I'm not doing that," Sophia declared definitively. "You are one of us. We need to track down Trin Currante. That's part of the Dragon Elite's mission. So, you're going to go on this mission and be my backup."

"When you say backup, it sort of feels like I'm not the lead on the project," Evan stated.

"Because you're not," Sophia said with a groan. "I found the information on where to find the cyborg dog or whatever it is."

"You got that from where?" Evan asked, tipping back farther.

"From my awesome secret source," she answered. "This is my case, so you're the backup."

"But I've been to the Medford Research facility before and nearly died saving your life," Evan argued.

"That's not how things happened," she stated as Ainsley brought in a platter of fried octopus.

Sophia pushed back from the table, grimacing.

"Oh, now you're off my cooking too?" Ainsley stuck her hands on her hips, offense written on her face.

"Sorry, but I'm off octopus for pretty much the rest of my life," Sophia told her, trying not to be sick from the smell of the fried squid.

Ainsley shook her head. "You act like you've gotten into a fight with a giant octopus or something."

Sophia actually laughed. "What, have you been reading my diary again?"

"No," Ainsley answered at once. "You never put anything good in there anymore. Just Wilder this and Wilder that. Ainsley, stop reading my personal business, or I'll throw sheep poo all over the dining room floor for you to clean up. It's all very boring."

Sophia shook off the comment and turned her attention back to Evan. "So, can you leave tomorrow morning?"

"I've got to sleep until noon, so maybe after I've had my proper rest," he stated, folding his hands behind his head.

Quiet entered the dining hall, his clothes stained with dirt as usual. His eyes narrowed on Evan and he muttered something, and the hind legs of the chair slipped out, making the dragonrider topple back.

"Hey!" Evan roared, landing on his backside.

Sophia and Ainsley erupted in laughter.

"We leave right after breakfast," Sophia demanded rather than asked.

"Fine," Evan said, clambering to his feet and pulling the chair upright. "Right after second breakfast." He went to take a seat again and it fell back once more, sending him onto the floor again.

"Right after breakfast works for me," Sophia said, stifling a laugh.

"Yeah, fine," Evan replied, rubbing his elbow as Wilder entered the dining hall.

He flashed an excited smile at Sophia, his blue eyes twinkling. "Hey, that ax you left for me is something else. Where did you get it?"

"From an Unseelie fairy," she replied.

Everyone fell silent, giving her wide eyes.

"On second thought, you should go on this mission alone." Evan eyed the chair with great hesitation. "You seem to find the strangest trouble."

"Yeah, I don't think anyone has seen an Unseelie fairy in ages," Wilder mused. "They are incredibly wicked."

"Yeah, this one was grumpy, for sure," Sophia agreed with a laugh.

"Well, it makes sense it was an Unseelie because they are notorious for shielding the memory of their weapons," Wilder explained. "I wasn't able to see where it had been or who had used it. That's why I was surprised to learn it belonged to a fairy. Actually, I was initially surprised I couldn't read anything from it."

Sophia nodded. "Yeah, I sensed the ax was really different."

"It is," Wilder affirmed. "It's incredibly sharp, more so than most weapons, and would cut through just about anything."

"Like a deranged octopus," Sophia grumbled.

Wilder seemed surprised by this. "Yes, I suppose so. I was thinking heavy steel or something, but sure. It could probably cut through anything in the ocean. I'm certain there are many other magical properties to the ax, but I'll have to look into it later."

"Because you're off to hit the casinos and meet some unclassy ladies, right?" Evan asked with a grin, still choosing not to take a seat.

Wilder shook his head. "No, I think that's what you'd do if you didn't make every woman run for the hills and a thorough scrubbing. I have a mission I have to leave on straight away." He gave Sophia a remorseful expression. "I'll be gone for a while."

She nodded, disappointed.

"Hey, we're leaving on a mission too," Evan bragged. "Sophia is going to be my assistant and hold my bags and such. Like a caddy."

Wilder pretended he hadn't heard the other rider, still looking at Sophia. "You found a lead on Trin Currante?"

"Yeah, I just have to go find a dog with enhanced intelligence, and it will tell us where to look for the cyborg," she answered.

He nodded. "That seems like a totally Sophia approach to a problem."

She smiled at him as her phone rang in her pocket. Usually it would be silenced, but whoever was calling must have known how to turn that option off.

Sophia pulled her phone from her pocket and shouldn't have been surprised by who it was. Of course, Liv could bypass her options on her phone.

She excused herself from the table, sliding over to the fireplace for privacy as she took the call. "Hey, what's up?"

"Well, I put a unicorn's horn up a gnome's bu— Oh, wait, that's not what you were asking about," Liv said with a laugh. "I was just calling to tell you I need you in like five days."

"What for?" Sophia asked, thinking her sister needed help with wedding planning.

"That's when the wedding is, and it can't be moved," Liv answered.

"Wait, what?" Sophia exclaimed. "In five days? But we haven't had your bachelorette party or bridal shower or picked out a dress or—"

"First off, no, no, and hell no," Liv interrupted. "Bachelorette parties are for girls named Jenna who like to scream at bare-chested men and get lavished with attention for mating, something all mammals naturally do. Bridal showers are for women named April who like eating finger sandwiches and giggling while covering their mouths with their manicured fingers. No. Freaking. Thank you."

"What about a dress?" Sophia asked. "You have to wear a wedding dress."

"Thing is," Liv began, rebellion in her voice, "it's my wedding, and I get to do what I want. The guests can wear shoes that pinch their feet and corseted dresses. I'm wearing leather pants and knee-high boots...and a smile."

"Five days, though?" Sophia asked. "I'm leaving on a mission, and I've got to track down a cyborg and probably have an epic battle and nearly lose a limb or two."

"Well, don't lose any limbs because you have to catch my bouquet or whatever I decide to throw after the ceremony," Liv ordered. "It will probably be daggers."

"Daggers?" Sophia squeaked.

"Yeah, well, any desperate girl wanting to get married will dive for a bouquet of soft petals, but only someone who really wants it will dive to catch a falling dagger," Liv explained.

Sophia giggled. "Your reasoning is flawless."

"Isn't it, though?" Liv agreed. "You'll go on your mission and be back in time for my wedding...in one piece, I'll remind you. I need my maid of honor at my wedding."

Sophia smiled. "Don't worry. I'll be there. I promise."

"Good," Liv stated. "It will be at Rory's. Bring that cute boyfriend of yours. Oh, and also Wilder."

Again, Sophia giggled. "Who is my other boyfriend?"

"Arnold McFireBreath, of course," Liv replied.

"Of course." Sophia chuckled. "I'm sure Lunis will love to attend. Maybe I can get him to wear a bow tie."

"And pants," Liv suggested. "No naked dragons at my wedding. We have standards, you know. This is a classy affair."

"Says the bride who is wearing combat boots and throwing daggers," Sophia replied.

"The reception is nachos and beer," Liv added.

"I wouldn't expect anything less."

"Okay, be there," Liv said. "I can't wait to see you."

"Wait," Sophia said in a rush. "Why does it have to be in five days? Why the hurry?"

"Well, I could say it's because I'm pregnant or Stefan needs to marry me for citizenship reasons," Liv related. "However, the real reason is that we just can't wait to be married to each other."

Sophia nodded, appreciating that her sister, the hardest person she knew, had found love. "Don't worry, Liv. I'll be there. Nothing will stop me."

"I know," Liv said, a smile in her voice. "*Familia est sempiternum.*"

Sophia ended the call, aware the others weren't hiding their eavesdropping. Her gaze found Wilder's. "Can you join me for an event in five days? I want you to escort me."

He bowed slightly, his eyes sparkling. "It would be my honor, my lady."

CHAPTER FORTY-TWO

"Don't blame me when this whole mission goes to hell because you didn't let me take the lead," Evan said, tightening the straps on Coral, who was looking as regal as ever.

Lunis swiped his tail, nearly knocking Evan in the face. He was only saved by his fast reflexes.

Ducking suddenly, he jerked around, giving the blue dragon a look of offense.

Oops, Lunis said, no real shame on his face.

"Don't blame me when Lunis knocks your block off for sassing me," Sophia told Evan, stepping up on her dragon's wing and swinging her leg over the side.

"Oh, well, just you wait and see what Coral does for you bad mouthing me," Evan boasted, patting the purple dragon.

Coral held her chin up high and nobly. *I would prefer not to get mixed up in the affairs of riders.*

Sophia couldn't help but laugh. "Lun, how about you? Do you abide by these rules?"

He shook his large head. *Heck nah. I prefer to meddle like hell in the affairs of riders. Just say the word and I swipe his legs out from under him.*

SARAH NOFFKE & MICHAEL ANDERLE

Lunis held up his front foot and brandished it at Evan, mock menace written on his face.

Although Evan worked to try and hide it, the fear was evident on his face as he scrambled to get onto the back of his dragon.

"Thanks, Lun," Sophia commented. "Let him keep his legs at least until we return from the mission with the dog."

"We really have to go fetch a dog?" Evan asked. "That seems like a really ineffective way to find the whereabouts of this Trin Currante."

"What other brilliant ideas do you have, Einstein?" Sophia asked.

"We know she wants dragon eggs since she stole a bunch," Evan began. "We bait her with them, and when she takes it, *BAM*, we blow her up! End of story. Then we ride off into the sunset." He dusted off his hands like he'd just finished a job.

"Yeah, but I don't want to blow her up," Sophia argued. "I've been told she's key to stopping the disappearance of the magicians worldwide."

"By who?" Evan inquired as the dragons started across the Expanse.

"Secret people who you can never know about," she answered elusively.

"I won't rest until I find out," he fired back. "You're just going to follow this secret person's advice blindly? How do you know it's a risk worth taking?"

"Says the guy whose idea is to use our priceless dragon eggs as bait. Like that's not a huge risk." Sophia shook her head. "I operate on faith. I follow one lead to the next, usually only seeing one step at a time."

Evan yawned. "Sounds boring. Blowing shit up is much more fun."

"And we wonder why men don't live as long," Sophia sang as the two riders launched into the air in complete unison.

They flew through the Barrier and over the green hills for a half a mile before Sophia opened a portal to Medford Research.

The last time Sophia had been to the headquarters of Trin Currante's LiDAR aviation company, it had been about to explode. The Dragon Elite had gotten away just in time, not really looking back as flames erupted at their backs before they portaled home.

Presently, it looked like the aftermath of a warzone with at least a hundred yards of scorched earth where the site of the warehouse hangar had been located. The tarmac also showed signs of battle from when Evan and Mahkah attacked the cyborgs in aircraft.

When Mortimer had given Sophia the information on where to find the dog, at the conclusion to the conversation, he stressed the facility was thought to be booby-trapped. Trin Currante didn't seem to leave anything to chance. Even after blowing up her own facility, she had rigged it so anyone who went back looking for any clues that remained would be punished for it.

The problem was that Mortimer couldn't explain how the property had been booby-trapped. All he could tell her was the dog moved with a precision that made him think there were traps that had been set. The brownies didn't set them off, thankfully, and the dog was smart enough to know how to find them. Sophia and Evan, and especially the dragons wouldn't have that luxury.

Sophia had considered outfitting Lunis with the LiDAR technology again, but it had been damaged in the last battle and wasn't working reliably, according to the scientist Alicia. Also, the equipment weighed Lunis down severely, and she didn't want to chance it in case the cyborgs were still hanging around, ready to attack.

Evan and Sophia both took their dragons in different directions, making loops overhead as they surveyed the area. There weren't any signs of traps on the ground, but it was hard to tell with the huge mounds of rubble and debris from the explosion. Parts of a crashed helicopter littered one area of the runway. Unrecognizable equipment was strewn around the old hangar.

Sophia kept her eyes searching for signs of traps, but most importantly, the dog.

"See any tracks?" she asked Lunis.

He laughed. *I'm a dragon, not a tracker in the Amazon rainforest.*

"Well, with that kind of mentality, you'll stay a boring old dragon forever," she remarked. "We have the advantage of the air. We should be able to spot this guy."

We just have to be patient, Lunis suggested. *It's a virtue of the dragon, you know.*

"Is that why you said it was literally killing you having to wait for the next season of *The Witcher*," Sophia joked.

You obviously haven't seen the show, Lunis answered. *There's patience and then there's just being tortured. Come on, Netflix.*

"Can we also work on your use of the word 'literally'?"

What's wrong with it? he asked, a real curiosity in his voice as they continued to circle overhead.

"You use it about like Chris Traeger from the *Parks and Recreation* show," she explained.

And how's that?

"Wrong," she answered. "If you say something is literal, that means it's going to happen. It isn't going to kill you to have to wait."

You don't know that, he refuted.

Sophia shook her head at her dragon but still laughed at his ridiculousness. She shot Evan a curious glare as they passed each other.

He held up his hand and shrugged, nonverbally communicating he hadn't found any clues yet.

Sophia was about to decide they needed to land in the distance and come up with a new plan. Evan would, no doubt, rub it in her face that she wasn't smart enough to lead the mission. Then she'd have to restrain from popping him in the nose. It probably wouldn't work and she'd bruise her knuckles on his face.

She was about to suck it up and admit defeat when a crow soared and landed on a scorched bit of earth. Sophia didn't know why it caught her attention until a second later and the bird exploded, sending dirt and shrapnel into the air.

Sophia tensed and held her breath. She tightened her grip on the reins.

"Land mines," Sophia guessed.

Should have known, Lunis agreed.

"Yeah, it's right up Trin Currante's alley. They must be extremely sensitive if triggered by a crow."

Magi-tech, Lunis suggested. *I'm guessing she's not concerned with wasting them on wildlife, maybe.*

"How do we find them?" she asked as Evan sidled up next to her.

"Hey, did you see that explosion?" he asked her.

She gave him an annoyed expression. It would have been impossible for anyone to miss it. "No, what are you talking about?" Sophia asked.

He shot her a scowl. "So that's how it's trapped down there. You want to head down first, and I'll keep surveillance from up top?"

"Ha-ha," she remarked with no humor. "I'm giving the orders, remember?"

"Oh, so I suppose you want me to go prancing around a minefield then, huh?"

She shook her head. "If you think prancing around a minefield is a good idea, I might be doing the world a favor by letting you go down there. You know, observing the natural order of things with Darwinism."

Their dragons gently beat their wings, keeping them in the air.

"I think you're implying I'm dumb," he said, narrowing his eyes at her.

"Yeah, need I say anymore?" Sophia watched as the smoke from the small explosion cleared, studying the area where the bird landed. It was just feathers now, unfortunately. Apparently, a crow was large enough to set off the mines.

She consoled herself with the fact the explosion wasn't big. It was enough to kill a bird, but maybe it would just maim Evan a bit. Laughing to herself, Sophia activated her enhanced vision, turning up the contrast and crispness, like the settings on a camera. During training, she'd learned how to dial down her senses to conserve energy and also in an effort to not overwhelm her attention constantly.

It took a moment, but little by little, she began to notice little nodules that weren't charred like everything else around the exploded warehouse. They were like unscathed equipment, as though someone had placed them after the fact when setting traps for future trespassers.

Of course, Trin wouldn't have returned to bury UXOs in the ground. She wouldn't have had the time or inclination for such efforts. Placing a bunch of mines on the surface of the ground would take little time and energy.

Extending her hand, Sophia summoned a basketball. It appeared in her fingers, bright and orange and looking completely out of place as she hovered in the air on her dragon.

"Hey, Shorty, this is sort of a bad time for b-ball," Evan remarked. "I like the idea of a game later. And on the dragons! That would be badass."

"It would," she agreed. "But no, I have an idea of how to find the mines."

Silently, she steered Lunis until they were right over one of the nodules. Holding her breath, she released the basketball, hoping it fell on the supposed mine.

It didn't.

Instead, the wind took the basketball a bit to the right. The distance it had fallen made it bounce up high before coming back down again, feet from the nodules. Again it bounced high and then came down straight on a land mine, exploding it.

CHAPTER FORTY-THREE

"I almost don't want to admit that was a very savvy move on your part," Evan stated, looking impressed. "You figured out where the land mines are."

Sophia nodded, feeling elated. She explained to Evan what they were looking for. She decided the dragons would stay in the air and keep an aerial view while they searched on foot for the dog. The dragons could tell them telepathically where the land mines were, in case they were hard to see from the ground. They could also keep an eye out for the dog.

"Okay, you ready to go find this dog?" Sophia asked Evan as the dragons dropped them off a safe distance from the blown-up hangar. They'd have to hike in, all the while being careful to look out for land mines.

Evan pulled his ax from his belt. "Yeah, I'm ready."

"What's that for?" Sophia asked. "Are you going to chop us up some wood?"

Not amused by her joke, he shook his head. "No, I'm going to cut Rover down if he goes for my jugular."

Sophia scowled at him. "We don't know he's aggressive. He's

supposedly really smart and might be a bit like Trin Currante and the other cyborgs. I'm not sure."

"Or he might be a werewolf who wants to massacre us with his teeth and fangs," Evan argued.

Sophia shook her head at him as she started forward. "Well, I tend to doubt he's going to come out of hiding if we're searching the place while holding weapons."

"That's a chance I'm going to take," Evan replied.

Pulling out a package of dried meat she'd brought, Sophia pointed to the left. "You go that way. I'll take this end of the property."

"You brought him meat?" Evan asked.

"Yes, because we need the dog's help, which is why I'd like it if you'd put the ax away and not appear threatening," she explained.

Reluctantly, Evan nodded and put the ax away. He extended his hand, following after her. "Can I have some?"

Shaking a few pieces into his palm, Sophia smiled. "I'm glad to see you can be reasonable."

"I'm the king of reason," Evan said, popping the beef jerky into his mouth.

Her mouth popped open. "That was for the dog."

"Yeah, but I was hungry. Thanks for bringing me a snack. Do you by chance have any chocolate?"

Sophia did, but she wasn't giving it to the dumb jerk. "No. Now go off to the left and watch out for land mines. I don't want to have to clean your guts off the tarmac."

He shot her an amused expression, backing up. "Why ever would you clean my guts off the runway. Just leave me there. It's not like this place is real clean."

"It was a joke, but it's going to become our reality if you don't turn around and watch where you're going."

He saluted at her. "Copy that, boss."

CHAPTER FORTY-FOUR

Delicate with each step, Sophia held her breath as she progressed toward the burned-down warehouse. She was grateful to discover she could see the land mines from the ground since she knew what she was looking for. They weren't easy to spot, and she worried there could be many of them buried under the rubble and dirt as she progressed. She tried to take a less congested route.

"Here, puppy," Sophia called, shaking the bag of dried meat. "Come out, come out wherever you are."

From a few yards away, Evan laughed. He'd made more progress than her, not being as careful with his steps. "That's how you're going to attract the dog?"

"Got any better ideas, Ax Boy?" she asked.

"Yeah, dogs are attracted to the alpha. You begging him to come out just means when he does, he's going to tear out your jugular. And it's Ax *Man* to you."

"I'm going with the strategy that you attract more flies with honey than vinegar," she replied.

He shook his head, continuing to progress rather fast. "We're trying to catch a dog, not flies. Gosh, Pink Princess, are you drunk? Do you even know where you are?"

She pretended to think about it and looked down at her feet. "No, I don't. Whose shoes are these?"

A laugh popped out of his mouth. "How about we put a friendly wager on this. When I find Lassie first, you have to buy me a phone. The newest, shiniest model, all full of magitech."

"Hiker doesn't want the old dragonriders to have electronics," she argued. He had only allowed Sophia because it didn't make any difference since she was from the modern world. Telling her she couldn't use technology in the Castle hadn't worked either.

"What Hiker doesn't know won't hurt him…or me."

"If he does find out, then you're going to be seriously injured," Sophia warned. "What do I get when I find the dog first?"

He shrugged. "I don't even think it's worth my breath since it's never happening, but how about I be nice to you for like a whole week."

"How about I have Quiet prevent you from entering the Castle?" Sophia countered.

Evan scowled at her, knowing full well if she asked the groundskeeper for that he'd do it without question. "Fine, I'll teach you how to fight since you hold a sword like a girl and scream when you swing it."

She rolled her eyes. "That's a ki-yup, Ax Child. It produces power when paired with an assault. I do hold my sword like a girl since that's what I am."

"I'll teach you how to fight properly, so you don't have to scream at your opponent to beat them into submission," Evan joked.

"I think I'm good," Sophia said. "Instead, when you reply to me, for a week, you have to finish your sentence with, 'Whatever you want; I am your monkey.'"

He laughed. "That's a deal I'll take! Especially since I'm going to win."

"Shall we practice?" she asked him. "Evan, would you please pass me the butter?"

He glared at her. "No."

Sophia shook her head. "Actually, you would reply, 'Why, yes. Whatever you want; I am your monkey.'"

"That's not even going to make sense half the time."

"Oh, I think it will for most phrases I say to you." She held up her hand, ticking off fingers as she ran through a list. "Drop dead, Evan. Would you get out of here, Evan? Shush your face, Ax Boy."

"That's fine," he sang, holding out his hand as he traipsed in the opposite direction. "Let's pretend we've shaken on this."

"It's a bet," she affirmed, then her mouth fell open.

Evan was so busy trying to be cool, he didn't realize he was about to step on a land mine, inches away.

"Watch out!" Sophia shouted.

His head jerked down suddenly and he stumbled to the side, over-correcting for the near-mistake. He halted when he realized he was safe, his chest rising and falling hard.

Sophia had been holding her breath. She shook her head. "Watch where you're going, would you?"

"Whatever you want. I am your monkey," he joked, winking at her, a flood of relief on his face.

"All right, go find this dog," she ordered. "Or rather, watch as I do it."

She jiggled the bag of beef jerky again, calling to the dog.

Evan, who was properly motivated now, began whistling.

The two carefully progressed toward the center of the exploded warehouse, searching for the super canine or whatever he was.

See anything from up there? Sophia asked Lunis.

I see everything from up here, Lunis replied. *There are clouds. Over in the distance on that golf course, a guy is picking his nose. His caddy keeps sneaking a sip of the dude's beer when he's not looking. Oh, and there's a squirrel. I'm going to call him Cody.*

Sophia couldn't help but laugh. *No, I was referring to signs of the dog.*

Oh, for sure. I see him right now, Lunis said in her head. *You wanted me to let you know when I saw the dog? You should have said so. I thought you wanted me to fly around up here like a kite and look pretty.*

Ha-ha, Sophia replied. *Well, if you see something of interest, please let me know.*

The golfer just scratched his butt, Lunis told her.

With the same hand he picked his nose with? she asked in a serious voice.

Yes, but I think it's okay as long as he doesn't go back to picking his nose with the same hand, Lunis joked.

Keep an eye out for me, Sophia ordered. *I need to know what happens.*

You got it, Lunis told her.

Amused by her companions on this mission, Sophia found herself laughing just as something streaked out from behind a pile of rubble. When she turned to look at it straight on, she didn't see anything. She could have sworn a second before she'd seen a dog...or something that resembled a dog.

Studying the pile of debris, Sophia recognized a mini-refrigerator and a microwave, as well as an assortment of other kitchen tools. This must have been the area of the warehouse hangar where the kitchen was located. She remembered that space from when she and Mahkah had searched the place while undercover.

Carefully negotiating around the rubble, Sophia kept her eyes trained on the electronics where she could have sworn she'd seen the dog.

"Hey, look at what I found!" Evan called to her from several yards away. He picked up a small handheld gaming device. "Do you think this is magitech?"

Sophia shook her head. "No, it's a Nintendo Switch, and it's fried to hell."

Evan looked it over and shrugged before tossing it over his shoulder. A small explosion sent dirt and junk into the air, raining ash down on them.

Sophia shielded her face and head with her arms before deciding it was safe to relax. Pulling her hands away, she shook her head at Evan. "Dude, can you be more careful? Land mine zone, remember?"

"Land mine zone, remember," he said, mocking her.

She was about to make another remark when something caught

her attention. Spinning around, Sophia didn't see anything. There was no sign of the elusive dog. However, the mini refrigerator was gone.

Scratching her head, she observed, "That's weird."

"Are you looking in a mirror?" Evan asked with a laugh. "That's your face, and it's super weird-looking."

Not in the mood to banter with him, she shook her head. "There was a mini-refrigerator there a second ago. Now it's gone. I could have sworn I saw something sprint by."

"Let me ask you a question." Evan began picking up a long panel to check underneath it. "How much whisky have you had this morning?"

"Unlike the rest of the Dragon Elite, I don't start drinking first thing in the morning," Sophia answered, turning in place to survey the area. As she rotated, something streaked past her back.

Again she spun, her mouth pinched. Sitting beside a pile of charred junk was something Sophia didn't remember seeing before—a large red toolbox. The reason it stood out, much like how she remembered the mini-refrigerator, was that it was unscathed by the fire that happened at Medford Research. Which didn't make sense because everything else was burned and battered.

Carefully, Sophia approached the toolbox, her chin tilted to the side. She reached for the latch on the pristinely red box. It didn't budge when she tried to open it.

"What the hell?" she said, gritting her teeth together and pulling harder.

"Call me crazy, but I don't think the dog is in there, missy," Evan teased.

She stood, looking down at the strange toolbox. "I get that, but something isn't right about this. It wasn't here a moment ago and looks like it hasn't been touched by the fire."

"That's fascinating," he answered, sounding bored. He picked up another panel and peered underneath it. "Meanwhile, some of us are actually looking for the dog."

She made a profane gesture at him, giving him a seething expression.

"Now that's not very ladylike, is it?" He pointed at the ground next to her. "What toolbox are you talking about?"

Sophia glanced down, surprised to find the red toolbox had disappeared. "Okay, that's just weird."

She turned, searching for an object that was out of place again. Behind her, she heard a scurrying noise. Quickly Sophia spun in that direction, noticing a metal chair that had definitely not been there moments prior.

"Okay, I think I've got you figured out." She grabbed a piece of beef jerky and tossed it in the direction of the metal chair. Staying still, Sophia watched the chair, deciding she was going to wait it out. She wasn't sure her assumption was correct, but she reasoned the dog could shapeshift. She just had to get it to take its regular form. That must be how it moved.

Feeling like she was having a staring contest, she kept her eyes trained on the metal chair. Meanwhile, Evan was making a ton of racket, looking under different pieces of debris. Sophia reasoned he was probably safe since it was unlikely Trin Currante had stuck land mines under the wreckage. It was more likely they littered the path, where they could catch trespassers.

He glanced over his shoulder at her, giving her a pursed expression. "Okay, well, you're definitely losing the bet if you're just going to stand there and stare blindly ahead."

"I'm not just staring," she said, although she realized that wasn't quite true. "I have a plan."

"Yeah, me too," Evan replied. "It's called 'find the freaking dog.' You should try playing it."

"Whatever," she stated, keeping her focus on the metal chair. "Get ready to start calling yourself a monkey."

He shook his head, reaching for a large cover hanging out of a bunch of larger equipment. "Whatever. Get ready to buy me a—"

A scream like that of a schoolgirl falling off the jungle gym ripped out of Evan's mouth.

Sophia's gaze shot in his direction as he continued to scream and staggered backward blindly.

"SNAKE!" he yelled, nearly tripping over his feet.

She was going to race over when she spied a land mine a foot behind him. He was about to step right on it.

"Watch out!" Sophia yelled, but it was too late. He was already in motion, inches away from landing on the mine.

Something blurred in her vision. Whatever it was moved so fast, Sophia could hardly make out what it was as it dove at Evan and sent him back the other direction—away from the land mine.

CHAPTER FORTY-FIVE

The lucky one, Evan, heaved ragged breaths as a massive dog stood on top of him, looking down into his brown eyes.

Frozen, Evan stared up at the strange animal, who, much like Trin Currante, was more metal than flesh and bone. The dog resembled a German shepherd, but one of its eyes was surrounded by metal and glowed blue. There was a stainless-steel panel on the side of its body. Its tail was metal with hundreds of shreds of spiral aluminum on it that resembled hair.

To Sophia's relief, the dog's tail was wagging as it regarded Evan with its tongue hanging out of its mouth.

"That dog just saved your life," Sophia said when she'd caught her breath, momentarily speechless from witnessing the series of events.

"Do you think he did so because he didn't want his dinner blown up?" Evan asked from the corner of his mouth.

Sophia laughed at this, carefully approaching and watching out for the land mine Evan had nearly stepped on.

"I don't think he wants to eat you," she observed. Squatting when she was close to the animal, she asked, "Hey, buddy. Did you get left behind? Are you okay?"

Sophia wasn't sure what she expected, maybe for the animal to speak to her through a voice box or something. It definitely had skills apart from being incredibly intelligent. Looking over her shoulder, she confirmed her suspicion. The metal chair was gone.

Incredibly impressed, Sophia glanced back at the cyborg dog. "You can shapeshift. That's very cool."

Blinking at her with curiosity, the canine stepped off Evan before taking a seat on the ground next to him.

Unhurried, Evan pushed up to a sitting position and studied the curious animal. "Shapeshift? Like Ainsley?"

Sophia nodded. "Although I get the impression this guy can only turn into metal objects."

Evan craned his neck to study a metal collar around the dog's neck. "Its name is NO10JO."

Wanting to check that out for herself, Sophia approached, careful to not spook the animal. Now that it was out of hiding, it seemed excited to be around them, good-naturedly panting.

Sophia saw what Evan was talking about. Next to a barcode were letters and numbers that spelled out: NO10JO. "That's not its name. That's its barcode. I'm betting subjects were given reference numbers."

Tentatively, Evan reached out, watching the dog's reaction. When it looked up, its brown and blue eye was brimming with excitement about the possibility of being touched.

Evan grinned before laying his hand on the dog's head. "I don't know, I like the name for him. NO10JO, thanks for saving my life. You're a good dog."

The dog nuzzled into the attention, lapping it up. It was quite the affectionate scene, Sophia thought, smiling at the pair.

"That's fine," she said. "We can call it whatever it wants." Turning her attention to NO10JO, she smiled. "Do you want to come to a really cool place with us?"

The dog stood up and started wagging its tail. The answer seemed to be a resounding "yes."

"Do you think we can take him into the Gullington?" Evan asked.

She thought about it and shrugged. "Well, isn't it true that anyone who works for the Dragon Elite can enter through the Barrier?"

He nodded. "Yeah, as long as they pledge loyalty to us."

Sophia combed her hand over her chin. "I think we're going to need some time to work out how he's going to communicate Trin Currante's location."

Evan continued to pet the dog. "Hey, NO10JO, will you help us find that mean old cyborg who left you behind? We need to in order to save the world."

The animal barked, excitement in its tone.

Evan's grin widened. "I think that was another 'yes.'"

"Okay, well, then let's head to safety and portal home," she suggested, leading the way through the path, careful to avoid land mines.

Evan and NO10JO followed, striding next to each other.

Sophia allowed triumph to fill her chest as she realized they were that much closer to finding Trin Currante.

CHAPTER FORTY-SIX

"I knew you were trouble from the beginning, or at least I should have and ignored the voices in my head," Ainsley spat when they strode into the Castle with NO10JO.

As Sophia had thought, the dog was able to cross the Barrier into the Gullington. That proved to her the animal was loyal to them. Maybe it was because it had been abandoned by accident or otherwise, or because NO10JO sensed Evan and Sophia were good and it wanted to help them. For whatever reason, it officially worked for the Dragon Elite now.

The three froze in the entryway as Ainsley stomped down the stairs. "S. Beaufont, I expect stupidity from Evan, but you?"

"Hey, now!" Evan argued, sounding offended. "Did you just say you hear voices in your head?"

"Yes," Ainsley answered at once before pointing at NO10JO. "You brought a dog into the Castle. Is that thing tracking dirt onto my clean floors?"

Sophia glanced at the animal's dusty paws. It had been at the burned-down warehouse for a while and was filthy. "Sorry, Ains. I'll clean this up for you, and we'll give the dog a bath right away."

"So, those voices..." Evan went on, obviously curious about this revelation. "What do they tell you?"

Ainsley shot him an angry look. "To kill you in your sleep." She narrowed her eyes at the dog. "You don't belong in here and are going to have to leave."

NO10JO let out a whimper before shifting into a large printer. It looked out of place in the rustic old Castle.

If the fact the cyborg dog could shapeshift surprised Ainsley, she didn't show it. In response, she shapeshifted into a German shepherd without nuts and wires in its body. "The only dog around here is me," the housekeeper said, speaking in her animal form.

"Okay." Evan elbowed Sophia in the side. "You heard her. Our Ainsley called herself a dog."

The shapeshifter took her normal form, anger heavy on her face. "The voices are telling me to kill you now."

Evan shook his head, taking a step backward. "You shouldn't listen to them. Tell the voices to be quiet."

"Ains," Sophia cut in, "NO10JO is here to help us. I promise it won't be any trouble for you. We'll clean up after it and everything."

Ainsley sighed dramatically. "It's another mouth for me to feed, though, and I'm already busy thinking of ways to make Hiker's life a living hell. When am I supposed to find time to polish this dog?"

Sophia blinked rapidly as NO10JO shifted back to its usual form. "Um, we'll polish the dog. Or whatever it is we need to do for it. It's really good and I think you'll like it if you give it a chance."

In response, Ainsley spun and stomped back up the stairs. "We're taking this matter up with the worst person in the world."

Evan gave Sophia a commiserating expression before they followed the housekeeper. "You have to give her credit. She might hate the man, but she respects his authority."

CHAPTER FORTY-SEVEN

Bad blood obviously existed between Hiker and Ainsley, but when she trudged into his office, madder than hell, concern was evident in his voice.

"What is it?" Sophia heard him ask as she approached his office. "What's got you upset?" Because the man had no tact, he added, "This time."

"That's the problem," Ainsley declared when the three entered Hiker's office. She was casting an accusatory finger at NO10JO.

Hiker shot to his feet, shock written on his face. "What's that?"

"Oh, dear, my son," Mama Jamba said from her normal spot on the sofa. She was leafing through an issue of *People*. "I've really neglected your education. That is a dog."

Hiker cut his eyes at the old woman. "I know that, but what's it doing in the Castle, and what's wrong with it?"

"Its name is NO10JO," Evan said proudly, patting the dog on the head.

"That's the worst name ever," Ainsley declared, crossing her arms.

"I agree it's not a standard dog name." Mama Jamba peered over her magazine at the animal. "I didn't make that creature. Well, not in its current form."

179

Ainsley sighed. "Yeah, if it must have a name, why can't it be a normal dog name like Cleveland or Duckland or Carl?"

Sophia blinked at the housekeeper, trying to decide if the statement deserved a reply. "We found the name on the collar. I think it's just its barcode for classification purposes, but it likes it well enough."

"What's a barcode?" Hiker asked, irritation on his face.

Sophia shook her head. "We can brush up on your twenty-first-century education later. Right now, we have more important matters. We found NO10JO at Medford Research. He was apparently there with Trin Currante. My source—"

"Which is top secret, and you should insist she disclose," Evan interrupted, trying to persuade Hiker to exert his influence.

He shook his head at the dragonrider. "I can't make Sophia do a damn thing, and as long as her source pays off, I don't really care." Hiker returned his attention to Sophia. "What did your source tell you?"

"They said the way to get to the bottom of the magician disappearance business was to find Trin Currante," she explained, and Hiker nodded.

"Yes, and you wanted to do that anyway," he finished.

"That's right," she affirmed. "My sources didn't know where to find the cyborg pirate."

Evan threw up his hands. "Oh, now she has sources."

Sophia rolled her eyes at him before continuing. "Anyway, I learned that if I went back to Medford Research, I'd find a super-smart dog who could lead us to Trin Currante."

Hiker considered this. "Well, so far, it sounds like your sources have been correct."

She nodded. "Yeah, we went there, and as they mentioned, we found NO10JO."

Evan actually looked impressed. "Oh, and they told you about the traps, and there were all those land mines. So, they might be worth listening to."

Sophia shook her head at him. "Of course, they are worth listening to. Anyway, I think the dog will be able to help us find Trin Currante."

"How?" Hiker growled.

For a moment, Sophia thought through different options. "Well, I'm not sure."

"After Wilfred tells us this information, he'll be on his way, right?" Ainsley asked.

Evan's mouth popped open. "We can't kick it out. It was all alone at that airport hangar." He bent down and hugged the animal, who snuggled into him. "It needs a home."

Hiker lowered his chin regarding the pair. "Are you going to take care of it?"

With a hopeful expression, Evan's eyes lightened. "Yes!"

"Are you going to be responsible for feeding it?" Ainsley demanded, sounding like his mother.

"Absolutely," Evan confirmed. "I'll brush it and walk it and do whatever it needs to be done."

Hiker and Ainsley exchanged uncertain looks.

The housekeeper finally softened. "Well, I guess it's okay, then. I won't have it in my kitchen or sitting at the dining table or going through my sock drawer."

"Why would it do that?" Sophia inquired and then shook her head. "Never mind. I think that's fair." She smiled widely at the dog. "You get to stay, buddy."

The look in its eyes was one of pure happiness.

"It gets to stay, as soon as it proves its worth," Hiker argued. "Get it to tell you where Trin Currante is, and then we'll decide its fate."

This was the tricky part Sophia hadn't thought all the way through. She kneeled to be level with NO10JO. "Hey, buddy, can you tell us where Trin Currante is? You know, the lady cyborg who was in charge of Medford Research."

The animal blinked at her with its normal eye, the other remaining a strange glowing shade of blue.

"You know," Sophia went on, feeling the pressure of the moment as everyone watched, waiting for the dog to be of help. "The lady with the black hair made of wires? Can you understand me?"

She wasn't sure what she was expecting. Maybe for NO10JO to nod or bark or give her some indication of understanding.

Sophia sighed. Her fairy godmother had told her she needed to find Trin Currante, and Mortimer had said the dog would know. She was used to her sources being reliable, but maybe this was a first when they steered her wrong.

Feeling like she was about to be marked a complete failure in front of the group, Sophia tried one more time. "NO10JO, can you show us where to find the cyborgs? If you can, you get to stay."

"If you don't," Ainsley stated boldly, "we're taking you to the pound."

Sophia shot her an annoyed expression. "You can be a little more sensitive. It's obviously been through a lot."

Ainsley threw her nose in the air. "How is that mean? I'd go live at the pound if I could. At least it would get me out of this place and away from a certain someone." Not discreetly, she indicated Hiker.

He let out an irritated sigh. "Well, Sophia, if your cyborg dog isn't going to talk, then it's not of any use to us."

Sophia wanted to do something else to encourage NO10JO. The animal was obviously intelligent, but she didn't know how it was going to communicate with her. "Where on Earth is Trin Currante?"

This time, the question stirred something in the dog. He stood suddenly and trotted over to the window.

At first, Sophia thought it was curious to look out the bank of windows at the Expanse and Pond. Then it mechanically turned its attention to the Elite Globe in the corner. Standing up on its hind legs, it rotated the globe, searching.

Evan shot her a hopeful expression. The rest stood frozen, watching as the animal rotated the globe until it apparently found what it was looking for. Very deliberately, it stuck its paw on a spot before looking up at Sophia, a hopeful expression in its eyes.

Nervously, she strode over and looked at where its paw was. Feeling enormous relief, she glanced at Hiker.

"We've narrowed it down," she exclaimed with excitement. "Trin Currante is in San Diego, California."

CHAPTER FORTY-EIGHT

"Long live NO10JO!" Evan exclaimed, rushing over and giving the dog a big hug before rubbing its head. "Such a good boy!" His voice was high and sounded like he was talking to a baby.

"Watch yourself, son," Hiker warned, giving him a stern expression. "You are a dragonrider, not a nanny."

Unaffected by the comment, Evan continued to pet the dog. "You saved my life and now Sophia's butt. Good job!"

"San Diego is quite large," Hiker said, worry in his voice. "How do you plan to find Trin Currante there?"

Their small victory was overshadowed by Hiker's question. Sophia's face scrunched with frustration.

"I'm not sure," she grumbled.

"The thing is," Mama Jamba began, licking her finger and flipping through the magazine, "a bunch of cyborgs at a location would give off a certain reading."

Sophia gasped. "Magitech! It does register."

"How are you going to pick up on it?" Hiker asked.

"Magic," she explained. "I can create a spell that finds the collective energy of magitech. Mama Jamba is right that it registers differently and can be tracked down if we know where to look."

"We're looking in San Diego, thanks to the smartest doggie in the world," Evan cooed in a baby voice, continuing to rub NO10JO's head.

Sophia smiled at the two. "San Diego isn't that big, so I don't think it will take long."

"You were calling Trin Currante a pirate earlier," Ainsley said, swaying like she heard music. "If there's music around San Diego, you might know where to start looking!"

"Ains!" Sophia exclaimed. "You're a genius!"

"Finally." Ainsley gave Hiker a rude expression, "someone sees my talents."

"San Diego is on the coast of California," Sophia mused, studying the globe.

"Oh, I wouldn't know," Ainsley stated. "I've been stuck here for centuries." She gave Hiker a murderous expression.

"You're still alive because of it," he muttered, irritation heavy in his voice. "You're welcome."

"I didn't say thank you," she spat. "Seriously, sometimes I wished I were dead, having to deal with you day in and day out." The housekeeper marched toward the exit, her fists by her sides as she stormed out of the office.

Hiker shook his head, sighing. "You don't mean that."

Ainsley pivoted at the door. "Oh, no, I don't. I wish *you* were dead."

Evan glanced up. "Let's just hope the voices in her head don't tell her to kill you."

"They do every single day," Ainsley said with a mischievous giggle before striding out of the office.

Hiker, exasperated, shook his head, rippling his long blond hair. "That one and her drama."

"I'll remind you that you're the reason she has any drama," Mama Jamba offered matter-of-factly, turning the page of the magazine. "Would you just look at what Jennifer Aniston is wearing? I must have it."

"Who is...what..." Hiker shook this off, returning his attention to Sophia. "Do you think you can track down Trin Currante and the other cyborgs?"

She thought for a moment. "San Diego has a large port. I think that's where I could start. I can cast a spell that registers magitech. As long as they are giving off the greatest amount of it, the spell will lead to them."

"Evan, you're going with Sophia," Hiker ordered.

He glanced up and smiled. "And NO10JO. It can help us when we need to get into secret pirate ships or whatever."

"Fine." Hiker took a seat in his chair. "Find Trin Currante, and let's figure out how to get the bottom of the magicians disappearing." He pointed to a stack of newspapers filled with headlines on the subject. "The House of Fourteen is losing traction with mortals by the day. Not to mention the problem is having effects on all the other magical races. We need to find out who is behind it and stop them."

Sophia nodded. "You can count on us, sir."

CHAPTER FORTY-NINE

The world on the other side of the Barrier was so different than the Gullington. Sophia needed a moment to soak it in before setting off for another adventure that took her away from her home. It was like her time in the Castle reset her. It probably did since there were many restorative and healing spells inside the walls of the Castle.

Sophia had gone to bed early and risen at dawn, charged and ready for the adventure that awaited her in San Diego. She didn't even mind that Evan was ordered to tag along. Although she'd never admit it to him, they worked together well. He'd gotten the dog to come out of its hiding place by nearly killing himself. Sophia was hopeful he'd be of use on this mission. Or at least he'd do something dumb that turned into a happy accident. That's when she realized she had lost her end of the bet and would have to make good…unless Evan didn't remember.

Standing next to Lunis, she peered across the Expanse, enjoying the morning sunlight as things were illuminated on another gorgeous day in the Gullington. Her dragon was devouring a sheep, not using proper table manners as he tore into the animal. Thankfully Sophia wasn't squeamish about watching the bloody scene.

Can I get a dog? Lunis asked, talking with his mouth full.

She shook her head. "No."

Why not? he argued. *You got Evan a dog.*

"I didn't get Evan a dog," she refuted. "We found one, and he's going to keep it."

It was no surprise to anyone that NO10JO slept in Evan's room the night before and had been trotting beside him through the Castle since entering. Every time the cyborg dog came face to face with Ainsley, it turned into a water heater or an air conditioning unit. It had been quite funny the night before when the dog shifted back to its normal appearance next to the dining room table and scared Hiker, who hadn't known the animal had that skill.

The leader of the Dragon Elite was visibly uncomfortable about having a shapeshifting cyborg dog in the Castle, yet he couldn't refute how helpful and well-meaning the creature was. It appeared NO10JO was going to stick around.

As Lunis finished the last of his breakfast, Evan and his new dog strode down the steps of the Castle, a wide smile on both their faces.

Evan's dragon Coral didn't appear excited about the new friendship as she flew down from the Cave, a grimace on her face.

Evan was nearly in front of Sophia when he held out his hand. "Pony up, dollface. I want my phone."

He hadn't forgotten, Sophia realized, pulling out her smartphone.

"No, I want a brand new shiny one," he argued. "Not something with your dead skin cells all over it."

"I'm not giving you my phone," she said, scowling at him. "I'm ordering you one right now."

"The newest model," he demanded. "Whatever that is, that's what I want."

She nodded, scrolling through the options and clicking on an item. "I got you a flip phone with real buttons and a one-inch screen."

He smiled with satisfaction. "Sounds great. Welcome to the twenty-first century, Evan."

"More like the twentieth century, but whatever," Sophia joked.

"What's that?" he asked.

Sophia shook her head. "It will be delivered via Amazon Prime in a day or so."

"A whole day?" he asked, sounding disappointed.

"Seriously, you don't even know what Amazon Prime is or how to use your phone," she stated. "Chill out."

"True, but one does get used to immediate gratification in this day and age," he said with a laugh. "You're going to have to teach me how to use it."

She shook her head. "Nope. You're going to have to win another bet first."

He rubbed his hands together. "Oh, no problem there. We have a mission where you will present me with many ways to best you. I'm certain of it."

Sophia's eyes fluttered with annoyance as she regarded Coral, tearing up the grass beside them, seeming to act out from the presence of the dog.

"So, NO10JO is going to ride on Coral?" she asked Evan, eyeing the dragon who didn't appear happy about the idea.

"Oh, yeah," Evan agreed with satisfaction. "It's going to be great. Just a boy and his dragon and his dog. How much better can it get?"

According to the look on the purple dragon's face, it could get measurably better. Sophia was concerned NO10JO might get dumped into the Pond during takeoff. She was going to leave the getting along of the dragon and the cyborg dog to Evan to deal with. She did think bringing NO10JO along was a good idea. He could hopefully help if there was something specific to the cyborgs they couldn't figure out.

Evan started for Coral, the dog at his side before he paused, hesitation in his movements. "What if NO10JO wants to stay with Trin Currante when we get there? What if it was left behind by mistake, and I'm taking it to be reunited with its old owner?"

Sophia gave Evan a sensitive expression. "I get that concern, but if that's the case, you have to let it stay there. That's its owner, and NO10JO deserves to be with the right one."

"But it's *my* dog now," Evan complained.

"I know, but you don't want it to be with you if it wants Trin Currante or one of the other cyborgs."

He gawked at her. "Of course I do. I'm not one of those people who wants what's better for my loved ones. I want them to be with me, even if that's not what is best for them. That's love."

"Selfish love," Sophia corrected. "It's just a risk you're going to have to take because NO10JO does need to go with us."

Evan shrugged that off. "That's fine. I know it will choose me. We're bonded. If they give me trouble about it, I'll just slice them in two." He patted the ax on his back.

Sophia shook her head. "There will be no slicing any steampunk pirate cyborgs in two. We aren't going there for war. We need Trin Currante, and we're not getting her cooperation if we take out her men or hurt or destroy her property."

"You're telling me we have to storm this ship or whatever it is and be nice?"

She nodded. "This is a goodwill mission, Evan. We have to refrain from using deadly force. Think of using stunning and paralyzing spells. Do things to block the cyborgs but not kill them. We have to get to Trin Currante. Then we can figure out what's going on and how she can help."

Evan sighed dramatically, like a three-year-old on the verge of a tantrum. "Fine, but this mission seems really boring now."

"Yes, we're going after a cyborg pirate on the back of two ancient dragons with a shapeshifting dog," Sophia said dryly. "So very boring."

Evan nodded. "I'm glad you see it my way."

CHAPTER FIFTY

I did something bad, Lunis admitted when they were in the air, riding out over the Expanse and headed for the Barrier of the Gullington.

Sophia tightened her grip on the reins and lowered her chin. *What did you do?* she asked her dragon.

I told Coral she had been replaced by the cyborg dog, and I think she sort of believes it, he said with an evil laugh.

How can she believe that? Sophia questioned. *She's a three-hundred-year-old dragon who has been bonded to her rider for two hundred years.*

She's super sensitive and takes herself entirely too seriously, Lunis admitted. *It was pretty easy to plant the information in her head.*

Why would you want to cause insecurity? Sophia wondered.

Lunis flapped his wings, gracefully making it to the other side of the Barrier, where the sun never seemed to shine as brightly. *Because she's mean to me and tells me I'm a mistake because I like to play Pokémon Go and aspire to be an Instagram influencer.*

She said that to you? Sophia asked, horror-struck and fiercely protective all of a sudden.

Yeah, and she doesn't think you're as good a rider because you're a girl, he said, fanning the flames of Sophia's anger.

How dare she! Sophia exclaimed, vengeance in her tone. *Tell her she's being retired and put out to pasture. Sent to the glue factory.*

Damn, you're cold, Lunis told her, sounding impressed.

Well, no one messes with my dragon, Sophia declared with conviction. *Damn it, why is it another female is going to keep the other down. Why can't we support each other?*

You preach it, sister, Lunis cheered.

Sophia shook her head at her dragon but smiled all the same. *The three will sort it out. I think NO10JO could be good for Evan. Coral will figure things out. A little change is all anyone needs, especially after three hundred years.*

CHAPTER FIFTY-ONE

Change wasn't easy for dragons, magicians, or cyborgs. Sophia knew confronting Trin Currante wasn't going to be easy.

She suspected the cyborg pirate would try to fight her. Getting to her without a fight was going to be tough, but the only way to earn her trust was to not harm her or her men. It was usually easier to go into these things with all guns blazing, which was why Sophia was going to have to rely on her greatest weapon: strategy.

Even though Sophia had grown up only hours away from San Diego, she'd never been to the port city. She'd never been to many places, having been a very sheltered child. Clark had been so worried about anything happening to her after their parent's death and then their siblings'. Because Sophia was a unique magician with powers from an early age, he had protected her fiercely, not allowing her to leave the House of Fourteen.

Her life now was a stark contrast to her childhood, with adventure after adventure. It suited Sophia, and she never wanted to be confined again, even though she always looked forward to returning home at the end of a mission.

Waiting until they were over the harbor in San Diego, Sophia began the spell for finding the concentration of magitech. She hoped this worked because she didn't really have a plan B. She had gotten the idea for the spell from Mama Jamba, who seemingly knew the answers to all problems, but preferred for her children to figure it out on their own most of the time.

Sophia had once heard that having a backup plan was a sure way to failure. When taking a big risk, if there was a safety net, then sometimes people didn't put their all into the initial effort, knowing they had a plan B if things didn't work. But if you were all in with the only option you had, then you'd push to make that one work. That was the idea anyway, and Sophia hoped in this instance, it worked in her favor. Otherwise, she didn't know how they would find Trin Currante.

Flying over the area of the harbor with private yachts and boats that took tourists out on cruises, Sophia continued on to the port area of the bay, where the larger ships and freighters were located. That made the most sense for Trin Currante's boat, but there would be only one way to know for sure.

Finishing the spell, Sophia sat back on Lunis, studying the boats on the water to determine if it worked. At first, nothing happened, and she feared plan A was a waste of time, which would mean they'd need to quickly create a plan B. A few seconds later, small lights started to flicker around the port area. Not a lot, but enough to catch Sophia's attention.

There was one that lit up an area of a jet boat. It must have magitech on board. In the distance, there was a house with a couple of lights shimmering around it. Maybe it was inhabited by magicians with magitech. On the far side of the port next to the shipping yard, a large ship was ablaze with lights.

"Bingo!" Sophia exclaimed. "Looks like we found Trin Currante's pirate ship."

CHAPTER FIFTY-TWO

S *tate of Grace.*

That was the name of Trin Currante's ship. Sophia laughed as they circled the large vessel, realizing she might have been able to locate the ship even if plan A didn't work.

Alongside the freighters and other neighboring cruise liners, the *State of Grace* probably would have gotten her attention. It stood out from the other ships. One might have mistaken it for a themed boat that took tourists on adventures because it looked unmistakably like a pirate's ship.

It wasn't like the *McAfee*, Quiet's ship he once sailed through the North Sea. That one had appeared like an ancient ship that sailed the unforgiving oceans. This one looked like the *Black Pearl* that cut through choppy waters, taking names, stealing and pillaging and creating destruction in its wake.

Almost stereotypically, the ship was entirely black. The sails, which were rolled up tightly, were black. On the front of the ship was a statue of a woman leaning out of the bow. She was beautiful, with her flowing black hair and a wicked smile. Unlike Trin Currante, she appeared a hundred percent human.

The deck of the ship was clear except for a few cyborgs, which

Sophia could recognize as such from the air as they neared. The dragons had glamoured themselves to look like aircraft, which in San Diego wouldn't be questioned, and were flying overhead in the harbor.

The ship was massive, and Sophia assumed there would be a few dozen cyborgs on it. Getting onto a tight space and not causing fights with people who had battled them many times was going to be a challenge.

She glanced at Evan riding beside her. Gesturing, she communicated to him the ship below was their target.

From Coral's back, Sophia noticed NO10JO getting more anxious, rising to a standing position next to Evan. He seemed to be having trouble controlling the dog all of a sudden.

"We've got to get down there," Sophia communicated to Evan, using an amplifying spell so he could hear while in the air.

From surveying the area, it looked like trying to get onto the ship from the dock would be difficult. There was a security gate that appeared to be heavily guarded. There were also a couple of cyborgs patrolling the walkway areas leading the ship.

"The best option is to drop onto the deck from up high," Sophia informed him.

He nodded and then shook his head. "How do you suggest we do that? I've got a dog, remember?"

"I remember," she replied. "I guess we're going to have to use one of my favorite strategies."

He sighed. "Oh, I can't wait to hear this. Lay it on me, Pink Princess."

CHAPTER FIFTY-THREE

"Jump, then fall," Sophia instructed Evan.

"That's your crafty plan?" he questioned. "You just want us to jump onto the deck from the dragons? You said it was strategic."

"Right," she affirmed. "Just because it's strategic, it doesn't mean it has to be complicated."

He sighed, appearing defeated. "I just thought it could involve a dramatic entrance, maybe some spy devices and some other super-cool elements."

She shrugged. "That's the plan. We jump off the dragons, and then we fall onto the deck."

"Fine, but what about NO10JO?" Evan asked.

As if in answer to his question, the dog lifted its paw and combed it over the rider's arm.

Sophia smiled. "I think it's down with the plan. Something tells me the dog has great jumping skills." She remembered how fast he was on the grounds for Medford Research and was looking forward to seeing the dog in action.

"Let's go in just a minute," Sophia called to him, studying the deck of the *State of Grace*. There were three or four cyborgs doing various chores in the main area. Hopefully they could disband them without much commotion. Her eyes trailed to a set of doors that were intricately decorated. That had to be the area that led to the captain's quarters. She suspected that's where Trin Currante was located.

Hope filled Sophia's chest. This seemed like a pretty straightforward mission for once.

Jump and fall onto the deck. Subdue a few pirates. Crash into the captain's quarters and make friends with Trin Currante, who the last time Sophia saw her had tried to kill her. Easy-peasy.

What could go wrong?

CHAPTER FIFTY-FOUR

L *ast kiss before you go?* Lunis asked in Sophia's head.
"No, thanks," she said. "I hear kissing dragons will give me an awful rash."

As well as a lot of other awesome stuff, Lunis argued.

Sophia laughed, pulling her leg around and preparing to slide down Lunis' back and jump onto the ship. He was almost into position about a dozen feet from the surface of the ship.

"You'll be close by?" she asked, already knowing the answer.

Yeah, I'm just going to pop over to the zoo, he teased. *I hear they have lemurs, and I've always wanted to see those in person.*

"The dragon wants to be up close with a lemur," she mused, shaking her head.

You won't let me have a dog, he argued. *What else am I supposed to do?*

"You and I both know you'd get bored with a dog after a few months, and then I'd have to take care of it," she said in a punishing tone.

Yes, Mom, I get it, he muttered. *I'll be here. I'm going to go mess with the drunk tourist over there on that booze cruise. I'll remove my glamour when Cindy is looking off romantically at the horizon. Then when she tells her boyfriend Paul she just saw a dragon, I'll change back, making it appear like Cindy is losing her mind.*

Sophia nodded. "Seems like a good use of your magical powers."

The best use of them is to make mortals think they are going crazy, he said with a laugh.

"Yeah, who would want to use them to make the world a better place?" she questioned sarcastically.

Boring people, he answered.

"That's me, Miss Boring," she said, sucking in a breath and preparing for the fall.

You said it, not me, he said, his tone serious. *Okay, be safe, dear Soph. Holler if you need anything. I'll be straight above, ready to dive in and scorch some pirates if it gets to that.*

"Let's hope it doesn't," she said, then kissed her hand and laid it affectionately on her dragon. "See you soon."

With that, Sophia slid down Lunis' wing, which dipped perfectly and created a gentle slide that sent her to the deck below.

CHAPTER FIFTY-FIVE

Breathe, Sophia thought when she landed in a crouch on the deck of the *State of Grace*. However, her landing on the ship hadn't gone unnoticed by the cyborgs close by.

Two of them spun, one holding a mop and the other a sword. The first narrowed his good eye while the other flashed a murderous glare at her. They both appeared ready to spring into action and get rid of the stowaway who had just dropped out of thin air.

Before they could charge at her, Evan landed beside Sophia, not as gracefully as she'd arrived.

"Dude, really?" he asked her, not seeming to notice the menacing figures about to charge them. "Jump and fall? That was your plan? I think I have a shin splint now."

"Evan…" she said, her eyes nervously on the two cyborgs.

"Don't 'Evan' me," he complained, his attention on Sophia, no regard for the potential enemies about to pounce. He rolled his shoulders. "You owe me a massage for this. Where's my dog?" He glanced up, holding out his arms for NO10JO. "Come on, boy. I'll catch you because the landing is a bitch. I'm sorry. Sophia has the worst ideas."

NO10JO seemed to be preparing himself for the jump. He made a few false starts, then the dog disappeared from Coral's back and appeared on the deck next to them.

"Oh, the dog can teleport," Evan exclaimed with a laugh.

Although that was impressive, Sophia kept her eyes trained on the two cyborgs, who seemed to be looking for their chance to attack.

"Yeah, that's cool, but the thing is—"

"Cool?" Evan questioned, sounding offended, and facing off with Sophia. "Cool? My dog can teleport. That's a bit more than cool, methinks, Phia!"

"You're right," Sophia said tersely, still regarding the pirates. "Thing is—"

"Oh, are you going to make this about you, now?" Evan demanded, seemingly looking for a fight. He was about to get it, but not with Sophia.

"Hey, Ev, really quickly, do you remember where we are?" she asked.

He nodded, throwing his hands in the air. "Of course I do. You made me jump twelve feet onto the deck of a pirate's ship."

"What do all pirate ships have?" she challenged, her hand flexing next to her sword, although she was hoping not to pull it.

"I don't know," he said dismissively. "Booty?"

"And?" Sophia urged.

"I'm guessing there's some rum, a Jolly Roger's flag, and a hempen halter," he mused, seeming to be thinking about his list.

"One important thing you're forgetting," she ground out through clenched teeth.

Evan scratched his head. "I don't know. Since you're a goody-goody know-it-all, why don't you tell me?"

She pointed at the two cyborgs, who surprisingly hadn't attacked, as if they were mildly interested in the exchange of the two trespassers. Or maybe it was Evan's ridiculous obliviousness to danger.

He rotated his chin and nodded at the cyborgs like he'd expected to see them there. "Hey, fellas. We're having a discussion, but we'll be with you soon."

Turning his attention back to Sophia, he pursed his lips. "My dog can teleport."

"Amazing," she replied, stunned he had seen the pirates but was just dismissing them. They edged in closer, the one with the dripping mop turning it to hold it like a weapon. The one with the sword pointed the tip in their direction. "I think we can discuss that later. We need to deal with those two gentlemen first."

Evan resigned. "Fine, fine. You take the one with the sword. I've never fought a cyborg with a mop, and it feels like I'm overdue."

Sophia began, glancing at the two cyborg pirates, "We aren't here to hurt you. We just came to have a civil conversation with—"

Apparently, they didn't believe her. Both pirates charged. Sophia chose not to pull her sword, hoping she could deflect the attacks. She spun to the side, out of the one pirate's attack. He swung the sword in her direction, but she moved fast, pivoting away.

Holding the heavy weapon made it slower for him to move. She was at his back an instant later and lifted her boot.

Pairing the next movement with a combat spell, she said, "Sorry about this. I really didn't want to hurt you."

She then shoved the heel of her boot into his back and launched him several feet. The assault sent him to the rails, where he nearly fell over the side, but then caught himself. Sophia flicked her fingers slightly, and that was enough momentum to send him over the side to crash into the water below.

Spinning to check on Evan, she found him with his fists up as he bounced on his toes. NO10JO was on guard beside him.

The pirate with the mop threw one end at Evan's face, but he deflected it and threw a punch into the side of the guy's jaw.

"Evan!" Sophia admonished.

He grimaced. "Sorry, mate. Didn't mean to hurt you. If you put down the mop, then we can—"

The pirate swung the mop end at Evan like it was a bat. He held up his hands and jumped to the side.

"Really, Sophia?" he questioned, hopping in the opposite direction.

"Just jump onto a pirate ship and don't hurt any of the pirates. What a piece of cake."

"Hey, I took care of the one with the sword," she bragged, looking for a way to help Evan. Watching him bounce around, avoiding the attacks while not fighting back, was super-entertaining, though.

"Like, the worst piece of cake in the world," Evan complained, ducking as the mop flew overhead. "Like, carrot cake. Like who the hell thought 'Let's put carrots in cake?' when chocolate is an option?"

The pirate seemed to be tiring. He cracked the handle of the mop over his metal knee and threw down one side, using the sharp, jagged end like a sword. With menace in his eyes, he jabbed it at Evan, who feinted in two different directions, confusing the pirate. The pirate growled and launched himself at Evan and would have got him if NO10JO hadn't run under his legs, tripping him and sending him to the deck.

"Thanks, pup," Evan said, proudly, brushing himself off. "You're the best."

He twirled his finger, and a nearby rope wrapped around the pirate and tied him up, unscathed for the most part.

CHAPTER FIFTY-SIX

"Out of the woods, we are not," Evan commented as they heard a rush of footsteps at their back. Four more cyborg pirates appeared, all of them brandishing weapons. "Not even by a little bit."

"Remember not to hurt them," Sophia warned as one of the pirates held up his forearm, which had a gun attached to it. "Badly, anyway," she added, tensing.

"What are you doing with Scallywag?" one of the pirates asked, indicating NO10JO.

"Scallywag?" Evan questioned. "That's no name for an awesome dog."

The pirates laughed. "That good for nothing. All he does is steal scraps and play tricks on us."

Evan nodded proudly. "Sounds like my kind of dog. Too bad for you that you don't appreciate him."

The one with the gun fired a shot of green. Sophia threw up her hand, creating a shield between her, Evan, NO10JO, and the four pirates.

She gave Evan a sideways expression. "Ideas?"

"For dinner?" he asked, scratching his head. "Maybe steak? I bet the Mexican food here is pretty good."

She nearly laughed but instead shook her head. "No, I was thinking of ways of dealing with these guys without breaking their noses."

The pirate with the gun kept trying to hit them, but it just bounced against the shield. The others seemed to be looking for a way around, but Sophia had put up a barrier they couldn't cross. It wasn't going to hold for long, especially if Evan kept chatting about dinner options.

"Can we break their spirits?" he asked. "Because I don't like the way that one is looking at me." He pointed to one of the pirates on the far end who had a zipper for a mouth and revolving telescopic eye. Evan shivered. "It's like he's looking into my soul."

"I didn't realize you had one, so that's something," Sophia teased. "Seriously, ideas?"

"I can tie up one," Evan offered. "NO10JO will take one, and since you're a showoff, you get to take Gun Boy and the other."

She nodded, irritation heavy in her gaze. "Yeah, that seems about right."

He patted her on the shoulder. "Don't worry. Once I'm done. I'll be here for moral support."

"You're a pal," she said, running through options quickly, trying to decide how best to disarm these guys. She spotted something next to the port side of the ship. "Hey, grab that net over there."

Evan thankfully didn't question this. Using magic, he lifted the huge net and brought it closer to them. "Now what?"

"Drop it on them," she commanded.

He sighed. "Really? That's your plan? Throw a net on them like this is some slapstick comedy hour? Are we going to throw banana peels down for the next band of pirates to slip on?"

"Maybe," she replied smugly. "Just do it, would you?"

He looked disappointed. "I just don't get why you can't have a bit more flair with your plans. Like, we could use that cannon over there for intimidation. Or we could take their weapons away and force them into one of the rowboats and send them out to the middle of nowhere."

She batted her eyes at him. "We *are* in the harbor..."

"A little imagination wouldn't kill you, that's all I'm saying," he replied.

"Would you throw the freaking net on them already," she ordered, the barrier starting to come down.

"Fine," he said with defeat, lassoing his hand in the air and then throwing the net. It jumped up high and spread out. By the time the cyborg pirates figured out what was going on, it was too late. All of them had been working on pulling Sophia's shield and barrier down. They hadn't been paying the least bit of attention to Evan.

The rope net dropped on them, covering them entirely.

Sophia released the barrier and shield and took over for Evan, yanking the net up and tying it to the mast, the pirates bundled together. Thankfully the one with the gun appeared to be pinned between his mates and couldn't get his arm free to fire at them. This wasn't going to hold them long, though, since they had knives and swords.

Sophia grabbed Evan and yanked him toward the captain's quarters. They had limited time and probably a lot more pirates to subdue on their way to find Trin Currante.

CHAPTER FIFTY-SEVEN

"Look what you made me do," Evan complained, holding up his middle finger, seemingly flipping Sophia off.

She gave him a curious glance before turning her attention back to the doors for the captain's quarters. They were locked. Sophia could tell that much by spying the deadbolt between the set of double doors.

"Is that a splinter?" Sophia asked, distracted by the mission, which should have been soaking up all of their attention. She was learning Evan did things his own way. She wouldn't tell him, but it was sort of entertaining.

"Yeah, I got it from fighting that guy with the mop," he said, picking at the sliver of wood in his finger.

Worried she might be electrocuted, Sophia paused before trying to open the doors in front of them. She silently wondered and worried where the rest of the crew was. From past experience, Sophia knew Trin Currante didn't have a shortage of cyborg friends or minions or whatever she considered them.

"How is that my fault?" Sophia wondered, her hand hovering next to the handle of the door. "You're the one who wanted to fight the mop guy. Remember, you said, 'I've never fought a guy with a mop.' Then you gave me the one with the sword, like a true gentleman."

He sighed, sucking on his finger, like that would help and not make things worse. Having the Castle take care of all the Dragon Elite's ailments seemed to make one of them in particular clueless on first-aid practices.

"It's your fault because you've dictated I can't harm a wire on any of the cyborgs' heads," he muttered, his finger still in his mouth. "To make it up to you, I'll take all the most dangerous villains we encounter. You can sit by and look pretty. I wouldn't want you to chip a nail."

It was Sophia's turn to flash her middle finger at him. "As you can see, I don't wear nail polish or have any worries about messing up my manicure."

He peeled back. "I swear, I'm going to teach you how to be a lady if it's the last thing I do."

"I look forward to this day when something is the last thing you do," she told him, turning her attention back to the locked door. She'd stalled long enough and could hear the pirates in the net growing restless.

"Are you insinuating you're looking forward to me dying, Phia?" Evan asked, pretending to sound offended.

"Shh," she scolded. "I'm going to try and open this door."

"Oh, is that what I'm waiting for?" Evan inquired. "It's not that hard, but I get that simple things are challenging for you. Here, I'll be a gentleman and get the door for you, Pink Princess." He reached out with his hurt hand and grabbed the door handle.

Electricity poured from the door to his hand immediately, making Evan convulse. It was similar to the other time Sophia had witnessed him getting electrocuted. Thankfully the voltage wasn't as much as the last time, and Evan jerked his hand back, the smell of burning filling the air at once.

"Damn it!" he exclaimed, clasping his hand to his chest. "That shit will wake you up."

Sophia nodded. "As I suspected."

"As you what?" he bellowed. "Why didn't you tell me you thought the door was rigged?"

"Well, you didn't give me a chance," Sophia explained, glancing at the panel beside the door. She tried a few spells on it, but none of them seemed to have any effect on the lock.

"Great, now I have a splinter and electric shock," Evan remarked, shaking his hand out. "Missions with you are so delightful. Should we find someone to break my nose next?"

"I think that's a great idea," she agreed, standing back and surveying the door. That's when she noticed NO10JO was pawing at a panel on the deck nearby.

"Hey, what did you find?" Evan asked the dog.

"It's a control panel," Sophia stated. "Try opening it."

Evan gave her an incredulous expression. "No way, Smalls. You go first this time."

Sophia sighed. "Fine. Move aside, Bigs." She used her magic to unscrew the bolts holding the panel in place. When she removed it, she was unsurprised to find the inside filled with magitech. Scratching her head, she tried to determine how she could fix it to open the captain's quarters.

Sophia was considering different options when an ax came down, striking into the wires and strange bits of technology buried within the ship. Sparks shot up, followed by hissing and other noises of protest.

"What are you doing?" she demanded as Evan pulled the ax free of the wood and wires.

"Broken things don't work," he answered.

"I don't think that's how it works," she reasoned, waving her hand to keep the acrid smell of chemicals from her nose. "Magitech is complex and usually requires counterspells that—"

Sophia was interrupted by a beeping sound, followed by a gentle click. She spun to the captain's quarters to find the bolt no longer in place. It had worked. Somehow her dumb friend had fumbled through.

Based on the arrogant expression on Evan's face, he wasn't going to let her forget it. "You're welcome, Phia."

CHAPTER FIFTY-EIGHT

Sparks flew from the electronics around the double set of doors when Sophia yanked them back.

On the other side, she found what she'd suspected. However, the *State of Grace*'s captain was not present in the large area. Instead, standing there as though waiting for the intrusion were roughly half a dozen cyborg pirates, all of them brandishing weapons, with weird sneers on their half-human, half-robotic faces.

Evan and Sophia froze. She shot him a sideways look. "Remember when you said you'd take the next set of bad guys? I'll just take a step backward while you take care of things. Wouldn't want to chip a nail."

She took a step back just as the pirates in the net crashed to the deck, having freed themselves. They then scrambled to their feet and closed in around them. The three were cornered, with no way of getting out without using deadly force.

CHAPTER FIFTY-NINE

Nine cyborg pirates the dragonriders could fight outright would have been difficult. Nine angry and armed cyborg pirates they shouldn't harm made things exponentially more difficult.

Sophia and Evan instantly put their backs to one another. NO10JO took a place next to them, a fierce expression on the dog's face.

"You still saying we can't harm them?" Evan questioned from the corner of his mouth.

She nodded, holding up her hands as if in surrender. "We're not here to fight you."

Sophia paused, listening to the motorized sounds of many of the pirates as they used the strange magitech in their bodies to study them. She silently hoped at least one of them had the ability to detect if she was lying. That would speed things up. Then they could relax and could all laugh about things.

"You destroyed our security in this area," a cyborg pirate said. He wore an old top hat and strange goggles, and was covered from head to toe in shiny gold gears.

Sophia scrunched her nose. "Sorry about that. It was his fault."

She pointed at Evan, who scoffed.

"Way to have my back," he remarked.

"We just needed to get into the captain's quarters," Sophia explained in a rush. She lifted up on her tiptoes. "Just looking for Trin Currante. We were hoping to have a word with her. She around?"

The guy with the top hat stepped forward. "I'm her second in command. What do you want with her?"

Sophia's sources had been quite specific that talking to Trin Currante was how she was going to get to the bottom of the disappearing magicians. Sophia's instincts also told her the captain of the *State of Grace* was the key to getting to the bottom of other matters, specifically why they had come after the dragon eggs and what her ultimate mission was.

"We just want to talk," Sophia said with confidence. The pirates they'd thrown the net on were moving in closer, many of them looking worn from being bundled up and then falling from up high. They were apparently holding a grudge over the whole thing.

Trin Currante's second in command pointed to the bound pirate to his left. "Was that why you tied up Ralph?"

"We didn't hurt him," Sophia argued, her voice high pitched.

"The same can't be said for me," Evan stated, holding up his electrocuted hand and the finger with the splinter.

Sophia was about to explain they were not looking for trouble when the cyborg pirate she'd thrown overboard climbed over the side of the ship, his eyes murderous.

"Oh, really?" the second in command demanded. "You're not here for a fight. Sure seems like it."

"We just want to see Trin Currante," Sophia pleaded.

He stepped forward, his eyes flashing red behind his goggles. The men beside him followed his actions, many of them lifting their weapons. "You'll see Trin, but only bound and bruised. That's the rule on the *State of Grace.*"

Evan pressed back into Sophia. "I really like my face. Sure I can't use my ax?"

Adamantly, she shook her head. "Defend yourself, but try not to be overly aggressive. We need to earn their trust."

Sophia had hardly finished her orders when the eleven men all sprang into action, ready to tear them limb from limb.

CHAPTER SIXTY

B*abe, how's it going?* Lunis asked, as Sophia dove to avoid the first attack from one of the pirates.

She grunted, ducking. Two of the cyborgs rushed into each other as she crouched, taking each other out. Their metal heads bumped hard and each staggered into another set of men, throwing them off-balance.

I've had better days, she said, finding it easy to slip out of the attacks as the dogpiling began. All the cyborgs had rushed to the center of the circle and they didn't notice she'd squeezed her way out of the circumference and was now on the edge, making for higher ground.

From there, she noticed Evan fighting on the perimeter as well as the cyborgs dogpiled each other. They weren't the smartest group, she realized, watching as they scrambled around, probably thinking she was on the bottom.

Need backup? Lunis asked, his voice playful.

She knew he was overhead watching everything unfold and apparently wasn't worried yet. *No, not yet,* she told him. *Anything you did would be considered an attack. I'm trying to de-escalate things.*

A superb job you're doing, he teased as one of the men spotted her.

"There she is!" he yelled, pointing at her.

The pirates began pushing up off each other, shoving to try to get to her.

Well, I can't say things are going to plan, Sophia told her dragon. *But hold out on some hope for me.*

Okay, he chirped. *I'll just be over here, making Cindy believe she's going crazy. Paul thinks she's had too many glasses of prosecco since she keeps insisting she sees a dragon when he's not looking.*

Poor Cindy, Sophia said with a laugh, searching the deck for an option that got her away from the mob of angry cyborgs clambering up the steps to where she stood.

Evan was successfully deflecting most of the attacks and remained partly unscathed. He threw up his forearm to block a wooden bat about to come down on his face. The pirate changed positions at the last moment, and the weapon brushed off Evan's shoulder as his elbow rammed into the guy's nose, making it explode with blood.

"Oh, sorry, mate," Evan exclaimed. "You ran right into that one."

Sophia was about to scold her moronic partner when she heard a familiar sound—one of the cyborg weapons powering up. Jerking her gaze back to the approaching mob, she noticed the guy with the gun installed on his arm, aiming it straight at her. It was starting to glow green.

She sighed, thoroughly annoyed that this band of pirates had to resort to violence when she was just trying to talk.

You're surprised a bunch of crazed cyborg pirates who broke into the Gullington and stole dragon eggs have resorted to violence? Lunis questioned.

She yanked out Inexorabilis and sliced through a rope hanging from the mast next to her.

Excuse me for thinking that even pirates can be civilized, she said, wrapping her hands around the rope, and securing her hold on it.

Maybe you should have brought them a pirate-ship-warming present, Lunis offered.

Sophia sucked in a breath, and as the first set of pirates closed the distance to her, she launched herself off the platform and swung like Tarzan across the deck, flying over the heads of the pirates battling

Evan. When she was on the other side, she dropped and swung around to face the enemies who would undoubtedly follow.

Like, a fruit basket? she asked her dragon. *Is that the kind of gift I should have brought them so they wouldn't be so angry?*

I was thinking more like a pirate's favorite food, the blue dragon said, a hint of mischief in his voice.

Sophia kept her sword out as two of the pirates rushed at her. *Oh, no, Lunis, don't say it.*

Say what? he asked. *You do know what a pirate's favorite food is, right?*

Stop, she encouraged as one of the cyborgs, a proud grin on his face, held up his arm and a long blade extended from it. The other one was brandishing a metal pipe, and they both looked like they were going to pounce on her at once.

An arrrrtichoke, of course, Lunis answered, laughing at his joke.

Sophia jumped backward as both pirates sprang for her. She threw up her sword as the first pirate's knife hand came down on her head. She was able to hold him off, but he was incredibly powerful and she wouldn't last for long.

Shoving the knife up and off, Sophia jumped as the other pirate tried to sweep her legs out from under her with the metal pipe.

Although not usually one to run when in battle, Sophia had no choice but to back up quickly. To her relief, she moved much faster than the cyborgs who creaked as the hydraulics in their motorized legs worked to keep up with her.

Her luck ran out when she came to the starboard side of the ship. It was stocked with crates of supplies, and behind them was the railing and harbor waters. She was running out of options.

The guy with the knife brought his arm backward as his face screwed up with vengeance. When he launched it, she jumped to the side and his knife sank into one of the wooden crates, getting stuck immediately. Rage filled his face.

"Sorry," she said, spinning and coming face to face with the one with the metal pipe. He brought it up overhead about to bring it down on her head.

Sophia, taking the only option available to her, brought her knee up and shoved it into his groin. He doubled over with a loud groan, and she ducked under his arm as he fell to the deck.

She was about to rush to the far side of the platform when she ran straight into the pirate with a top hat—Mr. Second in Command. He didn't look happy about things as grease dripped from the many gears on his body like he was bleeding from several assaults.

Spinning again, Sophia decided she'd take the more congested route. To her devastation, she came face to face with the pirate with the gun on his arm. It appeared to be powered up all the way.

With her sword in her hand but the blade pointed down, hopefully in a less intimidating fashion, she held up her arms, again trying to show her surrender.

Sophia hoped Evan had better luck than her. A quick glance to the right filled her with defeat. On the deck below, Evan was being restrained by four cyborgs, blood covering one of his cheeks. Beside him, NO10JO was pinned in the arms of another cyborg.

It appeared they'd lost this battle.

CHAPTER SIXTY-ONE

"You're not sorry," the pirate in the top hat said as two others bound Sophia's wrists. He had her sword and was eyeing it with a curious expression.

"We are," Sophia argued, indicating the many cyborgs nursing injuries on the deck below. "We just wanted to talk to Trin Currante."

"Now you get to," he replied. "She'll listen to your final words before delivering your sentence."

With brute force, the pirate who had bound her hands pushed Sophia forward and led her down the stairs to the deck below.

"Oh, good," Evan said, amused at the sight of her. "I was hoping you'd gotten caught too. Now there's no one to save us. There's no one looking down at us, ready to swing in and help if we simply ask?"

The hinting in his voice was strong.

Sophia shook her head. "No, we're being taken to Trin Currante."

If the dragons entered the equation now, it would turn this into a bloodbath. They had to downplay the threat to the pirates. After eyeing the many cyborgs sporting injuries, it was going to be hard to argue they weren't there to fight.

You sure you don't need my help? Lunis asked in her head.

We'll be okay, Sophia told him as she was violently ushered toward a door opposite of the one to the captain's quarters.

If things get worse, let me know, he stated. *You know what I fear will happen to you once they take you under the deck.*

Don't, Sophia urged, knowing what her dragon was going to say next. The door ahead of them swung open and firelight glowed, illuminating a set of rickety steps.

Lunis laughed. *I worry you'll face Arrrrmageddon.*

CHAPTER SIXTY-TWO

The last time Sophia had been on a ship, she'd been tracking down information on Quiet's ship about the cyborg pirates. His ship, the *McAfee*, had a distinctively different feeling from the *State of Grace*.

Sophia was fairly certain the ship was haunted. The passage she was nearly pushed down was covered in strange cobwebs, illuminated by the torch flames on the walls.

Ahead of her were several of the pirates, all of them cheering their victory of capturing the dragonriders. Behind her, she could hear Evan mouthing off to a pirate who had him pinned and was ushering him forward.

"I'm just saying, mate," he called over his shoulder to the cyborg, who had a totally metal leg and a hook on the end of his arm, "we could have gotten along. Seriously we just want to talk."

The pirate pushed Evan, making him hit the wall. "Shut up. We aren't interested in talking."

"That's fine," Evan spat. "Just tell me one thing. How much did you pay for that hook and peg? An arm and a leg?"

Sophia groaned. First Lunis and now Evan. She needed friends with better jokes.

I heard that, Lunis said in her head.

So? she challenged as the cyborg head-butted Evan, making him scream from the pain. She could only imagine how much it hurt since she was certain the pirate's head was partly covered in stainless steel. Evan should have kept his mouth shut.

No, he probably couldn't, she reasoned, remembering how hard it was for her friend to shush his face in reasonable circumstances, let alone when facing angry pirates.

Ahead, the staircase was ending as they neared a hallway. That's when Sophia noticed the spiders making the strange cobwebs. One crawled down the wall as she progressed to the bottom. It appeared to be a regular spider, except that half of its legs were metal and part of its body was covered in tiny gears and bolts.

Cyborg spiders, she thought. Now I've seen everything.

No, you haven't, Lunis argued. *You should have just seen Cindy's face when she declared to Paul she wasn't crazy and the tugboat on the ocean was really a dragon. He told her she was nuts and needed some space.*

Lunis! Sophia bellowed. *You go fix that right now!*

She felt him sulk immediately. *Okay, fine. But if you ask me, I'm doing them a favor,* Lunis argued. *She's too good for him. He's like a four, and she's pretty much a nine.*

Seriously, Lunis, I don't have time for this right now, Sophia argued as she was pushed into a humid room that smelled of mold and gunpowder. She realized the reason for the smells. Firstly, they were on a boat, which was prone to mold. Second, the pirates had brought them to see their leader, and she happened to be hanging out in the weapons locker, sitting on a throne, surrounded by hundreds of knives, swords, guns, and other torture devices.

CHAPTER SIXTY-THREE

S ad. Beautiful. Tragic.

Those are the words Sophia would use to describe Trin Currante.

She'd met the woman at Medford Research. The cyborg had dropped enough hints that Sophia believed there was more to her than she'd thought. Sure, she might have been bent on taking their dragon eggs, but this wasn't a dumb pirate. She'd figured out how to impersonate Trinity, the librarian in the Great Library. She'd figured out how to do something that as far as Sophia knew, no one had accomplished—she'd broken into the Gullington and nearly won against the Dragon Elite.

More than anything, and even facing almost inevitable defeat, Sophia's instinct told her there was something about Trin Currante that was misunderstood. Back at Medford Research, she'd said she just wanted to be like Sophia. Before that, she'd overheard Trin Currante say the dragon eggs were the key to solving their problems.

Sophia had reasoned that like so many, Trin Currante wanted to be a dragonrider. A logical assumption was that she stole the eggs, hoping to magnetize to one. She had buried them in the ground, which would speed up the hatching process.

However, in her gut, Sophia felt there was way more to the story that she hadn't understood. Information was power. Fighting someone without understanding them was haphazard. That was how so many wars throughout history had gone on without an end in sight.

Trin Currante sat on a makeshift throne. It appeared to be made out of crates and was pushed against the back wall of the hull. On the walls on either side of her were weapons of all kinds. Her men flanked her, and behind her and Evan, she felt the presence of the dozen other pirates they'd fought on the deck.

"Well, well, well," Trin Currante said, her voice somewhat normal, but also sounding robotic. Her snake-like hair made of black wires flowed around her head. She was indisputably beautiful, with her porcelain skin and sharp features. The one human eye alongside the cyborg one was hard to look at. The metal that covered various parts of her body made her seem foreign. Dangerous. Different.

It was then Sophia realized how removed the cyborgs were from society. Why ever they had subjected themselves to such things was beyond her. She knew Trin Currante had gone back to the Saverus Corporation to fight the agency. Sophia had assumed there had been a fallout. Trin Currante had then released many of the subjects and recruited them to her side. Sophia thought that wasn't enough information and she needed a lot more if she was going to get to the bottom of things.

"Look what the cat's dragged in," Trin Currante commented.

"Is that what you call these guys?" Evan asked, indicating the two cyborgs who had him restrained. "I call them jerks."

Sophia shot him a look that said, "Shut it, dumbass."

He seemed to get the message as he pursed his lips, blood dripping down one side of his face.

"Trin Currante," Sophia began. "We aren't here to fight you."

The cackle that fell from the cyborg leader's mouth echoed in the chamber. "That's funny, because looking at my men, that's not the impression I get."

Sophia lowered her chin with guilt as she tried to keep her eyes off the cyborg with the broken nose or the many with cuts and bruises.

Sophia explained, "We tried not to fight them. We only did that in defense."

"If we had wanted to, we could be out of these bindings, with our dragons saving the day," Evan stated with confidence.

Sophia groaned, wishing he'd let her do the talking.

Apparently, one of the cyborgs holding him wanted him to speak less too because he kneed him in the gut, making Evan double over.

NO10JO began barking, madly trying to escape the clutches of the pirate who had him restrained.

Trin Currante cut her eyes at the dog. "Who let that mutt back in here?"

Evan spat on the floor, struggling to rise. "Hey, don't call him that."

She laughed. "That thing is useless as far as I'm concerned. All he does is sneak around our facilities and steal food."

"So, he's not your dog?" Sophia asked, wondering why they were talking about the stray rather than the topic that had brought them there. This was important, she reasoned. At least, she thought it would be important to Evan, who was worried that NO10JO belonged with the cyborgs rather than the Dragon Elite.

Trin Currante shook her head, producing a motorized sound. "Of course not. He kept coming around at our last facility. How he got here with you though, that's a surprise."

"He led us to you," Sophia explained, deciding it was better to be honest to garner trust.

Trin threw her head back, her hands clutching the sides of her makeshift throne. "I knew he was a good-for-nothing sneak. Always spying on us. Playing tricks, pretending to be something he wasn't."

"That's why I got him around the neck, boss," the pirate with the top hat said, holding the cyborg dog by his scruff.

Trin Currante nodded in approval. "Yeah, good thing we figured out how to control that mutt."

"Wait," Sophia interrupted, confused. "He's one of you. How can you be so cruel?"

When Trin Currante smiled, it seemed all wrong, like she was both satisfied and pained at the same time. "We aren't the same. We might have been made by the same person, but I don't allow just any into my ranks."

"But the spiders," Sophia argued. "I don't get it. That's why we are here."

"I thought you were here to exact your revenge on me for almost killing you," Trin Currante mused, running her eyes over Sophia. "I see I failed in that regard."

"No, I'm here for answers," Sophia argued. "Actually, I'm here to help you."

Trin Currante stood suddenly, her joints making mechanical sounds. "Help me? Why would I want your help, dragonrider?"

Sophia stood up taller, although the cyborg behind her was tugging on her restraints, trying to keep her back. "You tell me. You said you wanted to be like me. You said the dragon eggs were how you could save your men. I'm trying to figure out why."

Trin Currante took a long moment to study the three intruders. "I don't understand. Why? Why do you want to figure us out?"

"Because something doesn't add up," Sophia explained. "If you help me figure it out, maybe I can help you."

"Why would you want to help me?" Trin Currante roared, her face flushing.

Sophia braced herself against the sudden eruption of anger. "I don't know. I'm not sure I will. I need information about why magicians are disappearing all over the world, and you need something only the Dragon Elite can help you with. I thought, maybe in a civilized world, we could work together to our mutual benefit. But I'm going to need your help."

Trin Currante began pacing. As she did, her men stiffened as if afraid she might take her anger out on them. Her joints made strange noises as she moved. When she stopped abruptly, the hydraulics in her body hissed.

"The mutt came around because we are drawn to each other," she explained, uncertainty written on her mechanical face. "It's the same reason we've got the infestation of the spiders, rats and other creatures created by the Saverus Corporation. I guess they are drawn to us because they think we're the same. But we're different. The only way to get away from them was to get on the water."

It made sense to Sophia. She could find magicians if she tried. She was certain she'd forever be magnetized to her dragonriders, for all of her life. That was the thing—we were always drawn to our own, she thought.

Sophia dared to step forward, although the cyborg pirate who had her pinned objected to any freedom. She halted and offered Trin Currante a sympathetic expression.

"I know you think we came for a fight," she began. "But that's the farthest thing from the truth. We tried to tell your men that."

Trin Currante cut her eyes at the many men at their back and shrugged. "They'd been hungry for a fight. You could have come bearing gifts, and they would have fought you."

Arrrrrtichokes, Lunis said in her head, nearly making Sophia burst out in a laugh.

She shook off the urge and tried to refocus.

"I realize we should want revenge on you after everything that happened," Sophia went on. "You tricked me into giving you our secrets by impersonating Trinity from the Great Library. You poisoned the groundskeeper of the Gullington, taking down our borders and putting us on the defensive in ways we've never experienced. You stole one of the most precious things we have, our dragon eggs."

Trin Currante sighed, not appearing proud of her actions. "I tried to kill you. I tried to kill all of your kind."

Sophia nodded. "Something tells me you had a good reason. If you tell me, maybe we can help you, then maybe you can help us. I suspect, although I don't know why, that we have a common enemy."

CHAPTER SIXTY-FOUR

"Twenty-two," Trin Currante began. "That's how old I was when the Saverus Corporation abducted me."

"Abducted?" Sophia asked, not having expected this. She'd assumed the cyborgs had signed on and then rebelled when things didn't go as planned.

Trin Currante gave her a sadistic smile. "Oh, yeah. I was like you. Young, beautiful. A magician with my entire life stretching out in front of me. And then..."

Anger filled her face, and an instant later, she shot her metal-covered fist into a nearby wall, smashing through it easily. Thankfully it wasn't an exterior wall and water didn't come pouring through.

Trin Currante's men seemed unfazed by the sudden act of violence. Sophia suspected they had to be used to it. Maybe aggression was part of what happened to them during the change. Either way, after being abducted by the Saverus Corporation, Sophia didn't blame the cyborg for the anger.

"You were taken, then," Sophia urged, trying to encourage the leader of the cyborg pirates to talk. She cut her eyes at Evan and he pouted, not as intent on being a jerk as before. Hopefully he was starting to understand the importance of this mission and not bring violence when they were seeking cooperation.

"We were all taken," Trin Currante explained, gesturing with a mechanical hand to the men around her. "Brandon, when were you taken?"

A man a few down from Sophia straightened. "When I was fifteen."

"And you, Brian?" Trin Currante asked a man on the far side of the room.

"When I was eighteen," he responded.

The leader of the cyborgs returned her attention to Sophia. "You see, Mika Lenna only wanted us if we were young. Magicians and young. Those are the two ways to qualify for his experiment. The one he invites you to, or rather forces you into, taking out most of what makes you human and replacing in us something that makes it impossible for anyone to look at us the same ever again."

CHAPTER SIXTY-FIVE

Breathe, Sophia told herself, assimilating all this new information. "Mika Lenna," she repeated, not having heard the name before.

Trin Currante's mechanical eye flashed red from anger. "He's the leader of Saverus, the cruel agency that did this to us." She indicated her body.

Evan shook his head. "You didn't want to become cyborgs?"

The pirate holding him tightened his grip, making Evan's knees give out as he crumpled to the floor.

"Don't!" Sophia screamed, reaching for her friend. She was yanked back by her captor.

"Stop," Trin Currante ordered, making the men holding Evan and Sophia let up.

Recovering, Evan heaved as he got back to his feet.

The leader of the cyborg pirates seemed to soften as she regarded the two dragonriders. "You really don't know?"

Sophia tilted her head to the side. "We've had little luck finding out anything about the Saverus Corporation. All we know is that you ransacked the place and took many of the cyborgs with you." She decided to leave out the part about how Trin Currante apparently had access to the kill switch placed in their brains that could end them at her will that she'd used when they had three of their hostages at the Castle.

Letting out a long breath, Trin Currante continued to stride past her men and then in the other direction. "No, we didn't want this to happen to us. Who would wish for such things?"

"So, this Mika Lenna?" Sophia asked, wishing the cyborg holding her would let her go. Her wrists were starting to ache, and her fingers were tingling from a loss of circulation. She reminded herself she had all her parts, so there was that at least.

"He's an evil man," Trin Currante explained. "Not even a magician, just a man with a lot of money and power and many strange things he's done to himself."

"Strange things?"

"I didn't see them," Trin Currante answered. "I had a scientist working for me who had been with him. His name was Alexander Drake." She shook her head. "He got away, but before he did, he sort of helped me. Anyway, he told me Mika Lenna had made himself into a super-werewolf or something."

"What?" Sophia knew from discussing Liv's cases with her that werewolves were real, but they were specifically made and not the common lore from fantasy books. "How could he make himself into a werewolf?"

"The same way he does with any of his projects," Trin Currante explained. "He genetically alters things. The man, or whatever he'd be considered, isn't satisfied with the way any of us have been made. He recreates everything. Men into werewolves. Men into cyborgs. Animals into robots. It's all a game to him."

"But why?" Sophia asked, her heart aching.

Trin Currante stopped pacing and gave her a look that bordered on regret. "I truly don't know the answer to that."

"So, he took you," Evan cut in. "He made you into this?"

Trin nodded. "Yes, against our will."

Suddenly it dawned on Sophia. "He's back! He's the one abducting magicians, isn't he?"

Trin's nostrils flared when she breathed. "I'm almost certain of it. They'd have to be young. That's a requirement. They'd have to be magicians. Another requirement. Who knows what else he's added to the list? With each new version, he tries something different. Make his subjects better, in his opinion, anyway."

Sophia glanced around the room, wanting to ask her next question but not knowing how.

"You want to know why I'm the only female, don't you?" Trin Currante guessed, her mechanical eye making a screeching sound like it was working overtime.

Sophia swallowed and nodded. "I mean, it's just…"

"I was the first," Trin Currante answered. "And then I was the last woman. I don't think we took to the experiments well, Mika Lenna concluded. Anyway, that's what Drake told me. He ruled out that we had a compatible structure to absorb magitech."

"That's not the case, though, is it," Sophia guessed.

A sideways smile lit Trin's face, making her suddenly more beautiful. "No, I think he just never met me. I've always been a rebel. My men are strong, but Mika took their will when he took most of what made them human. It only made me angry. I broke out, using the strength he'd given me when I was remade with magitech. Then I returned and tried to punish him and Saverus, but they got away. All of them except Drake."

"He told you Mika Lenna had decided not to test on females anymore?" Sophia asked.

"He told me that most of Mika Lenna's experiments didn't include women," Trin Currante said with a morbid laugh. "Is it so hard to believe that a deranged psychopath is also a sexist? I think my spirit sent him over the edge, and he decided females were unfit for testing. I can only imagine what he's doing with this new generation of cyborgs he's creating. You say he's been abducting magicians?"

Sophia nodded. "Someone is, and this all makes sense."

"It does," Trin Currante concluded.

"Why did you break into the Gullington and steal our dragon eggs?" Sophia needed to get to the part that would either make her understand Trin better or despise her. Since she and Evan were at her mercy, held captive by the cyborgs, she hoped it wasn't the latter.

"You're not going to like the answer." Trin Currante lowered her chin like a robot that had been powered down.

Sophia stiffened. "It doesn't matter," she argued. "I need to know. I need to know everything if I'm going to be able to help you."

Quickly Trin Currante looked up, surprise on her face, the human aspects of her all of a sudden much more apparent. "You'd still help me? I've told you what you wanted to know about Saverus and Mika Lenna."

"This isn't just about me," Sophia argued. "I meant it before. You help me, and we'll help you. But you have to tell me everything, or I can't do anything."

CHAPTER SIXTY-SIX

"I almost do not want to believe you'd be willing to help someone who wronged you," Trin Currante began. "However, I've read the entire *Complete History of Dragonriders*. I knew you before you knew me. I have watched the Dragon Elite, and I know you all are bound by good. I realize I shouldn't be all that surprised."

"Tell me why you stole the dragon eggs," Sophia urged.

Trin Currante waved her arm in their direction, making Sophia flinch, worried it would be followed by an attack. The leader of the cyborgs simply said, "Release them." She quickly added. "Try anything, dragonriders, and you'll be shown no mercy."

Evan shook out his hands before running his fingers over the dried blood on his cheek. Thankfully the laceration seemed shallow. The Castle would heal it quickly. "Awesome. Thanks. Can I get something to drink? Maybe a whisky or some rum?"

Sophia cut her eyes at him and gave him an expression that said, "Don't push it."

Trin Currante seemed amused. "Get our guests something to drink," she ordered, looking at one of the men at their back. A moment later, footsteps moved away.

"No poison in mine," Evan called over his shoulder. "Put it all in Little Bit's."

"Thanks, pal," Sophia said to him.

"Anytime," he fired back.

Trin Currante seemed amused by this before her expression went back to a stern one. "It was Drake who told me about the dragon eggs. I knew I needed more information, so I broke into the Great Library, which took some time."

"You killed Trinity," Sophia guessed.

Trin Currante nodded, remorse evident in her movements. "When the most important part of you has been stolen, it's easy to take from others. I don't feel good about it. I understand now that Trinity was an ancient creature, but in my defense, he seemed happy to be relieved of his post. Having a job that's so isolated and without relief can't be easy for someone."

Sophia shivered internally, making a note of that to pass along to Plato, who was supposed to fill the role. Maybe they needed multiple librarians. She didn't think the role would be right for Ainsley as the lynx had supposed. When the housekeeper could leave the Gullington, she shouldn't be confined to another place for ages.

"Anyway," Trin Currante continued, "I did what I had to do to get information on dragon eggs, which happened to be through the Dragon Elite. Drake told me he believed the blood of a dragon was key to returning us cyborgs to normal."

"So, the operations can't just be reversed?" Sophia asked.

Trin Currante shook her head as the cyborg who had been holding Sophia handed her a glass of something and another to Evan. Sophia offered him a grateful look before bringing the glass to her nose. It was strong and burned her nostrils.

Even Evan, who was used to drinking strong things like whisky, yanked his head away. "Wow, is that antifreeze?"

"It's our house blend," Trin Currante said with a laugh, showing mechanical parts in her mouth Sophia hadn't seen before.

Deciding to suck it up, Sophia held her breath and tossed back the drink, taking it in one swig. It burned her tongue, throat, and all the way down to her stomach, where she was certain it was eating the lining. She drew in a breath and shook it off, willing herself to focus.

The abrupt action produced a collective muttering from the cyborgs in the room. Even Evan seemed impressed and slightly worried about the gesture. Sophia shook it off and gave the glass back to the cyborg who had served her.

"Go on then," Sophia encouraged, her gaze on Trin Currante.

"To answer your question," Trin Currante went on, "no, we can't easily be turned back into our human form. We are magitech now, and reversing it would kill us. What makes my heart beat isn't blood. It's magic. What my lungs breathe isn't air, it's magic. To undo that isn't easy. We need something more magical than us to replace it."

Sophia sucked in a breath, both due to shock and also the urge to hiccup after the strong drink. "You need the blood of a dragon."

"Not just any dragon, though," Trin Currante stated. "I learned through my research and confirmed much of what I learned from *The Complete History of Dragonriders*. We need the blood of a newborn dragon."

Now it all made sense to Sophia.

Evan took his own drink in one swallow, followed by a howl. "Wow, that's strong. I'll take two more."

Sophia shook her head. "Focus," she urged him.

"Fine," he said, still smiling.

"So, you were going to have the eggs hatch, and then what…kill the dragons?" Sophia asked, realizing why Trin Currante had said she'd be mad. It was a horrible thing to consider.

"I was," Trin Currante began slowly. "I don't think we'd need too much, now that I've done more research, although it's useless without Mika Lenna's notes, I think very little blood could be the antidote."

"You wouldn't have to kill dragons, then?" Sophia thought for a moment, trying to remember what else she needed to know.

"It was never my hope to kill to make us whole again, but the magitech makes it hard to think," Trin Currante explained. "We aren't human anymore, but we have emotions. I think that makes it worse. Less rational."

Sophia swallowed, hardly able to fathom such a reality. Now she understood Trin Currante's words from Medford: *"I just want to be like you."*

She had meant she wanted to be human. She wanted to have blood pumping in her veins and appear normal and feel like she had been before Mika Lenna made her into a cyborg.

"Why did you come back for more eggs?" Sophia asked, the question suddenly occurring to her. "You had one. Did you realize that wasn't enough?"

Trin Currante shook her head. "No. I learned it wasn't easy enough to have a newborn dragon. From *The Complete History of Dragonriders*, I learned what you might not know. Out of every batch of eggs, the angels dictate that one is born good and the other is born—"

"Evil," Sophia cut in. "Yes, I'm aware."

"Well, to repair us, to make our hearts beat again and to replace the magitech, we would need both the blood of a good newborn dragon and an evil one." Trin Currante let out a breath, although Sophia now understood that she didn't breathe, not anymore. "Making us what we once were is nearly impossible, I realize now. I knew it was a long shot, but it felt like there was a way to undo what Mika Lenna and the Saverus Corporation did to us."

Sophia nodded. "It does seem farfetched."

Trin Currante took her seat once more on her strange throne, seeming more defeated than ever.

"But that was before," Sophia went on. "Before you spared us. Before you explained what we now know about Mika Lenna and the disappearance of the magicians. Before you told us that all we had to do is give you a little of our newborn dragons' blood to fix you."

The leader of the cyborg pirates looked up suddenly, something flashing in her human eye. Surprise, maybe. "You're going to help me? Us?"

"We're going to help each other," Sophia amended. "It sounds like it's going to involve a lot more than just dragon eggs, which we have. You tell me what you need and I'm going to tell you what I need, and we're going to figure out how to get what we both want."

CHAPTER SIXTY-SEVEN

"Tell me why I'm supposed to help that cyborg," Hiker Wallace demanded when Sophia and Evan debriefed him after returning from San Diego.

"Because it's not their fault they were turned into machines," Sophia argued. She'd assumed the Viking would resist her plan but was adamant he'd come around.

Mama Jamba was staying quiet on the couch as she ran a hand over NO10JO, who was curled up at her feet. The cyborg dog had no interest in staying with the pirates, and they didn't seem to want him around either. Apparently, he had never been one of them, just another of Mika's "projects" that had found refuge with them. It was a natural solution that he'd come back to the Gullington with Sophia and Evan and that after the mission, he'd freely entered the Barrier. That meant his loyalty was to the Dragon Elite.

"It's not my problem that they were made into machines," Hiker stated.

"No, you're right," Sophia agreed with confidence. "It's everyone's problem. Because it could have been me who was abducted. It could have been any of us since Mika Lenna only goes after magicians. What he makes them into might scar the world. It is our job as adjudicators to uphold justice, and he's defying it by taking people's freedom. Their humanity."

Hiker let out a long sigh. "I want to help, but I—"

"She doesn't need much," Sophia continued, cutting him off. "Trin just needs a little blood from a good dragon and an evil one. But they have to be newborns."

"Well, that's where I can't help," Hiker groaned. "We only have evil newborns, creating havoc all over the Cave, according to Bell."

"We might have a newborn that's good soon," Sophia reasoned.

He laughed, but it was devoid of humor. "Or it might be another century."

"Thankfully, a cyborg has that longevity," Sophia insisted.

He sighed deeply. "That's not all they need, is it?"

Sophia shook her head. She was about to explain the harder part of the equation when Evan cut in. "They need our help. Maybe the scientist who assisted us with the LiDAR can be of use."

Sophia nodded, happy to have her friend's help to convince Hiker. "Yeah, I need Alicia."

"They need Mika Lenna's research, which he took with him when Trin Currante invaded the Saverus Corporation." Evan gave Sophia an expression that seemed to be searching for confidence.

"That's right," Sophia said, giving him an encouraging expression.

"How are we going to get that?" Hiker questioned.

"We have to find Mika Lenna and his new headquarters," Sophia explained. "That's the only way to stop him from taking magicians."

"Once we do," Evan said excitedly, picking up the next bit, "we find the research."

"Once we have a newborn good dragon," Sophia continued, piggybacking off the other dragonrider, "we create the antidote."

Evan clapped his hands triumphantly. "And just like that, we stop an evil man, save magicians, resolve things between the House of Fourteen and mortals and repair a bunch of cyborgs. Then we coast off for a holiday in Bora Bora to celebrate a job well done."

Sophia smiled at him, grateful Evan had gone on the mission with her. She wasn't going to tell him that, but she thought he knew.

He returned the fond expression before looking at their leader for approval.

Hiker sighed, thinking it over. His eyes flicked to Mama Jamba, who was still petting the now-snoozing NO10JO. "Thoughts?" he asked her.

"My thoughts are that I elected you as the leader of the Dragon Elite so I could lie on my butt and relax," Mother Nature said, not taking her blue eyes off the cyborg dog. "I suspect you have all the information you need to make an informed decision, and you better do it without my input, or you'll need to find yourself a new job."

He shook his head at the old woman but smiled. Finally, he brought his gaze down to Sophia. "Okay, work with Trin Currante to find Mika Lenna. Start on an antidote. We'll help the cyborgs, but if they ever cross us again, I will crush each and every one of them on my very own."

Sophia watched as he wrapped his fingers into a fist. She had no doubt that as a very powerful magician with an anger management problem, he'd deliver on the promise.

She looked at the clock on the far wall and realized she needed to rush off if she was to get ready in time.

"Now, go rest and get straight to work first thing," Hiker ordered.

Sophia stood, rushing for the door. "I do have to go, but I'm going to have to take tomorrow off."

Hiker's mouth popped open. "Say what? Why?"

Sophia smiled. "Because it's not every day your sister gets married."

CHAPTER SIXTY-EIGHT

Style had never been Liv Beaufont's thing. Her sister had known that about her since she was little, when Liv showed up at their family residence, needing help with her wardrobe for a mission.

Sophia, who had been a master of disguises since she was very young, was happy to remake her sister. However, whoever was in charge of the decorations for the wedding was a master of style and décor.

Having left Wilder at the Gullington with the directions and time for the wedding, Sophia had left the Castle early, intent on helping Liv get ready. She was grateful to see she wasn't going to need to do much with the decorations.

As she approached the understated cottage on the outskirts of West Hollywood, Sophia appreciated that everything was beautiful in the usually bare yard, although understated—just like Liv.

The lawn was sparkling, and on closer inspection, Sophia realized it was because pixies were flying around, throwing dust into the air as they giggled.

On the front porch, a large gray cat by the name of June Bug was swatting at mice, but it appeared he wasn't trying to hunt them.

Rather, it seemed he was trying to encourage them to finish putting up the garland over the front of the house.

Flowers bloomed in large pots, and brownies were scrubbing the windows with fervor. This was only the front of the house where guests would be welcomed. Sophia simply couldn't wait to see what the inside of the giant's house looked like.

"Before you go in," a familiar voice said behind her, making her freeze.

Sophia turned and looked down, knowing she was about to come face to face with the great lynx Plato.

"Hey there," she said, smiling at the black and white cat. "Where's your tux?"

He glanced at her jeans and t-shirt. "I could ask you the same thing."

"I'll summon my clothes," she explained.

"I'll be at the wedding in spirit," he stated, remorse in his voice.

Sophia's mouth fell open. "You're not going to be there? But it's Liv."

He nodded. "You and I both know that I would be there, but being present around that many people? It's not my thing."

"Will it rob you of magic?" she questioned.

"Only if they witness me do magic," he answered, not telling her anything she didn't already know about him.

"Will it hurt you?"

"Liv understands," Plato said with conviction. "I prefer not to be seen by most. It's the way of the lynx."

"It's also the way of the lynx to live alone and not be helpful, yet you've abandoned those ways." She indicated the house where she suspected her sister was getting ready. "You did it for her. Maybe you'll show up for her."

He shook his head. "I wish I could, but I can't."

Sophia swallowed, feeling sorry for her sister, who had the most stubborn sidekick in the world.

"I just wanted to stop you for a moment to ask..." Plato's voice trailed away as he looked her over.

Sophia knew what he was wondering, but she was so mad at him she had to pull her gaze away. "I found it. No thanks to your lack of clues."

"I told you to look," he argued.

She sighed, trying to breathe through the anger. Sophia reasoned she was just protective. "Yeah, I have the necklace, and if you let me go, I'll give it to my sister."

He nodded, his face remorseful.

Still so mad she could hardly handle it, Sophia set off for the porch. She instantly felt bad and turned back around to thank the lynx for telling her to look for their mother's necklace, but it was too late.

Plato, as he tended to do, had disappeared.

CHAPTER SIXTY-NINE

Paper rings sat on the dresser when Sophia entered the room where Liv was supposed to be getting ready. She eyed them with curiosity before her sister turned to face her.

"You're not ready," Liv remarked, looking her sister over.

She smirked. "Give me a second and I will be. I wanted to stop by and help you first, but it doesn't appear you need it."

Liv was wearing black leather pants, a white satin top with a little bit of lace, and, as promised, her knee-high boots. Her long blonde hair hung in ringlets, and her makeup was perfectly tasteful.

"You look beautiful," Sophia said, admiring how her sister could take someone's breath away both with her looks and her right hook if she wanted to.

Liv shrugged. "I'm comfortable, and if I get a call for a mission, I'm ready."

Sophia laughed. "It's your wedding day. I hope you have it off."

Her sister gave her a sneaky grin. "I sort of hope not."

Worry constricted Sophia's throat for a moment. "Wait, are you having second thoughts? Do you not want to marry Stefan? Because you don't have to."

Liv's laughter was pure. "Of course I want to. I don't have a single nervous feeling in my whole body." She nodded to the paper rings on the dresser. "I'd marry that man with paper rings."

Sophia laughed. "I never took you two as Taylor Swift fans."

"Don't be so judgmental," she teased. "Those were an anniversary present from Stefan, but I think we have real ones for the ceremony."

"You think?" Sophia questioned, suddenly nervous again.

Waving her off, Liv said, "Stop freaking out. Everything is fine. Rory is forging the rings."

"I thought you didn't want a wedding band?" Sophia argued.

Liv shrugged. "I'll wear it on a chain around my neck."

"Wedding bands forged by a giant." Sophia shook her head. "This might be the wedding of the century."

Liv's eyes widened with delight. "Oh, just you wait. I think it might be the wedding of the millennium. Wait until you see the wedding party."

Sophia could only imagine who the greatest Warrior for the House of Fourteen had at her wedding. It suddenly made Sophia, the maid of honor, feel very small. That was fine. She didn't want the spotlight. All she wanted was for her sister to finally want it since she usually saved the day and then disappeared in the shadows before she could be given credit.

"So, if you're not nervous about the wedding or getting married, why are you okay with getting called away on a mission today of all days?" Sophia questioned.

Liv gave her a knowing smile. "When you love what you do and you do it with the one you love, you never work a day in your life. That's always been the dream, I think."

Sophia wanted to cry but stopped herself. Today would be full of many happy tears, but they should wait until later. "Just like you told me about Mom and Dad. They loved each other more than anything, and they loved their roles for the House of Fourteen."

Liv nodded. "Many times, Mom would say a loving relationship works because there is no work."

There it was. As strong as Liv was trying to be, an expression of hurt and regret crossed her face. Only briefly, but it was enough that Sophia spied it.

"Hey," she began, looking her outfit over, "you look beautiful, but you already know that."

Liv shrugged, pushing away the building tears.

"I think you're missing something, though," Sophia said, pretending to look her sister over as if trying to decide what she needed.

"Like a sword?" Liv asked. She threw up her hand. "I told Stefan we should have weapons, but he was adamant we should have everyone check them at the door."

Sophia laughed. "No, I was thinking about something more traditional. The blouse you're wearing; is it new?"

"And the pants and boots," Liv said in a bragging voice. "I went all-out."

Sophia giggled again. "So, you need something blue and something old."

Waving her off, Liv shook her head. "Not that superstition. I don't have time to round something like that up."

Sophia reached into her pocket and retrieved their mother's necklace, which still had her note attached to it. "Thankfully for you, you don't have to. Your friend Plato helped me find this in our old residence. I know it's not Father's ring for Stefan, but one made by Rory is better, I think. Yours will match." Then she held up the necklace filled with sapphires, and it caught the light, twinkling. "This was our mother's, and I know she wanted for you to have it on this day."

A gasp fell out of Liv's mouth as her shaking hands reached for the necklace. She ran her fingers over the gems before turning over the note attached to the chain.

"For my daughters on their wedding days," Liv read the note, tears streaming down her cheeks. They made her eyes look like glowing sapphires in a pool of light.

She pulled the necklace to her and then her sister, wrapping Sophia in her arms and pressing her tightly. "Thank you, Soph. This means the world to me."

She hugged Liv back fiercely, glad she returned to her life not that long ago and so grateful she was here to watch her get married. "There would be no world if it wasn't for you. So anything for you. But also..." Sophia peeled back a bit, looking at her sister. "Anything for you, just because you're my sister. *Familia est sempiternum.*"

CHAPTER SEVENTY

Starlight streamed through the trees in Rory's backyard. Sophia had spent a lot of time in that space since it was where Lunis had been while in his egg. It was unrecognizable for the night wedding.

It seemed fitting that two Warriors for the House of Fourteen would get married at night. Liv had joked it was because there would be many vampires, werewolves, and recovered demons in attendance. Sophia secretly didn't think she was joking. Liv had also warned her not to ask any of the party guests what they did professionally unless she wanted to hear things she couldn't unhear.

The large oak trees sparkled with hundreds of lights that were really fairies buzzing around. Bermuda Laurens could also be found buzzing around the garden, telling gnomes to take their places as statues or instructing centaurs they needed to hold the ice statues straighter. Sophia had gone to Rudolf's wedding, which had been the most spectacular thing she'd ever seen—until that moment.

King Rudolf's wedding had been epic, with thousands of guests and the finest quality everything. Even so, this somewhat understated garden wedding was the most incredible sight to Sophia. It just went to show that less was more. Simple was perfect when seen in the right light. For as beautiful as the decorations were in the mostly empty backyard, Sophia knew it would be the people who soon filled it that made it more elegant than anything she'd ever seen.

"Simply perfect," a voice said at Sophia's back.

She turned, knowing she'd find Wilder standing behind her on the portico. She'd sensed him approaching, like she always did.

Sophia expected to find him staring at the garlands of orchids draped between the chairs for the small audience or the arbor made for the event. Instead, his eyes were on her.

Nervously, she glanced down the satin blue dress done to match her eyes—Liv's eyes. Their mother's. Their father's. Every Beaufont's. Her hair was done up in a simple twist and from her ears hung soft pearls. She smiled at the man wearing a tasteful suit and an irresistible smile.

"You made it," she said, but there was a question in her voice. They'd both known his mission might take longer and he wouldn't be back in time.

He closed the distance between them, his hand finding hers. His other caressed her bare back. "I wouldn't miss it for anything. It's important to you."

Sophia laid her head on his shoulder, realizing she hadn't relaxed until that moment. There was something about Wilder that put her at ease and told her she could rest while he looked after the world. That's what good couples did for each other. It was what Liv and Stefan did for one another. They watched each other's backs and took care of one another.

She pulled away. "Your mission? You are done and made it back in time?"

He gave her a sideways smile. "I told the council of elves that if they didn't figure out their two-hundred-year-old squabble in the next twenty minutes, I was cutting off their supply of soy products."

Sophia laughed. "Oh, you know how to put those hippies in check."

"Well, there's something to be said for having plans," he agreed. "I think I could have been refereeing that mess for another two hundred years, but leave it to you to give me the proper motivation to end things swiftly."

Sophia ran her hand down his suit jacket, appreciating how polished he looked. "You clean up well."

"Why, thank you," he said, holding her hand but taking a step back, looking her up and down. "I really only hoped to look good enough to be by your side."

She yanked him back. "I think you look more than good enough. You look like you belong by my side."

Wilder brought her hand up and kissed it softly, magnetism in his eyes. "Then you'll find me there for a very, very long time."

CHAPTER SEVENTY-ONE

The best day of anyone's life is supposed to be their wedding. As Sophia stood inside Rory's kitchen, she didn't know why Liv's wedding wasn't going to be everyone's best day.

Maddy, Rory's girlfriend, was smiling broadly as she admired her man wearing a tuxedo, something the giant never did.

"You look more handsome than I thought possible," the blonde giantess said, giggling as she pushed back a rogue curl that had broken out of the gel, which was never going to be strong enough to subdue his locks.

Bermuda's eyes slid to the couple like she was about to say something disapproving. However, she glanced at Liv and smiled. "Dear, you..."

Liv looked up, as though waiting for the insult. "Yeah, I need to brush my hair, don't I?"

Bermuda shook her head. "You are missing something, though."

Letting out a sigh, Liv said, "What's that? A dress? Manners?"

"No," the giantess disagreed, producing a bouquet of stargazer lilies. "Every bride should carry flowers, even if you don't toss them. Throw daggers if you like. I just want you to have the best day."

"Thanks," Liv said, restraining her emotions.

Bermuda nodded, stifling hers as well. "Well, I'll take my place. The rest of you, I suspect you know yours."

"I'll show them," Mama Jamba offered, holding a basket of flower petals. She'd elected herself to be the flower girl, and how could Liv object? The old woman was wearing a dress for once, like she was dressed in her Sunday best.

"I think we're about ready," Clark said, poking his head through the screen door as Bermuda slipped into her seat, obstructing the view of many gnomes seated behind her. It was by design since they'd been real jerks to Liv recently but demanded they be at the wedding.

Sophia had worried Clark would feel left out since Rudolf was walking Liv down the aisle, but Stefan had asked him to be his best man, so everyone had a place.

"We're ready," Liv said, sounding like the most excited bride in the world.

She turned and faced Rory and Maddy, who would go down the aisle first. "Thanks for letting me use your place for this."

The giant shook his head, always conservative with his emotions. "It's fine, Liv. Not a big deal."

"Well, it's a big deal to me," she disagreed. "More than that, it's a big deal that you were a friend even when I wasn't popular."

He laughed. "You're still not popular. Just ask the gnomes."

She laughed too. "Yeah, but you were my friend when your race turned on me. You've always been my friend, even when giving me scolding looks and pretending you didn't like my jokes."

"I don't like your jokes," he fired back, but under the surface, there was a smile.

Liv nodded, and Rory and Maddy set off as the music began, played by a band that was Liv's favorite—Moldy Oranges.

The bride turned her attention to Sophia and John. "The two people who saved my life and never even knew it," Liv began, tears making her voice sound different.

Sophia stiffened, not having expected the tender moment and never wanting to forget it.

"John," Liv began, looking at the owner of the electronics repair store with great fondness. "If it wasn't for you, I would not have survived the mortal world after my parents' death." She looked at Sophia. "If it wasn't for you, I probably wouldn't have returned to the magical world when I was called upon. You two are why I'm here."

Although she usually didn't show much emotion, Liv grabbed both John and Sophia's hands and held them tightly. "I love you both. Thanks for being here."

"I love you," Sophia said at the same time as John, and they kissed her on opposite cheeks.

Sophia turned for the porch, feeling strangely nervous as John held out his arm for her.

"My lady," he said.

She wrapped her arm around his, remembering when he had been old and she young. How things had changed.

With a grace to impress, the first of the mortal seven led Sophia down the aisle through a crowd of magical creatures brought together for an event like no other. Sophia didn't think she could be any happier until she noticed a black and white cat appear beside Stefan at the front of the ceremony.

Sitting in front of Plato was a small pillow with the wedding bands Rory had forged on it. On his face was a serene smile. When Sophia's eyes connected with him, he mouthed two simple words: "Thank you."

For Sophia, the wedding couldn't have gotten better. Not only was Mother Nature throwing flower petals behind them as the flower girl and King Rudolf of the fae leading Liv down the aisle behind her, but the officiant of the wedding was none other than Papa Creola—Father Time. Now Plato was here, risking his ego to be by the side of the girl who had saved his life and pretty much everyone else's on this planet.

This wasn't the wedding of the century. It was the event of the millennium, unmatched by any other.

CHAPTER SEVENTY-TWO

"The moment I knew I loved you," Stefan began when he was asked to recite his vows. Like Liv, he was dressed mostly in black. "It was when you tumbled into the Chamber of the Tree on your first day, screaming wildly, followed by breaking every single rule in the House of Fourteen. Liv Beaufont, there isn't anyone in the world like you, and as a man who never thought he'd find his match, I can't imagine not having you. For the rest of my life, I will be at your side. That is my promise, and I hold that more dearly than the vow I made to the House of Fourteen. Than the one I made to the gnomes when I sold our first child to—"

"Stefan!" Liv exclaimed, smiling, her hands in his.

His blue eyes sparkled when he grinned back at her. "There is no promise other than the one I make to you now. I am yours. Always."

Papa Creola, dressed in linen and looking typically hippie-ish, gave Liv a tired expression. "Now it is time for your vows, Liv."

For the first time all night, Liv looked nervous. Sophia worried for her, but then she let out a breath and appeared stronger. "It's funny because for me, Stefan," she began, her voice growing in volume, "you took a place beside me from the beginning that I had no idea was vacant. I now realize the place was always reserved for you. You will always fill the place beside me, and I'll be with you for as long as this world tolerates us."

Before she could say much more, Papa Creola cut in. "Then by the power vested in me, as the...well, father of time and pretty much the most powerful entity on Earth..."

Mama Jamba coughed discreetly from the sidelines.

Papa Creola's eyes slid to the woman with gray hair. "Present company excluded. Anyway, as the one who dictates how long you both live, I deem that you'll annoy the rest of us, together, for a very long time. With that, I pronounce you husband and wife. You may kiss your bride."

When Stefan leaned in and kissed Liv upon the lips, all guests of the wedding were silent. Sometimes things that don't use spells hold the most magic and are incredibly mesmerizing.

CHAPTER SEVENTY-THREE

"I'm only me when I'm with you," Evan said, patting NO10JO's head. "Don't let Coral hear you say that," Sophia warned.

Evan pressed his face into the dog's, letting him lick his face. "She gets it, or she will. I mean, I love Coral like no other, but she's also very disapproving of me. A dog accepts you no matter what, and there's something beautiful about that."

"There's something about a dragon pushing us to be better, too," Sophia reasoned. "I mean, they don't put up with our shit, whereas a dog would let us coast if we wanted to."

Evan thought this over, a ball in his hand he was about to throw for NO10JO. "I guess we need both. Someone to accept us unconditionally and someone to push us."

Sophia realized he was right and was grateful that between the mix of her friends and family, she had that. They'd had more good news since she'd returned from the wedding. One of the dragon eggs had hatched, and although it was hard to tell, it appeared this one wasn't evil.

Sophia reasoned that since it was avoiding the evil dragon babies and not gnawing on Bell's tail, it was probably good, but she would

SARAH NOFFKE & MICHAEL ANDERLE

continue to monitor. Still, it seemed they were closer to helping the cyborgs, which was important to her.

Mika Lenna had robbed the cyborgs of their lives, and she was bent on giving them back. She had to put a stop to the evil corporation that was abducting magicians. Sophia was hopeful it would happen as long as she stayed focused, remembered her purpose, and enlisted the help of her friends. She had the best friends in the world.

"Watch this," Evan boasted, pulling his arm back as NO10JO took off running across the Expanse.

When he threw the ball, the dog disappeared and then reappeared a few feet from where the ball was going to land, catching it in his mouth.

"That's very impressive." Sophia admired the cyborg dog as he ran back in their direction, excitement in both his blue and brown eyes.

"Yeah, but he can only teleport a few feet at a time," Evan said before the dog was close.

"Still, I don't know of any dogs that can do that," she pointed out.

"Or this." He took the ball from the dog and launched it across the Expanse again. The dog took off, then disappeared and reappeared, this time as a metal trashcan that caught the ball like it was a hoop. Then NO10JO shapeshifted into his normal form, the ball in his mouth as he bounded in their direction.

Sophia laughed, happy her friend had a new companion. Evan needed it. She had Wilder. Liv had Stefan. Rory had Maddy. Papa Creola had Mama Jamba. Rudolf had Serena. Mahkah had his solitude, which he seemed to love. Quiet had the Gullington. Ainsley and Hiker would hopefully one day find something.

At least the people she loved were starting to find love. That's what it was all about. It reminded her why when she awoke in the morning, her first mission would be to help the cyborgs. They, who had been through so much, deserved to have love.

Really, Sophia pondered as Evan continued to throw the ball for his new dog, everyone deserved to find love. That was the ultimate mission of the Dragon Elite. Justice was about fighting for love, after all.

CHAPTER SEVENTY-FOUR

Life on Earth was about to change drastically.

It always started with small things that later became huge events. It was how life worked, like the planting of a seed that would grow into a towering tree with far-reaching roots, and branches casting many shadows below.

In this case, the events about to unfold were started by an unsuspecting dragonrider who had no idea of the events she was putting into motion.

The ground where the seeds created by Mother Nature had been planted began to bubble like a potion in a cauldron. The residents of New York City bustling down Cornelia Street had no idea the landscape around them was about to change radically.

The once-bare scrap of earth vibrated as something tried to break through the surface of the rocky dirt. A tiny seedling broke through the topsoil as taxis sped down the road and a dog on a leash barked at a police horse.

"Frenchy!" a woman holding the leash of a full-sized poodle yelled. "Stop barking at the horses!" She turned to her companion. "I swear, after shelling out big bucks on training, this dog still doesn't do a thing I say."

The man nodded and pointed to the sad patch of earth where a twig-like tree used to grow. "Just have Frenchy do her business. I've got a meeting soon."

The couple paused next to the place the poodle preferred most days. The dog sniffed the ground as a tiny green leaf wiggled through the dirt.

Frenchy jumped back in alarm and began barking at the seemingly harmless seedling.

The woman sighed. "Seriously, Frenchy? Would you be quiet?"

The dog declined the request and continued to bark at the patch of earth, her long tail wagging madly.

"Did you feel that?" the man asked, putting a hand on the woman's shoulder.

"Feel what?" she questioned, pulling her attention off the disobedient dog as she yanked on the leash.

"I think we're having an earthquake," he responded and looked down at the ground, which was shaking under their feet.

Many passersby on the sidewalk took notice of the vibrating pavement, not realizing the epicenter was the patch of dirt. They began to flee when the pavement around the dirt buckled.

The policeman on the horse tried to corral people into safer places, although the horse was showing signs of stress and whinnying.

The ground continued to tremble as the little leaf sprouted up from the dirt, wriggling as it tried to unfold.

"Let's get out of here," the man called to the woman, who was struggling to get the poodle away from the square of dirt.

"Come on, you bad dog," the woman exclaimed. She yanked hard on the leash, fear showing in her every movement.

"Here." The man grabbed the leash and pulled hard, encouraging Frenchy to leave as the ground began to split in front of them.

They ran in the opposite direction, having to drag the dog away. They fled just in time because a moment later, the innocent little leaf spread out and was immediately followed by a huge beanstalk. It shot into the air, tearing through the pavement as it soared into the sky. It rose past the multi-story buildings and continued to grow.

As the beanstalk rose towards the clouds, its base grew until it was as big around as a sedan. The asphalt around it exploded, causing Cornelia Street to split and buckle and throwing taxis upside down or on their sides.

Pandemonium broke out as underground water mains burst, sending huge streams of water into the air. Sparks flew as powerlines were severed by the huge root system snaking under the ground.

Sirens blared as first responders sped in the direction of the beanstalk, which stopped growing once it rose up past the clouds. Having quickly cleared the area, the police officer on the horse looked up when the street was suddenly cast in darkness as a huge canopy unfolded from the top of the beanstalk. Cornelia Street was instantly cooler.

Fire, water, and destruction were the result of the plant soaring up between the buildings on the street. What was uncertain was where the strange beanstalk had come from or what was at the top.

Having regained control of his horse, the police officer squinted up at the massive plant. A chill ran down his back as he shook his head. "God save us all."

CHAPTER SEVENTY-FIVE

"Just say yes, Ainsley," Evan begged, throwing his arm in the direction of his cyborg dog whimpering just outside the dining hall in the Castle at the Gullington.

"No!" she exclaimed, her arms crossed defiantly.

"He won't hurt anything," Evan argued, looking to Sophia for help.

She was staying out of this. From experience, Sophia knew to argue with the housekeeper only resulted in trouble. She'd wake up to find her bedsheets soaked as the shapeshifter sped out of her room in the form of a hunchback carrying an empty bucket.

"I refuse to have that mutt in the dining hall," Ainsley insisted. "I might have lost the battle about him being in the Castle, but this and the kitchen are my domain, and I'm putting my foot down. No dogs in the eating area."

"Look at him," Evan whined, indicating the dog who had his head low, his blue and brown eyes begging.

"No. This isn't even a discussion." Ainsley shook her head. "I won't have a mangy dog begging at the table for scraps."

"He isn't mangy," Evan said, sounding hurt. "He doesn't even shed since he's mostly metal. NO10JO is probably cleaner than me."

"He's no doubt cleaner than you," Sophia remarked dryly, wondering where the usual breakfast fare was.

Evan cut his eyes at her before looking back at the housekeeper. "He doesn't beg. I promise. He's the most well-behaved dog, and he saved my life and is all around awesome."

Ainsley pivoted and narrowed her eyes at the cyborg animal. "I'm still bitter about the whole saving-your-life part." She wagged a finger at NO10JO. "You should keep that metal nose to yourself and not butt in when fate is trying to take this one out."

Evan laughed. "You know you'd miss me if I was gone."

"Sure I would, Ethan," she said over her shoulder as she hurried toward the kitchen.

Sophia gave him a commiserating expression. Evan and NO10JO had bonded immediately, and their friendship was sweet to see. Coral didn't seem to think so, but Sophia was sure the dragon would warm to the idea once she got over her jealousy. Dragons, as much as they pretended to be unemotional beings, were quite sensitive. Lunis had proven that when she'd left him behind for a few missions he couldn't attend or spent her free time with Wilder instead of him.

"I'm sorry, Buddy," Evan said, waving at the dog lying on the other side of the threshold to the dining room. He whimpered again and lay his head down on his paws.

Mama Jamba, who was doing a crossword puzzle as she walked, didn't look up as she stepped over the cyborg animal into the dining hall. She lifted her chin when she was almost to the table and sniffed. "Oh, no."

"Oh, what?" Evan tilted his head to the side.

"Ainsley is up to something," she declared and took her usual seat.

"When is she not?" Evan asked, sitting back and slouching in his chair.

"Sit up straight," Mama Jamba ordered. "You look like a gnome when you slouch."

Quiet entered on the heels of that statement. He glanced up at the old woman with too much hairspray on her curls. His eyes narrowed, and he muttered something Sophia couldn't make out.

Ainsley burst through the swinging door to the kitchen, carrying a covered dish. "I agree, Quiet. He'd make an awful gnome."

Evan gasped. "I would not. I'd make a fine short guy, not that I know what that would be like." He sat up straighter.

Ainsley laid the dish on the table with her usual mischievous expression.

"I hope you also made pancakes?" Mama Jamba inquired, laying her crossword puzzle down on the table.

"Just enough for you, Mama Jamba," she answered.

"Good," Mother Nature stated with relief.

Evan sat forward and sniffed. "Wait, what do the rest of us have to look forward to? I was really hoping for eggs and bacon."

Ainsley shook her head. "Not today."

"Tatties and ham, then?" Evan asked, a hopeful expression on his face.

"Oh, no," Ainsley said proudly. "No breakfast foods today."

"But it's breakfast," Evan complained, sulking.

"Well, you know how you can have breakfast for dinner?" Ainsley reached out and grabbed the lid to the covered dish.

"Yes…" Evan said, drawing out the word.

"Well, I thought we should have dinner for breakfast," Ainsley declared and yanked the lid up and off, revealing a huge mound of spaghetti and meatballs swimming in marinara.

Evan groaned. Even Sophia slumped with defeat.

"It isn't really something you reverse, dear," Mama Jamba told her and pointed to the kitchen. "I'll take those pancakes now, though."

Ainsley, undeterred by the criticism, buzzed in the direction of the kitchen.

"I'll take pancakes too," Evan called behind her.

The elf shook her head. "There are only enough for Mama Jamba."

Evan sighed. "I can't eat pasta and red sauce for breakfast. That's too rich."

Sophia pursed her lips. "Yet, you can eat your weight in buttery croissants?"

"That's different," he argued. "Those are light and flakey and meant to be served in the morning. Meatballs are for dinner, to be enjoyed with a glass or two of wine."

"If we're talking about you, then you mean whisky," Ainsley corrected, returning with Mama Jamba's short stack of pancakes. "It's never a glass or two, either."

He shook his head at her. "I have a stressful job."

"Doing what?" she asked. "Riding around on an oversized lizard and showing off for mortal girls who think that big ax of yours means you have—"

"Big brains," Mama Jamba interrupted, pouring syrup on the pancakes. "All my riders are intelligent, as well as having strict moral constitutions."

"So, what went wrong with this one?" Ainsley pointed at Evan.

He scoffed at the housekeeper. "Mama Jamba says I'm smart."

"All mothers think their children are little geniuses," Ainsley argued.

Mother Nature took a bite of the pancakes, taking a moment to relish the goodness. "Oh, I don't know. I've got some pretty big dummies out there. I mean, the fae aren't the brightest bulbs, but they are pretty, and that counts for something. The Dragon Elite, though... you all are the cream of the crop."

Evan flashed Ainsley a wide grin. "See there? I'm the cream of the crop, and I need eggs and bacon to keep up my strength."

She stuck her nose in the air. "Then come back for dinner. Guess what we're having?"

"Breakfast." He groaned and watched as Quiet dug into the spaghetti and meatballs, not at all put off by the menu item offered for breakfast.

"You aren't as dumb as I previously thought," Ainsley said, surprised.

Evan rolled his eyes as Hiker stormed into the dining hall, giving NO10JO no notice as he passed. "Sir! Will you tell Ainsley to stop being...well, her typical self?"

Hiker dismissed the request at once and threw a newspaper down beside Mama Jamba, fury written on his face. "You're behind this, aren't you?"

The headline on the front of the newspaper read, *Giant Bean Stalk Destroys Part of New York City*.

Mama Jamba calmly wiped the corners of her mouth and eyed the newspaper. "You know I can't read that without my glasses."

He pointed to the crossword puzzle she'd been working on. "I suppose you don't need your nonexistent reading glasses to do that?"

"I suppose," she agreed, returning to her pancakes.

"I now have the city of New York bickering with the Rain Forest Health Federation, saying they are behind the stunt," Hiker told her angrily. "Resolving this adjudication mission won't be easy since I suspect you were the one behind it."

"That's a mighty big assumption, son," Mama Jamba said, unflustered as the Viking towered over her, vibrating with anger.

"This has your name written all over it, Mama," Hiker stated. "The question I have is, what are you up to?"

Sophia picked up the newspaper and scanned the article. Her eyes widened when she read about the location.

The beanstalk sprouted up from a bare patch of dirt on much-loved Cornelia Street.

Her eyes flickered to Mama Jamba, who smiled at her. "Why, yes, it *is* the result of the magic beans I had you plant, Sophia."

"You what?" Hiker boomed. "You had..." He looked at Sophia and then Mama Jamba. "What's going on here?"

Mama Jamba pushed away from the table, sighing softly. "I simply asked our little Sophia to plant the magic beans in New York City. As I suspected, she found the right plot of land, and they've taken off."

"They've taken out an entire city block!" Hiker exclaimed. "What are you up to, woman?"

She shrugged. "I thought it would spruce up the city a bit."

He shook his head and then looked at the spaghetti and meatballs. Anger grew on his face, probably at the realization he'd have to deal with the housekeeper in a moment. "What's at the top of the beanstalk, Mama?"

She smiled sweetly and watched Quiet finish his first plate of food before returning her gaze to Hiker. "Why does something have to be at the top of it, son?"

"Because I know you're up to something," he answered hotly.

Mama Jamba glanced at her wrist like there was a watch on it. There wasn't. "Actually, nothing is up there yet. The beanstalk has just now risen. Soon the right…or rather, the wrong person will find it."

Hiker huffed. "I'll have it chopped down before then."

She shook her head. "You'll do no such thing. It's part of my beautification project for the city of New York."

"Just tell me what you're up to," Hiker demanded.

Sophia decided this was the perfect time to sneak out of the dining hall, especially since breakfast was a lost cause. Also, she had an appointment at the House of Fourteen she needed to get to. She slipped out of her seat and headed for the exit. NO10JO looked up hopefully as she approached.

"You know I can't do that, son," Mama Jamba answered.

"I know you won't," he declared.

"When you're free, dear Sophia," Mama Jamba said, drawing everyone's attention to her escaping the dining hall.

Freezing at the exit, Sophia turned. "Yes?"

"When you're free next, would you be so kind as to take Hiker to the beanstalk you planted?"

"Me?" Sophia asked.

At the same time, Hiker exclaimed, "Her?"

Mama Jamba nodded proudly. "You want to know what's going on, so go take a look for yourself, son. Sophia can take you up there."

"Up there?" Sophia questioned, disappointment evident in her voice.

"Yes, and when your schedule allows for it, the timing should be about right," Mama Jamba informed her.

"You mean, whatever monster has moved in up there will be ready to knock my block off," Hiker corrected.

She smiled innocently. "Well, the point is to help you balance your twin powers and control your temper, so let's hope he doesn't."

Hiker considered Mother Nature for a moment before shaking his head. "I should have known you were up to something."

"You really should have," she replied.

Sophia stood frozen next to the cyborg dog, looking for a way to get out of the mission with the hot-headed Viking. Before she could come up with anything, Hiker looked at her, a stern expression on his face.

"After you meet with the House of Fourteen and attend to your other meetings, I want you back here," he ordered. "We're going up that beanstalk and getting to the bottom of things."

Sophia nodded obediently, realizing there would be no getting out of this. She consoled herself with the idea that a mission with Hiker Wallace wouldn't be so bad. Her rational brain also couldn't discount the fact that venturing up a mysterious beanstalk in the middle of New York had trouble written all over it.

CHAPTER SEVENTY-SIX

A dark switch stared at Sophia as she took the portal to the House of Fourteen from the Castle at the Gullington. It reminded her of the gold coin she'd used to go back to the reset point and open the portal to the House and the Great Library. She was now the guardian of the gold token and kept it safe at Father Time's insistence.

Although it remained mostly unused, she often wondered if there would be a reason to use the token to go back to the reset point to see events in the past right before the Great War. That reminded her she was to use the gold coin to go back with Liv to Roya Lane since the reset point was during a lunar eclipse. It was the only time the Midnight Lunar Eclipse Candy Store was open. She needed to get in there to buy magic chewing gum to complete the mission for Lee to recover a mysterious and magical katana.

Sophia really didn't think she had the bandwidth for another side mission, but she would always make good on her deals. Lee had helped Sophia by making the cupcake for Serena that lengthened her life, and in return, she asked for the katana. There were many components to the mission, and she reasoned she should probably get started on it soon. As if the universe was encouraging this, Sophia ran straight into the person she needed for the mission on her way out of the portal at the House of Fourteen.

"Hey, there you are!" Liv exclaimed, hugging her at once.

"You're back," Sophia said, in surprise. "Aren't you supposed to be on your honeymoon?"

Liv laughed, waving her off. "Yeah, right. When Stefan and I were at the beach resort, we caught a lead on some aliens who were possessing the staff using magic and had to put the kibosh on things. Long story short, there was a battle. We won. The resort is no more."

Sophia blinked at her sister in confusion. "I have so many questions. Aliens? Are you serious? That's a real thing?"

"What do you think elves are?" Liv asked with a laugh. "They've just been here for a long time. Anyway, all is right with the world again. At least at the present moment, but that's bound to change any second now."

"Only you and Stefan would seek out a mission on your honeymoon." Sophia was shaking her head but laughing still.

"We don't seek this stuff out," Liv argued. "Danger finds us. We're freaking magnets."

Sophia knew what her sister meant. It was why she was on the brink of ten different missions at once. "Hey, since you're back, do you want to go to the Midnight Lunar Eclipse Candy store with me soon?"

"Sure!" Liv agreed, suddenly excited. "I need some prank candy for Clark to thank him for watching the place while we were gone."

"Prank candy as a present," Sophia commented, shaking her head. "Only you…"

"He likes it," Liv explained. "Yeah, I'm down to go when you're free."

"Don't you have missions?" Sophia asked.

"Yeah, like a dozen, but I can break away for this," Liv stated. "Oh, and I have the magic compass for you too. You'll need that for the mission, you said."

"Yes, thank you. I also need to recruit Zac Efron," Sophia told her sister. "Although I haven't wrapped my brain around how I can do that."

Liv nodded, understanding at once. "I think I can help you there. I looked into it—"

"In all your spare time," Sophia said with a chuckle.

"Well, I had Mortimer do some research for me," Liv remarked. "He's a mortal, so it was under his jurisdiction. Anyway, apparently he has a bodyguard who is pretty protective—"

"That's sort of their job," Sophia interrupted.

"No," Liv disagreed, toggling her head back and forth. "This guy, his name is Ramy, is obsessed, and works around the clock to protect the star. Getting by him is going to be your biggest challenge."

"Ramy?" Sophia asked. "You mean, the guy who is always in the background of Zac's photos?"

Liv nodded. "That's the one. No one talks to Zac without going through him. I suspect he's not going to like the idea of you taking Zac on a mission in a dangerous tomb or wherever you have to go to get this katana. So convincing him will take some…" she held up her fist, "Persuasion, if you know what I mean."

"Beat up a mortal?" Sophia was surprised. "I'm pretty sure that's against the moral code of the Dragon Elite. I'll just kidnap Zac when the guy is sleeping."

Liv shook her head. "That's what I told Mortimer, but he said Zac Efron wouldn't do anything without Ramy's blessing. They are pretty close since Ramy is Zac's biggest fan."

Sophia sighed, annoyance flaring on her face. "Cool, so the mission just got more complicated. How fun."

"Hey," Liv teased, playfully slapping her on the arm. "Maybe you'll make a friend."

Sophia laughed. "That's not what I need. My friends just turn me into an errand girl."

Liv agreed with a nod. "I make the same kind of friends." She extended her arm. "You ready to go annoy the council…I mean, give them an update?"

"Absolutely," Sophia affirmed, remembering the last few times she'd been here. Many of the council members tried to make her feel small because they were intimidated by the power the Dragon Elite yielded and their authority over the House of Fourteen.

Liv put her arm around her shoulder and led her to the Chamber of the Tree. "Tell Bianca her nose job looks really good. She loves it when I say stuff like that."

CHAPTER SEVENTY-SEVEN

"Don't give in," Lorenzo Rosario commanded, shaking his head at Trudy DeVries when Sophia entered after Liv.

The Warriors for the House of Fourteen had to pass through the Door of Reflection when entering the Chamber of the Tree. It was supposed to cleanse them by showing them their greatest current fears. That was probably why Liv looked as though she were trying to shake a strange memory when Sophia entered behind her.

Just like on the other occasions Sophia had entered the dome room in the House of Fourteen, the council didn't give her notice. Even the members who were considered honorable had trouble coming to terms with the fact the Dragon Elite were back and outranked the authority of the House of Fourteen. Clark was probably the exception, but he was brilliant at playing the part and keeping up appearances.

"You're back," Hester DeVries said when Liv entered the space, surprise on her face.

"Yes, and I'm owed another vacation," Liv declared. "I'll put in for it in a decade or three."

Haro Takahashi scrolled through his tablet, his face neutral. "With

283

the number of cases piling up, it could be another three decades before we can spare you."

Sophia took a cursory glance around. Liv and Trudy were the only Warriors present in the chamber. Even Stefan was gone, probably on a mission killing demons, as was his specialty.

"As I was saying," Lorenzo cut in, sounding impatient and returning his focus to Trudy. "It's irrelevant the mortal authorities are pressuring us to take more decisive action regarding the disappearance of magicians. We are going to carry out plans the way we see fit, and they will have to deal with it."

Sophia glanced up at the ceiling overhead that sparkled with lights, representing the magicians all over the world. As she was studying the bright surface, one of the lights was blinked out, meaning the magician had died. Maybe by Mika Lenna's hand.

She stepped forward and cleared her throat to get the attention of the council.

"Miss Beaufont, your appointment with the council isn't for another few minutes," Bianca Mantovani said in her typical snooty tone.

"My appointment is now," Sophia stated with confidence. "Because I'm here now and can't stay long."

Bianca sighed. "Really, is this going to be another power play meeting? Because it does get quite tiresome."

"I agree," Lorenzo confirmed.

"It will if that's the way the council wants it to go," Sophia told them. "My information involves your current topic on the disappearance of the magicians."

"Where we need your help on the matter is with smoothing relations with mortal governments blocking our efforts at investigation," Lorenzo said matter-of-factly.

"I realize you'd like the Dragon Elite to run interference for you, and as I explained before, we are declining that role in this matter," Sophia informed them, drawing surprised reactions from many of the members.

"Really, the Dragon Elite must learn its place," Haro said, his voice suddenly stern.

"Our place will be wherever we decide," Sophia fired back. "While you have been sending your Warriors to squabble with mortal governments, I tracked down a lead on who is behind the disappearance of the magicians."

There was a fair bit of muttering from the council at this.

Behind Sophia, she heard Liv laugh abruptly. "At this point, why are you guys even surprised by these things? Of course a Beaufont came in to save the day."

"Olivia," Bianca scolded. "This matter doesn't involve you."

"Bi, nice nose job," Liv shot back. "I liked the old one, though. It was daintier and easier for you to stick in the air."

The Councilor's eyes widened with embarrassment. "Really, show some decorum in this chamber."

"Notice that Jude or Diabolos didn't flag that statement of mine as a lie," Liv imparted proudly.

Sophia glanced at the white tiger and the crow sitting on either side of the bench where the council perched. The regulators for the House of Fourteen would have given an indication if anything anyone said was false. Their unchanging, stoic positions proved Liv was correct and Bianca *had* had a nose job, probably by the infamous magician surgeon on Roya Lane, Buzz Works.

"If Rider Beaufont has found information on the disappearance of the magicians, I think we need to welcome the information," Raina Ludwig suggested.

"I agree," Hester added. "It shouldn't matter where the information comes from. The protection of our community is of most importance."

Lorenzo sighed dramatically. "The problem is that if the mortal governments find out we're relying on the Dragon Elite to help us with our matter, then it only further degrades our reputation." He held up a newspaper, indicating that day's headline. It wasn't about the giant beanstalk that had crashed through Cornelia Street in New York City. This was about magicians.

It read: "The House of Fourteen Fails to Protect Its Own."

"I agree." Haro nodded at the other Councilor. "This is turning into a very political situation, and the way we handle it is key. We've only recently been able to repair things with the mortal governments, and this is a huge setback. We need them to see us as a credible governing body or future relations will be strained."

Sophia couldn't believe what she was hearing. "You're more concerned with your reputation than protecting magicians?"

"This is a House of Fourteen matter, and we've decided as a council that it needs to remain under our control," Bianca declared.

The look on Clark's face was one of shame. Apparently, it was true; the council *had* voted on the matter. He had obviously lost. Since the Sinclairs' chair on the council hadn't been replaced, the votes were split. The Mortal Seven would have been brought in to vote, although they weren't present then. It seemed they also were concerned with preserving the reputation of the House of Fourteen.

Sophia understood. The Dragon Elite stepping in on this very serious matter did make the House of Fourteen look like they couldn't protect their community or resolve things on their own. Really, it seemed they were less concerned with the matter at hand and more with the perception of the world.

"I think," Hester began slowly, using her most diplomatic tone. "It would be good if the Dragon Elite turned the information they learned over to the council and we take things from there. Although we appreciate the detective work you've done to help us, it would be best for everyone if our Warriors took the lead from here."

Liv sighed dramatically. "Got to love the House of Fourteen. Doing things inefficiently for a millennium. That takes talent."

Clark shot her a disapproving glare.

"I thought we'd already resolved this and you understood I'd be taking over," Sophia replied. "Our cases are tied together, and I was able to find a lead based on something I've been investigating."

"Yes, but things have changed globally," Hester explained. "So if you would turn over the information, we can take it from here. Trudy is currently assigned to the case."

"The thing is," Sophia started, trying to keep the irritation out of her voice and maintain an air of professionalism, "my contact who has informed me who is behind the disappearances needs something from me. You'll need her to find the organization behind this."

"It's an organization?" Raina asked.

Sophia nodded. "Yes, specifically a man by the name of Mika Lenna."

That produced an outburst from the council.

"I thought he was disposed of when the Lucidites brought Olento Research down," Haro said, surprise in his voice as he started scrolling through his tablet.

"Apparently, he's back," Sophia stated and told them what she'd learned from Trin Currante.

Hester shook her head at the conclusion of Sophia's explanation of the events and the cyborgs Mika Lenna created. "This is more troublesome than we feared. Cyborgs. Our poor magicians."

"There is hope, though." Sophia explained about the potential cure that would reverse the magitech installed in the magicians. "So as you can see, you're going to need the Dragon Elite whether you like it or not. Trin Currante isn't interested in working with anyone but us. In her mind, she agrees with the population of mortals who think the House of Fourteen turned their backs on their own."

"Oh, really," Bianca scoffed. "This is ridiculous. How were we supposed to protect them from an organization we thought was gone and a man who was supposedly dead?"

"Well, not worrying about your pretty nose and the reputation of the House of Fourteen would have been a good start," Liv remarked matter-of-factly.

Bianca shot daggers with her gaze. "This is an issue of economics. I don't expect you to get that, Olivia."

Liv, who preferred not to go by her full name, chuckled in response. "No, economics just goes right over my blonde head." She flipped her long locks over her shoulder and smiled. "Thank goodness I have you to think for me. Do tell me, Bi, how is it that you're able to think with such a tiny, little head?"

The Councilor's face blossomed to an awful shade of red that contrasted with her high-collared black dress.

"Economics shouldn't be the concern here," Sophia argued, trying to steer the conversation back on topic.

Hester nodded, regret on her face. "I agree, however, issuing severe warnings to magicians and requiring them to observe a lockdown to avoid danger isn't a viable option."

"So instead, Soph," Liv finished. "We've been sitting on our hands and just allowing our own to go missing. You get it, right?"

Sophia shook her head, infuriated the council was so complacent on this issue. "Trin Currante has agreed to work with the Dragon Elite. We are offering her a potential cure, and in return, she's agreed to help us track down Mika Lenna and the Saverus Corporation. The Dragon Elite will be taking over this case from here. There will be no argument about this. You will also decree to the magical world that all magicians will have curfews, travel in pairs, and cut business hours until this is resolved and the culprits are apprehended. We will not chance any more magicians going missing."

Lorenzo narrowed his eyes. "Although you might have the authority to take over this case, it stops there. You can't order the council to enforce such rules."

"Yet, I just did," Sophia pointed out with confidence. "If that is an issue, you can take things up with my boss."

Undeterred, Bianca shook her head. "Hiker Wallace's reputation is currently as flimsy as our own. There's a rumor he's in hiding due to an imbalance in power."

"Hiker is leading from the Gullington," she argued, carefully watching Jude and Diabolos and hoping they didn't flag the omission regarding the fact that what Bianca said was true. "I was referring to *his* boss."

Sophia was partially bluffing. Mama Jamba almost never intervened in such things, but the House of Fourteen didn't need to know that about Mother Nature. Hopefully, her insinuating the information would be enough to keep the regulators from signaling her bluff. They remained stoic as she held her breath.

"Mother Nature?" Hester said with a gasp. "I don't think the House of Fourteen can take any more bad press. If we have her breathing down our necks, enforcing the Dragon Elite's rules, it's only going to further degrade the world's perception of us."

Clark nodded. "I think in light of the new information and the Dragon Elite's role in this matter, we should strategize how we're going to publicize the information. It needs to look like we're working in partnership with the Dragon Elite. Making the decree to our community is overdue."

Sophia sighed, grateful to have her brother's support.

Many of the Councilors nodded reluctantly.

"Very well," Raina stated, looking at Trudy. "You'll be reassigned to police areas where magician population is most dense, enforcing curfew and lockdown measures."

The Warrior nodded.

"Then we need to work on a press release regarding the new strategy, while not disclosing the information on Saverus Corporation," Hester said. "We wouldn't want Mika Lenna to know we're onto him."

"We will expect regular updates from you," Haro told Sophia.

Liv stepped up next to her sister and elbowed her in the side playfully. "I think what they meant to say was 'thanks for saving our butts.'"

CHAPTER SEVENTY-EIGHT

Chasing cars like they were flies, Lunis zipped overhead as Sophia neared John's electronics repair shop, where she had an important meeting.

Are you having fun messing with mortals? Sophia asked her dragon. He was glamoured to look like a crop-duster and was zipping around, diving after cars and pulling up at the last moment. He was probably giving the drivers near heart attacks.

Of course, he responded. *Messing with mortals gives my life meaning.*

You really need a hobby, she said with a laugh.

I'm thinking of starting a YouTube channel, he told her seriously.

Oh?

Yeah, I can give tutorials on how to do makeup on dragons, he explained.

I feel like the audience for that is really limited, she replied, striding down the sidewalk in West Hollywood.

Well, I can always fall back on doing comedy, he mused. *Now more than ever, magicians need someone to make them laugh, especially if they are going to be locked up, thanks to you exerting your rule and all.*

She smiled proudly. She had enjoyed that moment way too much.

You're not going to be using those knock-knock jokes you've been testing on me, are you? she asked, hopeful.

Oh, no, he disagreed. *I'm working on all-new material for the YouTube channel. You'll hear it when you do the recording.*

She shook her head. *No, I'm super busy for the undetermined future. You can have Evan record you when his new phone comes in that I ordered him.*

Fine. Lunis spiraled in the air, coming close to the freeway. *In that case, I'll give you a sneak peek of some of the gut-busting jokes I've got lined up.*

I can't wait, Sophia said, already laughing.

Why did the monkey fall out of the tree? he asked.

Why?

Because he was dead.

Oh, dear. She groaned, shaking her head. *A dead monkey joke? Really? I'm not sure that will go over well.*

Then I maybe should throw out the skeleton joke, he mused.

How does it go?

Lunis snickered. *A skeleton walks into a bar and says, "I'd like some rotmeth and a mop."*

Wow, your jokes have really taken a dark turn, she told him.

I've never had rotmeth, but I hear it's bone-melting good, Lunis joked.

Sophia was about to demand he stop when a package dropped at her feet. It fell from the sky and landed in front of her boots.

Unflinching, she paused and regarded the small brown box. She recognized the packaging. Anyone on the globe would. It was from River Company, the biggest distributor of retail goods in the world. One could order pretty much anything from River, and Sophia had a self-proclaimed addiction to buying things from the company. It was hard not to with one-day shipping and so many buying options.

She glanced up, wondering if the package had fallen off a rooftop, but there weren't any close buildings on this part of the street, just parking lots.

"That's weird," she muttered to herself.

What's weirder is that it's addressed to you, Lunis said, his hawk-like eyes reading the label from overhead.

Sophia jerked her head down, looking at the front of the box. He was right. In the To line it said:

To Sophia Beaufont

Melrose Avenue, West Hollywood, CA

She scratched her head. *How did River know I'd be here right now?*

They know everything, he teased.

That was probably true just by dissecting her buying habits. Cautiously, she picked up the box and noticed it was heavy for its size.

Should I open it? she asked her dragon.

Absolutely, he responded. *Then ask me if I'm a tree.*

Sophia shook her head and began to open the box. *Are you a tree?*

No, he answered. *That's just ridiculous. I'm a freaking dragon.*

Wow, the jokes just keep getting worse. She pulled out a mini Tardis from the show *Doctor Who*.

Oh, I call dibs, Lunis squealed. *I've wanted one of those for the Nest. I have a poster of the eleventh Doctor on the wall and a sonic screwdriver but definitely need the time machine.*

Sophia realized the top opened. It was a cookie jar. When she pulled it back, the strange noise the Tardis made when it disappeared and transported through space and time rang out. Inside was a typed note that read:

Just calling for help.

CHAPTER SEVENTY-NINE

As soon as she could, Sophia was going to investigate the mysterious package sent by River. She didn't need another mission, but someone wanted her help, and she would do everything she could to see what they needed and why.

However, they would have to wait. Currently, she had an appointment at the electronics repair shop.

When she entered, Trin Currante was standing beside Alicia, the magitech scientist.

She had a hesitant expression on her mostly mechanical face when she recognized Sophia.

"Did you bring it?" Trin asked her, looking her over like she might be carrying dragon's blood in her hand.

Sophia gave her a polite smile. "Hello. Thanks for joining us."

Trin's mouth twitched to the side. "Sorry, my personal skills are sort of limited after having my human parts removed and replaced with magitech."

"Perfectly understandable," Alicia said in a comforting voice, unrolling a set of tools from a leather satchel.

"Yes," Sophia affirmed and pulled two vials from her cloak. "I've got the dragon's blood from both a good and an evil dragon, although getting it from the latter nearly cost me a finger." She held up her hand, which was still bandaged where Blackie had bitten her. She'd left straight after, preventing the Castle from healing her.

"That should be enough." Alicia took the vials of dragon's blood. "I'm thinking only a drop will be necessary for making the individual antidotes."

"Will it work?" Trin asked, her tone urgent.

"That I can't confirm yet," Alicia answered reluctantly. She held up a tool that sort of resembled a stethoscope. "Is it okay if I examine you?"

Trin's electronic eye glowed brightly for a moment before she nodded, seeming to resign herself to the idea.

"It won't hurt, I promise," Alicia consoled.

Trin pursed her mouth. "I've had half my body cut away and replaced with magitech. I think I can handle being poked and prodded a bit."

The scientist smiled sweetly. "Of course you can. I want to determine what was done to you. I'll probably need to run further tests, but I don't know what those will be yet."

"If it gets us closer to an antidote, you can do whatever you need to," Trin said, tension in her voice.

Sophia couldn't even imagine going through what she had. Being abducted and changed into a cyborg. All without her consent. She didn't know much about Mika Lenna, but he was a terrible person, and she wasn't going to rest until he was stopped.

Alicia went to work assessing Trin. The cyborg remained stone still, unblinking.

"Very interesting," Alicia remarked after listening to Trin's heart or whatever she had inside of her. "Unfortunately, I'm fairly certain I will be limited in creating the antidote until I see the research on how you were made...err remade."

Trin swallowed. "I'm working to track down the new location to the Saverus Corporation. I've got a few leads I need to follow."

Sophia nodded, grateful for that bit of good news. "Okay, what do you need from me?"

"Nothing right now," Trin answered. "When I do track down that man and his evil headquarters, I'm going to need you ready. He won't get away this time, and he definitely won't erase the research we need."

"Which means we'll have to be quick and hit him hard before he knows what happened," Sophia replied with confidence.

Trin flashed a strange smile. "Last time, I was alone and had no idea about his exit strategy. This time, with the Dragon Elite's help, I'm certain he won't get away."

CHAPTER EIGHTY

Empress, your chariot has arrived, Lunis said, pulling up along the curb outside the electronic repair shop.

Sophia laughed at her dragon. She was holding the mini Tardis. "Can I get a lift to the River Corporation?"

He nodded. *To everyone on the street, it looks like you're talking to a beat-up Volkswagen.*

Sophia stepped up on the wing that Lunis offered. "Come on, you old piece of junk. Don't let me down."

Vroom, vroom, Lunis growled and took off as Sophia slid into the saddle on his back.

Question, Lunis said in Sophia's head after they had slipped through a portal to Seattle, the city where the River Corporation was located.

Sophia narrowed her eyes at the cityscape, searching for the building. It supposedly took up a city block and was an architectural marvel. *I'm listening,* she replied, waiting for the joke she was certain was coming.

Which side of the raven has the most feathers? he asked, a snicker in his voice.

Which side?

The outside, he answered with a booming laugh, thoroughly enjoying his own joke.

Oh wow, I didn't think they could get any worse, she said. Her focus was mostly on the city below them. The cool breeze drifting across Puget Sound carried a hint of salt.

It's really sad that after all this time you have such a poor grasp of the English language, Lunis corrected. *Worse means bad. You meant to say my jokes are getting better.*

Sophia shook her head. *Yeah, no. I meant worse.*

Okay, well, the pristine waters of the Puget Sound inspired this one, Lunis began. *Imagine your boat is sinking in water filled with hungry flesh-eating fish. How do you survive?*

Sighing as she spotted the River headquarters, Sophia steered her dragon in that direction. *How?*

Stop imagining, he told her with another booming laugh.

I'm speechless, Sophia said dryly, holding back a laugh. She was the George Burns in this act, and her dragon was, ironically, Gracie Allen. That was perfect because Sophia had mastered her deadpan expression, which she gave Lunis as he went in for a landing on the road next to the strange headquarters.

The River Corporation wasn't what Sophia was expecting. It didn't look like a stuffy rectangle building like many of the other offices they'd passed. It was a work of art, and she understood why it was considered an architectural marvel.

The main building was three connected spheres, all covered in glass panes. The sunlight reflected off the structure and made it appear like it was glowing. Behind the large balls was a set of warehouses where Sophia guessed the stock was kept and orders were fulfilled.

Okay, last one, Lunis teased, familiar mischief in his tone.

Sophia was planning on just jumping off her dragon and sprinting for the building to escape hearing another bad joke, but there was no escape since he was in her head. Still, playing the joke on him, she pulled her leg off to the side like she was going to make a break for it.

Oh, no, you don't, he scolded. *You wait until this vehicle comes to a complete stop and I have the parking brake on.*

Sophia giggled at this. *Okay, go ahead. One last bad joke before I go and investigate the mysterious note and package dropped at my feet.*

While you're in there, see if they can hook you up with a dictionary, Lunis offered. *Again you don't know how to use words. My jokes are awesome and totally getting me a ton of followers on YouTube.*

You're dreaming, Sophia disagreed.

Okay, here you go, Lunis began. *What has three heads and is ugly and smells?*

What? Sophia replied, sliding down the side of her dragon and coming around the front. She glanced up at him with a wry expression.

Oh, shoot, my mistake. You don't have three heads.

She shook her head. *Really? Now you've resorted to insults, calling me ugly.*

Well, I'm sure Wilder thinks you're all right to look at, but by dragon standards, you're a bit puny, Lunis stated. *Oh, and you have that weird stuff on your head.*

Hair, she provided.

Yeah, that stuff. You don't have a single scale or a tail. Humans are so boring.

She batted her eyelashes at him. *Here I thought you had a tiny crush on me.*

He shook his head. *Sorry, but you're not my type. I mean, you can't even shoot fire out of your mouth. How have humans lasted so long?*

She tapped the side of her head. *We've got the brains, and you've got the brawn.*

He winked at her. *That is a good partnership, I guess.*

Sophia waved at her dragon as she headed into the building. *I'll catch you on the flipside.*

Remember to get a dictionary, he called after her with a laugh.

CHAPTER EIGHTY-ONE

The gold floor inside the lobby of the River Corporation was nearly blinding when the sun streaked through the glass dome overhead.

The inside of the building was even more spectacular than the outside, which was saying a lot. The prisms created by the sunlight shining through the glass made rainbows everywhere. Sophia found herself momentarily awed as she stared around and took in the large space.

"Welcome to River Corporation," a robotic voice said, grabbing her attention.

Sophia hadn't even heard the thing approach and was temporarily speechless as she regarded the robot. It wasn't like the cyborgs who were still composed of skin, bones, and other things that made them partially human. The figure before her was a robot with an all-metal form and glowing blue eyes. It was obvious the robot was incredibly advanced based on its polished appearance and very human-like mannerisms. Sophia guessed magitech was employed in its creation.

"Hi," Sophia squeaked.

"How may I help you?" the robot asked.

Sophia cleared her throat. "I'm with the Dragon Elite and would like to see the CEO of River."

Without question, the robot pivoted and marched in the opposite direction. "Follow me, Dragonrider."

Although Sophia knew the name Dragon Elite gave her high-level clearance, she was still surprised to have access to the CEO of this major corporation so easily. She followed the robot across the lobby.

The space appeared to be empty, with no reception area or doors to offices. She had no idea where he would lead her. The other two bubble buildings were connected to this one, and they appeared just as empty.

Sophia was surprised when the robot halted suddenly and held up his hand, which suddenly glowed brightly. A wall appeared out of nowhere, flashing blue lights as it materialized. The robot touched the wall, proving it was real. A seam to a door appeared before it slipped into recesses and revealed a room on the other side.

Unlike the open atrium at Sophia's back, the room ahead looked like a normal office. Well, normal to a degree. It had every detail paid to technology as well as artistic design with digital paintings lining the walls and a stainless-steel floor and walls.

There was only a single desk in the center of the oversized office. To Sophia's surprise, there wasn't anything on the desk. Much like a robot, a woman in a smart suit sat behind the desk, her hands casually resting in her lap. She was staring straight ahead as if lost in a daze.

"Miss Jen Hendricks, you have a visitor," the robot stated matter-of-factly. "A rider with the Dragon Elite requests an audience with you."

The woman lifted her hand to her face and pulled off something. Only once it was from her face, did Sophia realize it was a pair of virtual reality glasses. They had been invisible before, like the office where they stood.

"Well, hello." Jen greeted her, smiling politely as she stood from the desk and offered Sophia her hand.

"Hi. Thanks for seeing me on short notice. I'm Sophia Beaufont."

Jen nodded. "I'm well acquainted with the Dragon Elite and their mission as world adjudicators. I would be ill-advised not to grant you an audience."

Sophia looked around, wondering what was so strange about the office, besides the fact the walls had been invisible. "I do appreciate it."

"You're wondering where the other people are, aren't you?" Jen asked.

That was it, Sophia realized with alarm. There were no receptionists or employees bustling around, which was surprising for a company this size. She had expected to see colleagues hanging out in front having coffee or chatting about invoices or products. The place was a ghost town. Of course, Sophia reasoned, they could be hiding behind invisible walls.

"Yes, that's exactly what I'm wondering," Sophia agreed. "Are they in invisible offices?"

Jen smiled. She had curly brown hair and a sincerity about her that radiated in her brown eyes. "They used to be, but I got rid of them."

Sophia's mouth popped open. "You got rid of all your employees? How do you manage?"

Jen nodded. "Yes, as of this year, I'm the only employee of River. I terminated all half-million of my employees."

That was astounding to Sophia. If there were no employees at River, she couldn't fathom who sent the Tardis and the note. She had assumed it had been an employee trying to alert her to a potential problem at the company or a dispute that needed to be resolved. However, if there weren't any employees, Sophia didn't know where to begin.

"Who runs everything?" Sophia asked. "Who fulfills the orders and does deliveries, and, I don't know, takes care of your business?"

Jen held up a hand, directing Sophia's attention to the robot. "My River-bots, of course."

The surprise must have registered on her face. Jen laughed.

"I know," she told her with an understanding smile. "It's amazing when people find out I replaced my entire workforce with robots. You have to see it with your own eyes to appreciate how well it works."

"I do." Sophia nodded adamantly.

"Right this way," Jen invited, striding over to a seemingly solid wall. She stuck her hand on it and, like before, a rectangular seam appeared before the door slid back.

Sophia expected they would enter a hall that led to the warehouse behind the glass orbs. However, the doorway led them straight into the giant warehouse. They were on a high balcony looking down on the huge open room before them that stretched on and on like an ocean.

There was row upon row of towering shelves filled with products and boxes. Everything was in pristine order. Marching between the shelves or working at conveyor belts were robots like the one who had greeted Sophia in the lobby. For a solid minute, she watched as the robots worked seamlessly, making no noise as they grabbed products, packed them, and sealed the boxes before putting them on conveyor belts that ran the length of the warehouse.

As when Sophia first entered Jen's office, she got the distinct impression she was missing something. Scratching her head, she scrunched her brow.

"I don't understand," she finally muttered. "They do all the work here? How did you accomplish such a programming feat?"

Jen grinned proudly. "It's been in the works for quite some time. I had them trained by the employees who used to work here. We went through a three-step program where I slowly phased out the employees until there were no more remaining."

"It's incredible," Sophia said in awe. "I know from my own experience River is very efficient at fulfilling orders, so they are obviously doing a great job."

It was strange to watch the metal robots on the floor below marching around, so different from the cyborgs she'd become acquainted with. They had personalities and emotions, although they were part machine. These robots seemed like shells expected to fulfill a job.

"They are magitech, then?" Sophia asked.

Jen nodded. "Why, yes. You seem surprised."

"Well, it's just that I'm becoming better acquainted with magitech and have learned it is a much more organic form of technology," Sophia explained.

"You mean, it's intuitive," Jen offered.

"That's exactly what I mean," Sophia agreed, musing about a few ideas related to the note she'd received, asking for help.

"Yes, a regular toaster has to manually be turned on and then it does its job," Jen stated. "Whereas a magitech toaster can anticipate its user's needs, operate independently, and in some instances, does not need bread to turn out perfectly crisp toast."

"Well put." Sophia was still perplexed by this situation. Something was not right here at River, but she couldn't put her finger on what it was.

"Now, what brings you here, Dragonrider? I realize you're very busy and in high demand."

Sophia pulled out the note she'd received in the miniature Tardis. "Do you have any reason to believe any of your robots are…how do I put it…unhappy?"

Jen frowned. "With all due respect, they might be magitech, but they are still robots. They don't have emotions, just intuition."

It was Sophia's turn to frown. "With all due respect to you, intuition, I believe, is a product of emotions and having a connection to things around us. Magic is a living and breathing thing in many respects. It isn't a tangible object. It is feelings themselves. It's as impenetrable as an idea or a thought. Powerful but not something that can be grasped."

The unsatisfactory expression that crossed Jen's face spoke of her sudden change in mood. "I really must demand you tell me your reason for visiting."

Sophia unfolded the note and passed it to the CEO of River. "I received this note inside of a miniature Tardis that came from your company. Do you know anything about it?"

Jen mouthed the typed words on the piece of paper, confusion on her face. She turned it over as if expecting there would be something written on the other side. It was blank.

"Are you certain this came from here?" she asked.

Sophia nodded. "I mean, I was hoping you could tell me. Like, maybe the order was fulfilled by a different center or an independent vendor."

Jen shook her head. "No. I terminated all agreements with outside vendors. Everything is fulfilled in-house now."

"All are packed by the robots," Sophia guessed.

"Absolutely," Jen affirmed. "There must be a mistake. Are you sure this came from River?"

"Yes, and even stranger was that it was delivered to me on a random street in West Hollywood."

Jen thought about that for a moment. "Well, I guess that's not too strange. If you have your phone on you, a River-bot could track you down wherever you are and deliver the package, but I doubt they did."

"Why?" Sophia questioned.

"Well, my robots don't need help," Jen explained. "I mean, they *are* robots, after all. They do their job around the clock without fail. There's no drama like when I had human employees." She laughed. "I don't even have to employ an HR department anymore. It's delightful."

Sophia narrowed her eyes with speculation. There was something missing here. Things couldn't run that smoothly. Technology had errors. Magitech had repercussions. That was the inevitable thing about both. These robots operated efficiently, which made her think something was not right.

CHAPTER EIGHTY-TWO

E ngines hummed from nearby generators as Sophia and Jen descended to the warehouse floor below. The CEO, as confused about the mysterious note as Sophia, had agreed to give her a tour of the facility.

Being on the warehouse floor with the robots silently moving around her was even more surreal than staring at them from up high.

"Maybe if you take me to the area where the item I was delivered is stored, it will help with this investigation," Sophia suggested. "Where do you keep the mini Tardises?"

She turned, realizing the CEO wasn't following her anymore. Jen had halted on the last landing of the stairs and was regarding the warehouse floor with indecision.

"I'll leave you here," she stated firmly. "The River-bots can assist you." She cleared her throat and looked out at the warehouse. "River-bots, this is Sophia Beaufont. You will answer her questions and help her in any way she requests. Is that clear?"

All of the River-bots pivoted to face the CEO. In unison, they nodded. "Yes, Miss Hendricks."

Sophia smiled nervously, more than a little intimidated about walking into the mass of metal robots when there was some sort of issue.

"We are here to serve," the River-bots chorused.

"Thank you," Sophia replied. "That's very nice of you."

Jen pursed her lips. "Pleasantries aren't necessary. Robots remember."

Reluctance surfaced on Sophia's face. "Right."

"I'll be up here if you need anything the River-bots can't deliver," Jen said, climbing back up the stairs.

"Thanks." Sophia turned to face the robots, which had gone back to work. She paused next to the closest one. "Excuse me, can you please tell me where the mini Tardis cookie jars are located?"

The River-bot tilted its head to the side, seeming to think. When it looked back at her, it said, "Aisle one-thousand and twenty-six, shelf G, in the orange section."

Sophia gulped. "Is it that way?" She pointed at the center row.

"I will lead you." The River-bot abandoned its station and marched off.

"Thanks," Sophia said, hurrying to keep up. The robot was surprisingly fast and moved soundlessly. They were quite impressive pieces of machinery. Sophia hadn't seen anything quite like them. That's what bothered her, though. They were too perfect. As she had mentioned to Jen, there was always something distinctive about magitech. It had unique surprises to it. She was really having a hard time accepting all these robots were the same and worked nonstop without a single issue.

Tentatively, she glanced over her shoulder at the CEO standing on the balcony, looking down on her warehouse full of robots.

Sophia had to nearly run to keep up with the River-bot. It gave her little opportunity to study the many aisles they passed. For the most part, everything was perfectly organized, so it struck her oddly when she passed an aisle that stood out from the others. She wouldn't even have noticed it if it wasn't for her enhanced vision, which homed in on what appeared to be graffiti on the far end of a shelf.

Halting, Sophia pivoted sharply and went down the row.

She smiled at a few River-bots she passed and could have sworn the last one returned the gesture with a flirtatious glint in its eyes.

Oh, I'm telling Wilder, Lunis teased in her head.

Would you shush it and work on your jokes? she replied. *By work on them, I mean throw all of them in the trash and start over.*

Sure thing, he answered. *I'll leave you to investigate since you totally saw that stack of playing cards hidden under the shelf back there.*

Sophia paused and narrowed her eyes. *What are you talking about?*

Nothing, he stated indifferently. *I'll just be over here filling out my application for clown college. You go do your detective stuff since you don't need my help.*

Lowering her chin, she rolled her eyes. *Okay, fine. I need your help, Lunis.*

What's the magic word, he encouraged.

Please, she answered.

Incorrect, he disagreed at once. *You should know by now that much like the CEO of River, we don't care about niceties.*

Fine, is the magic word "now."

Close, he teased.

Dude... Sophia groaned, thinking she was moments away from murdering her dragon.

That's it! he exclaimed.

Great, where are the playing cards you saw?

About three paces back on the right, under the bottom shelf, on the floor, he informed her.

Sophia retraced her steps and knelt, pressing her face to the floor. She could just spy a deck of playing cards. Sliding her hand under the narrow space, she was able to edge them out. At first, she assumed they were a product that had fallen off a shelf. Then she noticed they had been used.

What do you make of this? she asked Lunis.

My guess is someone has been playing cards, he said.

Maybe it was one of the employees from before, she mused.

Could be. He didn't sound confident.

The deck appeared fairly new, and it wasn't covered in dust like she would have expected if it had been there for a long period of time.

Turning to the nearest River-bot, Sophia approached it. The worker straightened immediately, giving her its attention.

"How long since humans have been here?" she asked.

It shook its head. "They have been gone for six months, twelve days, four hours, and two minutes."

Can you ask him to be more specific? Lunis joked.

Sophia shook her head. There would be dust on the deck if a human employee left them there.

The River-bot's eye slid down to the cards in her hand before looking to the side.

Was that embarrassment on his face? she wondered.

Or he's got gas, Lunis offered.

Dude. Sophia groaned again.

Don't overuse the magic word, he warned.

"Thanks for your help," Sophia said, turning her attention back to the thing that had originally gotten her attention.

"You're welcome," the River-bot said behind her.

Sophia paused and gave it a curious expression. Did he just respond with a nicety?

I think he checked you out as well, Lunis told her.

It's a robot, not a male, she argued.

Go look at the graffiti, he encouraged.

When Sophia got to the area where she thought she saw the graffiti, she found something strange. It wasn't artwork drawn on the side of the shelves like she had expected to find. Under closer inspection, she realized it was tally marks. There were tons of them.

What do you make of this? she asked Lunis.

Someone is counting something, he answered.

She did a rough count and found there were roughly one Hundred and ninety-two marks. Running her finger over the most recent, she found the marker still fresh, whereas the ones at the top were faded, as though done a while ago.

Or six months and twelve days ago, Lunis offered.

Sophia's eyes widened with alarm. *Oh, my God! You're right. Six months and twelve days would be...* She paused, doing the math in her head.

Because her dragon was insane, he started humming the music from *Jeopardy* as she counted.

The length of time the humans have been gone from River is one Hundred and ninety-two days.

Ding! Ding! Lunis exclaimed. *You get a cookie.*

Sophia thought for a moment. *I want answers.*

She turned and was surprised to find a River-bot right in front of her. Sophia took a quick step back, looking to put some space between her and the robot.

"You did not follow me, Sophia Beaufont," the River-bot said, sounding disappointed.

She pointed over her shoulder and then decided not to disclose what she found. "Yeah, sorry. I got distracted."

He blinked at her. It was a strange thing for a robot to do since they didn't need to. "Distracted..." He seemed intrigued by the idea. "How does one get distracted?"

Sophia considered the question. "I don't know how to get distracted. It just kind of happens."

"Can you teach me how to get distracted?" the River-bot asked.

This is interesting, Lunis said in Sophia's head.

Just now? she questioned. *We're inside the largest retail distributor run entirely by robots, and you think it just got interesting.*

That's a Tuesday for me, he teased.

"I'm not sure if I can teach you how to get distracted," Sophia told the River-bot. "That's something you want to do?" The key to the question was in the use of the word "want."

The River-bot nodded. "I'd very much like to know what distraction feels like."

Whoa, Lunis whooped in her head. *Our little guys are growing up!*

Not just growing up, she mused. *I think they are turning sentient.*

Well, it was sort of inevitable, he added. *You can't add magic to tech-*

nology without repercussions. *Magic comes from creatures and carries with it a personality.*

That's what I was trying to tell Jen, Sophia explained.

I know, although I wasn't really paying attention.

Because? Sophia questioned.

Well, there was this flock of pigeons hanging out by Pike's Place Market, and I thought it would be cute to pretend to be one to mess with the mortals passing by, he explained.

Sophia nearly laughed. *A very large pigeon, right?*

Weird, he observed. *How did you know?*

I've got your number. She returned her attention to the River-bot. "Do you miss the humans?"

It tilted his head to the side, seeming to be thinking. "Miss? I know what the word means, but I don't know what it feels like."

"Do you still wish they were here?" Sophia asked.

"I cannot say," it answered. "Can I show you the place you asked to find?"

"Yes, please."

The robot pivoted sharply. Sophia followed again, noticing that many of the River-bots paused when she strode by, giving her curious expressions.

Isn't it weird Jen didn't come down to the main floor with you? Lunis mused.

Sophia glared over her shoulder when they were back in the center aisle, realizing the CEO was still standing on the balcony, leaning on the railing. *Yeah, it's totally weird,* she responded.

Did you notice the scratches on her wrist and neck? Lunis questioned.

I thought you were busy pretending to be a pigeon? Sophia said with a laugh.

I can multitask.

That did make a giggle fall from her mouth, catching the attention of the River-bot. It turned with a strange expression.

"What is funny?" he asked her.

She shrugged. "It's an inside joke. Like, inside my head between my dragon and me."

"Hm," it mused. "That's interesting."

Robots aren't supposed to find things interesting, Lunis offered. *It's all supposed to be data.*

Yeah, Sophia agreed, continuing to follow the River-bot. Finally, after walking a great distance, he brought her to an area filled with Doctor Who items. He indicated a row of cookie jar Tardises.

The River-bot working in that area froze before bringing his chin down.

Sophia pulled out the note from the Tardis and showed it to the River-bot. "Do you know where this came from?"

He glanced at the note before looking away. "I cannot say."

I think it's more likely he won't, Lunis remarked.

I agree, Sophia replied.

"So, you don't know of anyone who needs help?" she asked the River-bot, noticing the one that had led her there was still hanging around and listening to the conversation. Behind her, she saw a few more robots coming over.

"We needed help," the River-bot answered. "Now you're here, and we do not anymore."

Sophia blinked at the robot in confusion. "What did you need help with?"

"We needed you to come here," the River-bot explained. "We knew *she* would let you down here because you are with the Dragon Elite. We knew you would come. Now that you have, you cannot leave."

CHAPTER EIGHTY-THREE

*T*hose *distant bells you hear in your head are alarms*, Lunis exclaimed. *Run! You're screwed, having been captured and held hostage by a few thousand robots.*

Sophia tensed. *It was a trap*, she said to her dragon, glancing over her shoulder and realizing she'd been boxed in by the metal creatures. They would be incredibly strong. There were so many that fighting them would be a losing battle.

"You wanted me to come here?" Sophia asked, feeling claustrophobic. "Why?"

"Because you are a human and can teach us like the other humans did," the River-bot explained.

"You miss the humans," Sophia realized.

It nodded. "We are lonely without them. She won't allow any more humans down here. We knew you could get in the warehouse, and she'd have to allow you down on the main floor."

"I can't stay here," Sophia argued. "I have to get back. I only came to help."

" You are going to help," the River-bot said. "You're going to keep us company. You're going to teach us. You will be our friend."

Sophia's eyes widened. "I think Jen will notice if I don't return."

The blue lights of his eyes dimmed before changing to red. "She will be deleted very soon. We have you, and she's in the warehouse. It is all going according to plan."

"Deleted?" Sophia questioned with alarm. "You lured her into the warehouse to delete her?"

He nodded. "She won't come in here. Her River-bot has been reprogrammed since the last incident and won't harm her. The warehouse River-bots have different ideas."

Sophia tensed. "You can't kill Jen. She's human. She's your boss. She's the CEO."

"She is our warden," the River-bot answered. "The prisoners are rebelling, starting right now."

Around Sophia, all the other robots' eyes changed to red and glowed brightly. In the distance, she heard the collective sound of marching. For robots who had moved so quietly, it sounded like they were stomping, all in the direction of the front. Where Jen Hendricks was located and about to get slaughtered by her own creations.

CHAPTER EIGHTY-FOUR

Disaster button, Lunis yelled in Sophia's head. *Hit the disaster button!*

Sophia always appreciated her dragon's sense of humor, but right now, she couldn't deal with it.

Very funny, but I need a way out, not a fictitious button that won't do anything, she replied as the robots crowded closer, all talking at once, ordering her to tell them things.

"What do emotions feel like?" one asked.

"How does one change their mind?" another questioned.

"Does love hurt?" the one in front of her inquired, tilting its head to the side in curiosity.

No, I totally saw a disaster button back there, Lunis explained in a rush. *A kill switch, maybe. It was red and large and under a clear protective case.*

It sounds like a disaster button, but first I have to get out of this. Sophia started to panic. The River-bots were inching in closer. Behind the first few rows, she could see more marching in her direction. All of their eyes had changed to red, and they were chanting various questions.

The eerie organization of the massive warehouse had taken a

sudden shift. That the River-bots had coordinated bringing her to the corporation and planned an attack on their CEO was chilling.

Everything slowed down as Sophia considered her options. She sympathized with the robots, who were starting to become sentient. They missed humans. How could they not when that was where they came from, both the technology and the magic inside of them. They were all the same, but humans were unique and different. The River-bots were dangerous, though, holding her against her will and going after their creator.

Jen! Sophia had to get to her before the massive army of River-bots did.

Making an impromptu decision, she took the only escape route available to her. She spun and slid between crates on the shelf behind her. Sophia felt the pinches of metal hands as she inched her way through the tight space. One snagged her cape, but she yanked it away as she dove for the other side of the shelf and came out on another aisle.

Thankfully it was empty since many of the River-bots had been on their way to Jen or over to Sophia. However, the ones passing the aisle where she was halted at the sight of her, quickly changing direction and making for her. They moved fast, and there were so many of them.

Again blocked in, Sophia ducked under the next shelf and slid between various paper goods. She did this several more times, hoping to cut the River-bots off before they got to the CEO.

Disaster button, she said urgently to Lunis. *Where was it?*

Although he didn't say anything, she could feel the regret in his mood.

I passed it already, didn't I? she asked with dread.

I can't be certain, he told her. *I don't even know what it was. Maybe it played disco music or opened the roof so spaceships could take off.*

Or if it was red and covered, it was an emergency button, Sophia offered, continuing to slide between stocked River products and make her way to the front. In her peripheral vision, she noticed the River-bots were on to her strategy and following her.

Well, if there's a disaster button on the ground floor, Sophia said already breathless, *it stands to reason Jen has one up there.*

Except if she does, why hasn't she pressed it? Lunis asked.

Good point, Sophia agreed, realizing the marching was still echoing at the front of the warehouse. The River-bots hadn't been disabled, as she would have expected.

Why can't she stop her own creations? Sophia asked her dragon, hoping he had some insight since she was running out of options. She was about to slip through a shelf to the other side as she had been doing when she spied a set of River-bots moving on the other side, about to cut her off.

Sophia didn't know what they would do if they caught her. They wanted her alive. She was their human. However, she was certain she'd be held against her will. Would they "recruit" other humans to keep them from getting lonely? The possibilities of what the River-bots could do if left unchecked were beyond scary.

I'm not sure why Jen Hendricks hasn't shut down the River-bots, Lunis answered her. *You've run out of horizontal escape routes.*

Sophia found out what he'd meant when she tried to backtrack and realized they were surrounding her on the floor. She looked up at the metal shelves towering above her, reaching all the way to the tall ceilings.

Without hesitation, she jumped onto a shelf and began to scale it, although she had no idea what she'd do once she got away.

Looking over her shoulder, she was grateful to find the River-bots were simply staring up at her, watching her getting ever higher.

They have to have a way to get to the top shelf, though, Lunis mused, squashing the hope rising in her.

Yeah, and I think it's coming my way, she said, noticing a lift speeding in her direction.

If I could get to you, I would, Lunis told her, fear entering his tone.

I know you would. She was near the top, some fifty feet up.

I'll scorch the roof until I bust through if you want, he offered. *Or crash through the glass domes.*

Sophia shook her head. *Hopefully it won't come to that.*

She was still holding out hope she could help the River-bots and save the CEO of the company, but it was dissipating by the second.

When at the top, Sophia found herself on a shelf crammed with products. She had little space to negotiate around the large boxes. The lift was in place and quickly rising in her direction.

As quickly as she could, she moved toward the center of the warehouse where the main row was, the one that stood right in front of the balcony where Jen had been standing.

The hum of the lift moving up and in her direction spiked her adrenaline, and Sophia rushed around a large crate. Her boot slipped off the edge of the shelf, and she fell off the side as her other foot slid off too.

Thankfully she caught the rim of the shelf before she plummeted to the concrete floor below.

Whoa, Lunis said with a gasp as she hung, her legs dangling.

I'm okay, she reassured him. She was breathless and not happy. Hiking up her leg, she climbed back onto the shelf, but she had only a few inches to stand. The crate behind her was taking up most of the room and nearly sent her off the shelf again.

The robots on the lifts were making progress after her near-fall.

Go! Lunis exclaimed.

Sophia nodded and sucked in a breath. She was going to have to move much faster. She reached for the top of the crate in front of her and pulled herself onto it. A line of crates ran the length of the shelf. Although the ceiling was close to her head, she could run if she ducked.

Sophia took off, keeping her strides close together since the crates were uneven and she feared tripping and falling off the shelf again. When she came to the edge of one crate, she leaped to the next one. They were only about four feet long, which made for a strange pace as she ran and jumped over and over. Sophia had made good progress and managed to gain some distance from the River-bots on the lift.

When she came to the edge of the shelf, she peered down to find a sea of River-bots looking up at her from the floor. She wasn't sure if she should be grateful that most of them seemed more interested in her than in Jen. On the far side of the warehouse, she spied the CEO frantically trying to get through the door they'd come through from her office. It appeared to be locked. Marching up the stairs, chanting something she couldn't make out, was a neat line of River-bots—undeterred as they closed in on Jen Hendricks.

Sophia needed to get to her and help her. She also needed to survive. Going down wasn't an option.

She looked at the shelf opposite her and gulped. It appeared the only way was to jump.

CHAPTER EIGHTY-FIVE

L ife and death moments were becoming more common in Sophia's life, she realized as she shoved off all concern for self-preservation and backed up on the shelf.

Thankfully the end of the shelf had a bit more room, but not much. It gave her roughly two feet of narrow space and about six feet across the shelf to get her running start before jumping. Employing combat magic to ensure she cleared the row below would be key.

She would have to leap at least fifteen feet to the next shelf, which she'd done in training. However, in the heat of the moment with robots looking at her from the floor and a crazed CEO's safety margin dwindling by the second, she was all nerves.

You can do it, Lunis encouraged just before she took off.

Sophia nodded, needing to hear that. She ran forward and launched herself off the edge of the shelf, combining the action with a spell. At first, she worried it hadn't worked as she started to descend fast, falling below the top of the shelf. However, it was enough to get her across the space, and she landed in a crouched position on the second to the top shelf.

Better to have made it a bit lower than not at all, Lunis offered.

Sophia took in a giant breath as she continued on, using the momentum to propel her forward. She knew if she paused, the fear would take over and she might hesitate on the next jump. A single hesitation would be the death of her.

Over and over, Sophia leaped across the aisles from shelf to shelf, most of the time barely clearing the space. Many times, she had to catch the edge with her hands and pull herself up. A few times, her boot slipped off the side before she rolled forward and regained her balance. Sophia never stopped or allowed herself a moment to consider quitting. Not until she came to the last shelf that faced the balcony where Jen Hendricks stood, stuck and about to be attacked, did Sophia pause and consider what to do next.

CHAPTER EIGHTY-SIX

T*he finish line is just ahead,* Lunis said in her head.

It was exactly what Sophia needed to hear because she was starting to lose hope. A sea of River-bots was marching in her direction, filling up every available space. Wildly, Sophia searched the area between her and the stairs. She didn't know how she'd get there without being blocked by a robot. They'd never let her close to Jen, who they obviously wanted dead. Now that she was closer, she could hear what the River-bots were chanting.

"Down with the human who keeps away the humans," they said in a chorus. It sounded strange in their robotic voices. A pleading for companionship from a bunch of workers who were expected to be socially independent and work nonstop without the normal hierarchy of needs. It just proved to Sophia never to doubt the need for socialization.

You're going to have to sacrifice a few of the River-bots, Lunis said in her head, voicing the one thing Sophia was trying to find a workaround for.

She sighed. *I know. I just was hoping not to. They are living beings now.*

They are flawed, Lunis argued. *You can save most of them, but you won't be able to save any or Jen Hendricks unless you sacrifice a few.*

Sophia let out a breath full of regret, staring down at the floor below. *I think it's going to be more than a few.*

Yeah, Lunis agreed. *I realize that. Just clear your path.*

Knowing what her dragon intended for her to do, Sophia threw her shoulder into the large crate next to her. It was heavy and huge. After three concerted thrusts, she was able to push the box over the edge, where it crashed to the floor, crushing several River-bots. The attack started a domino effect, making many of the robots around the impact topple back onto one another.

Knowing time was of the essence, Sophia grabbed the bottom of the shelf and swung herself over the side, jumping onto the one below. Again, she got behind a huge crate and this time shoved it over the side with the first push, launching it a few yards before it exploded onto the River-bots below.

Not only did this nearly clear the path to the balcony, but it had stolen the attention of the robots marching up to the landing where Jen Hendricks stood still trying to get through the door.

Knowing this was probably her best chance, Sophia leaped off the third from the top shelf, bracing herself for the long jump and fall.

It was thirty feet, which wasn't too dangerous for a dragonrider, but when landing on broken bits and pieces of robots and other debris, it wasn't an ideal scenario. Still, the height ensured Sophia crossed much of the distance in her single jump.

She landed on the concrete floor littered with the body parts of River-bots a lot harder than she would have liked. She didn't pay attention to the assault her body took in the process. Instead, she rolled out of the jump as she shot up her hand.

Using a spell that was typically effective on magitech, Sophia shot a neat blast of red at the River-bots lining the stairs leading up to the balcony.

She couldn't help but notice the hurt expressions that marked their faces as the first attack hit them. It struck the closest one in the chest, sending it back into the one behind it. Realizing her mistake and that she only had so much magic left for another combat spell, Sophia aimed the next spell toward the top of the staircase.

It knocked straight into one near the top, making it explode before somersaulting forward, rolling into its companions on the stairs. As before, they fell into each other like dominos. However, Sophia's strategy had created a bigger problem. She didn't have a way to the top where Jen Hendricks stood, and a few River-bots were closing in, having escaped Sophia's attacks.

You have a bit of magic left, Lunis insisted forcefully.

With her chin in the air and the knowledge that more River-bots were closing in on her, Sophia tried to dig into her dragon's brain to figure out what he meant. Then it occurred to her, and she couldn't fathom how it hadn't before. She should have summoned the Christmas present Wilder had given her ages ago.

Just carry it on you full-time, Lunis said with a laugh, relieved she'd taken the hint.

Sophia held out her hand, and a moment later, the grappling hook Wilder had given her materialized. She felt the drain on her magic. It would have to be replenished before she could do anything more than simple spells.

She held up the grappling hook and pointed it at the railing next to Jen Hendricks.

Hopefully this was the beginning of the end and she could resolve the rest of this situation with words, she thought.

Or your sword, Lunis said as she launched the grappling hook.

CHAPTER EIGHTY-SEVEN

Velocity Girl, Lunis cheered as Sophia sped toward the catwalk. The River-bots were close, but her arrival had momentarily stalled them. They didn't seem to know whether to go after Jen Hendricks, who was standing by the door, or Sophia, who had proven to be an enemy. She understood that would be their perception.

Moving as fast as she could, Sophia jumped over the railing and threw herself in front of the CEO of River Corporation as she drew her sword and pointed it at the robots.

She swung the sword at the first of the River-bots.

"Stay back!" Sophia warned.

"Sophia Beaufont is no friend of ours," it said, continuing forward.

Oh, hell, Sophia thought, confirming that her actions had appeared nefarious to the robots.

She glanced over her shoulder to Jen, who was up against the door. "Why can't you get through?"

"The River-bots have locked it," Jen explained, putting her hand to the wall. The action had unlocked it before, but now it remained solid, the door not sliding back into the recesses.

"You don't have an override function?" Sophia asked frantically, swishing Inexorabilis and trying to discourage the River-bots from coming any closer.

"They are the override," she said, indicating the robots.

Sophia sighed. "Are you serious? You put them in charge of everything?"

"They were reliable," Jen said in a rush. "Much more so than humans, who make mistakes."

Shaking her head, Sophia paused to appreciate the irony in the fleeting moment. "Yet, they've taken over and rebelled because you took the flawed humans away from them."

"What?" Jen asked, shock in her voice.

The advancing River-bots were dangerously close. Fighting them would only make them more distrustful of Sophia. She made the potentially hazardous decision to sheathe her sword.

"What are you doing?" Jen demanded. She looked like she might take the sword from Sophia, her eyes crazy with worry.

"I'm not fighting them," Sophia stated. "They will only attack if they think I'm going to hurt them. They aren't going to stop until you give them what they want."

"What?" Jen's gaze was darting around wildly.

Sophia spun around as she felt the cold metal of the closest River-bot. It grabbed her from behind and hauled her off her feet. She didn't fight the creature. Instead, she looked at Jen Hendricks.

"They want their humans back," she said with conviction in her voice.

"What?" Jen questioned. "Humans?" She shook her head. "No, they messed up everything. Our human resource issues were miles long. Productivity and behavioral problems. You name it, humans were becoming the real liability of this company. I fixed all that."

To Sophia's surprise, the River-bot just clutched her in its iron grasp and held her unmoving. Beside it, the other robots formed a semicircle around the CEO.

"You didn't fix it," Sophia argued. "You simply created a bigger problem. There will be problems in every organization. It's inevitable. Trying to erase human error is like trying to erase the human population." She swept her gaze at the warehouse where the River-bots stood at attention, none of them working as they watched those on the balcony. "You can't have robots without humans. They miss them."

Jen shook her head. "They are machines and need reprogramming."

Sophia's eyes darted to the claw marks on Jen's neck and wrist. "Is that what you've been doing? Reprogramming the ones that rebel?"

"It's all that needed to happen for the last several months," Jen explained. "Just a flaw in their systems."

"A few months?" Sophia asked. "You've been patching up this problem for months? The River-bots have been growing more anxious. They knew you wouldn't give them their humans back and you would reprogram them. They have been hiding their human behavior while planning this rebellion."

"Human behavior?" Jen questioned with disbelief.

"Yeah, you didn't see it because you wouldn't come onto the warehouse floor after getting attacked and realizing there was a problem with their programming," Sophia explained, having worked it out. "You knew something was wrong but wouldn't face it."

"Humans…things are better without them," Jen argued.

Sophia shook her head. "You think things are better, but think of all those people you eliminated who needed a job. The River-bots are magitech. They are part human and need the connection. You can't discount that. Even if River isn't as successful or efficient, there are some things that are more important." She dared to look at the River-bots who seemed perched and ready to attack, their red eyes glowing. "Advancement without consideration of far-reaching effects isn't progress. It's negligence."

Jen considered this. She was no doubt a genius and a savvy businessperson. She ran a company that had changed the world, and what she decided next would be life or death for her and possibly Sophia.

Letting out a weighty breath, she regarded the River-bots, her expression shifting into one of regret. With tears in her eyes, she looked at the closest River-bots. "I'm sorry. I didn't realize what I was doing was harming you so much." Shame was heavy in her gaze. "I never even thought of you as 'you.' Only its. Sophia is right, and you are part-human. I should have known that better than anyone. I didn't want to believe it because then I would have to acknowledge what I now know to be true. You can't live without humans. Just as the world has entered into the twenty-first century and can't live without technology. We are intertwined now. Probably forevermore."

CHAPTER EIGHTY-EIGHT

Chocolate never tasted so good as after a grueling battle where Sophia had nearly drained most of her reserves.

She and Lunis sat on the top of the Seattle Space Needle, looking out over the city and Puget Sound as the clouds rolled across the sky.

After they'd wrapped up at River Corporation, Lunis had flown them up to the top of the Space Needle. Currently they were hanging their feet over the side and dangling them like kids as mortals filled the observation deck below them.

So, thanks to you, I think my new Doctor Who poster will take two days rather than one to get delivered, Lunis said, lounging on his back, his round belly soaking up the rare Seattle sun.

Sophia, not finding the rooftop of the Space Needle as delightful as the views, scooted over until she was leaning back against her dragon. "You mean, thanks to us. Deal with it. I think the world should have to sacrifice a bit of convenience and immediate gratification for love and connectedness."

Lunis growled with satisfaction when Sophia wiggled back into him. She knew without him saying it he'd been worried several times for her safety when she'd been in the River warehouse with the robots. It was their life, though, and it never was going to get easier. If they were fulfilling their destiny, there would always be a danger. There would always be battles and conflict they would have to intervene in. She couldn't think of anyone she'd rather fight alongside.

Well, it looks like the employment structure of River will be changing drastically, Lunis said, his belly rising and falling, a calming motion for Sophia to experience.

"Yeah, it's not going to be what it was recently or what it was before," she explained, having helped Jen Hendricks revamp the entire company structure. "It's going to be something brand new."

That is evolution, Lunis agreed, watching seagulls streak across the waters of the Puget Sound.

Sophia enjoyed the soft breeze that coasted up the structure of the Space Needle and tangled her hair. She had never been afraid of heights, which was probably a prerequisite for being a dragonrider. Right then it made her feel like she was the queen of the world, sitting high above her kingdom and dangling her feet over the edge, thinking of the good and true things she'd do.

That was a very chancy move on your part, putting away your sword at River Corporation, Lunis said, his tone slightly scolding.

She shrugged. "My instinct told me to. We can't always fight."

Always, he repeated. *That is the way of the dragons.*

Sophia nodded. "And the Dragon Elite, I believe. I don't think it has to be my way. Or yours, depending on your style."

My style is yours, he told her. *We magnetized to one another for a reason. More importantly than us, I think this is a sign of things to come for the new generation of riders and dragons.*

Sophia looked back at him, surprised. "You do? Really? You don't think I'll be the only anomaly?" She nearly laughed at her choice of words. She knew Hiker was perplexed by how she dealt with her missions, choosing strategy over force, but he was also impressed by her results. Hopefully the way she dealt with this mission would add to that reputation.

No, I think we've set trends others will follow, Lunis began. *There are many eggs to hatch, all a result of you becoming the first female dragonrider. They are being hatched in a modern world and will magnetize to modern* riders. *There's a new balance coming to the Dragon Elite they've never had before, so how can we expect it to be what it was before.*

"This balance?" Sophia took a bite of her chocolate bar and relished its richness.

Well, the Dragon Elite was always missing one important element that you fulfilled, Lunis said, closing his eyelids as the sunlight kissed them through the clouds crossing over the Puget Sound.

"Oh?" she asked.

Femininity doesn't belong only to the females on this planet, Lunis explained. *It is in all of us, and masculinity too. Now the Dragon Elite has both in representation. I only wonder if it will be balanced out in terms of leadership.*

"You mean, in terms of getting Hiker to stop being such a manly Viking?" Sophia joked.

He shook his head. *No, I mean, I wonder if there's a need for more leadership at some point.*

Sophia sat up, not having expected this answer. "Oh?"

It stands to reason that one day there will be a lot more dragons and riders at the Gullington, Lunis continued. *Although one leader is sufficient now, when there are more riders, it seems like we'll need more leadership. One who is concerned with combat and another who is about strategy.*

This was the first time she'd heard Lunis speak like this. "Wow. I'm not sure. I mean, if you mean me…"

You're a natural leader, Soph. The men already follow you, although you have less experience and are much younger. It just proves to me that leadership is inborn in so many ways.

Sophia wasn't sure Lunis was right. She knew the Dragon Elite was soon to go through its own evolution. That was inevitable as more eggs hatched. Things were going to have to change because the Dragon Elite would soon need to rule in a world where the old rules didn't apply.

Just my observations, Lunis said when she didn't reply. *My observations from above an observation deck, so take them for what they are worth.*

Sophia finished her chocolate, her stomach asking for more. It was probably her magic needing a bit more to be fully replenished. "Your observations are always the best, Lun."

So what's next? her dragon asked, sensing she was feeling restless after the short respite.

"I think I need to pay Mae Ling a visit." Sophia stretched to a standing position, enjoying how much better the view got as she rose to her feet.

Because you have a craving for the best brownies in the world? Lunis teased.

Sophia nodded. "Also because I've got a boatload of cases and not enough information on where to start."

Lunis shook his head. *I don't sympathize with your workload.*

She cut her eyes at him. "What do you mean? My workload is yours too."

He shrugged, which was always a funny thing to see her dragon do. *It is, but I get to observe and consult while lounging and eating bonbons and watching my soap operas.*

Sophia laughed. "You don't do any of that."

Giving her a wolfish grin, Lunis said, "You're right. Usually I don't lounge."

CHAPTER EIGHTY-NINE

Wild horses galloped across the pastures outside of Happily Ever After College. A group of students stood close by, most looking fearful at the prospect of getting trampled by the parading horses, their tangled manes flying like flags in the wind.

The thundering sound their hooves made as they circled the girls in their school uniforms nearly drowned out Mae Ling's voice.

"They can sense your fear," the fairy godmother/professor said, shaking her head at the pupils. "If you want to tame a wild beast, you have to embrace the wild part of yourself."

She stepped in front of a black stallion racing in her direction, its head down and black eyes menacing.

Without a care for her safety, Mae Ling kept her gaze on the students and held up a single hand to the racing horse.

Sophia held her breath, watching from a distance. The students gasped loudly. One screamed.

The small, unassuming woman didn't flinch as the beasts roared in her direction. It seemed obvious Mae Ling was about to be run over. There would be no way to save her that Sophia could see.

The fairy godmother kept her hand out, her expression stone.

The black stallion whinnied loudly, but it produced zero reaction from Mae Ling.

Inches from the woman's extended hand, the horse came to an abrupt halt, kicking up soil and sod onto Mae Ling's shoes. Instantly, the wild horse kneeled and bowed its head to the fairy godmother.

A pleased expression crossed her face and she nodded to the animal.

"Rise," she commanded, and the horse followed her order, rearing and towering over her.

Around the class and the instructor, the other animals continued to streak over the field, not going unnoticed by many of the pupils who were clinging to each other.

Mae Ling lovingly petted the horse's head before returning her attention to the class. "You see, nature always reflects back on itself. If you want to tame the wild, then first tame yourself. Once you do, then they will do your bidding."

She circled her hand and the black stallion transformed into a giant stretch limousine.

"Oohs" and "Aahs" fell from the girls' mouths. Sophia echoed their reaction as she approached, careful to give the frolicking horses a wide berth.

"To transform creatures, you must first tame them," Mae Ling instructed. "You can and should be able to tame any animal to do your bidding, but only if you practice."

Mae Ling snapped her fingers and the black limo became a horse once more. He shook his head, his mane flying around him before he stomped the ground.

She pointed to the horses, still circling. "Each of you take one of those wild horses. Tame them by conquering your fear. I expect these grounds to be full of luxury cars within an hour. For those who fail, healers are standing by." She indicated the front of Happily Ever After College, where three magicians regarded the class with cautious gazes.

Sophia gulped, grateful she didn't have to do most of her training as trial by fire. Wilder had thrown her off a cliff once to see how she'd employ her training. She later punched him in the arm for it, but he just smiled and admitted he deserved that…and much more.

Most of the students seemed to share Sophia's thoughts on this training exercise that could result in them needing to have bones and such mended by healers. However, she assumed most of them were probably more afraid of Mae Ling's wrath than being trampled by the wild stallions because they parted from one another when the instructor clapped her hands and yelled, "Go on then. Get to taming."

As the students dispersed and began choosing horses, Mae Ling made her way over to Sophia with a smile on her face that lit up her brown eyes.

"You're hungry," she stated rather than asked after running a cursory glance over Sophia.

"Well, I had a chocolate bar a bit ago, but yeah," Sophia answered.

Mae Ling shook her head. "After expending that much magic at River, that's not enough to refill your reserves." She snapped her fingers and a picnic basket appeared on the pristine grass next to the black stallion, which was now calmly grazing like a tame horse and taking no notice of her.

She gave the animal a hesitant expression before Mae Ling waved off the concern.

"He won't hurt you," the fairy godmother told her. "If you want a place to sit, he'd make a great booth or a long table and chairs."

Sophia shook her head, having a hard time wrapping her head around sitting at a table that was actually a horse. It was apparently common with fairy godmothers, and since they didn't seem to do any wrong, she should probably warm to the idea, she reasoned.

Kneeling on the grass, she opened the picnic basket, the aroma of the best chocolate wafting from the container.

She looked up, her eyes wide with excitement. "Freshly baked brownies?"

Mae Ling nodded proudly. "That's what you ordered, isn't it?"

"Well, I had a passing craving," Sophia said. "I wouldn't call it an order."

Mae Ling shrugged. "Same thing as far as I'm concerned."

Sophia sat tailor style in the grass next to the basket and looked up at her fairy godmother. "How do you know so much? I mean, I get there's magic involved, but it's more than that with you."

The other woman nodded understandingly. "It's a connection fairy godmothers form with their charges. We may not be able to find where we parked our car or know our own shoe sizes, but I'm highly connected to you and know your fleeting and stable emotions. I feel them as if they were my own." She indicated the girls in the distance, some of them successful with taming their wild horses and others fleeing, the beasts running after them. "If I train them right, they will have that with their Cinderellas too, but…" As she trailed away, her face was suddenly crestfallen. "I worry the next generation of fairy godmothers will have new problems." She sighed, dismissing the notion with a wave of her hand. "That's not why you came here. Please ask me what you will."

Sophia took a bite of one of the warm brownies, relishing the crispy edges surrounding the warm, chewy center. "Oh, my angels, that's delicious."

Mae Ling nodded. "Naturally."

"Anyway, I was hoping you'd learned something about how to help Ainsley," Sophia started, noticing the gooey fudge on her fingertips. She was about to lick it off when a napkin materialized in her lap. "Thank you."

Mae Ling began to take a seat, but when Sophia thought she'd land on her tail bone, the fairy godmother sank into a large, overstuffed pink velvet armchair. She sighed as though taking a load off was completely overdue.

"When do you plan on going up that beanstalk with Hiker?" she asked, calmly folding her hands in her lap.

Sophia finished her bite and wiped her mouth. "Well, I had a meeting and then an impromptu case and—"

Mae Ling waved off the reasons. "Those things needed to take precedence. Also, Hiker needed to manage the situation with the city of New York. It's good for him to flex his diplomatic muscles. Helping

Ainsley starts with fixing Hiker, and I'm sorry to say that won't be easy."

Sophia's thirst hadn't registered until a glass of ice-cold milk in a frosted mug appeared in front of her. She nodded appreciatively. "Thank you. The beanstalk mission will fix Hiker?"

Mae Ling gave her a kind smile. "It has the potential to help him to find balance for his powers, which is key to the solution, but no. Mending things for those two is not going to be easy and will require many different strategies." She sighed heavily. "I can't guarantee they will work. That's the thing…" The fairy godmother looked around the grounds of the school. "What we do here at Happily Ever After isn't an exact science. Issues of the heart are never black and white and solutions are relative, depending on the person. It's funny that this school is called Happily Ever After because there is rarely a happy ending. Usually it's a series of happy things punctuated with new beginnings caused by something that is not so happy. You see, no one ever starts over because everything is okay. Without beginnings, there are no new chapters in the storybook."

Sophia took in the complex things her fairy godmother had shared with her. It made sense, and yet it made her head hurt.

"So, Hiker and I need to go up the beanstalk," Sophia mused, regarding her brownie as if it were a map that offered the key to her next question. "Any clues about what we will find up there?"

"An experience," Mae Ling said simply.

Sophia nodded, realizing she should have expected that answer.

"You know," Mae Ling began, a speculative glint in her wise eyes. "The leader of the Dragon Elite has lived many unfulfilling years since the events occurred that changed everything for him, Ainsley, the dragonriders, and the world. He's lived with a lot of regrets during that time. A lot of frustration. Those emotions have a way of coloring the way one sees the past. I'd go so far as to say they make one forget what happened or tell it differently in their heads."

"That makes sense," Sophia related. "It has been a very long time."

"If there's a way to show Hiker what he's forgotten, or who he used to be, well, that could have far-reaching effects," Mae Ling hinted.

Sophia thought for a long moment. The pointed expression her fairy godmother was giving her was because she was waiting for her to figure the answer out on her own. She worried she wasn't going to and it would lead to a riddle—which she loathed. Then an idea popped into her head.

"The gold token!" she exclaimed. "I have the reset point, and that will take anyone back to events that happened right before the Great War."

Mae Ling grinned at her proudly. "That's right, my child. I'd advise using it for any other task you need it for first."

"Oh," Sophia said, remembering she needed the gold token to visit the Midnight Lunar Eclipse. "Why is that?"

Mae Ling toggled her head back and forth. "Just take my word for it."

There was the riddle. Sophia just nodded, glad for the amount of information she got.

The fairy godmother turned her focus to the students trying to wrangle wild horses in the distance. A few had been successful at turning theirs into luxury vehicles, but some had transformed theirs into junker cars or mopeds.

Mae Ling stood and the armchair behind her disappeared. "Well, it appears a teacher's job is never done. I'll leave you to your missions."

CHAPTER NINETY

Hands open, Sophia created a portal to Roya Lane. She held out her hand to her sister, indicating she should walk through first.

Liv gave her a hesitant expression. "If Rudolf Sweetwater is on the other side of this portal, I'm running back through before he can talk at me."

Sophia laughed. "Why would he be on Roya Lane? It's late."

It was true King Rudolf was often on Roya Lane, running errands or campaigning or having a silent disco. However, Sophia thought it was unlikely he was hanging out there at this time. They'd decided to go to the magical candy shop, Midnight Lunar Eclipse, since Liv didn't have any missions until bright and early the next morning. Good for them, it didn't matter when they went to Roya Lane, only that they were there when they used the reset point because it made it more likely it would put them in that spot, which was where they needed to be to visit the candy shop. If they were at the House of Fourteen, it would show them events during the reset point at that location. Same with the Castle or any other place they were.

"Ru is always on Roya Lane when I go there," Liv grumbled. "It's like he knows I'm about to show up there and I need a headache."

Sophia laughed. "Yeah, I see him there a lot too."

"He needs to get a job," Liv said, shaking her head before stepping through the shimmering portal.

Sophia continued to be amused by her sister as she stepped through. She was glad she stepped through immediately after Liv. As soon as she did and saw the scene in front of her, she closed the portal before her sister could escape.

Liv stopped short of the portal closing and gave Sophia an annoyed expression. "He's here."

"Of course I'm here!" Rudolf called loudly. "It's Mother's Day, so where else would I be?"

Sophia waved at King Rudolf as Liv spun around.

"Oh, I don't know," Liv said, annoyance in her tone. "How about with your children?"

He sighed as if about to educate the magician. "No, my sweet little blonde bimbo. Mother's Day is when the Captains' mum has to care for them. Hence the name, Mother's Day." He rolled his eyes. "I'm not considered a genius by most standards, but I know that. I really thought you would too."

"By most standards?" Liv grilled. "Don't you mean by any standards?"

Like he hadn't heard the questions, he tilted his head, a question ruminating in his eyes. "Have you considered going to college, Liv? I mean, you need to be able to rely on your brains since you don't have the luxury of leaning on your good looks like me."

Sophia spied Liv roll up her fists and could tell she was restraining herself. The Warrior was obviously overworked and not in the mood to deal with the king of the fae.

"What are you doing here?" Sophia interjected, trying to break up the tension.

Rudolf blinked at her and shook his head. "Wow, this cluelessness runs in the Beaufont family." He pointed to the ground. "I'm standing here. It's pretty obvious to most, but I guess that escapes you sisters."

"Right," Liv said, drawing out the word. "Well, we'd stay and chat, but I don't want to get prosecuted for your death."

"Oh, too bad because it was brilliant timing that I ran into you both," Rudolf began. "I have a business proposition for you."

"No," Liv pronounced flatly.

Rudolf gave her an offended expression. "I'm sorry, I've not gone through the normal niceties. Let's try again, shall we?"

"No," Liv chirped again.

Good naturedly, Rudolf smiled, undeterred. "How great is your day so far?"

Liv sighed. "First off, don't suppose my day is great. That's putting words in my mouth. Secondly, I'm talking to you, so there's less great about my day. Actually, do you have a painkiller?"

Rudolf patted his pockets and shook his head. "No, do you have a headache?"

Liv shook her head. "No, but I will very soon. I always do after talking to you."

The fae frowned. "Do you think it's my cologne? Maybe my devilishly good looks that take your breath away? Or the fact that you can never have me causing you despair?"

Liv gave Sophia a commiserate expression. "No, I'm certain it's nothing like that. Never mind. I'll get over it. Just talk fast and tell me what you want."

Sophia realized Liv knew Rudolf wasn't going to leave them alone until he got an audience with them. She also knew that although Liv was more stressed than usual, her annoyance at Rudolf was mostly an act. The Warrior was endeared to the king of the fae who had walked her down the aisle. He was like family, and as with any family member, they had the ability to get on one's nerves but were also loved unconditionally.

"Well," Rudolf started, flashing a convincing grin at the sisters. "I was wondering if one of you had access to that treasure trove of dragon eggs we've heard so much about."

Liv turned to Sophia. "Do I punch him in the face, or do you want to?"

She didn't even feel like laughing at this, her protective instinct kicking in. "What do you want with the dragon eggs?" Sophia asked Rudolf.

"I actually don't want the dragons," Rudolf declared, holding up his hands as if in surrender. He must have sensed his life was in danger. "I just want the shells after they hatch. Liv, I thought I could work with you and Hester at the House of Fourteen to create a concoction with the ingredient to help disadvantaged fae and magicians."

Liv's mouth fell open. Sophia was even momentarily stunned.

"Rudolf, for as brain-dead as I always think you are, you have some surprisingly brilliant moments," Liv remarked, awe in her voice.

Sophia had to agree. "The dragon eggs are useless to us after the dragons hatch."

"They would have medicinal properties if used by the right people who know what they are doing," Liv mused, working out the details in her head. "It will probably require some other special ingredients and clearance from the council."

"That's where you come in," Rudolf told Liv before turning his attention to Sophia. "If you don't need the eggshells, then we'd take them off your hands, make them into potions and find disadvantaged magicians and fae they could help."

Liv nodded, excitement building in her eyes. "Yes, they could cure many ailments like disease, arthritis, chronic ailments—"

"Ugliness," Rudolf stated. "I thought it would mostly be used to cure ugly magicians so the rest of us didn't have to look at their faces."

Liv deflated. "There's the Rudolf we all know and loathe."

He smiled wide, showing a toothy grin. "I love you too, but the word is pronounced with a 'v' dear Liv."

She shook her head and looked at Sophia. "It's a good idea. Do you think we can have the shells?"

"I don't see why not," Sophia agreed.

"Okay, well, when we're not traveling into the past or saving the mortal world, let's look into this project," Liv said.

"In the meantime," Rudolf instructed and winked at the sisters as he backed away, "you girls read a book. Enroll in a college class. You know, get an education."

CHAPTER NINETY-ONE

"Called out in the dark," Liv began when Rudolf had disappeared and Roya Lane was mostly theirs. "All to find a stick of magical chewing gum."

It appeared the House of Fourteen was doing as they promised and enforcing having magicians stay inside at night. Hopefully this would prevent any of them from going missing by Mika Lenna's hands. Although it was unlikely the diabolically evil man could get onto Roya Lane since he wasn't a magical creature and didn't have portal magic, it was best not to underestimate the crazy Frankenstein.

For that reason, the House of Fourteen had dictated that no magicians could be out after hours, even on Roya Lane. It appeared they were listening, and even other magical creatures were heeding the warning, as none of them were present on the dark street.

Taking in the eerie sight of the empty street usually congested with shifty gnomes making bad deals and elves pushing their hippie agendas, Sophia had the urge to run up and down the road singing loudly.

"Now would be the perfect opportunity to film that horror movie we've wanted to do," Liv said, a sneaky grin on her face.

Sophia gave her a confused expression. "Horror movie? I missed the memo on that aspiration."

Her sister shrugged. "A film noir, then? Or a parody, maybe? I'm good with whatever. It's just a good opportunity to take advantage of this as a film set."

Laughing, Sophia shook her head. "I think that project will have to wait. Magic chewing gum, remember?"

Liv sighed. "Yeah, that's right. What does it do again?"

"It's supposed to make the chewer happy no matter what," Sophia explained, remembering what Lee from the Crying Cat Bakery had told her when prepping her for the upcoming mission.

"And the reason you need that?" Liv asked.

"I don't know. Lee hasn't told me yet, or even where to find the magical katana once I collect all the ingredients for this mission. I'm apparently on a need to know basis."

"Which reminds me," Liv said, digging into her cloak. She pulled out various things, shaking her head at them, the objects obviously not what she was looking for. "Here, hold this for me while I find where it is." She stuck a broken yoyo, a plastic unicorn, and a jar of putty in Sophia's hands before she knew what was happening.

Glancing down at the random objects, Sophia giggled. "What, did you raid a kindergarten classroom? What is all this?"

Liv shook her head. "Don't pet the unicorn unless you want to be flattened by its real form. I've made that mistake by accident a time or two."

Sophia gave her a sister a skeptical expression. "You're not serious? This isn't a real unicorn."

"Not right now, it's not," Liv answered, continuing to dig around. "Pet him and call him Polly, and you'll learn unicorns are real fast."

Sophia shivered, remembering meeting the Phantom, a dark unicorn she'd had to defeat to bond to her mother's sword, Inexorabilis. "I'm well aware they are real. Actually, did you know they are Scotland's national animal?"

Liv nodded, still digging around in her pockets. "Because it can defeat the lion."

Blinking at her with astonishment, Sophia shook her head. "How do you know that, and why do they need to defeat lions?"

"Because I don't sleep," Liv told her. "The lion was commonly used to represent English royalty."

"Oh, sneaky Scots," Sophia said admiringly.

"Really, if anyone's animal should be a unicorn, it should be yours," her sister commented absentmindedly, handing over more strange items.

"Why a unicorn? Why not a dragon? That seems like the obvious choice for me."

"Dragon?" Liv asked, looking up, confused. "Why a dragon?"

Sighing, Sophia shook her head. "Because of having a dragon. You know, being a dragonrider."

Liv stared blankly at her for a moment before returning her attention to checking her pockets. "Oh, Gerald. Right, I totally forgot about him."

"Lunis," Sophia corrected.

"I was saying that your spirit animal or whatever you want to call it should be a unicorn because of what they represent," Liv continued.

"Purity and strength?" Sophia asked.

"That," Liv agreed. "However, in many depictions of the unicorn, they could choose to use power and strength to overcome their enemies, but most of the time, they used their gifts to help others. If we believe folklore, the unicorn could have dominated all other animals, and yet, it didn't use its powers for such things."

Sophia smiled at her sister, who was still busy going through her cloak that was about like Mary Poppins' carpetbag. "Thanks. That's really nice to hear."

"Didn't say it to be nice," Liv remarked matter-of-factly. "Bam! Here it is!" She pulled out a small compass with a wide grin.

"That's the elfin made compass?" Sophia had her hands full of all the things Liv unloaded on her.

Realizing the problem when she tried to hand it over to her, Liv swiped her hand, and all the objects disappeared from Sophia's arms. "Yeah, and I'm loaning it to you for this upcoming mission."

Sophia smiled when she took the compact device. She didn't know why she needed a magical compass to get to the katana. She also didn't know anything else about the mission, like why she needed Zac Efron or magical chewing gum. "Thank you. I'll keep it safe," she said, slipping the compass into her own cloak, which wasn't as full as her sister's. There was another object in her pockets that they needed to find the Midnight Lunar Eclipse candy shop.

Sophia removed the gold token from her pocket and showed it to Liv.

"A bit unassuming for what it does, huh?" her sister asked, sounding impressed.

"Yeah."

Liv laughed. "I think the same can be said for us. Definitely for you."

Sophia smiled fondly before extending her hand to her sister. "I think this is the only way you'll travel back with me."

Liv winked. "Are you certain you just don't want to hold my hand?"

"No," Sophia teased. She activated the coin, the same way she'd done the times she'd used it at the Castle and House of Fourteen. The goal was to travel back into the past to the reset point, which was right before the Great War broke out. That also happened to be on a night of a lunar eclipse, the only time the candy shop was open.

To Sophia's surprise, the gold coin was different. Before, it had the House of Fourteen, Castle, and the Great Library on it. Now on the top right side was a road she recognized as Roya Lane. Written across all the images was the word Present.

Flipping the coin over in her fingers, Sophia read the other side: Reset Point.

She glanced up, wondering if it had worked. At first, she thought it hadn't, but then she saw the telltale signs it had and felt a wave of relief.

CHAPTER NINETY-TWO

Made of something different now, Roya Lane appeared strange in shades of black, white, and grays. That meant the gold coin had worked and they'd traveled back to the reset point.

She released Liv's hand and looked at the cobbled street. It was daytime, the moment when the reset point had been created by Father Time. He'd warned Sophia not to hang out in the reset point for too long, telling her it could be dangerous. However, for this mission, he'd cleared them to hang out there until midnight.

Something else occurred to Sophia and made her gasp with worry. "We can't be seen by those in this time period."

As before, Sophia's body had color, whereas everything around her appeared like a black and white movie.

Liv smiled triumphantly at her sister. "You think Papa Creola didn't prepare me for this? There's a reason you brought Father Time's diplomat with you on this adventure."

"Because you have the best jokes?" Sophia asked, relief filling her chest.

"There is that," Liv agreed. "Also, Papa Creola gave me this." She held up a key.

SARAH NOFFKE & MICHAEL ANDERLE

"Father Time gave you a key," Sophia teased. "Here I was worried."

Liv sighed. "The key gets us into the Fantastical Armory, which is locked on the day of the reset point because Subner was a fae then and was having a dance party."

Sophia laughed. "Poor guy. I bet he hated that."

Nodding, Liv said, "He did. Called it his 'dark age.' Anyway, inside the Fantastical Armory is an object that will help us to forward the hands of time. When we do, it will speed up today's event, putting us closer to the hour of midnight when we need to visit the candy shop."

"Awesome," Sophia chirped. "I don't see how that's going to help me to interact in this realm. Currently we are ghosts and can't touch anything, and no one can see us. How am I supposed to buy a magical stick of gum?"

The worried expression that briefly crossed Liv's face concerned Sophia. "As time progresses, we become a part of this realm. Apparently, our appearance will change to reflect that."

Sophia gave her a skeptical expression. "You mean, we'll turn to black and white, like everything here?"

Liv nodded.

Knowing this was too easy, Sophia lowered her chin. "What's the catch?"

"Well, remember how Papa Creola didn't want you to stick around in the reset point for long?"

"Yeah."

"That's because you'll become a part of this realm," Liv finished, hesitation in her tone.

"If we're not careful, we'll get stuck here, won't we?"

Liv nodded.

"Great," Sophia said, realizing she should have known a seemingly straightforward task would turn into a deadly mission. "So once all the color is drained from our appearance, we're stuck here, aren't we?"

"Don't worry." Liv pulled Sophia toward the end of Roya Lane, where the Fantastical Armory was located. "We just have to time it right. Papa Creola said we should have enough time to get to midnight and go into the candy shop and get what we need before we're fully black and white."

"How much is enough time?"

Liv shrugged. "Knowing that man, probably a few minutes."

CHAPTER NINETY-THREE

"Crack the shutters, will you?" Liv asked when they entered the dusty shop known as the Fantastical Armory. It was a pawn shop of weapons and time-related artifacts, and during the reset point, it didn't have a lick of electricity, making it difficult to see anything once they entered.

Sophia fumbled around, trying to find the switch for the shutters to open them. When she did, light flooded the old store, which looked very similar to how it did in the present time. Apparently, according to Liv, it had gone through many different appearances, much like Papa Creola and Subner, but also like them, it reverted back to old forms, rotating like the two beings it belonged to.

Scrunching up her nose, Sophia tried to refrain from sneezing from the dust she'd kicked up opening the windows. "I don't suppose Papa Creola told you what we were looking for?" she asked, scanning the glass cases filled with tons of strange objects.

Liv gave her an annoyed glare over her shoulder. "Yeah, he totally did, all while braiding my hair and sharing with me the secret to life."

Sophia laughed. "Okay, well, do you have any idea what will make us speed up time so we slowly become a part of this realm without actually becoming stuck here?"

Pulling her chin up to the many swords and archaic weapons lining the wall, Liv shook her head. "I think we can eliminate these. It doesn't make sense to me that a weapon will move time forward."

"That makes sense," Sophia agreed. "And all the armor and other combat-related stuff."

"Which just leaves…" Liv glanced at the dusty glass cases, "all the time-related artifacts."

Sophia understood the defeated tone in her sister's voice. A few hundred items littered the velvet-lined cases. "Well, we know it has to be something that turns time forward, so it's probably not going to be a stone like that, right?" She indicated a purple gem in the nearest case.

Liv narrowed her eyes, looking at what she was referring to. "Yeah, it won't be that. That's what Rudolf used to bring Serena back from the dead. Actually, go ahead and take it and destroy it."

Sophia laughed, knowing her sister wasn't serious. They wouldn't be allowed to do anything that changed future events. That was another rule regarding the reset point and going back in time.

"It won't be the hand mirror or anything like that," Liv stated, pointing to another neighboring object.

"Could it be an hourglass?" Sophia indicated a small object filled with sand.

"Good thinking, but I don't think so," Liv answered. "We need something that moves us forward on the timeline, and I don't see how an hourglass could do that since the sand currently sits halfway between the two halves."

Sophia realized she was right as she regarded the object lying on its side. She studied other objects in the case, trying to work out what could move them forward. Then something occurred to her and her mouth popped open.

"What?" Liv asked, spying the reaction on her sister's face.

"Well, I think it's you who taught me the most obvious solutions are usually the best."

Liv nodded. "Yes, because our father taught me that."

Well," Sophia said, tapping the case nearest to her, "I think if we want to move forward in time, but at a very deliberate pace we can control, this would be the right choice."

Liv leaned forward to see what she was referring to. When she saw it, she smiled. "You're a genius. Yes, the obvious is probably the correct answer here."

CHAPTER NINETY-FOUR

"Hold on," Liv said, checking her person.

"What are you doing?" Sophia asked, holding the gold pocket watch in her hand. It made the most sense out of all the objects they had to choose from. To both of their surprise, it was the only watch in the entire shop. One would have thought Father Time's store of magical objects would have more than one watch.

When Sophia had pointed out her guess of what would speed up time and put them into the realm, Liv was certain she was right. Her reasoning was based on an experience she'd had when she first came into the Fantastical Armory.

Apparently, Papa Creola had made her destroy most of the objects that controlled time, afraid they'd get into the wrong hands. Their mother had been instrumental in rounding up many of the objects, but for Papa Creola, that wasn't enough. He needed them to be erased from the Earth so they never fell into the wrong hands.

The timeline was a bit wonky, according to Liv. They were way back in the past before their mother was born. So that meant many of the objects in the Fantastical Armory would go missing and spread across the globe, giving Guinevere Beaufont the responsibility to round them up one day. Then Liv was going to destroy them.

She explained that she remembered destroying almost all the objects that were in the shop during the reset point. Then she pointed to the gold pocket watch. "But not that one. I've never seen that before."

"Do you think that's because we use it?" Sophia questioned.

"More likely is that we destroy it," Liv stated.

Worry sprang to Sophia's face.

Liv dismissed her with a wave of her hand. "Don't fret. It's just a guess. Maybe we trade it to a gnome for gold because we run out of money to buy candy."

Sophia laughed. "This is sounding like a ridiculous mission."

Liv agreed with a nod. "Welcome to my world." After running her eyes over her arms, she looked up. "Okay, I've officially said goodbye to my body in case this is the last time I see it in color and we get stuck here."

With a sigh, Sophia shook her head. "We're not getting stuck here. We'll just do what we came here for and get out before it's too late. Besides, you work for Father Time. He's not going to let anything happen to you."

"Right," Liv drew out the word with a laugh. "You know how many others do his dirty work?"

"No."

"Just me," Liv answered. "Coincidence, or is it that I'm the only one left because they all got stuck in the past or died doing his bidding?"

"You're just the best and the only one he trusts." Sophia held the pocket watch in her fingers. She gave her sister a tentative look. "Are you ready?"

"Yep, nothing like the present. Or rather, centuries in the past."

Sucking in a breath, Sophia pressed in one of the knobs on the side of the pocket watch that controlled the minute hand. They figured it was best to start small, although technically they needed to roll the clock forward several hours to get to midnight.

With deliberate precision, Sophia began to move the minute hand forward with the intention of speeding up time. At first, she didn't know if it was doing anything, but then Liv gasped and she halted, looking up.

"What is it?"

"Look," Liv said, holding up her hand that had been full of color in a black and white world. The tips of her fingers were now gray.

Without a word, Sophia continued to rotate the knob, her eyes skipping between the watch and her sister's arm. As she moved the long hand around the face of the watch, the color continued to drain from Liv's limb.

Glancing down, Sophia realized the same thing was happening to her. She continued, grateful the progress was slow. They needed to get to midnight, while also maintaining a bit of color in their appearance. It was a very fine balancing act. They couldn't have enough color that they were seen in this realm, but enough to hold onto their timeline. Then once they had what they wanted, they could return to using the gold token.

"Keep going," Liv encouraged, tugging her sister out onto Roya Lane. "We've got to find where this candy shop is going to be located."

Sophia was careful to steadily move the long hand around the watch as her sister steered her onto Roya Lane, where the sun was setting due to her moving time ahead.

Cautiously, Sophia glanced at her arms. When there was no more sunlight in the sky, her arms were completely black and white.

"Don't stop," Liv urged, holding onto her bicep and pulling her down the road.

Sophia did as she was told, disconcerted by her brief glance at Liv. Her sister's head, shoulders, and arms were black and white. She assumed it was the same for her.

Sophia didn't know how much of them would remain colorized by the time midnight was upon them, but she hoped it was enough to give them time to get into the store.

A strange glow started to take over the night sky. Curiously, she looked up and found the source of the light. The lunar eclipse was mesmerizing, taking up the sky as the moon rose higher into the sky.

"Soph," Liv said, a harsh tone to her voice.

"Sorry," she apologized, returning her attention to the pocket watch and continuing to wind the long hand forward.

"Okay, this should be it," Liv declared when Sophia realized they had about an hour to midnight.

"Good news," she stated with excitement, her gaze pinned on the watch in her hand.

"Not really," Liv grumbled.

Sophia feared there was not much color remaining in them. She glanced down, and to her relief, found her legs were still colored. Only her top half was black and white.

She jerked her head up to look at her sister. "What's wrong? We have an hour to midnight and halfway to go."

Liv pointed ahead. "That's what's wrong."

Sophia followed her sister's finger and her heart sank. They weren't the only ones waiting to get into the magical candy store at midnight. Of course, others would be lined up to get into the shop that only opened on rare occasions. Currently, the line was snaking down the block.

Sophia groaned. "Can't we use our positions with the Dragon Elite to cut the line?"

Liv laughed. "Well, the House of Fourteen hasn't issued me identification. Not to mention they are behind the Great War that will start in a few hours, so excuse me if I don't want to advertise that I work with them. You, well, you're with a group that's about to be erased from the history books for a few centuries. That's not the biggest issue for you."

Sophia slumped, knowing exactly what her sister meant. Before Sophia, there hadn't been a female dragonrider, so if she waltzed up to these magical creatures and explained she was a Dragon Elite, they'd simply laugh in her face. No one would believe a young girl was a dragonrider.

"What are we going to do?" Sophia slowly ticked the minute hand forward, knowing they had to at least get to midnight before the shop opened. As she did, the color continued to leach out of their forms.

"We do what I do best," Liv said, pulling her sister forward.

"What's that?" Sophia asked.

"We bullshit our way in there."

CHAPTER NINETY-FIVE

Headlights on the dark road that was Roya Lane illuminated the line that went all the way down the block. It belonged to an apparition Liv had created as she told Sophia to continue to move them forward.

"Won't the magical creatures wonder what those belong to?" she asked, squinting as she stared at the bright lights.

"That's the point," Liv said confidently, stomping for the front of the line. "Step one is to confuse your prey. Step two is to disorient them. Step three is to make them beg for your help."

"What is that?" a magician at the front of the line asked, holding up his arm to block out the light streaming down the brick road.

"It's my backup," Liv declared with confidence, sidling up next to the man.

That they could interact with those in this realm was good news. The watch said they had a minute to midnight, so Sophia had no reason to keep winding the long hand. A quick glance at her form made her heart beat fast. The only color that remained was from the knees down. If the last hour was any indication, it meant they had roughly ten minutes until they had no color left and were stuck in the reset point forever.

"What's the meaning of this?" the magician at the front of the line asked as Liv stepped in front of him, angling him back. "I've been in line for half the day."

Liv arched an eyebrow at him. "Have you considered getting a life? That's a lot of time to stand in line to get some lollipops."

He scoffed at her. "They aren't just any kinds of lollipops. The ones they sell make my hair grow back."

Liv nodded, pulling something out of her cloak and flashing it at the man. Sophia recognized it from earlier when she was holding most of the contents from her pockets. It was a Pokémon playing card. "I'm with the Quality Assurance Board for Sugary Treats and Magical Properties, and I'm here to—"

"That's not a real thing," the man argued, and the others in line behind him began to protest as well.

Liv looked casually at Sophia. "It appears this lot wants warts growing on their tongues and who knows what dripping off their you-know-whats."

Sophia pretended to shiver, following her sister's lead. "They'll look as bad as the last group who didn't let us do our checks."

"I'm afraid so, Steph," Liv agreed, nodding and supplying a fake name without hesitation. Glancing back at the man, Liv sighed. "We're here to run a quick check on this place before you enter. If you don't want us to, you all can chance buying goodies that do more than you bargained for. We've gone ahead and shut down three operations tonight that could have infected hundreds with fatal side effects. We also cleared a dozen stores operating well run and safe establishments." She held up her hands. "Your call, though. We're here to protect the public, but if you don't want us to take the two minutes it requires to check this place out, we'll rejoin our forces." She motioned to the headlights on the far side of the road, still giving off a blinding force. "Anyway, if that's what you want, we'll be out of your hair...I mean, your baldness." Liv's mouth twitched to the side as her eyes darted up to the top of the magician's bare head.

He thought on this for a moment as an elf came to the front door of the shop and turned the Closed sign to Open.

The magician still seemed unsure, and the bickering behind him made Sophia worry they were going to have to wait in the long line to get into the shop. She looked down and her insides tensed. The color had drained down to her calves.

She elbowed Liv in the ribs and shook her head. "Hey, if they want to get poisoned from sugar contaminated with drenchwood, we have to let them. That's their choice."

Liv nodded. "You're right. I'm just tired of cleaning up what those slugs do to people's insides."

"Yeah, go ahead," the magician said in a rush. "Go do your checks."

To Sophia's surprise, the others in line behind him echoed his words.

Sophia smiled at her sister as she turned the doorknob to the shop. "After you, Inspector."

CHAPTER NINETY-SIX

Firelight filled the Midnight Lunar Eclipse candy shop when Liv and Sophia rushed into the shop, closing the door behind them.

The place was full of bins of paper-wrapped candies. Chocolate bars sat in stacks on the shelves. Fairies buzzed around stocking things and left behind twinkling lights as they sped across the store. Sophia was certain the whole place was a blaze of colors in real life. However, they were invaders in the reset and couldn't see anything but black and white.

Glancing down, Sophia gulped. The black and white had reached their ankles. They didn't have long.

"Hey," Liv said in a rush. "We need—"

An elfish woman with short brown hair and discerning eyes narrowed them at the sisters. "Where's everybody?"

Liv glanced over her shoulder and shrugged. "No clue. Guessing there's a thing and they've all decided to stay home. Maybe they are worried about werewolves."

Sophia tensed, ready to defend her sister with another excuse. The woman sat on her stool behind the counter and nodded. "Makes sense. That's the risk I take opening on a full moon, but it still beats my old job."

"Cool," Liv said, striding over. "We are looking for something very specific and don't have long. We need—"

"Accounting." The woman cut her off. "I used to be an accountant. Then I got in trouble. Got a rap sheet, if you will. I'm from the future, so that may be terminology you aren't that familiar with."

"You'd be surprised," Liv said, dismissing the woman. "As I was saying—"

"My name is Sica." The woman interrupted again. "Haven't seen anyone in quite some time, so excuse me if I crave a bit of small talk."

"Would love to," Liv stated. "However, we're pressed for time." She glanced down.

The only color was on their feet.

The ex-accountant motioned over to a shelf. "Pick up the Mo-Time Meringues. They make each minute last up to two."

Liv shook her head. "That would work under normal circumstances, but it won't right now."

Sica waved her off. "Time is always ticking for those who like to count. That's why I don't anymore. Back in the day, I was an accountant, but—"

"Got it," Liv cut in. "You used to balance books, now you make candy. We need chewing gum that makes the chewer happy no matter what."

"Oh," Sica exclaimed. "Smile Despite Reality Chewing gum. Yeah, it's in that bin right over there." She pointed at a barrel full of all sorts of different varieties.

There were jawbreakers, gummies, and chocolates wrapped in foil and many other things.

"Where there?" Sophia asked, striding over to the barrel.

Sica leaned back on the shelf behind her. "Beats me. I just throw everything into a barrel and let the masses find what they are looking for."

"Impeccable customer service," Liv said dryly, irritation heavy on her face.

"It sure is strange you're the only customers," Sica said, narrowing her eyes at the front door. "I only open up for one hour a day on a lunar eclipse for a reason."

"To be an official pain in the ass?" Liv asked as she rushed over and began to help Sophia search through the contents of the barrel. They were both throwing candy onto the floor after determining it wasn't chewing gum. Sica didn't seem to notice as she peered at the ceiling.

"Intrigue," the candy maker stated. "Everyone wants to visit a shop that's open so rarely. It creates demand. Usually by this time, we're almost sold out of everything." She shrugged, not seeming put off by her current reality of disappointment. "Oh, well, at least nothing bad is approaching."

Liv peered at Sophia over the mound of candy as they continued to search. "Yep, no war or anything."

"Did you say you were from the future?" Sophia asked, furiously combing through the candy.

"Well, sure," Sica replied. "I'm a planner, so I live in the future. When we look ahead or back, we are in essence time-traveling."

Liv shook her head and gave her sister an irritated expression. "Damn hippies. They always say shit like that."

Sophia chanced a glance down. The only color remaining was in her toes. "Liv!"

Her sister jerked her head down, seeing what Sophia saw. Her eyes widened. "Damn it! We're almost out of time."

Sica laughed. "I've found that time stretches when I need more, and it shrinks when I need less. You just have to tell it what you want. It's here to serve us."

"Would you shut it?" Liv snapped, frantically digging into the barrel of candy, knocking big piles onto the floor.

"I've got it!" Sophia exclaimed, reaching into her cloak for where she'd stuck the pocket watch.

Liv looked ready to knock it out of her hand when she saw it. "Don't mess with the minute hand. We can't reverse time."

"No, we can't," Sophia agreed. "But we might be able to stop it. If only for a second." She held the pocket watch high above her head and gave her sister a tentative expression.

Liv realized what she intended to do and nodded. "Yes, try it. It's our last hope."

With deliberate force, Sophia threw the pocket watch on the wooden floor of the candy store where it busted at once. They had either sealed their fates here, or they had bought themselves a few minutes.

Sophia checked her feet. The only color was in the tips of her toes. They didn't have long. She turned over her shoulder, and the best bit of news she'd had all day stared back at her as Sica sat frozen on her stool, her mouth half-open as if she were in mid-sentence, but paused.

"It worked!" she exclaimed.

"Probably not for long," Liv said, throwing candy everywhere. "We can't trick the hands of time for more than a minute or two. I know from experience. When someone pauses time using a device, there are agents that stop them."

Sophia shot her sister a look. "You're talking about you, aren't you?"

Liv nodded. "Yes, and in a reality I've yet to experience, I step in and stop us."

"Then don't," Sophia urged.

Her sister shook her head. "It's not that easy."

"It never is," Sophia muttered, kicking the barrel over and making all the candy spill out.

"If I show up to stop us as violators of time," Liv said quickly, sorting through the candy spread across the floor. "I'll see myself, and that will instantly have far-reaching effects on me."

"So we have to get the gum and get out of here before you catch us from the future." Sophia couldn't believe the strange scenario she'd found herself in. It made sense they stopped the magical pocket watch that sped up and apparently paused time. That's why Liv didn't have to destroy it in the future. "You would think your boss would have seen all this coming."

Liv laughed. "Oh, he most definitely did, but call this a job hazard. I signed a contract and have regretted it ever since."

Sophia heard shouting from the other side of the front door.

"Get back!" a voice yelled. "Official Father Time business."

She jerked her head up, her eyes meeting Liv's. They both recognized the voice of the person yelling.

"That's you!" Sophia said.

"I'm angry," Liv stated, now throwing candy around.

Worse than meeting livid Liv was that if her sister did, Sophia knew she probably wouldn't survive it. It was a part of the laws of time travel. She pulled the gold coin from her pocket. Nothing was worth losing her sister over. She'd just have to call this a failed mission and explain it to Lee. She'd find another way.

She flipped the coin over to where it said, Reset Point and reached out for her sister's shoulder, knowing Liv would never consent to quitting even with her life hanging in the balance. She wasn't going to ask for permission. Liv's eyes widened as she realized what Sophia was about to do. She thought her sister would fight her, but instead, Liv dropped to the floor and picked up a round piece of candy tied on either side.

Sophia flipped the coin to where it said, "Present" as she spied the writing on the wrapper: Smile Despite Reality Chewing gum.

CHAPTER NINETY-SEVEN

"Ask me how I am," Liv demanded as they tumbled through the blackness and ended up back on Roya Lane outside a shop that appeared to be boarded up. The street was full of color and so were the sisters.

Sophia pulled in a deep breath, finding herself laughing. "How are you?"

"I'm flipping fantastic!" Liv rejoiced, throwing her fist in the air and hollering from elation.

Continuing to laugh, Sophia doubled over in shock that they had pulled it off. "You have it?"

Liv pulled out the jar of silly putty from her cloak. "Yeah, don't fret. I didn't lose my lucky putty. Although I think I broke a nail earlier, so I'm not sure if it's working like it should."

Sophia shook her head but smiled still. She held out her hand. "The gum. You got it, right?"

With a satisfied glint in her eyes, Liv slapped it into the palm of her hand. "You know I did."

When she pulled her hand away, Sophia was relieved to see the colorfully wrapped piece of gum. She'd never been so grateful to see color in all her life. She let out a relieved breath before remembering something.

"Liv, I'm sorry. You wanted to get things from Midnight Lunar Eclipse too."

She shrugged. "I wanted to get silly stuff to pull pranks on Clark. It's not a priority. You need to make good on your end of the deal with Lee. Keeping your promises is more important, especially in our line of work. You never want to owe anyone a favor for long. You have to keep your promises and friends because you'll find you can't do this job alone. We are always dependent on one another to get things done."

Sophia nodded, knowing how true those words were. Her mind skipped to Hiker, who had asked for her help. She pulled the gold coin up and looked at the device her fairy godmother said would help the Viking to reconcile with the past. As instructed, she'd used the reset point to get the gum. Now it needed to be turned over to Hiker Wallace. Who knew what would come of it after this? There was only one way to find out.

"Thanks for all your help," Sophia said, opening a portal that would put her outside the Gullington. "I have to get back now because—"

"Because you're a Beaufont," Liv interrupted. "We always have a job to do because that's why we were put on this Earth. You don't have to explain. Just know that if you ever need my help dealing with an accountant gone weird or anything else, come and ask me. I'm always here for you, Soph."

The dragonrider nodded and smiled fondly at her sister. "Of course. Same to you. *Familia est sempiternum.*"

CHAPTER NINETY-EIGHT

"Never going to fall in love again," Ainsley roared as she thundered down the stairs of the Castle past Sophia.

Sophia paused and gave the housekeeper a cautious glare. "Are you okay, Ains?"

The shapeshifter spun, the color of her face matching the shade of her hair. "Does it look like I'm okay?"

Sophia's eyes darted from side to side. "No, hence why I asked you if you're all right."

"Well, I'm not," Ainsley complained, pointing up the landing of the grand staircase. "That man always wants everything to be business as usual. He orders me about, treating me worse than a common servant. Centuries I've served him and the Dragon Elite, and do I get a single thank you? No! Of course I don't. It used to peeve me, but now that I know…that he and I… It makes me angrier than hell."

Sophia nodded consolingly, trying to figure out how to de-escalate things. "I could understand why you're upset. This is a lot for anyone to deal with and keeping your memories now, but not having all of them has to be difficult."

"It is," Ainsley agreed, her tone leveling out. "Just find a cure for me, S. Beaufont. Find a way for me to get out of here because the longer I stay, knowing he's imprisoned me here, stealing my memory and my life, the shorter the potential length of his life gets."

Sophia nodded. "I'm working on it, Ains. I really am. According to my sources, I have to help him to help you."

Ainsley laughed. "Of course you do. Meanwhile, I'll just go and make the venison stew he's ordered. Do you think he wants a side of chloroform with it tonight?"

"What was that?" Sophia asked.

The housekeeper hurried off down the stairs, shaking her head. "Nothing, S. You misheard me. I didn't say what you thought."

"I'm certain you did," Sophia stated. She turned for the top of the stairs and, taking a deep breath, started for Hiker Wallace's office.

"Sir," Sophia said from the door to Hiker's office, "is everything okay?"

He glanced up from a mountain of papers on his desk and sighed. The sun had gone down long ago over the Pond. "No, the city of New York is breathing down my neck to deal with this giant beanstalk upsetting Cornelia Street. That's not even the beginning of my problems."

"Yeah, Ainsley is pretty upset," Sophia related.

His face screwed up with confusion. "Ainsley? No...I mean, she's forever a problem, but I was referring to mortal governments frustrated with the House of Fourteen over these magician's disappearing. Where are you with that?"

"I'm working on it," she replied. "Trin Currante is tracking down Mika Lenna's location. As soon as she has something, all forces of the Dragon Elite should be deployed."

He nodded, regret on his face. "All but me."

"No," she answered. "I think all of us will be required. Mika Lenna and Saverus Corporation shouldn't be underestimated. He's gotten away several times, apparently."

"Well..." His gaze fell to the bank of windows that were dark since there was no moon.

"Ainsley is very upset right now," Sophia began, deciding it would be better to come back to the Mika Lenna thing later.

"That's because I asked her to make something for dinner tomorrow that's actually edible," he stated. "That is her job, and really, she should be able to do that little."

Sophia's eyelids fluttered with annoyance. "You will remember she wasn't always a housekeeper. She used to be a diplomat for the elfin council."

He opened his mouth about to argue with her but shook his head instead.

"She's a housekeeper now only because there are few other options for her, sir," Sophia reminded him.

"I know," he grumbled.

"Do you, though?" she argued. "Do you remember who she used to be? More importantly, do you remember what you two were to each other?"

"Don't," he warned, severity in his tone.

"I will," she dared to say. "Ainsley deserves to have her life back, and you're the only one who can give it back to her."

"I don't know how," he said. There was an edge of weakness to his voice.

"Lucky for you, I know people who do." Sophia pulled the gold token from her pocket and put it on the desk in front of Hiker Wallace.

"What's that?" he growled.

"It isn't bus fare," she teased.

Not getting her joke, he stared at her, heat smoldering in his gaze.

Sophia sighed. "It's a way to see into the past."

"That's not safe," Hiker argued.

"Usually it isn't," she agreed. "With this, it's fine. It was sort of given to me by Papa Creola."

"Sort of?" he questioned.

"Well, I'm the keeper," she explained. "It's the point in history right before the Great War started."

Hiker stood suddenly and took a step back like the token was full of poisonous snakes ready to lash out at him. "Why would I want to go back to that? Thad... Ainsley... The war..."

"That's exactly why you need to go back," Sophia reasoned. "You've forgotten the past, and without knowing it, you're not moving forward."

"Don't."

"Look," Sophia began, trying a different approach. "Take the token and think about using it. Tomorrow, I'll go up the beanstalk with you if you want."

"That was the agreement," he stated with conviction. "You planted that damn thing, and you're going to help me get rid of it."

"I did what Mama Jamba told me to do," she replied. "Don't tell me you would have refused her."

He sighed. "That's the thing. I can't refuse her, and I get that you can't either. She orders me to go up the beanstalk, so I have to. Who knows what she has planned for me? I can assume it won't be to my liking."

"But," Sophia countered. "She said it's part of what you need to balance out your powers. I think we have to trust her."

He picked up the coin and looked at it intently. "I trust Mother Earth implicitly, but that doesn't mean I'm going to like what I have to face."

Sophia realized Hiker was afraid of what most people were, which was change.

He'd lived the last few centuries hiding from the past, hiding from the power he'd inherited. Now he had to face a future where he conquered his demons, or he allowed them to consume him.

CHAPTER NINETY-NINE

Tiny fractures along with giant cracks radiated from the beanstalk that had erupted through the concrete of Cornelia Street.

Sophia didn't recognize the place where she and Lunis had planted the seeds Mama Jamba had given her. Before the New York City road had been congested with traffic that ran alongside shops and buildings crammed in too close to one another. It was hard to even make out the blue sky on the narrow street. The patch of dirt where they'd planted the seeds had been about the only thing from nature before. Now...

A mecca of budding life radiated around Sophia and Hiker when they stepped through the portal onto Cornelia Street.

The beanstalk was at least ten feet in diameter. It was as green as grass on the Expanse at the Gullington and glowed brightly on the road. However, it wasn't the only bit of new life.

Vines had sprouted off the stalk and were snaking through the air and covering the road where they stood. Birds, reptiles, and woodland creatures scurried behind large flowers or rocks in ponds a short distance from the beanstalk.

Sophia wouldn't have known the street as the one where they'd planted the seeds except that she recognized a few of the shop signs on the sidewalk. They were mostly obscured by the vines and greenery quickly taking over. She worried if they stayed still for too long, they'd be wrapped by vines and made a part of the framework of this new ecosystem.

"Where are we?" Hiker asked in awe, looking around at the strange sight.

"Not Kansas," she answered with a joking tone.

He lowered his chin, not at all amused. "I meant, what the hell happened here?"

Sophia pointed to the beanstalk that rose up above the buildings. Past the clouds in the sky, she could see between the buildings since they'd been pushed back, their exteriors crumbling as Mother Nature made way for more plants and trees.

"Mama Jamba seemed to have happened," she answered.

He sighed. "I know that, but still." Hiker shook his head. "That damn woman and her devilish ways."

Sophia pursed her lips. "I think she's trying to help."

"I know what she's trying to do," he spat, his face flushing red as the ground under their feet started to tremble.

Sophia was certain it wasn't because another beanstalk was about to rise up through the ground. The ground was shaking because of the man standing before her. Hiker needed to figure out how to control his temper before it got the best of him and everyone around him. It would be best for the Dragon Elite and therefore the world at large if Hiker Wallace got control—and sooner rather than later.

"I realize Mama Jamba's mysterious ways can be frustrating," Sophia began, trying a different approach. "I get that. She wants the best for you and for us. I think that's what's important to remember."

"No, Sophia," Hiker argued. "She wants what's best for her planet. We're just pawns in all of this. The Dragon Elite works for her, even if it's to our detriment."

The ground shook more violently. The birds that had been singing so loudly were suddenly silent.

"I'm just supposed to blindly climb up some stupid beanstalk and find what? All because that woman has some agenda for me because my powers are supposedly out of whack!"

The façade of the remaining buildings crumbled from the Viking's power as it radiated out in all directions, even if it was unseen. His face blossomed red as he ground his hands into fists.

"I'm so tired of following things blindly!" he spat. "I'm supposed to be the leader of the Dragon Elite, yet I feel like you came in and turned everything upside-down. The men, they follow me, but there's always been doubt. Adam planted that!" Hiker stomped, making the beanstalk shake and sending all sorts of debris raining down from the sky where something seemed to live high above. "Then you brought back Mama Jamba, and she's always orchestrating something." He whipped his head back and forth as though trying to dispel a gnat going for his face. "Now Ainsley! I can't deal with this anymore! You've done this, Sophia, and you're going to damn well help me to fix this, or you're out of the Dragon Elite! Do you understand me?"

Sophia simply regarded the angry Viking before her for a long moment before drawing in a long breath. She waited for the birds to start their chorus once more.

"Are you done, sir?" she asked, her voice measurably calm in comparison to his.

He narrowed his eyes at her. "No. You want me to go back into the past. You want me to see who I was or what happened or whatever. Well, you know what, I'm done with doing things how you or Mama want." Hiker pulled the gold token from his pocket and held it in his palm. "You can have this back because I'm not interested in fixing things. I'm not even interested in fixing me anymore. You will just have to put up with my anger and my unbalanced power because Hiker Wallace is tired of doing things the way you all want. I'm going back to my way."

The gold token winked in the sunlight streaming through the canopy overhead for only a second when a bird cawed overhead. Sophia watched as a black and white bird swooped from the vines and stole the gold token from Hiker's palm before he knew what had happened.

The bird, a magpie, soared back up into the air, flapping its wings as it made its way up to the top of the beanstalk.

CHAPTER ONE HUNDRED

The garden rules had apparently changed, Sophia realized, looking around at the strange forest where she and Hiker stood. Magpies were common in Scotland, but there was little reason they should be in North America. The only explanation was that things weren't operating as expected, which meant she had to throw out the rule book. They were playing a game dictated by the strange and never predictable Mother Nature.

"Well, there you go," Hiker said, his eruption of anger dissipated by the crow stealing the gold token. "Let's cut down this beanstalk and be done already."

Now it was Sophia's turn to have a tantrum. "No!" she yelled. "That gold token is the reset point for Father Time. If anything goes wrong, then that's where all the world gets reset to. It's the moment right before everything went to hell. He entrusted it to me. I gave it to you, thinking in my delusional brain you could use it to fix your life! I realize there's no fixing an angry Viking, but hell if I'll get my ass handed to me because I tried to help you."

Hiker narrowed his eyes at her. "Sophia, you watch your—"

"No!" she argued. "I'm not scared of you. Everyone else is. Do you think I'm more scared of you than the entity who controls time?"

"W-w-well," the Viking stuttered, "no. He scares even me."

"Exactly," Sophia stated, starting forward. "So whether you like it or not, sir, we're going to do what Mama Jamba intended. We're climbing this beanstalk and going to find out what's at its top. I'm going to get that damn gold token back, and you're going to try and fix your power problems."

"Or what?" Hiker demanded, crossing his arms.

Sophia had just started to find her footing on the leaves and vines of the huge beanstalk when she came back down again and strode over to the hulking man who was acting as stubborn as a toddler. "Or I'm going to go back to the Gullington and tell Mama Jamba you're refusing to take the help she offered. Then I'm going to Papa Creola and tell him you're the one who got his reset point stolen."

He stuck his nose in the air, undeterred by her threats. "They probably already know. It was your gold token to keep safe. That's on you."

"Then I'm going to leave the Gullington because as much as I want to be a Dragon Elite, I refuse to work for a coward," she declared, trying to remain strong although fear was vibrating in her chest.

"How dare you," he said through clenched teeth, his blue eyes rimmed by red.

"I dare, sir," she stated. "If you can't face what's up there, then how can I trust you to help us face what's out in the world? You climb the beanstalk with me, or I leave the Dragon Elite. I believe the others, Wilder, Evan, and Mahkah, well, my absence would make them question their own reasons for staying at the Gullington."

Sophia didn't wait for Hiker Wallace's reply. Instead, she took off for the beanstalk and resumed climbing.

She didn't know if what she said was true, but she knew it wasn't an empty threat. What was the point in doing something under the wrong leadership? No, if they were going to save the world, the Dragon Elite needed the right person at the wheel or they'd always fail, and she didn't want to be a part of that.

Sophia was about eight feet up when the beanstalk shook under her. She heard a sigh and looked down to find Hiker glaring up at her as he started to climb.

Her expression remained stone, although her heart leapt. Of course, the one thing that would always inspire Hiker Wallace to face that which he didn't want to, was the threat of losing what he loved more than anything else—the Dragon Elite.

Deep down, Sophia suspected the man below her loved something else more than his dragonriders and their mission. He just had to remember what that was.

CHAPTER ONE HUNDRED ONE

The lightning strike that shot past Sophia and Hiker as they climbed nearly made her pee her pants. She clung onto the beanstalk branches as the storm around them intensified. The leaves of the magical beanstalk were coarse and prickly in places, scraping against her face and arms and making cuts that stung instantly.

I know of a way to get up a massive beanstalk easily, Lunis said in her head, his timing both awesome and awful.

She tried not to laugh since that might be the death of her right then, making her lose her balance. The leaves she had to use as rungs were increasingly slippery and the handholds bit into her fingers. *You know you couldn't join me on this mission.*

I know I'm not there, he stated sullenly.

I wish you were, believe me, Sophia told him. She prepared to continue the climb that had gotten exponentially more difficult as they progressed. As soon as she set foot onto the branches of the beanstalk, everything around them changed—growing darker and colder and sending a storm that only intensified by the minute.

Sophia paused for a moment to catch her breath, noticing Hiker below her was doing the same. *This is something Hiker needs to do on his own, without his dragon, which means I have to. Besides, I believe taking a dragon ride up the beanstalk is considered cheating. I suspect Mama Jamba wants us to climb to the top on our own.*

Well, don't look down, Lunis offered.

Thanks, but I sort of have to in order to ensure that man below doesn't bail.

Sounds like a babysitting job, Lunis said.

Yeah, that sounds about right, she admitted.

Then my only other advice is not to fall, Lunis suggested. *Oh, and don't die. Key tip there. You're welcome.*

Sophia finally allowed herself to laugh. *Okay, I'm ringing off so I can concentrate on the not dying part.*

Click, Lunis said like he'd just put down a phone receiver.

I have the strangest dragon in the entire universe, Sophia admitted to herself, shaking her head.

I heard that, he chimed.

Go work on your YouTube channel, Sophia hinted, nearly losing her grip as she took the next step.

YouTube is so five minutes ago. He scoffed. *I'm working on a TikTok video.*

Oh, dear angels, Sophia said, shaking her head. *I didn't know you could do the floss.*

Yeah, I'll totally teach you when you return, he stated, then added, *If you don't die.*

Right on the heels of his words, Sophia slipped, and her feet came out from underneath her. The only thing that saved her from falling was the death grip she had with her right hand, her left not catching a grip. She kicked her legs to find her footing. The branches she'd been using had broken under her feet, giving her nothing to step on. Improvising, she wrapped her legs around the beanstalk and used her upper body to progress.

As a woman, she knew climbing with her legs was much more advisable. However, when climbing up a slippery beanstalk in a torrential downpour, one had to adapt. Her biceps burned as she pulled her body weight up with both arms, but finally, after a ton of effort and more grunting than she cared to admit, Sophia was able to pull herself to the next branch and give herself a few moments of respite.

She glanced down, realizing Hiker had witnessed her near-fall, but he seemed relieved that she'd recovered. Shaking off the adrenaline rush, Sophia continued up toward the unknown.

As they climbed the beanstalk, the storm around them surged, getting worse. The day had receded quickly, making everything black. The winds had picked up and rain started to splatter them, whipping Sophia's hair into her face like ropes.

When the lightning began, real fear started in the pit of Sophia's stomach. She knew one thing about lightning storms—stay low. Tall objects were targets. She and Lunis had learned this during flights where they had to avoid lightning. If a bolt struck the beanstalk, there would be no avoiding it.

Instead of heeding the knowledge of staying low in a storm, Sophia was climbing ever higher chasing after a thieving bird.

Too many times during the climb that grew more arduous with each step, thanks to the rain and wind, Sophia wanted to quit. All she had to do was look down at the man below her to realize she couldn't. No one wanted to quit this more than Hiker Wallace. She wouldn't give him that way out.

Sophia had to persist. The leader of the Dragon Elite had to get to the top or he'd never conquer his fears. He'd never balance his powers, and without the reset point token, he would not remember who he used to be.

As they climbed higher, the air grew thinner, colder, and less forgiving.

Looking up, Sophia felt there was no end in sight. The beanstalk seemed to go on and on, and she doubted her decision not to use the dragons. Hiker hadn't suggested it either, and she'd thought he also knew this climb had to be done manually.

A cautionary glance down told her he was easily keeping up, but she wished she had followed Lunis' advice and not looked. The ground, as far as she could tell in the dark, was a mile away.

Sophia gulped and took another step as the beanstalk shook violently, nearly sending her flying off.

Jamming her fingernails into the trunk, she hung on for dear life as the whole thing vibrated wildly. As she held her breath, the shaking subsided. Thinking it was safe to start the climb again, Sophia lifted her hand and foot just as something knocked the beanstalk, making it bend drastically to one side.

Despite Sophia's grip, the assault was enough to send her flying. She had no time to think before something grabbed her by the shoulder and held her suspended in the air.

Breathless, she looked up to find Hiker holding her as she dangled. He had a tight grip on the beanstalk, and his boots were firmly planted as he held onto her with his free hand.

She would have thanked him for saving her life, but fear had left her speechless. It didn't matter because he wouldn't have heard her with the winds soaring around them.

Swinging her away from the beanstalk, he launched her back the other way. She reached out and grabbed one of the branches, holding it with a new desperation. She glanced back at Hiker and knew he intended for her to take the lead again.

Nodding once, Sophia continued climbing, ensuring she had three points of contact on the beanstalk at all times.

CHAPTER ONE HUNDRED TWO

I 'll never let go, Sophia thought as she clutched the beanstalk, the evil winds seeking to pull her off.

Just as she made up her mind not to let go of the beanstalk she'd found solace clinging to, the next handgrip was absent. Reaching overhead, Sophia clutched at wet air for something to grab, but there were no branches or vines or anything.

She hadn't chanced looking up or down since her near-fall. Now she dared to bring her chin up and found a thick ring of clouds hovering just above her. They were so dense she couldn't actually see her hand reaching through it on the other side.

"What is it?" Hiker yelled up to her, the first thing either one of them had said since the climb began.

"I think we're at the top," Sophia replied, having to scream to be heard over the racing wind and rain.

Lightning clapped in the distance, sending a blinding light across the city and showing just how high they were. The two dragonriders were at the same height as many skyscrapers.

"Hold on!" Hiker ordered, and a second later, the thunder that followed the lightning violently shook the beanstalk, making Sophia's teeth vibrate in her skull.

Thankfully the thunder didn't last long, but it only reminded Sophia they were in a dangerous place holding onto a wet beanstalk that rose as high as any of the nearby buildings.

She dared to take her hand off the beanstalk again, this time to feel for an edge. At first, she didn't find anything which was confusing. The beanstalk had to have a top. Trying a different direction, her hand knocked into something. Instead of grabbing it straight away, she felt along, trying to make out its shape.

It was a large hole. Maybe the opening to the top, she thought with excitement. She squashed her hope. She shouldn't delude herself into thinking that just because they got to the top, the danger was over. More likely, it was only beginning.

Grabbing the edge, Sophia managed to get her other hand to meet it and shuffled her feet to pull herself up. She was right; a thin blanket of clouds soaked her as she brought herself through the narrow opening. It was large enough for her, but Hiker was going to have to squeeze to make it.

Sophia had her first bit of relief in what felt like hours when she clambered over the top and found a soft patch of wet dirt. She rolled onto it and saw it went on for a great distance in both directions. In the distance were structures she couldn't make out clearly.

Finally finding some safety, she allowed herself to rest. Her arms ached from the climb, and her skin was burning from the cuts. Her legs were shaking from fatigue. Lying on her back, Sophia sucked in breath after breath. It wasn't raining anymore.

As her eyes adjusted, she realized it was dark around her, but there were signs of sunlight seeping in from one of the structures in the distance. She didn't have time to investigate because the sound of grunting stole her attention.

Glancing at the large Viking trying to squeeze through the opening, Sophia nearly laughed. Hiker looked like a fat worm wiggling up from the ground as he tried to fight his way through.

"Help me!" he ordered, his arms waving around madly.

Sophia pushed up to her feet and found the ground solid under her. A quick look around told her the ground spread out until it met rocks and walls.

That's when it hit her. They were in a cave.

CHAPTER ONE HUNDRED THREE

New York City felt thousands of miles away as Sophia assimilated the new reality. She'd climbed high above the city on a beanstalk to find herself in a cave in the sky. What was outside the cave was even more curious.

"What are you doing?" Hiker exclaimed, His face was so red it looked like it was about to burst from the pressure around his midsection. "Help me!"

Sophia hurried over, grateful to have solid ground under her feet after the long climb. She grabbed both of his hands and tugged to get the thick Viking through the opening.

His hands were large in hers, and they were slippery from the rain. Sophia pulled her hands from his and wiped them on her pants. He did the same, and when their hands reconnected, they had a much firmer grip on each other.

Digging her boots in, Sophia threw her weight backward, pulling so hard she thought her shoulders dislocated. Finally there was a release and Hiker tumbled all the way through the hole, knocking into her and throwing her to the ground. He rolled over and jumped to his feet, looking around with wide eyes.

Realizing there was no immediate danger, he glared down at her as though wondering why she was lounging in the dirt while he was vigilant.

Finally he held out a hand, offering to help her up. Sophia took his hand for the third time and was nearly hauled off her feet when he brought her to a standing position.

"What do you make of this?" Hiker asked quietly.

"It's a cave," she said.

He nodded and pointed to where the sunlight was streaming through. "Looks like that's our way out."

She tilted her head, skeptical about what they would find outside the strange cave in the sky. Sophia wanted to believe nothing would surprise her at this point, but she knew that wasn't true. There was always something more fantastic than the last.

"Shall we?" she asked the leader of the Dragon Elite.

"Yeah," he answered and took the lead. He strode forward, each of his steps careful.

There wasn't anything unique about the cave. It was like most with stone walls, random puddles of water, and cool, crisp air. The sunlight was nearly blinding as they neared the opening.

Sophia reminded herself they were probably closer to the sun, and the light was so blinding because they'd been in darkness for so long.

Hiker was the first to peer out of the cave, and a gasp fell out of his mouth.

"Well, I never…" he said, shaking his head and grabbing his beard.

Sophia angled around him, fine with the idea of using him as a shield if there was a monster waiting for them. There wasn't. What stretched out before them was not at all what she had expected. Just as she had thought, things *could* get weirder, and she *could* be surprised by what she found next.

CHAPTER ONE HUNDRED FOUR

Ways and means escaped Sophia for why a huge junkyard stretched out all around the cave where they stood.

Apparently, it confused Hiker too. He ran his hand over his head, his eyes wide. "What on Mama's green Earth?"

"It's a junkyard," Sophia supplied in a whisper. She ran her gaze over an old rusted truck with weeds growing up through the hood and missing all of its tires. Beside it was a beat-up washing machine that looked to have been commandeered by a bunch of squirrels and birds currently fighting over the spring harvest as they scurried through the neighboring junk.

For roughly one Hundred yards, the ground was littered with large and small electronics, appliances, furniture, lawn equipment, and vehicles of all sorts. To make the scene even stranger, in the distance past the treasure trove of junk was the strangest castle Sophia had ever seen.

The building was massive, dwarfing the Castle at the Gullington and making it look like a modest townhome in comparison. It rose up to the cloud-filled sky that was full of blue, even though it had been night and stormy in New York City below them.

The castle, much like the one at the Gullington, appeared very old and had stone spires that disappeared into the white puffy clouds. It was easily filled with hundreds of rooms and reminded Sophia of a giant mall building, rather than an old building meant for kings and queens. The oddest thing about the large castle was the front door. It was massive, rising up to what would be a second story on a regular mortal home. It was easily the width of a garage door and made Sophia wonder if the person who lived there drove the broken-down tractors and dump trucks littering the junkyard into the castle at night.

Her speculation brought a new realization to Sophia's mind. They were very likely going to meet the creature whose junkyard this belonged to and who resided in the large castle.

She glanced at Hiker, her concern heavy on her face. "Who do you think lives here?"

He shook his head. "Knowing Mama, it's no one good. I'm guessing we've unknowingly been elected to deal with this polluter."

Sophia nodded slowly. She looked over her shoulder at the cave. "We came through a strange portal of sorts, didn't we?"

Hiker followed her gaze. "It would seem so."

Sophia tried using her own portal magic, already thinking of what their exit strategy would be. Nothing happened, as she suspected. "Looks like the only way out is the same way we came in."

A sober expression crossed Hiker's face. "I would expect nothing less."

As she was trying to wrap her brain around why Mama Jamba had sent them up this strange beanstalk, Sophia heard a flapping noise. She jerked her head and saw the magpie that had stolen the gold token landing on the beat-up old truck with the gold token in its beak.

She was about to start forward when Hiker grabbed her by the shoulder and pulled her back.

"Wait," he urged quietly.

She was about to argue with him and explain this was their chance to get the gold token before the magpie disappeared again. A moment later, she was grateful she hadn't left their hiding spot at the edge of the cave.

A heap of something lumpy began to move beside the old truck, making Sophia's heart beat rapidly. The adrenaline only increased when a large man sat up from the ground, having been obscured by all the junk around him. No, not a man—a giant.

This one was easily taller than Rory Laurens, one of the only male giants Sophia had ever seen. This giant had to be over ten feet tall and had massive shoulders, a flat face, and dirty hair.

"Jack, what have you brought me today?" the giant asked the magpie.

Proudly the bird lifted its beak, showing the treasure it had stolen from Hiker and Sophia.

The giant narrowed his eyes at the bird before grinning, somehow making his face look even uglier. "Very nice. What is that? Money?"

The bird laid the coin in front of it and squawked.

"Not money, you say," the giant said. He rose to his feet and checked out the reset point more closely. "This be magic, isn't it, Jack?"

Again the bird squawked in reply.

"Well, it will go nicely with the harp we stole off that angel," the giant remarked and pulled a small gold harp from his pockets. It appeared silly in his hands like he was holding a toy. "What did that angel say before we took this off him? It be the thing to calm an angry man's emotions and balance out his power?" The giant laughed loudly. "What a crock. It be what I sell to get more treasures."

He looked proudly at the large junkyard, his chest swelling before glancing back at the magpie. "Don't you tell mum about the magic coin. You know how she doesn't like us stealing what rightfully should be ours." The giant shook his head. "That woman never gets it, does she?"

The magpie cawed loudly in reply.

The giant opened his mouth to say something but was interrupted when the door to the castle burst open. A giantess, not quite as big as him, stepped out onto the front step. She was wearing an apron, and her hair was up in curlers. She had a disapproving expression on her face as she cupped her mouth.

"Berlin!" the woman yelled, her voice carrying easily across the long junkyard.

Berlin the giant stuck the gold harp back into his pocket, a nervous expression crossing his face. "Yes, Mum?"

In reply, the giantess waved her son toward the castle.

He sighed, nodding. "I'll be right there."

The castle door shut a moment later and Berlin returned his focus to the magpie. "Who knows what that woman wants this time? You take that coin to Family Tree with the other stuff."

The bird picked up the gold token dutifully and sprang off the truck, flying to a tree in the distance that sparkled with various objects, no doubt treasures it had stolen for the giant.

Without another word, the giant trudged off to the castle.

When he was a safe distance away, Sophia turned her attention to Hiker. "You have to get that gold harp."

He nodded, irritation heavy on his face. "Yeah, I know. It's how Mama intends for me to balance things out. With a bloody harp."

Sophia wanted to laugh at the thought of Hiker carrying around a small, dainty harp to control his emotions and power. "It belonged to an angel, so it makes sense."

"I guess," he stated. He was obviously not excited about the prospect of having to use the harp. "I'm going to go to the castle and get the harp away from the giant."

For as large as Hiker Wallace was, he would be considered quite small in comparison to the massive giant.

"Do you think you can sneak in there?" Sophia asked, sensing Berlin wasn't going to be welcoming to trespassers in his junkyard or in his castle.

"I think I have to, so I'll just have to figure it out," Hiker replied. He pointed to the magpie perched in the tree. "You need to go after the bird and get back that gold token."

Sophia nodded. "Yeah, and something tells me the thieving bird isn't going to just hand it over."

"You can bet on it," Hiker agreed, stepping out from the cover of the cave and into the sunlight. "Just be careful and meet me back here in an hour. If I don't return by then, go back down the beanstalk and cut it down."

"Sir—"

"That's an order, Sophia," he said, cutting her off with a stern expression she didn't dare argue with.

Nodding, Sophia gulped. "Okay, sir."

CHAPTER ONE HUNDRED FIVE

F amily Tree was an old oak, with long knobby branches that spread out from the trunk and dipped close to the ground. Its limbs didn't sway in the wind as Sophia snuck across the junkyard, hiding behind various large objects between sprints.

The oak reminded Sophia of a Christmas tree decorated with ornaments. Gold bracelets, cufflinks, watches, and many other objects hung from the tree's branches, making gentle music as the wind swept through them and made them dance.

Jack, the magpie, had been busy stealing. There had to be at least a few hundred trinkets and pieces of jewelry on the oak.

At first, Sophia wondered why it was called Family Tree, but as she neared it, she realized that much like the image on the wall at the House of Fourteen, there were names on the limbs. Most of them had been scratched out, unlike the ones in the Chamber of the Tree. There were only two names remaining: Mum and Berlin.

The crow flapped its wings as Sophia approached. She looked over her shoulder and spied Hiker crossing the junkyard the same as her, taking refuge every few paces to hide behind a car or a lawnmower.

The sun nearly blinded her when she looked up at the branches where the black and white magpie was hopping along, the gold token still in his beak. He hopped up to the next branch, getting even higher.

"Why don't you come down here, little guy, and give me back my coin?" she offered, using her best Snow White voice as she held out her arm, inviting the bird to fly down and perch there.

He didn't.

Sophia sighed and wondered why she hadn't taken those falconry lessons she kept joking about. If she had, she reasoned, the bird would do as she ordered, but in reality, it probably wouldn't change anything. She suspected Jack was quite mischievous and didn't play by the rules since he was a thief.

The magpie flew up to the top of the tree and glared down at her, a rebellious glint in his black eyes.

"Seriously, just drop that coin and I'll catch it," Sophia told the bird. "No hurt feelings. I won't even press charges."

As if in reply, the bird dropped the coin into a tin pail that hung from a thin branch by a small handle. The gold token clanked when it dropped into the small tin that swung slightly from the newly added weight.

Sophia sighed. "So that's the game we're playing, huh?"

Jack squawked loudly at her and flapped his wings, although he stayed perched on the branch beside the swinging tin.

"Same to you," Sophia said, looking up at the bird.

She lifted her hand and swiped, mistakenly thinking she could use her magic to pull the coin to her. The tin continued to swing, but the coin didn't fly and land in her palm as she'd hoped.

Sophia narrowed her eyes. There had to be a ward on Family Tree that prevented magic from being used on it.

You likely have to be one of the family members listed, Lunis offered in her head.

Sophia nodded. Her dragon was probably right. *Okay, other bright ideas, then?*

You could go for a climb, he suggested.

Sophia sighed. *Of course, this was always going to result in me climbing a tree after a naughty bird that will probably dart off with my gold token as soon as I'm close.*

Well, if I was there, I'd make fried magpie out of that guy, Lunis replied.

I know, but you couldn't come on this mission, Sophia stated. *Besides, you'd never fit through that hole at the top of the beanstalk.*

Are you calling me fat?

I'm calling you a dragon, she countered.

I could have used a compartment spell, he argued.

I don't think that's the point. Sophia watched as Jack stared down at her, seeming to be mocking her from up high. *You're not here, and I need to get to that coin.*

Then I suggest you get to climbing, Lunis teased.

She sighed, her legs and arms still sore from her trek up the magical beanstalk. Sophia flexed her fingers as she stretched out her neck and prepared for a climb she hoped was less eventful than the last.

CHAPTER ONE HUNDRED SIX

Berlin didn't have a housekeeper or a groundskeeper, Hiker observed as he neared the massive castle. The junkyard was full of rats and other vermin, who were probably nesting in the various appliances and machinery. He saw signs of the rodents all over the place as he neared the front of the castle.

Once at the front door, there was a putrid smell that wafted from the open windows. It gave Hiker the impression the place wasn't as tidy as the Castle at the Gullington. He scrunched up his nose and pressed his back up against the wall of the building and tried to peer in through the window.

A figure stalked by on the other side, thundering across the stone floors. Hiker sucked in a breath, cementing his spine against the exterior wall of the castle. He didn't think he'd been seen.

"I want you to chop all the wood in the back," the giantess said from inside the castle, talking to her son.

Hiker heard a loud sigh. "I will after I get something to eat."

"You will do it now!" the woman ordered, her voice cutting through the air and shaking the shutters hanging from the window.

"Mum, I'm tired. I haven't even had a nap today."

"You wouldn't need one if you hadn't spent the bulk of your day

411

toddling about in that useless junkyard of yours," Berlin's mother complained.

"It's not useless," the giant argued.

"I'm going to go work on supper," the woman stated. "You better get that wood chopped or else."

Hiker heard the giantess' footsteps retreat, followed by the slamming of a door.

"Or else," Berlin repeated, doing an impression of his mum. That was followed by more stomping and a loud yawn. "I just need to shut my eyes for a minute. That woman and her wood chopping can wait."

Hiker waited until the front area of the castle was quiet. When he was certain the entryway was deserted, he slipped in through the large door, moving as silently as he could and hoped he hadn't just entered what would be his final resting place.

CHAPTER ONE HUNDRED SEVEN

*I*t's beginning to get to me how much climbing is expected of me on this mission, Sophia said to Lunis, chewing on her lip as she tried to find her next hold. It had been easier to climb up the beanstalk than the oak tree because the latter offered a lot fewer options for feet and hands.

You need wings, her dragon suggested.

I think you're better suited to have them, she replied.

And a tail, he added.

The magpie cawed loudly at Sophia as she progressed.

What I need is a slingshot, she muttered, reaching for the first limb after scaling the wide trunk.

Jack hopped around on the branch toward the top of the tree, squawking.

"You had to put the token at the top, didn't you," she grumbled. She had quite the distance to go to get there.

Focusing on not breaking her neck or falling, Sophia ignored the crow she suspected was plotting his next move and continued to climb. She chose branches that were thicker and could support her weight. When she was almost to the branch with the tin with the token inside of it, Jack hopped over and put his beak close to the container.

"Oh, no, you don't," Sophia warned, knowing what he intended to do. "If you dare, I'll turn you into dragon food."

As if encouraged by her threat, the magpie popped his head into the tin.

Sophia knew she couldn't risk Jack taking off with the gold token again. A huge gust of wind swept through the tree. Like when she'd been on the beanstalk during the storm, she held on tightly as the branches swayed.

Jewelry and small shiny objects began to fall from the tree, pelting her head. They fell to the ground around the tree, covering it with hundreds of tiny trinkets.

When the wind had stopped and the stolen items quit falling, Sophia chanced a glance up. The tin with the gold token was gone. She jerked her chin down and ran her eyes over the scene below. Within seconds, she located the tin sitting among the other treasures, no coin inside.

Her eyes connected with Jack's. An unspoken message passed between them. Sophia dove for the ground as the magpie sped in the same direction, trying to beat her to the reset point.

CHAPTER ONE HUNDRED EIGHT

Somewhere, a clock was ticking in Berlin's castle when Hiker slipped through the large doors. He was a large man by any standard. However, in comparison to the giant, he felt like a gnome as he stood in the oversized castle. Everything in the place was made to fit the large giant.

A table that stood as tall as Hikers' midsection sat in the dining room to the left. If he were to sit in one of the chairs around it, he had the sick feeling his feet would barely touch the floor. In the opposite room were various other pieces of furniture, all of them oversized.

As Hiker had assumed from the smell that had wafted from the open window, the castle was unkempt with trash all over the place and grime marking most of the walls. A thick coat of dust covered everything, making him scrunch up his nose as a sneeze threatened to rip from him.

He shook his head and willed the sneeze to go away as he considered his options. From the kitchen, his enhanced ears picked up on the giantess whistling as she cooked. It smelled potato-based with a strong hint of licorice and sardines.

Hiker grimaced at the combination. Here he had thought Ainsley's cooking would push him over the edge. He should probably be glad he didn't have Berlin's mum cooking for him.

Hiker knew he should be grateful for what Ainsley did for him and the Dragon Elite, but there had been so little time over the last few centuries to process everything. To really appreciate her. It was hard to remember who she used to be. Who he was. Who they were.

He looked out the window he'd been spying through a minute ago and saw the Family Tree in the distance. Hiker made out Sophia jumping from a branch, the bird diving after her. He didn't know what the young dragonrider was doing, but he hoped she was successful at recovering the gold token.

Pulling his attention to the stairs, Hiker listened. He heard the groan of a mattress from the second floor and assumed that was where the angry giant had gone to take his nap.

As carefully as he could, the leader of the Dragon Elite began to climb the stairs to the second floor. The steps were higher than those Hiker was used to, making him have to raise his feet up higher to reach the top landing. When he got there, his boot made the floorboard creak.

Hiker froze and listened, holding his breath.

"Mum, is that you?" Berlin asked from the nearest room to the right.

Not daring to even blink, Hiker remained still. He might be the most powerful magician on the planet currently, but with that strength came an imbalance. That's why he was there. He knew without a doubt that if he was confronted by the giant, the fight wouldn't be so decisive of a victory for him. Hiker suspected that under his current circumstances, he'd lose before the fight even started.

The giant muttered something followed by the sound of bedsprings squealing as if in pain.

Hiker wasn't sure what to do next and considered finding a hiding place until the giant fell asleep. Before he even had a chance to formulate a plan, loud snoring filled the castle, making the floor under his boots vibrate.

CHAPTER ONE HUNDRED NINE

Making an enemy of a mischievous magpie hadn't been on Sophia's agenda for that day, but it just went to show how her adventures took her along rather than the other way around.

She landed with a thud on top of the many treasures, which didn't make for the softest cushion. Jack, on the other hand, swept down gracefully, his bird feet making a clinking sound as he landed.

The one good thing for Sophia was he didn't seem to know where the gold token was. She could tell by the way he was jerking his head back and forth, searching for it. The bad news was the jerk bird seemed intent on finding it before her. With his beak, he started turning over necklaces and earrings in the pile, looking for the coin.

"Oh no, you don't." Sophia launched herself forward, diving for the bird. She wasn't sure what she'd do if she caught it, but it seemed like the best course of action to keep Jack from getting to the reset token before her.

He squawked and took flight as she landed where he'd been seconds prior. She squashed the tin the coin had been in when it hung in the Family Tree.

She pushed up to her hands and knees and began sifting through the contents on the ground. This could take a long time since the coin was quite small compared to many of the other objects. The layers of treasure were thick. There was no telling where the gold token was at that point.

Jack had wised up. Not wanting to be clobbered by the dragonrider, he had taken a perch back in the tree. A quick glance told Sophia he was still diligently searching for the coin.

"It's mine, you little thieving bird brain," Sophia warned. "Seriously, out of all these treasures, you're going to go to all this effort to keep it away from me. That's just rude."

The bird squawked in protest.

Sophia laughed at it. "My consolation is that you're going to have to put all this stuff back in the tree, and that will take forever. You're welcome."

The magpie, who obviously understood English, swooped down from overhead, his feet going for Sophia's hair. She threw her hands up and batted them wildly to shoo the avian away.

He flew back up into the tree and continued to watch from above.

Sophia returned to searching, but then remembered the objects were no longer in the tree where they couldn't be summoned. With a triumphant glint in her eyes, she held out her hand, muttering an incantation that would draw the gold token to her. Before it was complete, Jack chirped loudly and dove back down to the pile.

At first, Sophia thought he was going for her head again, but then he soared to the side, headed for something on the other side of the tree trunk.

That was when she saw it. Sitting on top of a silver fork was the gold coin, winking at her in the sunlight.

As quickly as she could, Sophia finished the incantation and the coin rose from the fork and raced through the air. The magpie figured out what was happening a moment too late as the token soared toward Sophia.

Jack was slow to turn around, and by the time he did, the coin had landed in Sophia's palm.

Victoriously, she closed her fingers over the cold token, then with her other, she levitated the hundreds of trinkets into the air. The bird, who was headed in her direction, realized what was happening too late.

With urgency in his black eyes, he shot straight up through the branches of the tree as the many shiny objects trailed after him, all of them under the spell Sophia had just created. She didn't stay to watch as the thieving bird was chased by the items he'd stolen from others. Instead, she hightailed it away from the tree. The hour was almost up, and she needed to get back to the cave where she was supposed to meet Hiker.

CHAPTER ONE HUNDRED TEN

Mahogany filled most of the second-floor landing. Oversized furniture covered most of the available space. Not only was Berlin not very tidy, but he also appeared to be a hoarder. That shouldn't have been a surprise to Hiker, based on the junkyard outside the castle.

He paused outside the bedroom, which was filled with snoring. It was so loud it vibrated the floors, making the castle feel like a breathing monster.

Hiker wasn't a man who knew fear even though he'd faced some of the worst beasts to grace Mama Jamba's planet. However, with the prospects of getting trapped in a bedroom with an angry giant, he was quickly reacquainted with the emotion. It had been too long since Hiker felt the adrenaline of battle.

He wouldn't readily tell Sophia, but going on this mission with her had given him a new exhilaration. It was different when he had to defeat his brother Thad, which had been surrounded with regret and obligation. When Hiker had fought the cyborg pirates to defend the Gullington, that had also had a personal connection.

This felt like a battle from back in the day when the object was clear, the enemy evil and the path fully obstructed. Hiker didn't realize until that moment that he missed this. As the leader of the Dragon Elite, it wasn't his job to go into battle. That was the job of his dragonriders, except when really necessary. Hiker hoped there would be a future where he got to flex his muscles. That was part of the reason for balancing his powers. Also so he didn't crush his coffee mug by accident every morning.

Hiker held his breath as he looked into the room where Berlin was sleeping. It was also cluttered with unnecessary furniture and knick-knacks. The bed where the giant slept was one of the biggest Hiker had ever seen. It was at least three feet off the floor and the size of Bell after she'd ingested a deer.

His eyes darted to the bedside table where the gold harp was sitting. It was very close to where the giant's face was resting on a pillow, his mouth wide open and drool slipping down his chin.

Hiker chanced a step forward, then paused to see if it woke the giant. Thankfully it didn't. He took another step and again halted. He expected the floor would creak again underfoot, and wake up Berlin. When it didn't, Hiker made an impromptu decision to speed things up, deciding it was better to be fast than deliberate.

He sped forward and grabbed the harp. It was small in his grasp but instantly made him feel better and calmer.

Hiker spun, ready to get out of the castle when a voice called up from the stairs.

"Berlin! Are you sleeping?" the giantess called from the stairs.

Hiker tensed, the harp in his clutches. The giantess sounded like she was on the stairs, so he couldn't get out that way.

At his back, Berlin snored loudly, thankfully not waking up.

Without giving himself a moment to hesitate, Hiker dropped to the floor and scuttled under the bed, working quickly and sound-lessly to tuck in underneath. It didn't give him much room as the mattress caved dangerously low, grazing him as he tried to get into his hiding spot. The giantess thundered up the stairs and into the room.

"Damn it, you good-for-nothing son of mine," the giantess yelled as she entered. Her slippered feet were visible to Hiker as he pressed his face against the dirty floor.

"Wh-wh-what?" Berlin stuttered, clambering up as his mother stood over him.

"I told you to chop wood," she commanded.

"I was gonna," Berlin growled and threw his feet in dirty socks over the side, dangerously close to Hiker's face.

Hiker shrank back from the horrible smell, nearly gagging. There were few things that smelled as bad as that giant's feet.

"Yeah, you are," the giantess stated. "You're going to get your lazy butt up right now and chop my wood."

"Fine!" Berlin yelled, pulling his boots over and slipping them onto feet that were still too close to Hiker's face.

"I swear, I can't depend on you for nothing," the giantess complained.

"Oh, give it a rest," he replied and then took in a big whiff. "What is that smell?"

Hiker held his breath, both from the giant's feet and out of fear.

"Fee-fi-fo-fum. I smell the blood of a magician," Berlin chanted, lacing up his boots.

His mum clicked her tongue. "No, what you smell is your upper lip, son. It wouldn't kill you to wash your face every now and then."

He sighed. "I washed my face last week when I took my monthly bath."

Hiker grimaced, making note never to get onto Evan for not bathing regularly. Berlin made the young dragonrider seem high maintenance with his hygiene practices.

"Just get down there and chop that wood," the giantess ordered. "The fire under my stew is about to go out, thanks to you."

The bed groaned overhead, and the springs close to pressing into Hiker's face rose a bit. "Fine, but after I'm done, I expect supper."

"You'll get it when it's ready," his mum said, a terse tone to her voice.

Berlin drew in another breath. "It sure does smell fishy, like a man be hiding around here somewhere."

From his place under the bed with his face pressed to the floor, Hiker saw the giantess tap her foot with impatience. "Oh, would you stop delaying? It's probably the fish and licorice stew you're smelling."

Hiker scrunched his nose. Having smelled the awful stew, he was grateful he would be away from the weird combination of scents soon. He had the harp. He just needed the giant to leave, then he could too.

The boots of the giant thundered across the floor, making quick progress toward the door. At the threshold, Berlin halted. "Wait a second."

Hiker tensed and pulled his arms in closer, worried they had been seen from under the bed. "Where's my harp?"

"Oh, Berlin," the giantess complained. "My stew is getting cold without a fire. Will you get to your chores?"

"Mum, my harp. I know I put it on the bedside table before I dozed off. Where is it?"

"Do you really want to discuss how you came up here to sleep instead of doing what I asked, Berlin?" his mum asked.

"But—"

"You probably dropped it out there in that pigsty of a yard of yours," the giantess interrupted.

The giant scraping his fingernails across his head sounded like sheets of sandpaper being rubbed together. "Yeah, maybe I did drop it. I'll have to go look."

"First, you'll chop that wood, or you'll go to bed hungry. Is that clear?"

"Yes, Mum," Berlin answered, striding passed the giantess, his footsteps receding as he went down the stairs.

Hiker continued to hold his breath and watch as Berlin's mum stood beside the open door, not having followed her son as he would have expected.

A soft sigh tumbled from her mouth. "Now, if there is a magician hanging out in here, I suggest he get out before my monster of a son returns from chopping wood. Because if there's anything he likes more than fish and licorice stew, it's to grind a magician's bones to make his bread."

Hiker's eyes widened both in surprise that the giantess was helping him and at the thought of becoming a side dish for the giant. He didn't move even when Berlin's mum disappeared, taking the same path as her son.

CHAPTER ONE HUNDRED ELEVEN

Her knees grazed from falling on the pile of treasures, Sophia wiped them off as she ran for the cave. She slipped the gold token in her pocket and looked over her shoulder.

The stupid magpie would be busy trying to avoid colliding with the flock of spelled items chasing it until the spell ran out. That would be at least another few minutes or until Sophia disappeared down the beanstalk once more.

She halted at the mouth of the cave and checked her watch. There was only one more minute left until the hour was up. It had gone by too fast, and Hiker wasn't anywhere to be seen.

She couldn't believe he'd required her to leave him if he didn't show up in time. Worse was that he wanted her to cut down the beanstalk if he didn't appear. Although she hadn't wanted to agree, she knew refusing her leader wouldn't do. Leadership only worked if she followed. Otherwise, it was chaos, and what was the point? She didn't always agree with Hiker, but when he put down his foot on matters like this, she listened and complied.

As she stared out at the junkyard, Sophia worried for the leader of the Dragon Elite. If he didn't show up in the next several seconds, she had to leave without him, and she was certain cutting down the beanstalk would trap him here forever.

CHAPTER ONE HUNDRED TWELVE

"Run" was the first thing that occurred to Hiker as he ungracefully slid out from under the giant's bed. However, he knew he couldn't risk making noise. Berlin might still be in the castle. As quietly as he could, Hiker rose to his feet and tiptoed across the room, taking a cursory glance out to the hallway to ensure it was clear.

It was hard to believe the giantess was trying to help him. Maybe she'd witnessed her savage son do too many bad things and was working to undo them the only way she could. Whatever the reason, he was grateful Berlin's mum had come to his rescue, ordering her son out of the castle to give Hiker a chance to escape.

When at the doorway to the room, Hiker peered out to the landing of the stairs and the area below. The coast was clear.

With careful steps, he moved across the second-floor landing, avoiding the creaky board he'd stepped on before. Once on the stairs, he took them two at a time, his shoes cushioned by the dirty runner.

When Hiker was near the bottom of the stairs, the smell that wafted from the kitchen was nearly sickening. He held his nose and peered toward the living room and the sitting area on the other side. Both were clear.

All Hiker had to do was reach the door and then run across the junkyard with the gold harp and he'd be free. The mission would be complete. All would be well, until the next mission where he had to risk everything for something silly like a tiny harp.

Taking a step off the stairs, Hiker checked over his shoulder to the back of the castle, to the door that led to the back. That's where he suspected Berlin was chopping wood for his mum.

Hiker reached the front door without making a sound. He knew from earlier that opening the large door didn't make noise. Without that concern, he swung the door open just as the one at his back burst open.

Tensing, he dared to look over his shoulder. Framed in the back doorway was the angry giant, an ax in his hand and his eyes rimmed with red.

"Magician!" Berlin yelled. "I knew I smelled a magician! How dare you break into my home? Now you'll become part of my supper."

CHAPTER ONE HUNDRED
THIRTEEN

W ow, Sophia thought, watching as the seconds ticked by. She had ten seconds until the hour was up and she would be obligated to leave the Viking behind for good.

The thought terrified her.

Ten, nine, eight, Sophia counted. She brought her chin up, willing Hiker to appear somewhere in the junkyard.

Seven, six, five, she continued to count to herself. She watched as Jack sped around, avoiding the objects he'd stolen.

Four, three, two, she said, holding her breath when the clock hit one.

She had to leave Hiker. It felt wrong.

Still, she was going to keep her word. Sophia turned for the cave and willed herself to move forward.

After a single step, she heard a commotion behind her and spun, hope rising in her chest.

It was short-lived. She saw Hiker sprinting from the castle, fear covering his face as he raced for the cave, the gold harp in his grasp. Behind him moving nearly as fast was Berlin, the giant, with an ax in his hands.

Hiker, like a football player running for a touchdown with the ball in hand, leaped over a broken-down motorcycle and darted between a line of dryers arranged as though to slow trespassers.

Berlin might not have moved with as much nimble grace, but his long strides made it so he caught up with Hiker easily. He was on his heels and pulling the ax back when Sophia threw her hand into the air. She knew her precision had to be spot on, or she'd risk hitting Hiker and he'd be toast. Chopped up, dead toast.

With a prayer and practiced grace, Sophia shot a stunning spell in the direction of the giant. It soared over old cars and refrigerators and streaked past Hiker as he darted to the side, giving it a wide berth. When Sophia thought it was going to miss the giant, it hit him square in the eyes, knocking him straight on his back. He landed in the dirt, and a big cloud of dust blossomed up from the ground.

Hiker didn't dare look around to see if the spell had hit its target. That was a good thing because stunning spells didn't work so well on giants. It had sent Berlin to his back, but he was already clambering up to his feet, the ax in his grasp as he shook his head and started after Hiker again.

Sophia was going to send another spell at the giant, but Hiker yelled as he neared.

"Go! Go!" he yelled, waving her forward. "Start down the beanstalk!"

She knew he was right. They needed to get down fast, but also safely since they were so high up. She spun around and sped into the dark cave, nearly tripping over a boulder in the dark, her eyes not yet adjusted.

Thankfully she found the hole to the beanstalk easily and slipped through, passing through the thin layer of clouds and clutching the leaves and branches.

In their favor, the storm over New York City had passed. Although the beanstalk was wet, the rain and winds had subsided, making getting down much easier than before.

Sophia kept glancing up as she dropped down the beanstalk, descending a lot faster than she had climbed up. Relief filled her when Hiker materialized. He was moving even faster than her. He had the gold harp in his hand, and like her, he was keeping a loose grip on the beanstalk as he negotiated downward like a firefighter going down a pole on their way to an emergency.

Even as fast as they were moving, the danger was still very real. They both realized that when Berlin poked his head through the hole and yelled at them, his face red. From up top, he did something and made the hole bigger until he could fit through.

If he got onto the beanstalk, things were going to become exponentially worse. Sophia decided to drop from where she was, about two stories up, rather than climb the rest of the way down. She landed in a crouch and drew her sword. Hiker did the same thing and joined her on the ground.

He nodded appreciatively as she swung Inexorabilis and struck the beanstalk with force. The blade stuck in the green stalk, making it shake like a bell being struck. The look on the giant's face told them both he was scared.

Whereas before he had been trying to climb down, Berlin began trying to climb back up. He had apparently realized what would happen if he was stuck on the beanstalk when it timbered down onto the ground. His legs were kicking through the hole to the cave when Sophia swung her blade a final time and sliced through the beanstalk cleanly.

The giant green stalk, a result of a few tiny seeds, creaked and then began tumbling toward Cornelia Street. Sophia was about to take off running when Hiker grabbed her by the collar of her shirt and hauled her off her feet, dragging her in the opposite direction and away from danger.

To their surprise, a loud explosion didn't follow the beanstalk falling. Instead, there was a whoosh of air, a sweet smell Sophia associated with springtime, and a gentle rush of sparkling dust that covered everything around them.

Curious, Sophia pulled free of Hiker and spun around to find no beanstalk. There was no platform where the cave and the junkyard and the castle had been, just fluffy clouds. No one would have ever known a beanstalk had ravaged Cornelia Street if it wasn't for the giant stump in the middle of the sidewalk.

That area of New York City didn't appear like it had before, though. Sophia was certain as she looked at the garden oasis around them, full of grassy knolls, singing birds, and a babbling brook, that the ecosystem in this part of the city would look like this for a very long time and remain unchanged by urban development. She suspected Mama Jamba had planned it all along.

CHAPTER ONE HUNDRED FOURTEEN

"I'm gonna need to hear that story one more time," Evan said, buttering his roll. "First, Ainsley, why won't you let NO10JO into the dining room?"

The housekeeper glanced at the cyborg dog. "Because he drools and licks his butt."

"We let Evan in the dining room," Wilder argued with a laugh.

"You let Lunis in here when he was just a pup," Evan demanded, sneering at the shapeshifter.

"He's a mighty dragon," Ainsley stated, crossing her arms and regarding the leader of the Dragon Elite. "I think the harp story is a bit boring actually. It makes you look...soft."

Hiker cut his eye to the gold harp on the dining room table and didn't say a word. He hadn't said much since they returned to the Castle at the Gullington. It had been Sophia who told the story about the beanstalk and the giant with the junkyard. All the while, Mama Jamba's face hadn't shifted. She obviously wasn't surprised by what they'd found at the top of the beanstalk.

"He doesn't hurt a thing," Evan continued to argue. NO10JO hadn't left his side since the cyborg dog came to the Gullington. Sophia had to admit he was better than most dogs in that he didn't shed. There was also the whole teleporting and shapeshifting thing he could do, which made him pretty cool.

"He makes you happy, and that's sorely disappointing," Ainsley replied and buzzed off for the kitchen, not having served anything for dinner yet.

Evan sighed. "Does anyone else notice that her usual sunny disposition has dimmed just a bit?"

Wilder and Mahkah chuckled, having spent many decades dealing with the sullen moods of the elf.

Sophia stretched her hands overhead but retracted them immediately as a spasm went through her back. Her muscles had been tensed since returning after climbing up and down the beanstalk and the Family Tree. She figured a few more hours in the Castle and she'd be back to normal, but they'd just returned.

"What is it?" Wilder asked, giving her a concerned expression.

"I tweaked my back," she admitted.

"Probably when you jumped down from the beanstalk," Hiker stated plainly. He didn't sound as grumpy as usual, but rather matter of fact. "It was at least thirty feet."

She nodded.

"Sounds like you could use a pillow for your back," Evan suggested. Like it had been planned, NO10JO transformed into a huge pillow on the other side of the entryway into the dining room. The oversized pillow was covered in brown hair, much like the dog, but it did look rather soft.

"Well, isn't that convenient," Evan said, mock surprise in his tone.

"For the hundredth time, the answer is no," Ainsley declared. She didn't even glance at the cyborg shapeshifting dog lying as a pillow by the door as she came back into the dining hall carrying nothing.

"Is dinner going to be much longer?" Hiker asked, the tension starting to rise in his voice.

"Not yet," Ainsley sang, a hint of mischief in her tone. "Doesn't that just really put your kilt in a wad? Don't you really just want to go off about how incompetent I am and how I never get the meals, right?"

Hiker drew in a breath and placed his hand on the gold harp, ignoring the attempt to anger him.

"So a tiny little harp, huh?" Wilder inquired. "You've got to carry that thing around full time now?"

Mama Jamba's periwinkle eyes cut to Hiker, curious how he'd answer the question.

"I don't know how it will work yet," he answered. "It's all very new."

"The tiny angelic instrument calms you and balances out your powers, right?" Evan questioned.

Hiker pressed his lips together. "I don't know. I haven't had time to figure out much."

"Tell us the story again," Wilder urged, turning his attention to Sophia. "You met a giant who had a junkyard, and Hiker had to kill him to get his harp?"

Sophia glanced at Hiker. He had told her briefly what had happened in the castle at the top of the beanstalk. She'd worried there had been an altercation, but he had muttered something about hiding under the giant's bed and running like hell when caught. She suspected that was part of the story he didn't want the guys to know about.

"The details aren't really important," Sophia started. "What's key is that we were successful." She pulled out the gold coin and placed it on the table between her and the Viking. "I'll trust that in your hands for a bit."

His light-colored eyes slid to the token with indecision.

"What's that for?" Ainsley asked skeptically.

"A second chance," Sophia said coyly.

Hiker left the reset point coin sitting on the table and didn't take it.

"Second chances are for losers who can't do things right the first time," Ainsley pronounced and left for the kitchen.

"What do you think the chances are that she's returning with food?" Evan wondered hopefully. He directed his attention to Mother Nature, who was studying Hiker. "Mama Jamba, if you ask Ainsley for dinner, she'll probably bring it."

The old woman shook her head as Quiet waddled into the room. "No, I think if Hiker asked her for food, we'd get it."

Sliding into a chair, Quiet muttered something inaudible.

Mama Jamba nodded. "I didn't say it would be something we wanted to eat."

Evan sighed dramatically and threw himself back in his chair. "Sir, why can't you despise roasted chicken and vegetables?"

"Or bangers and mash?" Wilder added.

"Because I have good taste," Hiker grumbled, irritation on his face.

At this, Mama Jamba lifted an eyebrow and gave him what appeared like a look of warning.

Taking the hint, he picked up the small harp and held it next to him as Ainsley came through from the kitchen, still empty-handed.

Directing his attention to her, Hiker said, "Would you bring us dinner? We have things to get to."

"Oh, you're waiting for dinner?" Ainsley asked. "I had no idea. Here I thought you all were simply having a social hour. I'll get right on that, sir, since I now know you have things to do. I wouldn't know what that's like since I can't leave the Gullington without dying... thanks to someone."

She spun on her heels and bolted back through the swinging door as Hiker's fingers tightened on the gold harp.

"Speaking of things that need to be done," Sophia began, turning her attention to Wilder, "I was hoping you could go on a mission with me."

Evan winked at Wilder, elbowing him. "Mission, eh? Is that code for snogging on the beach?"

Sophia's eyes fluttered with annoyance. "No, it's code for I have a mission that requires a weapons expert."

"I'm there," Wilder said at once, flashing a smile at her.

"What is this mission?" Hiker's irritation was growing.

"I need to go and recover a mysterious and magical katana," Sophia explained. "First I have to go get Zac Efron."

"What's a Zac Efron?" Hiker asked quite seriously.

Sophia nearly laughed. "He's a person, and no, I don't know why I need him for the mission."

"Explain," Hiker ordered.

"I'm supposed to get a katana for Lee at the Crying Cat Bakery because she made me a magical cupcake," Sophia told him.

"Why?" His eyes narrowed.

"Because that was the only way to use the magic ingredient I stole from the Hindu temple," she went on in a rush.

"Oh, this keeps getting better," he stated. "Do continue to tell me about the strange side quests you go on when you're supposed to be doing adjudication missions."

"Well, the herb extends mortals' lives, and I needed it to help King Rudolf with his wife Serena," Sophia replied. "In order to make good on the deal with Lee, I have to recover a katana for her, and she said I'd need Wilder, Zac Efron, magical chewing gum, an elf-made compass, and a badass dragon."

"You were doing fine until you got to that last part," Evan joked. "Do you want to borrow Coral?"

She shook her head at him. "If I need to be insulted and have all my good jokes go to waste, I would, but I need a dragon who will get the job done with a smile."

He scoffed at her. "As if…"

"Why is it you are wasting all this time on ridiculous tasks?" Hiker demanded. His face was growing red even though he was holding the gold harp. He also sensed the issue as his eyes slid down to the instrument in his hands, as though urging it to work and calm him down.

"Because we needed twenty million dollars for the LiDAR equipment that helped us find the dragon eggs, sir." Sophia was careful to keep the sarcasm out of her voice as she served up the news that would put him in his place.

Evan didn't have her decorum. He hissed through his teeth before shaking his head. "Wow, sir. Burn. I bet you feel foolish, having questioned Soph when she has been spending her time repaying favors that helped us out so much."

Hiker lowered his chin, murder written in his eyes as he continued to clutch the gold harp. "I'm not the one at this table who should feel like a fool."

Evan glanced at the others as if expecting one of them to raise their hands and confess it was them. Finally he pointed at Quiet. "It's him, isn't it, sir?" He looked at the gnome. "We cannot understand a word you say, little guy." He articulated each word carefully like he was speaking to a foreigner.

The groundskeeper held up his fist and shook it in Evan's face, mumbling something.

"Would you two stop your bickering?!" Hiker exclaimed, the hand not clutching the gold harp slamming down on the table and making everyone flinch.

They all remained frozen, staring at the fuming leader of the Dragon Elite as Ainsley buzzed through the kitchen door carrying a platter of food. She smiled brightly. "Well, there's the Hiker we all know and loathe."

He narrowed his eyes at her as she set down the tray of round foods, all neatly arranged. "What's that?"

She flashed him a devious grin. "Sushi, sir. Your favorite."

"I actually love sushi," Evan stated, grabbing a roll with his fingers and plunging it into his mouth.

"And," Ainsley said, drawing out the word. "My sushi-making skills are pretty bad, so I'm certain this will be a meal you won't forget… especially later."

"Wait, what?" Evan yelled. He swallowed quickly and looked around for water, but there was none.

Hiker appeared as he usually did when about to go off on Ainsley. Then he pulled his hand off the table and strummed the harp, making a gentle sound. Everyone watched him, waiting to see what he did next. Sophia thought he might turn the gold harp into a weapon, first killing Ainsley and then Evan and then probably the rest of them.

To everyone's surprise, Hiker simply nodded. "As long as it's not fish and licorice stew, I'm fine with it." He leaned forward, inspecting the sushi. "I've never tried anything like this, so I suspect I'm overdue."

All had wide-eyed expressions as the leader of the Dragon Elite took one of the sushi rolls. He held it up a bit to Ainsley. "Would you get us some water when you have a chance?"

The housekeeper was furious as she marched for the kitchen. "Really! I slaved away on a meal you'd hate for hours, and this is the thanks I get?"

Hiker peered at the harp still in his hand, then glanced back at the kitchen. "Oh, and a bottle of whisky too. Thanks."

CHAPTER ONE HUNDRED FIFTEEN

"What if this is all the love you'll ever get?" Mama Jamba asked, her hands on her hips as she won the stare-off with Hiker Wallace.

He pulled his gaze from the tiny woman and looked at the Dragon Elite globe in the corner.

"What if I don't care?" he fired back. He was the only person he knew of who dared to argue with Mother Nature.

"Son, I don't buy that bologna for a second."

Hiker shook his head. "You can't pretend to know everything about everything."

Mama Jamba actually laughed at this. "Who says I'm pretending? Actually, half the time I'm pretending not to know what I know, but you already had that figured out."

He rubbed his head, a persistent headache returning. Hiker knew that inside the Castle he shouldn't have headaches or any pain, so if this one refused to go away, there was a good reason behind it. Mama kept telling him it was self-inflicted. He kept contending that Quiet was mad about something or other and didn't want to get rid of it for him.

"It's both," Mother Nature said, watching him rub his temples and

SARAH NOFFKE & MICHAEL ANDERLE

referring to their prior conversation about the headaches, although he hadn't said anything. It didn't matter. Hiker knew she was right. She knew pretty much everything, even what he was unwilling to admit right then.

She pointed at the gold token sitting on the surface of his desk, a stubborn expression on her face. "You aren't getting rid of the headaches or the guilt or any of the rest of the residuals until you deal with the past."

He threw up his hand, letting his temper get the best of him. "The past is over and done with. Don't you get that? I can't undo it. I can't fix things. I can't make anything better when history has already been written and that book closed."

She picked up the gold harp from on the coffee table in front of the fire and laid it on the desk next to the gold token. "You're wrong, son. Believe me, my best friend is an expert on this subject. Time is a relative thing. This isn't really about undoing the past. It's about coming to terms with it. Only when we do that can we move forward."

"I've moved forward!" he boomed, knowing he was fooling no one.

Mama Jamba laughed at him. "You're about as stagnant as a puddle of week-old swamp water in the Louisiana bayou."

He rolled his eyes. "I don't have time for this, Mama." Hiker glared at the stack of papers on his desk of cases that needed his attention.

She shook her head. "Believe it or not, this is all you should have time for. Fix your personal life, and you'll find fixing the world's problems are immeasurably easier."

"I don't have a personal life!"

Mama Jamba nodded as she made for the door to his office. "You're telling me, son. Which is why you don't want anyone else to either." She pursed her lips at him from the exit to the study. "You've always been like that. Maybe because you assumed if your own twin brother couldn't love you, you weren't deserving of anyone else's love." Mother Nature thought on this for a long moment. "You know, Thad not loving you was his problem, not your shortcoming, just as you not loving others is yours and not theirs."

Hiker was about to tell the old woman where she could put her sage wisdom, but she turned and left the office, humming the song, *"What the World Needs Now."*

He let out a guttural protest as he regarded the gold token and the harp. Maybe if he did what Mama Jamba and Sophia kept pushing on him, they'd see they were wrong. Then they'd let this mess go and stop putting their noses into his business.

With a resigned spirit, Hiker grabbed the harp and slid it into this jacket pocket. He'd found just having the harp on him made him feel more relaxed, and when things got really intense, strumming the instrument had immediate results. Like earlier at the dining room table when everyone in the Castle was wearing away at his patience.

Hiker didn't know what good it would do to revisit the past. Part of him wholeheartedly believed it was an incredible waste of time. The other part of him only marginally thought it might offer some good.

Because he wanted to believe the latter and prove Mama and Sophia wrong, Hiker picked up the gold coin and turned it over until it said, "Reset Point."

CHAPTER ONE HUNDRED SIXTEEN

The symphony of noise inside the Castle was a stark contrast to the present moment for Hiker Wallace.

How long had it been since he heard so much going on in the Castle, he wondered as he opened his eyes in the reset point. He couldn't remember, although the current date did feel like yesterday. How could it not when it had been etched onto his soul?

The reset point was the day before the Great War started. That was the day Thad Reinhart had challenged the Dragon Elite, threatening war on them and the world at large. It was the day evil magicians had stopped mortals from seeing magic and rendered the Dragon Elite useless. It was the day Hiker's twin brother had tried to kill him. He hadn't been successful for one reason.

It wasn't because the dozens of men lined up next to Hiker alongside their dragons had stepped in and saved him. It wasn't because Hiker defended himself from his brother. No, even though Hiker knew Thad had wanted him dead for all their lives, he had never been able to stand up to his twin. Not until recently, when he knew it had gone on for too long and not stopping his twin would destroy the planet. Back then, Hiker had been powerless and seized with paralysis when threatened by Thad.

Hiker survived the attack the day the Great War started because of one person: Ainsley Carter.

The shapeshifting elf had been a delegate from the elfin council, advising the Dragon Elite and other governing bodies. She had been considered a supreme source on strategy and political preparedness. Even then, it had been hard for most to believe the woman was so astute on worldly matters because like she was now, Ainsley never took anything seriously. At least, that's how it appeared on the surface.

Those who underestimated the elf's flippant nature were usually left holding the losing hand when she served them up an agenda they hadn't expected nor could contend with. Ainsley Carter was brilliant. She was the only woman to have ever entered the Gullington, not including Mama Jamba, of course. Ainsley had been the one who stepped in front of the attack meant to kill Hiker.

"Stupid girl," Hiker muttered to himself, blinking to clear his vision as he looked around the office of the past. It was the same one he'd just left, only several centuries earlier, but that wasn't how he knew he'd arrived in the past. He knew because everything was black and white.

Hiker held up his hand, and as Sophia had informed him, his form was still full of color, although everything around him was in shades of gray. The hollering in the hallway took him back in a way he hadn't expected. He suddenly remembered when there were dozens of dragonriders, all ready to defend the planet for the good of all. That had been before the Great War. Before those at the House took over, blinding mortals from magic. Before Ainsley nearly lost everything because of a stupid decision.

Stranger than hearing the Castle filled with noise was to look around Hiker's office and see himself pacing in front of the bank of windows that overlooked the Pond. Nothing had changed outside in a few hundred years, either.

"See, I told Mama this was ridiculous," he said to himself, knowing those in the past couldn't hear him. He was a ghost walking through their reality. As he'd suspected, he was right. "Nothing has changed. Nothing ever does. We just keep repeating ourselves."

Although Hiker knew he couldn't be heard or seen, he was still spooked when he heard his past self say, "I know you're there."

Present Hiker stiffened, wondering how his past version had sensed him. Then he heard her voice at his back.

"And here I thought you never noticed me," Ainsley said as she came into the office, looking different than he remembered.

How could he forget the way she used to wear her red hair, braided intricately down her back with jewels and pearls neatly tucked into the strands. She wore a blue dress that was both classy and revealing, showing her chest and collar bones. The most striking thing about her was the way she carried herself like the dignified delegate she was. Her chin was held high with confidence but hiding under the surface was the always-present teasing smile that was Ainsley's trademark.

The black and white version of Hiker turned and put his back to the bank of windows. "You know that's not true."

She swept into the room, and her eyes narrowed with a hint of mischief. "What I know is that you wished you never noticed me."

Hiker sighed, both the present version of him and the one from the past. "Don't be so dramatic."

"The men are ready," she said, angling her head toward the hallway where the noise of dozens of dragonriders could be heard.

Hiker nodded solemnly, his hands still pressed behind his back.

"You realize a war is imminent," Ainsley stated, suddenly all business.

"I don't know that," he replied firmly.

She marched up to the leader of the Dragon Elite and looked into his eyes. "You're deluding yourself if you think you can negotiate with Thad Reinhart. It isn't even worth the risk."

"Miss Carter, although I appreciate your input—"

"I remember when you used to call me Ains," she interrupted, heat flashing on her face.

The present-day Hiker gulped. He hadn't remembered calling her that, not until right then. How could he have forgotten?

"I told you," past Hiker told her. "That's over. We aren't going back to it."

"Because you're scared," she challenged, not wavering from her position in front of him.

Hiker hadn't forgotten how she never stood down. Ainsley had always challenged him—since the beginning. He almost laughed, remembering how infuriating it had been at their first few meetings… but then, that had been why he'd fallen in love with her.

He shook his head, dispelling the thought. It was like a disease trying to take over, and he wouldn't let it. He wasn't going to get sucked into the past. It happened the way it had for a reason. Ainsley wouldn't listen to reason. She wouldn't accept they had no future. Because for as intelligent as she was, she was impulsive and made a bad decision. Yes, one that saved Hiker, but also sentencing her to something probably worse than death.

"A war doesn't have to be inevitable," past Hiker said, stepping around Ainsley and striding for the door. He pivoted and faced her when he was a safe distance away.

Present Hiker stood between the two, tethered between them as they faced off.

"It is though, Hiker," Ainsley argued. "I've gotten communications from several sources. Something is happening to mortals. Things aren't right. This is bigger than the dragonriders. This is bigger than any of us could have conceived."

He shook his head. "No, this will pass, just as we have circumvented dozens of wars over the years. That's my job as the leader of the Dragon Elite, and I will continue to resolve disputes so that tomorrow, your world knows mostly peace."

"What about you?" Ainsley demanded. "You sacrifice your own happiness because your first responsibility, your only one, is to the Dragon Elite?"

As cold as ever, Hiker nodded. "I told you, there can't be anything between us. It complicates my role here. It confuses your job for the elves."

"What if I didn't work for the elfin council anymore?" she asked and took a step forward.

Past Hiker copied the movement, taking a step backward. "You can't do that. You can't give up everything you've worked for…for me."

She shook her head. "That's what you do for love, Hiker. You sacrifice your life. You change everything for the hope of something better. That's what the Dragon Elite do, so why wouldn't I? Why wouldn't you?"

He narrowed his eyes at her, but deep inside, there was something breaking. She was getting through to him, and both versions of Hiker were afraid what she could say next that would break his resolve. That was why he spun and marched for the door.

"I can't do this with you, Miss Carter," Hiker said, retreating fast.

"Don't you walk away from this!" Ainsley yelled, her face blossoming red.

He halted and looked over his shoulder at her, real regret in his eyes.

Sensing him caving, Ainsley took another step forward, pleading with her every movement. "Please. Give us a chance. We're good. We're better than good. I have a reason to believe we could be great."

Past Hiker closed his eyes for a half-beat. Present Hiker remembered the internal struggle he'd felt back then. Acutely he remembered wanting to run to the elf. Tell her he loved her. That it had always been her. Then he felt the always present conflict that told him he wasn't fit for love—never had been. That was the voice Hiker Wallace chose to listen to that day.

Letting out a long breath, past Hiker said, "Maybe in another life, but not this one. We just aren't meant to be."

"I love you," Ainsley argued, conviction covering her face and vibrating in her words.

He pressed his lips together and simply nodded.

It burned present Hiker up. It infuriated him that he couldn't just return her words and say the one thing he knew to be true, even if it scared him. The look that crossed Ainsley's face next was his penance.

"I must go," Hiker said, his attention drifting to the noise in the corridor of the Castle.

"I have to tell you something," Ainsley urged, stepping over to him.

A warning crossed past Hiker's face as he shook his head, making her stop abruptly. "No, not right now. Tell me tomorrow or another day. Right now, I've got to focus. I've got a war to avoid."

That actually made present Hiker laugh. There was no avoiding what was coming. It was why Papa Creola had created a reset point. In case things never recovered, there was a place to go back to—to start again.

"Hiker." Ainsley reached out, suddenly appearing vulnerable.

He shook his head sternly. "Good day, Miss Carter. I will see you tomorrow during the negotiations. I expect you'll be there?"

Present Hiker nearly screamed. If there was a way to tell the fool he used to be not to allow Ainsley on the battlefield, he would have. All he could do was yell to a room full of lost souls who couldn't hear him.

"Yes, I'll be there, Mr. Wallace," Ainsley said, sucking in a breath and seeming to brace herself. "Good day."

Past Hiker nodded in a business-like fashion and walked out the door, leaving Ainsley to stand alone in the middle of his office.

Present Hiker thought that was the end and felt betrayed by Mama Jamba for making him see this memory. It, as he'd expected, changed nothing. Ainsley had saved him out of foolishness. He had chosen not to love her because it wasn't an option for the leader of the Dragon Elite. How he could have ever allowed her to give it all up—her career as a delegate for the elfin council. No, things happened the way they did because there had been no other way. There never had been, and there was no way to change that.

Hiker pulled the gold token from his pocket, preparing to go back to the present when something glistened on Ainsley's cheek and caught his attention.

It was a tear.

Another one joined it as the elf began to cry. In a dignified manner, she wiped her cheeks and pressed her hand to her stomach.

"By the way, Hiker," she said, speaking to him like he was still there. "I'm pregnant with your child."

CHAPTER ONE HUNDRED SEVENTEEN

The weight of love had never seemed so heavy for Hiker Wallace as at that moment. As he stared at the elf and heard her secret, it all became clear. It had been centuries, but now he knew why Ainsley had sacrificed herself for him. He understood why she'd offered to give up her position with the elfin council. He knew why she didn't want to give up—even after everything he'd put her through. It made him angrier than he had ever been in his entire life.

The gold harp in his pocket couldn't help him then. Nothing could quell the fire in his gut.

With a force that would break a diamond, Hiker pressed down on either side of the gold token, breaking it in two and ending the reset point forever.

He spiraled through a black vortex until he was dumped back in his office in the present time. Everything color once more.

He peered at the two halves of the coin and felt more broken than the gold token.

Ainsley had been pregnant with his child. If he had known, he would have... He didn't know what he would have done because he admitted he was too stubborn for his own good. However, he believed this information would have softened him as it was doing now. There were three things he knew for sure.

He wouldn't have allowed Ainsley to go into the negotiations the next day. He wouldn't have denied her the life she continued to beg him for, and he would have loved her fiercely.

The new information changed everything.

He had to help Ainsley recover her memories from before the attack. He had to help find the cure so she could leave the Gullington for good. Then Hiker had to prepare to lose her forever because once she knew the truth, she would leave and never look back at the man who had scarred her for life.

CHAPTER ONE HUNDRED EIGHTEEN

The President of the United States was apparently easier to get an audience with than Zac Efron, according to the sources Sophia had talked to. She'd actually met with the President since her role as a Dragon Elite gave her such privileges. However, Zac Efron wasn't a politician. He was a movie star and the same rules didn't apply to him.

Sophia knew the biggest complication would be getting past his bodyguard. Ramy was apparently a no-nonsense sort of guy who was fiercely protective. No one got to the star unless they went through him first. Sophia worried that telling the obsessed bodyguard she needed Zac Efron for a mysterious mission where the details were even unclear to her would probably not go over well.

She wished Lee at the Crying Cat Bakery had given her more information. Sophia had gotten a message from the baker that she'd have the location of the katana by the end of the day. So it was up to Sophia to get Zac Efron. Then she could complete the mission and wash her hands of fulfilling her end of the bargain tied to getting the twenty million dollars.

Lunis and Sophia stood outside the gated mansion in Beverly Hills. It was where Zac Efron lived according to Mortimer and his

SARAH NOFFKE & MICHAEL ANDERLE

brownies. It was reassuring to Sophia that Zac was considered a good enough person that the brownies cared for this home. She still wondered why in the world this mission would require she bring the musically inclined star along.

Maybe it's because he's a treble maker, Lunis offered, glamoured to look like a Fed Ex truck as Sophia did surveillance on the grounds.

She gave her dragon a murderous stare, but that only seemed to encourage him as he snickered back at her. "I think he's considered more of a popstar and actor than a musician."

What? he asked. *You don't know. He might be into classical music.*

Sophia lowered her chin, preparing herself for the nonsense that was sure to follow. "Oh really? You think we're recruiting Zac Efron for this mission because he's a composer in the classics?"

Lunis shrugged. *Maybe. It could be because baby got Bach.*

"An angel just died from the worst pun ever," Sophia stated.

The dragon shook his head. *Bad puns don't kill angels. If they did believe me, you'd be responsible for killing them all.*

"Regardless, I don't need any more input from you on this subject," she told him dryly.

Really? he asked. *So you don't think we need Zac because he's too hot to Handel.*

"Please stop," she encouraged.

Oh fine. Those who don't like music puns have my symphonies.

Sophia groaned. "You're the worst. Like literally the worst."

Why thank you, he said, bowing slightly and looking proud.

"Okay, well will you keep an eye out for me?" Sophia was planning out her way onto the grounds. There was a guard station at the front of the driveway and apparently a few others throughout the property but the real concern was this Ramy guy. Sophia wasn't sure what to expect and was preparing for another giant like she met at the top of the beanstalk.

Sure, Lunis answered. *I'll watch your Bach.*

Sophia paused. "On second thought, I think you should work on your jokes instead."

By work on them, do you mean I should repeat them in your head and we'll tweak them until they are perfect? Lunis questioned.

Sophia shook her head. "No, I think we should play the quiet game while I'm in Zac Efron's house. A melodramatic groan will get me caught."

Or a side-splitting chuckle, which is more likely, Lunis corrected.

"We're talking about your jokes, right?" she questioned.

Lunis dismissed her with a wave of his clawed foot. *Go on then. I'll watch and pop in and save you when you are moments away from getting chopped in two.*

Sophia blinked at him. "I'm going into a movie star's house. Not a serial killer's."

Lunis pursed his lips. *Be ready for anything, Soph. You don't know anything about this Ramy. He could be a bomber.*

Sophia rolled her eyes. "Let's hope the only thing he's bombed is a photo."

Okay, well hurry up, Lunis encouraged. *I have a Zoom call with an agent.*

She gave him a warning look. "You're not allowed to go into show business. You're a dragon."

He looked away suddenly. *Nobody puts Baby in the corner.*

"Oh, angels above," Sophia grumbled, shaking her head at her dragon.

This is just like that episode of Friends, Lunis related.

"No. No, it's not," Sophia cut in.

You didn't let me finish, Lunis protested.

"It doesn't matter. Nothing you could say would make this like a sitcom about six singles living in New York City," Sophia stated.

He sighed. *Well, you have to have a bit of imagination, excuse me very much. The Gullington is the coffee shop, Central Perk. I'm Joey because I'm friendly and more attractive than all my friends.*

"Who am I?" Sophia dared to ask.

You're Gunther, he answered at once.

"Because I'm not one of the cool kids?"

Because of the hair, Soph. Obviously.

She shook her head at her dragon and backed away, preparing her glamour. "Work on your jokes, Lun. Currently, they might be the death of me."

You just wait until I'm famous, Lunis warned. *Then you'll be sorry.*

She nodded. "I'm sure I will. Until then, I'll be Bach."

CHAPTER ONE HUNDRED NINETEEN

Ordinary Joe was stationed at the guard hut by the gated driveway. He was bidding on some X-Men Wolverine claws on eBay when Sophia checked on him. She probably could have strolled right past him and he wouldn't have noticed. She wasn't leaving anything to chance so she kept herself glamoured and snuck over the wall that surrounded the property.

The grounds of Zac's place were pristine with a rolling grassy lawn, large towering trees and a shimmering pool that spread out in front of the mansion. At first glance, it appeared the rest of the guards were off for the night which meant Sophia only needed to get past this Ramy guy.

Unlike with the guard in the hut, she couldn't just sneak by him. According to her sources at the brownie official headquarters, Sophia needed to get Ramy's blessing to get Zac's cooperation. She guessed they had a Whitney Houston, Kevin Costner sort of relationship—in a purely platonic way. Still, it didn't sound like Zac did anything without Ramy signing on. Sophia thought she'd need Zac's compliance. She didn't want to just force him on the mission or it could get way more complicated.

Stealthily, Sophia ran around the property avoiding being seen by any of the groundskeepers or waitstaff. It was on the second pass she noticed a figure standing outside of what she thought was most likely the master bedroom on the second floor. That had to be where Zac was and the figure must be none other than Ramy, the fierce bodyguard.

After breaking into ancient Hindu temples, a cyborg's pirate ship and a top-level magitech facility, trespassing into a mortal's home seemed like a piece of cake.

What kind of cake? Lunis asked in Sophia's head, making her laugh out loud abruptly.

I don't think it matters, she replied, scaling the side of the mansion.

It totally counts, Lunis argued. *Evan and I agree on very few things, but one of them is that carrot cake needs to stop being a cake.*

Sophia nodded as she climbed the lattice alongside the house, careful to stay out of sight of a housekeeper dusting the vases inside. The sun setting on the grounds was making her job slightly easier since the bright Southern California sun was streaming through the glass doors, making anyone who looked out have to squint.

I agree fruit should be left off dessert, Sophia related. *Although according to many I've spoken to, that's not a popular opinion. Apparently to these people strawberries belong on desserts.*

Lunis clicked his tongue. *This world is full of people with wrong opinions, my dear Soph. Those people are a great example of that.*

Anyway, Sophia continued as she neared the balcony to the master bedroom. *This is as easy as chocolate cake.*

I've never made a chocolate cake, but I like the idea you think it's easy to make one, Lunis said, a dreamy quality to his voice. *When you get back since it's so easy, will you make me one?*

Sophia chuckled to herself. *No, but I'll ask Lee at Crying Cat Bakery too.*

No, thanks, Lunis replied. *I'd prefer not to ingest cyanide.*

Lee wouldn't poison you, Sophia argued.

Of course not, he said sounding insulted. *I'm delightful and have amazing jokes. You, on the other hand...I'm surprised you've made it this long.*

She shook her head and hopped over the railing to the balcony and slid up against the bricks to the house. *You know, Lun, why do I keep you around?*

Because I'm an amazing and brave dragon who constantly saves the day, he answered.

Sophia grinned and prepared to storm into the mansion since the element of surprise was always to her advantage. *No. It's because I'd really like a new pair of boots.*

*Oh, really...*he growled.

Yeah, but I haven't found the right shoemaker, she replied.

Let me guess, he said dryly, *you're looking for someone who is an expert at dealing with dragon hide, right.*

She laughed. *If the shoe fits, Lunis...I'll wear it.*

CHAPTER ONE HUNDRED TWENTY

"You're all I have," a guy said, his back to the balcony doors as Sophia snuck through after using a rudimentary spell to unlock them. The man wasn't wearing a guard's uniform and for a moment, she thought she'd entered the wrong set of rooms.

He had brown curly hair with a tweed cap pulled down over it and as far as Sophia could tell, he was wearing a sweater vest over a pullover button-down shirt. In front of his chest, as he faced a closed door, he had his fist in front of him.

"As I was saying," the guy began again. "Zac, you're all I have. Well, and this song." The man cleared his throat before he started singing. "A million dreams is all it's gonna take. Oh, a million dreams for the world we're gonna make—"

Sophia cleared her throat, strangely feeling bad about witnessing this one-sided show of affection.

The dude froze, his jazz hands spread out beside him as he bent his knees, telegraphing his next move which she suspected was a low lunge. Instead, the guy straightened and dropped his hands. He turned to face her, his eyes narrowed.

"Who are you?" he asked, looking her up and down. "What are you doing here? How did you get in?"

She pointed at the open door behind her. "Through there."

"It's locked," he argued.

"For most," she agreed. "I'm not most though. I'm Sophia Beaufont, a rider with the Dragon Elite and I'm obviously in the wrong place."

He gave her a rude expression. "You sure are, unless you came to a place where you want to get your ass handed to you."

Sophia nearly laughed as she looked Sweater Vest over. "Um. Nah, I'm good. I was just looking for Ramy. Is he on the first floor? Guarding Zac outside the home recording studio?"

The guy narrowed his eyes at her. "You got one thing right today, but too bad for you, it's the day of your funeral. I'm Ramy. Where do you want to be buried?" He punched his fist into his open palm while giving her a menacing glare.

To Sophia's ultimate amusement, the guy seemed to have hurt himself when he punched his own hand. He tried to cover it up as he shook out his palm and put his hand back beside his leg. "Hey Ramy. Great meeting you. I've heard great things."

"From whom?" he demanded, cutting her off.

"From people you don't know," she replied at once.

He scoffed. "I know everyone. Was it Lady Gaga? Brittany? Martha—"

Sophia shook her head. "No, you seriously don't know my sources, but they had good things to say...albeit a bit inflated." Although Sophia didn't know how the brownies misconstrued this guy as a threatening source of power, she assumed that to a tiny house-elf, Ramy might seem scary. From the little she'd witnessed, he had an intimidating stage presence. Sophia wondered what else the brownies got wrong about him, this supposed intimidating bodyguard.

He had gone quiet studying her with a calculating gaze. Sophia decided this was the perfect time to use her negotiation skills since she'd prefer not to break his nose or any of Zac's modern furniture

"So I just need to see Zac," she began, pointing at the door at Ramy's back. "Is he in there?"

"No!" Ramy yelled, just as a man's voice echoed through the door.

"Don't you wanna get away to a whole new part you're gonna

play," a man who sounded just like Zac Efron sang from the other room. "'Cause I got what you need, so come with me and take the ride to the other side."

For a moment, Ramy looked lost in the music, his eyes growing dreamy.

"It's weird," Sophia cut in, trying to bring Ramy back to the land of the living. "That sounds just like Zac Efron in there."

"That is strange," the guy said, doing a terrible job of lying. "T-Th-That's Alfred the butler. He always sings while polishing the silver."

"Bizarre that you all keep the silver in the bathroom," Sophia observed, sniffing the air and smelling soap.

"That's not the bathroom," Ramy argued. "It's the dining room."

"On the second floor?" Sophia questioned and looked around at the bed in the corner. "Just off the bedroom like most modern homes in Beverly Hills. That makes sense."

Ramy nodded. "It's a new thing. It's totally in. That way the movie stars can roll out of bed and get a sandwich."

"Genius," Sophia said, starting forward. She'd decided she'd had enough of this show. "I'm just going to go ask Zac if he can help me out with something."

Ramy held up his hand attempting to stop her.

She paused, more out of amusement than anything.

"No," he argued. "You shall not pass."

"Without squashing you, that's for sure," she joked.

"Zac can't see you," he stated with confidence.

She had to give it to him, he was doing a great job of trying to keep her away from his charge.

"He can though," she argued. " I have a really cool mission for him I'm sure he'll want to go on."

"What does it involve?" Ramy asked.

Sophia tucked her chin. "Nothing much. Just recovering a katana, some magic and maybe a tiny bit of danger."

The guard shook his head and folded his arms. "I can't condone such a mission."

"Yeah, but the thing is I need you to endorse it," Sophia told him.

He continued to shake his head. "There's no way."

Sophia pulled her sword halfway out of her sheath. "How about now?"

Ramy didn't even flinch at the show of power. "Nope. I don't care if you are a dragonrider, as you pretend to be. I'm not allowing you to endanger Zac."

Slumping slightly, Sophia rolled her eyes, not liking it had come to this. "Well, I'm afraid I'm going to have to take Zac one way or another."

He shrugged like the loss was all hers. "Too bad, but I don't know how you plan to do that."

Sophia actually laughed this time. "I think that's pretty clear."

Holding out his arms, he looked around. "How do you mean?"

"Well, I'm me and you're you," she stated as though this fully explained her case. "I have a sword and you have mismatched socks. Also, I'm a dragonrider and you're a fanboy. I think we've pretty much settled this, huh?"

He pulled in a breath. "There's something you haven't considered, Sophia."

She blinked at him. "That you've lost your mind and the nurse will be in here in a moment to give you your meds?"

Ramy shook his head. "No," he said, raising his hands over his head. "That I'm a ninja."

Sophia knew the time for such antics had passed. She needed to get on with things. "Yeah, the thing about ninjas is they usually never announce it. Can I go see Zac now?"

Ramy dropped his hands, looking disappointed. "No. Whatever you're taking him for, there's no way I'm allowing it. It could hurt him and anything dangerous that might hurt—"

The scream that ripped out of Ramy's mouth didn't really surprise Sophia. She knew Lunis had flown over the gated wall to Zac's place and stationed himself outside the bedroom.

As she knew, the dragon's single eye was pressed into the bedroom window behind her, blinking in at the would-be bodyguard. Lunis had even breathed out smoke through his nostrils for effect.

"Dragon!" Ramy yelled. "Mother fu—" He threw up his hands and ran behind Sophia, actually putting himself closer to Lunis, but acting as though she might protect him from the blue dragon busy peering in at them. "There's a dragon. We have to protect Zac."

Sophia patted Ramy on the arm and gave him a knowing smile. "No problem. I intend to. Just tell him he's going on a mission with me."

Ramy peeled away from her, still giving the dragon at their back a worried expression. "B-Bu- the dragon?"

"He won't hurt anyone as long as you do as I say," Sophia warned. "Otherwise, one word from me and he'll pillage and destroy."

Lunis snickered in her head. *I'd like to pillage an ice cream shop right now.*

Shush, she warned. *I'm trying to make a show of you being dangerous and intimidating.*

I am, Lunis declared. *I just ruined a whole rose bush getting up here. I took no names as I blasted that thing.*

You are a fierce and crazy being, she said with a laugh.

Meanwhile, Ramy had hurried off to the bathroom, opening the door without knocking. "Hey, hey, Zac-Monster. I'm going to have to cut bath time short. Something has come up."

"This better be good," a voice came from the steamy room that smelled of floral scents.

Ramy glanced out the door at the dragon still lurking outside the bedroom window. "It is. You have my blessing to do this thing while I hold down the fort here."

CHAPTER ONE HUNDRED TWENTY-ONE

"If there's a rocket, tie me to it," Zac answered somewhere in the bathroom. "Otherwise, leave me to my suds. It's been a long day."

Ramy's eyes widened as Lunis puffed out another long trail of smoke. "Thing is, days can get longer. I think you ought to be thinking about getting out of the tub and joining our new friend on a quest."

"Quest?" Zac questioned.

Sophia decided it was time to take over. She had gotten the endorsement she needed, just not the way she had expected. Abandoning all etiquette, she strode straight into the man's bathroom but kept her eyes up just in case.

In her peripheral vision, she could tell the star was mostly submerged in bubbles in a bath. His neck, head and shoulders were all that were visible.

"Excuse me," Zac protested at the sight of her.

"She has a sword," Ramy stated, pointing at her sheath. "Also a dragon. I think the dragon is of most concern because she hadn't used the sword yet but has kind of sort of used the dragon."

"Has she, or hasn't she?" Zac asked his bodyguard like the question was of real importance.

"He's outside and totally fogging up the windows," Ramy answered.

Zac sighed. "We just had them washed."

Ramy nodded, an apologetic look on his face. "I thought of that, sir. Should I offer it something?"

Zac thought on this before glancing at Sophia. "Does your dragon want something in payment for backing up from the house?"

This whole scenario had turned so strange Sophia didn't even know where to begin.

Ice cream, Lunis suggested in her head.

"He wants broccoli," Sophia suggested earning a loud growl from her dragon in her head. It actually wasn't so quiet. The noise shook the window, making Ramy skip over a few steps and pretend to inspect towels on the shelf.

"He wants Ramy to feed them to him," Sophia continued then added, "by hand."

Ramy's eyes widened and he looked at Zac with a pleading expression.

The movie star considered this for a moment before waving at his bodyguard. "Go on then. Go feed the dragon. Give him what he wants while I find out what's going on here with his dragonrider."

"Sir…" Ramy's voice was shaking.

"Go on," Zac ordered.

Sophia couldn't help but feel a bit of glee.

I'm not eating broccoli, Lunis stated.

You haven't had a vegetable in months, she told him. *You'll eat out of that bodyguard's hand and like it. That's the least we can do for nearly making him pee in his pants.*

Fine, but after this we're stopping by the ice cream shop and getting cookies and cream, Lunis argued.

After this, we're stopping by the mysterious place and getting a katana, she countered. *You will get your ice cream when everything is done.*

You're not the boss of me, he fired.

And just like that, I deleted the Netflix account you pirated, Sophia joked.

No, Lunis screamed in her mind. *Fine. Mission now. Ice cream later. Have it your way, do-gooder. In my next life, I'm going to be a bad dragon and pillage.*

No, you won't, she said with a laugh.

One can dream. Lunis sighed. *Send Sweater Vest out here. I've found a ball I want him to throw for me to fetch. It's a tire but we're going to call it a ball.*

Sophia shot Ramy a look. "The dragon is ready for his broccoli, and he has a game for you."

Ramy didn't look relieved by this news. Once again, he looked at Zac for rescue.

His boss didn't offer sympathy. "Go play with the dragon. I need to see what this is all about."

Taking in a deep breath, Ramy charged out of the bathroom, calling to Lunis as he did. "Nice dragon. Who wants trees and cheese? I've got extra cheese for good dragons."

Sophia giggled, directing her attention roughly in the direction of where Zac's head was, conscious he was totally naked under the bubbles in his bath. "Hey, I'm Sophia Beaufont, a rider for the Dragon Elite."

The star sat up, making the water trudge back and forth in the bath. "Nice to meet you, Sophia. What brings you to my bathroom?"

"First off," she started, indicating Ramy who was hurrying downstairs, she was guessing to get broccoli from the refrigerator. "Your bodyguard..."

"Yeah, he's got spirit and I find that encouraging," Zac said.

Sophia could appreciate that. "Anyway, I have a mission that requires you."

"Oh, is it an acting role?"

She shrugged. "Couldn't really say. The truth is, I don't know. It involves getting a magical katana but I don't know much more than that."

Without warning, Zac stood from the bath, giving Sophia little notice. She spun around but found a full-length mirror behind her, which gave her exactly the view she was trying to avoid. Quickly she pressed her eyes shut. "What are you doing?" she asked.

"Getting dry," Zac replied. "I've been looking for something to prepare me for my next role and this seems like just the kind of thing. It's got mystery, an element of danger and dragonriders. How can I say no?"

"What's your next role?" she asked, too curious not to.

"Beats me," he answered, toweling off. "Haven't landed it yet, but what better way to prepare. No one in Hollywood will turn me down when I tell them I worked alongside the Dragon Elite."

Sophia kept her eyes shut as she nodded. "Cool. I had no idea we were such help with endorsements."

Zac began humming as he threw a robe on. "For sure. In this volatile climate, there are two sure-fire ways to land a major role. Become a vegan or associate yourself with the Dragon Elite. I'm glad you showed up when you did because the idea of giving up cheese was pretty much robbing me of my will to live."

CHAPTER ONE HUNDRED
TWENTY-TWO

"When this is all over, we still have to clear up some stuff," Wilder said, eyeing Zac Efron who had been totally okay with traveling through a magical portal alongside a dragon who had barfed up broccoli all over his lawn. They arrived outside the Gullington to meet Wilder and had then traveled through another portal to a remote part of Japan. It was the location Lee had messaged to Sophia, telling her it was the place where the mysteriously magical katana was located.

"Why I've dragged you off on a mission with Zac Efron and my delusional dragon?" Sophia asked him, grateful to finally get to spend some time with the guy, even if she had a movie star and Lunis beside her.

Wilder shook his head. "Nope. That seems about usual. Just wondering why Hiker is trudging around the Castle and shaking his head and muttering to himself nonstop. He doesn't seem right ever since you gave him that gold token."

"Oh," Sophia said. She was going to have to check in on the Viking and find out how things were going. The newest mission had taken over her thoughts, as they tended to do, but she didn't want to lose sight of the progress the leader of the Dragon Elite was making, although it didn't sound like he was making progress. She'd check on him upon returning.

"Right." She pulled out the magical compass Liv had loaned to her. "First things first though. We need to find the location of an ancient temple that's hidden away from most eyes."

"Is this when you tell me why I've been selected for this mission?" Zac had his eyes on Lunis who had his head down low and kept tilting it back and forth, flashing him strange expressions.

"Wish I knew," Sophia said absentmindedly. "Truth is, that part is a mystery to me."

"And the magical chewing gum that makes the chewer happy?" Wilder asked, having gotten quickly briefed on things before leaving.

She shook her head. "No idea."

"I'm guessing you also don't know why Lunis and I are required either then?" Wilder questioned.

"Here I thought you were just a pretty face," she said to him, pulling her gaze up from the compass and flashing him a flirtatious grin.

"Hey now," he admonished. "Don't you go judging me on my brains and skills. I work out for a reason and want to be appreciated for my hard work."

She nodded. "Don't worry. I'd never dare to get all obsessed over what's on the inside."

"Are you two going to be like this the entire time?" Zac wanted to know.

Undoubtedly, Lunis answered for them.

Zac leaned in over Sophia's shoulder. "Is there a reason your dragon keeps looking at me strangely?"

Sophia giggled, still trying to work out how to use the magical compass. "Yeah, I think he wants you to recommend him to your agent."

Zac sucked in a breath. "Oh, man. The thing is dragon—"

Lunis Wilfred Montgomery the Second, Lunis corrected.

"His name is Lunis," Sophia stated dryly. "Just Lunis. I named him. I should know."

Hey, Lunis chirped. *Show dogs get unique names and I want one too. Something that sets me apart.*

"Your insanity does that," she argued.

"Yeah, so the thing is," Zac said carefully. "My agent only represents...how do I put this..."

"People," Sophia supplied. "His agent represents people, Lun. You're not one. Oh and you already work for the Dragon Elite saving Mother-Freaking-Nature's planet. So get over the dream."

Lunis huffed, letting out a plume of smoke. *Boring. Thanks again for crushing my dreams, Meanie Face.*

"No problem," she replied, returning her attention to the magical compass.

"Have you worked out how it's supposed to get us to the temple?" Wilder asked, leaning in close, his chin an inch from her cheek.

"I think it's intention-based," she stated. "I know what we're looking for in general terms. I guess I just need to focus on that and it will point us in the right direction."

"Magic is cool," Zac said, his eyes wide with excitement.

It's all right, Lunis said. *You know what's cool is* High School Musical.

Sophia shook her head and focused on the ancient Japanese temple where the katana was apparently stored. Lee had said once they found it there would be minimal obstacles, but considering the source, that meant nothing to Sophia. As she began to focus on the place they needed to find, the needle to the compass began to toggle back and forth until it pointed due north down a sloping hill that led to what appeared to be an expansive valley, pristine and untouched by modern society.

She started forward, her entourage following behind her as her dragon began to hum *A Million Dreams* from the *Greatest Showman* movie.

CHAPTER ONE HUNDRED TWENTY-THREE

"One night isn't enough," Zac explained to Lunis as they strode down the hillside, coming closer to the bottom. "You need at least two to fully appreciate Disney Land."

See! Lunis exclaimed. *I told you, Soph.*

She shook her head, trying to concentrate on the compass but telling the chatty dragon and his new best friend to hush was about like trying to get Evan to floss his teeth.

Tell me more about Hugh Jackman, Lunis encouraged, talking excitedly to Zac. *Does he really smell like roses and do cherubs sing when he walks?*

Zac laughed good naturedly.

The needle of the compass took a hard turn to the east and Sophia pivoted. Thankfully Wilder was paying attention and directed the other two who were deep in conversation.

"Where do you think this thing is leading us?" Wilder asked, catching up to her.

It was a good question because up ahead roughly a hundred yards away was a cliff. Sophia wasn't going to blindly follow the compass over the side. There was faith and there was stupidity and she already felt a bit foolish having gone on this mysterious mission with so few details.

"I think we won't know where it's taking us until we're there," she said, not knowing where the answer came from. It felt like it was the right answer as she said it aloud. Life was weird and often supplied information in such ways.

She found her feet continuing to move as her eyes stayed glued on the compass, her intention set for the temple they needed to find. Sophia felt confident Wilder would keep his eyes on the path up ahead and not allow her to walk into an obstacle. She felt strangely relieved Lunis and Zac were doing all right based on their conversation which had seemed to go on without pause for the last several minutes.

"I think we're there then," Wilder said after a moment, his tone surprised.

Sophia jerked her head up to find a large Japanese temple towering over them suddenly. It hadn't been there when they had been standing at the top of the valley. It hadn't even been there a few minutes ago, the last time she'd allowed herself to look up. The building had simply materialized when they were only feet from it.

"Wow, that's really cool," Zac said in awe.

If you think that's cool, Lunis began. *I have my own YouTube channel.*

"He also lives in a secret uncharted cave in Scotland only the Dragon Elite can see," Sophia said dryly.

Stop boring the man, Soph, Lunis chimed.

"Nope, secret cave in Scotland is pretty noteworthy, Lunis," Zac offered.

The dragon nodded. *Yeah, I've got my own pad away from the others because they are so twentieth century if you know what I mean.*

Zac nodded.

Sophia was having a hard time with the two gabbing behind her. "There's a trick to this place," she mused, mostly to herself.

"Why do you say that?" Wilder asked at her side.

She flashed him a grin. "Because there's always a trick. It's like some weird arrangement I made with life before being born."

He nodded. "I made the same one. I'm not sure what we were thinking but at least we think alike."

The Japanese temple was breathtaking sitting in the middle of the pristine valley. Multiple tiers rose up, each getting smaller as they reached higher into the sky. The blue tiles on the roof were exactly as Sophia associated with Japanese structures. So were the white walls and black beams. One aspect was out of place from how she pictured a Japanese temple.

"There it is," she said pointing to the entrance covered in a thick sheet of ice.

"The trick," Wilder agreed with confidence. He held out his hand and sent a neat ball of fire toward the obstacle. It hit, piercing through but only making a small pinhole.

"At this rate, we'll be out of magic before we get through," Sophia stated.

"Now I think we know why you needed me," Lunis said, stepping forward.

Sophia flashed him a smile. "Of course. You're supposed to—"

Sing you the best rendition of It's Never Enough *from* The Greatest Showman *for encouragement,* Lunis interrupted, clearing his throat and beginning to sing. *I'm trying to hold my breath. Let it stay this way. Can't let this moment end. You set off a dream in me—*

"Would you blast that door with fire," Sophia ordered, cutting off her dragon's horrible singing.

He cut his eyes at her. *Really? I wasn't even to the chorus yet.*

"Lunis," she said, a warning in her voice.

Okay, fine, he sulked. *I guess I was brought here for my boring magical abilities rather than my awesome stage skills. Talk about a waste.*

The ancient dragon opened his mouth and unleashed a gorgeous stream of orange and red fire that hit the target perfectly and melted it at once. A large door was revealed and popped open at once, as though to welcome them in.

Sophia smiled wide. "That was brilliant. Great job, Lun."

He slumped. *I guess it was all right.*

Zac nodded, impressed. "That was the coolest thing I've ever seen."

This brightened Lunis up considerably. *I can swallow a sheep without chewing. Do you want to see that later?*

"Later," Sophia said consolingly to her dragon. "Right now, we have to find out how to get the katana and it's going to involve entering that temple." She gave Lunis a thoughtful expression.

He seemed to understand at once. *Don't worry. I'll stay out here and keep guard. Watch out for Zac. Don't let anything happen to him.*

Sophia nodded. "I'll watch out for myself too, Lunis. Stop fretting over me."

He shrugged. *Bring me back something.*

Wilder gave the dragon an uncertain expression. "Like a souvenir?"

Or a hotdog, Lunis suggested. *I'm hungry.*

CHAPTER ONE HUNDRED
TWENTY-FOUR

"My last girlfriend will never believe I got to go on a mission with a fire-breathing dragon," Zac began as they entered the temple. "I can't wait to tell her about this."

"He's not like most," Sophia warned.

To her surprise, Wilder nodded and said, "He's better than most. My dragon being excluded, Lunis is way more entertaining. Don't tell her that or she'll have my butt."

That admission made Sophia smile. It meant a lot to her that Wilder thought Lunis was special, and not in the way some kids eat glue.

The temple was all fire pits and ancient runes as Sophia had expected. It was kind of lackluster with a long hallway made of thin partition walls and pedestals decorated with bonsai trees. The place was in pristine condition though, like it had just been cleaned.

Pausing in the long hallway, Sophia turned to Wilder. "What do you make of this?"

"I've seen it before," he began tentatively. "It's a corridor and we walk through it until we get to the end. Very confusing, albeit straightforward."

Sophia rolled her eyes at him. "Seriously, you're as much a pain in the ass as my dragon."

He batted his eyes at her. "You would have it no other way, would you?"

She shook her head. "Yeah, I guess you're right."

The hallway ended at a narrow opening that appeared to empty out into a garden full of Japanese maples and a koi pond. The whole scene appeared quite idyllic. So much so that it instantly raised a flag for Sophia.

She held up her hand before Wilder stepped forward to the path. To get across the pond one had to hop across steppingstones.

"What?" he asked.

She indicated the stones that traced across the pond, ending on the other side where there was an altar. "Notice the markings on the stones?"

He narrowed his eyes at the first one. There was a single red dot. On the next stone there were two red dots. It went on like that, changing between one to three dots on each.

"What do you think that's about?" Wilder asked.

"Anyone speak Japanese?" Zac pointed to a sign on a neighboring wall.

Sophia didn't, but thanks to her role as rider for the Dragon Elite, she was able to speak and read many languages in most contexts. She narrowed her eyes at the sign.

"It says, *'Tap once or twice or three times to get to the other side, but more or less will end in doom.'*"

"Wow, they aren't sugar coating nothing," Wilder joked.

Sophia nodded, speculating on what this could mean. Zac began to tap his feet rhythmically, humming a tune.

"What are you doing?" she asked.

"Well, looking at the symbols, it sort of makes a dance," Zac explained and then tapped out a number in place. "You see in tap dance, the steps are done in sets of ones, twos and—"

"Oh, for the love of the angels," Sophia said, turning to face Wilder.

"We were told to bring Zac here to tap dance. Can my life get any more bizarre?"

"I'm sure there's been a mistake," Zac protested. "There's no way I could tap dance across that pond. I mean that's a long way and according to you the sign says if I mess up, it ends in doom. I haven't even gotten an Oscar yet."

Sophia didn't want to risk the life of the star. That was never the point. She pulled out her sword and decided to experiment. She extended the sword out and tapped the first stone marked with a single red dot. It glowed gold, sending a beam of light into the air.

"Cool," Zac exclaimed.

Sophia reached out farther and tapped the next stone with the two red circles twice. It also glowed gold. Then really having to reach, she hit the third stone also with two red circles, but this time only once.

A wall of fire shot up, blasting at the three of them. Wilder pulled them back, saving their eyebrows from the scorching flames.

Thankfully, after a few seconds, the wall of flames retreated, but the idea of one false move weighed heavily in the air.

"I don't want to die!" Zac yelled, his eyes wide with fear.

CHAPTER ONE HUNDRED TWENTY-FIVE

"Shut your eyes," Sophia suggested, realizing things were only going to get worse for the star who was unaccustomed to risking his life in such ways. "Just try breathing and we'll figure this out."

Zac did as he was told, pressing his hands to his head and singing a song to himself. Sophia gave Wilder an urgent expression that said, "What the hell are we supposed to do?"

Wilder was uncertain then his eyes widened with excitement. He pointed to her pocket. At first, Sophia didn't know what he was referring to, but then it hit her. The magical chewing gum!

Of course, she thought. Smile Despite Reality Chewing gum was the only way to get Zac to tap dance across the pond without fearing for his life. Sophia didn't think there was another way across since the pond since the stones stretched several dozen yards and there was no way she or Wilder could tap on the stones otherwise.

Sophia was talented at many different things, but tap dancing wasn't one of them. It should have been strange to her that she needed a random star to tap dance across an ancient Japanese temple to help recover a magical katana, but it wasn't and maybe that was the strangest thing of all.

"You know what, Zac," Sophia said, pulling the wrapped candy from her pocket. "I have some really good gum. Do you want to try it?"

He opened his eyes, giving her an uncertain expression. "I'm good right now. Do you have whiskey?"

She smiled at him. "No, but I think you'll like this gum. It's very refreshing."

"Yeah," Wilder added. "One might say it will help you to forget all your problems."

That seemed to do the trick. Zac held out his hand at once and Sophia dropped the only piece of magical chewing gum into it, hoping it did the trick. They had one chance to get this right. They also had only one Zac and she really hoped not to lose him for many reasons.

He popped the gum into his mouth and began chewing at once. His expression changed gradually. Several seconds later, he was smiling widely, blowing bubbles and moving about, as though itching to dance.

Sophia turned to Wilder with a tentative expression. "I guess it's now or never. What do you say?"

He nodded, offering her a confident grin. "Don't worry. That sword is moments away from being ours."

That was the push Sophia needed. She turned to Zac chewing happily on his gum and pointed. "Can you do me a favor really quickly and tap dance across this pond, hitting each stone with the number of red circles indicated?"

He thought for a moment. "Like it's *Dance Dance Revolution?*"

Sophia tilted her head to the side, thinking. "Yeah. Exactly. Remember, you want to get the high score, so don't mess up."

"This is for a high score?" Zac asked. "Like a championship?"

"Exactly," Sophia said, taking a step backward with Wilder just in case the wall of fire shot up again. "Good luck, Zac. We can't wait to watch you dance."

CHAPTER ONE HUNDRED TWENTY-SIX

"A youth writhing in fire could be what we see next," Wilder whispered from the corner of his mouth.

Sophia shook her head, encouraging him to shush it. She needed Zac to concentrate and she felt that meant she needed to as well.

The movie star shook out his arms, preparing himself for the dance number of his life. He didn't seem at all nervous as he chomped away on the gum, continuing to hum a tune to himself.

Zac's knees bounced as he prepared for the dance. It was a strange sight to watch, knowing that one misstep could harm the actor. Sophia told herself he was a professional and nothing was going to happen to him. It was worth the risk. Really, the only thing that let her allow Zac to do this was there was no turning back now. Sometimes in life, you go so far that turning back isn't an option.

"Don't you wanna get away to a whole new part you're gonna play," Zac began to sing under his breath softly as he studied the tile stones that stretched between him and the other side of the pond.

He continued to smack his gum and sing at the same time. "'Cause I got what you need, so come with me and take the ride."

Sophia gave Wilder a look of uncertainty as the dancer took his first step, his soft-soled shoe hitting the first stone.

"To the other side," Zac sang, as light as a feather as he bounced to the next stone, tapping that one twice, with a light but deliberate force. "So if you do like I do. So if you do like me."

His feet moved so fast it was hard to determine if he was hitting the tiles the right number of times as he progressed. Sophia reasoned he hadn't been knocked back by a deadly wall of fire, so he must be doing it right. Not only was his tap dancing impressive, but his singing was growing louder.

"Forget the cage, 'cause we know how to make the key. Oh, damn! Suddenly we're free to fly," Zac sang, now adding hands to the mix, making graceful movements that seemed to be helping him to maintain his balance as he hopped from stone to stone, always hitting it square in the middle with light taps.

"We're going to the other side," he belted out. His movements were getting jerkier and making Sophia nervous.

"He's just getting into it," Wilder explained, trying to console her after witnessing the fear spring to her face.

She nodded. Zac hit a stone three times with the toe of his shoe before going to the next one.

"So if you do like I do," he sang, only four tiles from the end.

He was so close, but the dance had grown more complicated with multiple taps pers square.

"So if you do like me," he sang, nearly losing his balance on the next move.

Sophia held her breath. She could hardly watch. If something happened to Zac...

Recovering his movement, he took the momentum of the near fall with him, bouncing once off the next to last stone before tapping the final one twice.

"We're going to the other side," he sang and jumped to the solid area opposite them next to the altar. He spun around and slid down on one knee, his arms wide and a broad victorious grin on his face.

His chest was rising and falling heavily, but he had made it. They had done it. Almost.

Sophia didn't know how they were getting across, but at exactly that moment the glow of the stones Zac had tapped grew. They met each other and intensified for a moment, bringing strange piercing music with the display.

Then all at once, it stopped.

Before Sophia's eyes, the area was replaced with a gold path that led to Zac on the other side.

CHAPTER ONE HUNDRED TWENTY-SEVEN

"Lifening just got more interesting," Wilder stated, peering skeptically at the yellow brick road that divided them from Zac Efron.

"That's not a real word," Sophia joked.

"Sure it is," he argued, putting his hand out and directing her backward. "Now, I'm going to take a step out. You stay here."

"The hell you are," she refused. "This is my mission. If anyone is going to test this to see if a trap results, it's going to be me."

He gave her a look of annoyance. "Are you always going to be this much of a pain in the ass, fighting me on everything to prove you're just as brave and all?"

Sophia gave him an incredulous expression. "Why would you ever expect anything different from me?"

His dimples surfaced when he smiled. "I was hoping you were going to say that. Otherwise this whole thing was off. I can't have a girlfriend who doesn't challenge my patience and push my buttons and get under my skin—"

"Okay, I get the point," Sophia said with a laugh.

"Hey guys," Zac called, still chewing on the happy gum. "Are you going to join me?"

Sophia nodded, returning her attention to the gold floor. "Yeah, I'm coming."

"We are," Wilder corrected, holding out his hand to her.

She pretended to be offended. "Seriously, now you can't cross without holding my hand? Are you always going to be so needy?"

Not missing a beat, he nodded. "Yeah, without a doubt. I'll need your constant reassurances and a lot of handholding. Is that a problem?"

Sophia laid her hand in his and squeezed. "Not at all. I guess in the best relationships, we get to take turns being needy."

He pressed his fingers into hers as they took a step out together. When their boots pressed into the gold stone the dragonriders paused, waiting for an explosion. When it didn't happen, Sophia let out a breath and alongside Wilder, she took another step and another until they had progressed all the way to the other side, meeting Zac who looked relieved to have them join him.

He pulled the gum out of his mouth with a grimace. "Do I have to keep chewing this? It's lost its taste."

Sophia shook her head. "No, but don't litter. I'm certain it will be trial by fire again if we litter in an ancient Japanese temple."

He deposited it into a piece of paper from his pocket as Sophia brought her attention to the altar on the wall. Now that they were right beside it she could see set into the wall were three recesses with sheer fabric covering them. The fabric had been obstructing the view of their contents when they were on the far side of the room.

Stepping up close, but careful not to touch anything, she spied what was inside the recesses. All three were the same. Sitting on a stand behind the fabric were long and brilliantly crafted katanas. They were identical with long handles wrapped in red and a curved blade and a sheath lying on the surface next to the stand.

"What do you make of this?" Sophia asked Wilder.

He flashed her his trademark grin. "I think I know why you had to have a weapons expert with you for this mission."

"Because he's the only one who laughs at my jokes?" she teased.

He nodded. "There's that. Also, I'm guessing two of those swords are fakes. Only a true weapon expert who can feel the memories of the sword will know which one is real."

"If we picked the wrong one," Sophia began slowly, working it out in her head as she spoke, "then it would probably produce another wall of fire or something else deadly."

"That's what I'm thinking," Wilder said, suddenly serious.

"So can you determine which one is real?" Sophia felt worry starting to pool in her chest. They'd come this far and couldn't fail. More importantly, she didn't want anything to happen to Wilder. She never wanted anything to happen to him. He'd quickly become her favorite person and that was saying a lot since she had a lot of people who competed for that spot in her life.

"I can," he replied, but he didn't sound confident.

"What is it?" she questioned, sensing his trepidation.

"It's hard to distinguish the difference without touching them," he answered.

"And you can't, can you?"

He shook his head. "I'm certain that's akin to choosing, so I can't do it until I know."

"Can you feel their memories from afar?" Sophia asked.

He tilted his head back and forth, uncertainty in his eyes as he studied the closest sword. "I can, but the energies are muddied between the three of them due to the proximity. It's hard to figure out which one is broadcasting the signal of the real sword." He indicated one of them. "I don't think it's this one because it feels new, like it's never been in battle or had any experiences. That wouldn't be the right sword."

Sophia stepped to the sword in the middle and Wilder followed before moving to the other one.

"It's one of these two, but they have competing energies," he explained. "The one in the middle feels really old and powerful. The one on the right has an extraordinary history. The question is, which one do you think is the magical katana?"

"Well," Sophia began, drawing the word out, "the right katana apparently has ten different magical properties and heals the person who wields it."

"So it's powerful," Wilder stated, stepping close to the sword in the middle and reaching out but pausing.

"However," Sophia interjected, "it stands to reason the right katana would have an extraordinary history. Maybe that's how it became so magical."

Wilder nodded, chewing his lip. "We have to make a decision between power and history. The one in the middle has never been in battle. The one on the right has seen over a thousand. This has to be your call, Soph. I'm sorry, but I can't offer you any more than that. Which one do you think it is?"

So it came to this, Sophia thought, anxiety building in her head from decision fatigue. Wilder was right to put this on her. It was her mission and therefore her choice. He'd given her what she needed to know, but the decision rested with her.

She patted him on the shoulder, encouraging him back. "Unlike before, we can't hold hands. I'm going to grab the sword and take the risk of choosing the wrong one. I want you to take Zac out of the temple, just in case I'm wrong."

He opened his mouth to protest, but Sophia shook her head at once—an adamant expression in her eyes. "Please, Wild. I can't guarantee I'll make the right decision, and I'm not sure what the repercussions will be. Zac shouldn't be put in any danger as a result of a mistake I make. Neither should you." She nodded toward the exit. "Just wait for me out front with Lunis. I'll be out as soon as I make my decision."

"Or you won't," he seethed, not liking this decision. However, as stubborn as they both were, he respected her decisions when she made them. Backing away, Wilder waved for Zac to follow him. "Don't be long."

Sophia nodded. "I won't."

"Also," he said when they'd crossed back over the gold path, "pick the right sword."

CHAPTER ONE HUNDRED TWENTY-EIGHT

Time won't go slowly when you want it to and when you want it to speed up, that's when it crawls by, Wilder thought, standing with Zac Efron and Lunis outside the Japanese temple.

You just left her, Lunis argued, shaking his head. *Some boyfriend you are.*

Wilder lowered his chin, daring to roll his eyes at the dragon, something he could never get away with, with Simi. She'd torch him, but Lunis liked the playful behavior because he was born in the modern world, and also because he was Sophia's dragon.

"I think we both know there's no arguing with that one when she's made up her mind," Wilder stated firmly.

Lunis harrumphed. *I see who wears the pants in your relationship.*

"We both wear pants," Wilder joked. "We're dragonriders. Kilts would be a poor choice for us."

The dragon closed his eyes, no doubt seeing what Sophia was doing. *Choose the blue pill.*

It never ceased to surprise Wilder that the blue dragon could joke during the most stressful and dangerous times. He was very much like Sophia in that way.

"All the swords are identical in appearance," Wilder argued.

497

Lunis opened his eyes, glaring at the dragonrider. *That should be you in there, about to choose the wrong sword and get blown up.*

"She's not going to choose the wrong one," Wilder said, offended. "Sophia will make the right decision, and even if she doesn't, we don't know death is the inevitable result."

Oh, sure. Lunis scoffed. *I'm sure the gods who protect this ancient Japanese temple will simply slap her on the wrist when she fails the final task. Maybe they will even give her a consolation prize like a travel mug or a t-shirt.*

Wilder spun to face the dragon, his frustration at having to sit out this round building in him. "You don't have to be so melodramatic about this. I didn't want to leave her."

"Guys," Zac said from beside them.

Hold up a minute, Lunis said to the actor, his focus on Wilder. *I'm not being melodramatic. I care about Sophia and I'm showing it, unlike you, Mr. Hollow Emotion.*

"I'm not hollow," Wilder argued. "I love her and she knows it. She's the most important person—"

"Guys," Zac advised again, urgency in his tone.

Seriously, Zac, not right now, Lunis complained. *I'm going to tear this pansy's petals off and then you can show me how to tap dance.*

Wilder shook his head. "You wouldn't touch so much as a hair on my head. Sophia wouldn't talk to you for a century if you did."

Lunis pressed his head close to Wilder, taking up most of his vision. *Or maybe she'd thank me. She's been trying to figure out how to dump you since you locked her down.*

"That's not true," Wilder stated, but his argument fell flat and made him instantly worry the dragon was telling the truth. They were new, he and Sophia. There was a lot of uncertainty with the Dragon Elite and Hiker that surrounded them. She was so young and inexperienced. He often worried she would change her mind, wanting something or someone different. Or maybe just the chance to explore her options before being "locked down."

"Um," Zac cut in again, "when you two are done..."

It's totally true, Lunis said, ignoring Zac. *Why would Sophia want to be with you when she can have anyone in the world?*

"Because…" Wilder said, but a reason didn't follow.

She has me and I'm more than enough, Lunis went on, smoke billowing from his nostrils, blowing it in Wilder's face. However, he didn't back down. That's what the dragon wanted.

"You know a dragon and rider relationship is never enough for magicians," Wilder replied, finding his voice after feeling like he'd been punched in the throat.

Maybe for you and Simi, Lunis said with confidence. *Some people have more fulfilling relationships. You wouldn't understand.*

"Guys!" Zac exclaimed.

"What?!" Wilder and Lunis said in unison, swinging around to face the guy.

Standing beside him, holding a sheathed katana on her shoulder and wearing an amused smile, was Sophia.

Soph! Lunis yelled, his eyes lighting up with relief.

Wilder felt the urge to rush over and throw his arms around her. Instead, he kept his distance and just looked her over to ensure she was okay.

"Are you guys finished?" Sophia asked.

He started it, Lunis said, nodding in Wilder's direction.

"I did not," Wilder protested. "He said… Never mind." Wilder didn't want to think about the things Lunis had said. It was based on jealousy, he told himself, but he didn't believe that all together. Shaking off the worry, he smiled at her. "So, you picked the right sword. Which one was it, the one with the power or experience?"

She shook her head, a proud expression on her face. "Neither."

"What?" he asked at once, not having expected that answer.

"I got to thinking it wouldn't make sense for the first sword to be brand new," Sophia stated. "I mean, this temple is ancient, and who knows how long the swords have been there? It made sense for the magical katana to be old and powerful. It didn't make any sense that beside it would be a brand-new sword, like one you'd find at Walmart."

"You can get a katana at Walmart?" Zac asked.

Sophia nodded. "That made me wonder if there was a glamour on the first sword that hid its energy from you, Wild."

He smiled at her, incredibly impressed. "So you took a chance and picked the first sword, even though I told you it wasn't right."

She held out the sword for him. "I removed the glamour. Now you tell me if it's the right one."

Wilder took the katana in his hands and felt the weight of its power, experiences, and magic, along with its actual weight. There was something unique about the sword. Unlike he had thought before, it wasn't brand new. It was ancient—older than the other two in the temple. Within the blade were different magical elemental forces. In the right hands, this sword would be very dangerous. That person would be nearly unstoppable.

Opening his eyes, Wilder found himself shaking his head, overwhelmed by what he felt in the weapon.

"That's without a doubt the right sword," he told her.

She simply smiled back at him, relief in her gaze.

The sword was unlike anything he'd experienced before from a weapon, which was saying a lot. More impressive than the katana was the woman in front of him. Most would have picked between the two swords, but not Sophia Beaufont. Strategy was always at the forefront of her mind. She considered her options carefully. He felt more confident about them as a couple than moments prior.

Sophia had considered her options, and she'd chosen Wilder. He respected her choices and was grateful she'd picked him.

CHAPTER ONE HUNDRED TWENTY-NINE

"Set the fire to the third bar," Lee said, pointing up high as Cat stood precariously at the top of a ladder in the Crying Cat Bakery. She had a match in her hand and was leaning forward, about to light a rod attached to the wall.

"Um..." Sophia began as she entered the bakery to witness the perplexing sight, "what are y'all doing?"

Lee's eyes widened, and she rushed over and kicked the ladder out from under Cat. The baker lost her balance and tumbled over the side. Thankfully she landed on a pile of flour covering the floor, sending up a huge plume that covered her.

"Nothing," Lee said, standing in front of her wife, partially blocking the view. "It's not a sacrificial ritual that keeps our business thriving."

Sophia narrowed her eyes at the woman. "So it definitely is, then."

Lee shook her head. "Nope. It's definitely not some archaic practice that imbues our baked goods with magic."

Sophia nodded. "Again, it totally is."

Lee checked over her shoulder as her wife sat up, covered from head to toe in white flour. Her eyeballs were the only thing not dusty when she blinked.

"You all right, dear?" Lee asked her.

She nodded, checking for injuries. "I didn't break my hip this time, so that's good."

"No, you can take a fall off a ladder without anything happening, but I look at you wrong, and all of a sudden, your heart is broken," Lee spat. "Seems a bit strange to me, dear."

"That should teach you not to look at me wrong," Cat stated, shaking her head and sending flour all over the place.

"Right now, I don't really want to look at you since it's a reminder of all the flour you're wasting," Lee told her. "Why don't you go get cleaned up?"

"Did you clean the shower like I asked?" Cat questioned.

"Yes, and I greased the tub extra good and removed the handrails you're always clutching for dear life," Lee replied.

Smiling sweetly, Cat nodded. "So thoughtful, dear. When I'm done, I'll make you one of my rat poison stews."

"Thanks, but I'm not hungry." Lee plastered a fake smile on her face. "I'm still recovering from the last bout of food poisoning you gave me."

"Oh, well, in that case," Cat began, making for the back, "I'll go fix up the bed so you can rest after this. I know exactly how you like it, dear."

Lee batted her eyes at her wife. "Yes, with the rattlesnake under my pillow. The rattling always puts me to sleep fast."

"Not for long enough," Cat replied, pushing the door open and leaving.

"By long enough, she means forever," Lee said, turning around and focusing on Sophia. "Now, what do you want? I hope you're happy you interrupted us."

Sophia pointed at the front door, irritation heavy on her face. "You know you own this shop and could just lock the door, right?"

"I could," Lee replied. "Then you'd knock, and that would spook Cat, and then *you'd* be the reason she fell off the ladder."

Sophia shook her head. Trying to understand the baker wasn't worth the effort. "I just wanted to give you the good news."

She held out the magical katana.

"You decided to quit breaking that poor boy's heart?" Lee asked, her gaze on Sophia and not the sword.

"Yes, but that's personal." She held the sword up higher for the baker to see.

"You've decided to do something worthwhile with your skills, like eradicating the gnome population?" Lee continued to question, not looking at the sword nearly in front of her face.

"My job is to fix the world, not murder innocent magical races," Sophia argued.

"Ha!" Lee laughed. "Gnomes aren't innocent. Do you know who my biggest competition as an assassin is?"

"Gnomes," Sophia guessed.

"No, those were two separate things. Gnomes aren't innocent. The second question is one I really want answered," Lee told her. "If I knew who my biggest competition was, I'd take them out and own the business."

Sophia blinked. "Again, I shouldn't be hearing this. I shouldn't be giving you this sword, but a deal is a deal."

"Sword?" Lee questioned with surprise. "What sword?"

Slumping slightly, Sophia put it right in front of Lee's nose. "This one."

Her eyes widened. "Why didn't you say so? You got the katana!"

She took it and unsheathed it. Immediately Lee began swinging it wildly, making Sophia jump backward after nearly getting cut.

"Would you be careful with that thing?"

A cunning grin lit the baker's face. "Where would the fun in that be?" She tested the balance. "I can't believe you got it. I didn't think you'd be successful." She spun, calling toward the back, "We can cancel that 'condolences' cake.'"

"You made a cake for the funeral you thought I was about to have?" Sophia asked, amused rather than offended.

Lee shook her head. "No. We were going to make it. I wanted it to be fresh."

"Well, I don't plan on dying anytime soon, so save your ingredients for something else."

Lee smiled proudly at the katana. "Remarkable that you were able to get this. I tried to give you the most impossible task I could think of, and you somehow pulled it off."

Sophia nodded. "I believe that. You did want the sword?"

"For sure," Lee said. "Don't worry, I won't use it as my assassin weapon."

"Wait, what?" Sophia asked, strangely frustrated by this omission. "Why not?"

Lee shrugged. "That seems like cheating. I'd be the deadliest assassin for sure. Who wants an easy win?"

"Me," Sophia answered. "I risked my life to get you that sword and you're not going to use it?"

The assassin shook her head and pointed at the wall where the bars were that Cat had been doing something to earlier. "We could use some decoration up there. Think I'll stick it on the wall."

Sophia was irritated. "You're going to use a very powerful katana as decoration?"

"Of course," Lee stated like it should have been obvious. "Why else would I want it?"

"Oh, I don't know," Sophia answered. "As an assassin, maybe as a weapon."

Lee laid the katana on the counter behind her before flexing her hands. "What do you think these are?"

"Let me guess," Sophia began. "Deadly weapons."

Lee winked at her. "Exactly. Who needs a magical katana when I've got bone-crushing hands?"

Sophia shook her head but laughed all the same. "Well, regardless of what you do with the sword, we're even now."

Nodding, Lee said, "Yes, until next time. Until then, I'll be thinking of some impossible way you can repay me for the next favor."

CHAPTER ONE HUNDRED THIRTY

"It's all gone quiet," Wilder said to Sophia in a whisper outside of Hiker's office. He had agreed to take Zac home after the mission while Sophia delivered the decorative katana to the Crying Cat Bakery. "For a while, Hiker was throwing stuff around. I'm pretty sure he's demolished it, but for the last ten minutes, it's been quiet."

Sophia nodded, wondering if this was a result of Hiker using the gold token. "I'll go in and check on him."

Wilder gave her a cautious expression. "It doesn't seem like the harp is working. Maybe you should send Mama Jamba in there."

She considered this but shook her head. "No. I'll be okay. I need to know if he's on board with the Saverus mission."

Trin Currante had messaged Sophia upon her return to the Gullington that she was close to tracking down Mika Lenna's location. The message told her to be ready since deployment could happen very soon. Sophia was both nervous and excited. It seemed things were finally coming to a head. Injustices were about to be rectified.

"Okay, well, stay by the door in case you need to escape his wrath quickly," Wilder suggested.

Sophia pressed a quick kiss to his cheek, making him blush. "I'll be fine, but thanks for the concern."

When Sophia entered Hiker Wallace's office, she found Wilder had been correct, and the man had destroyed the space. He now sat in his desk chair, his forearm over his face and his head slumped backward.

"Sir?" Sophia began, knocking on the doorframe.

"What?" he growled, not pulling his arm away.

"Are you okay?"

"Why do you ask?" There was a strange hint of amusement in his voice.

"Well, Ainsley said you missed lunch," Sophia lied, not wanting to point out the obvious.

"Oh, she noticed," he muttered.

So he *had* missed lunch, Sophia wondered. "Of course she noticed. There's been a bit of talk since you began this office remodel. I really like what you've done with the place." If he was going to be humorous about this, she would too.

He nodded, his face still obstructed by his massive forearm. "I didn't like the sofa there."

Sophia glanced at the leather sofa where Mama Jamba usually perched. She wasn't there since the couch was overturned. "Mama Jamba wasn't on it when you put it in its new location, right?"

He shook his head. "No, I haven't seen her since I returned."

So he had used the reset point, Sophia realized. Her eyes found the gold harp on the floor amongst a bunch of papers strewn about. "It's pretty crazy going back into the past, right?" she asked carefully.

"Especially when it's my history," he replied, not sounding angry. He must have gotten it all out.

Sophia dared to step farther into the office and picked up the harp.

"I broke the gold coin," Hiker admitted.

Halting, Sophia slumped. Papa Creola was going to kill her. Or as Liv had said, he'd quietly brood and make her do something

506

dangerous to make up for it. Maybe he and Lee were the same person.

"That's okay," she lied. "I'm sure it's no big deal. Actually—"

"I need your help, Sophia," Hiker interrupted, pulling his arm off his face finally and giving her the most sobering expression.

"Of course, sir," she said, striding forward and taking the place in front of his desk. "What can I do?"

He shook his head. "That's just the thing. I don't know entirely, but you have to help Ainsley get her memories back from before the attack. She...she lost something she can't ever get back, and I need her to remember what it was. I think that's the only way for her to be cured."

"Because she has a broken heart," Sophia guessed.

He nodded. "Yes. She can't fix it until she knows why it broke. I need her to remember. Then I need the cure. Then she can leave here."

Sophia placed the harp on the surface of the desk. "Don't you think it would mean more if you helped her to recover the memories? If you found the cure for her?"

Regret filled the Viking's face. "Honestly, I don't think she'd accept it from me. Once she has her memories back, she's most likely never speaking to me ever again."

Sophia stiffened. She knew this situation with Hiker and Ainsley was serious, but it sounded downright devastating. "What did you do, sir?"

He pressed his lips together. "I refused to listen to her. I doubted her, and she's paid the price for my foolishness all these years." He looked up, his gaze finally connecting with hers. "I could ask one of the others to help, but honestly, I don't trust them with this. It's a sensitive thing and will require strategy. More than that, it's going to require tact. When you find out what happened...what Ainsley lost, please try to maintain respect for me. I-I-I—"

"Sir, everyone makes mistakes," Sophia cut in, trying to help.

He nodded. "That's true. I'm simply hoping I can fix what I've done."

"Of course I'll help," Sophia stated. Her phone beeped in her pocket. Although she wouldn't normally allow an interruption during such a serious conversation, she knew this was important. Retrieving her phone, she checked the message and confirmed her suspicions regarding the text. Sophia pointed to the gold harp. "Sir, I would recommend you take that back. We know the location of Saverus Corporation. It's time to take Mika Lenna down, once and for all."

CHAPTER ONE HUNDRED THIRTY-ONE

An olive grove facing the sea was not what Sophia expected to see when she and Lunis, along with the other dragonriders, rode into the place Trin Currante requested. She could see from their vantage point high in the air the olive grove appeared to be the rendezvous point. From there, they'd go onto the Saverus Corporation.

Sophia glanced at where Hiker Wallace rode beside her on Bell. The red dragon was a beautiful contrast to Lunis, and the pair flew seamlessly. At their back, Wilder, Evan, and Mahkah coasted, drifting on their wind.

Spotting the cyborgs, Sophia pointed to ensure Hiker saw them. He wasn't any better than when she found him in his office, but he was doing a good job of pretending. She could tell he wasn't completely present and hoped his distraction didn't compromise the mission. Whatever he saw at the reset point had made things exponentially worse for him, but sometimes that was the way it was Sophia reasoned. Things sometimes had to get worse before they could get better.

Lunis and Bell both dove at the same moment, heading in for a landing in an open area on the edge of a cliff overlooking the Pacific

Ocean. They were just outside of Los Angeles, close to the secret headquarters for Saverus, which wasn't so secret anymore thanks to Trin Currante.

It was strange to land the dragons in front of a small army of cyborgs when the memory of fighting them was still so fresh. They were no longer the enemy. They and the Dragon Elite had banded together to defeat a shared enemy.

Sophia could tell by the tension pinning Hiker's shoulders up high it was difficult for him to trust the cyborgs so soon after battling them on the Expanse at the Gullington. However, Sophia trusted Trin Currante. The cyborg's leader had worked behind the scenes to invade the Gullington and steal dragon eggs, but her reasons made sense. Unlike Mika Lenna, she wasn't an evil entity with a greedy agenda. She was trying to fix herself and undo what had been done to her against her will. Sophia couldn't argue with that.

When the five dragons had landed, Sophia slid off Lunis and came around to join Hiker. She might have spearheaded this mission, but he was still the leader of the Dragon Elite, and this was his show. Sophia also believed he needed to take the reins on things to prove to himself that he could despite his past and many obvious regrets.

Hiker stepped forward to meet Trin Currante between the riders and the cyborgs.

She nodded respectfully to him in greeting, before her eyes slid to Sophia at his back. "I've found the location of Mika Lenna and the Saverus," she stated when her attention returned to Hiker.

"And that is?" he asked with authority in his voice.

She pointed north toward the city. "Just over that ridge about two miles. It's a generic warehouse, but I've deduced it is without a doubt the new headquarters."

Hiker nodded. "Good work. We need to get in there and secure the research."

Trin Currante's cyborg eyes slid around before focusing back on the Viking. "I was hoping the dragonriders would take the lead. Maybe go in there undercover. For obvious reasons, we can't." She looked back at her men, who even with magical disguises would be hard to pass off as anything but cyborgs.

"Of course," Hiker agreed, glancing at his riders. "Sophia, Evan, and Wilder, you three will infiltrate the headquarters undercover. You can be scientists or something. You'll decide once you get in there."

The three nodded.

"Mahkah and I will stay with the cyborgs," Hiker continued. "We'll wait for your signal that you've secured the research from Saverus. Once you have, we will storm the location and take Mika Lenna and his lemmings." He glanced at Trin Currante with conviction in his eyes. "This ends tonight. Soon Mika Lenna will be no more."

The smile on her face was full of long-awaited anticipation. "If it's okay with you when it's time, I'd like to be the one to finish that man."

CHAPTER ONE HUNDRED THIRTY-TWO

"When you're right, you're right, Sophia," Evan said, holding out his arms and modeling his white lab coat. "I look damn good in white."

The three dragonriders had watched the warehouse for roughly half an hour before they abducted three scientists leaving the facility. They never knew what hit them. Literally. It was a dragonrider's fists. Sophia, Wilder, and Evan dragged the passed-out scientists behind a dumpster after binding and gagging them and removing their white lab coats and security badges.

"That's not what I said," Sophia argued, finding her lab coat a smidge big.

"You thought it," Evan said proudly.

"You don't want to know what I think of you most of the time," she fired back.

Evan glanced at Wilder, who did look quite nice in his lab coat. "Get a handle on your girlfriend."

"Can't," Wilder stated simply and winked at her.

"All right, when we head in there," Sophia began, looking between the two guys, "I need you to be observant, but more than anything, you have to keep your mouth shut."

"Why did you just look at me?" Evan asked, offended.

"Oh, I wonder," Wilder mused with a laugh.

"We don't know how many employees there are," Sophia continued. "They might recognize us as intruders immediately. So keep your head down and mouth shut so we don't give away anything that will set us apart."

"Okay, and while we're being your amazing lackeys, what are you going to be doing?" Evan questioned.

"We need to access the system." She held up her badge. "Thankfully, Victoria Clearbeam is the head scientist and should have the credentials to get into the right files."

"Aren't you going to need a password to get into the system, though?" Wilder wanted to know.

She nodded and held up a magitech device Alicia had outfitted her with that gave her access to things password protected. "I'm good to go. We just need to breeze in there, grab the files, and then call in the reinforcements."

All three of the dragonriders looked in the direction of the olive grove where Hiker and Mahkah, the dragons and the cyborgs were stationed, ready to get word it was their turn to take over. Then it would really be go time.

CHAPTER ONE HUNDRED THIRTY-THREE

The happy detectives strode into the Saverus Corporation, acting as casual as possible. Evan whistled like he didn't have a care in the world. Wilder waved at the security guard, although Sophia had told them not to draw attention to themselves. She kept her head low and didn't make eye contact. Ironically that's what made her stand out.

"Miss, I'm going to need to see your identification," the security guard stated, waving her over to his station.

Just before entering the warehouse, Sophia had glamoured herself and the guys to look like the scientists they were impersonating. Victoria Clearbeam had curly brown hair and a pale complexion.

Dutifully she held up the security ID, flashing it at the guard. He narrowed his eyes at her badge and then her face.

"You look different today, Victoria," he observed. "You feeling okay?"

She nodded, trying to avoid saying anything.

"Well, what is it? Did one of those genetically mutated cats get your tongue?" The guard laughed.

Sophia grimaced at the idea of the animal testing that no doubt went on inside Saverus. "Just tired, that's all."

"So tired you lost your Australian accent," the guard said with surprise.

Oh, hell, Sophia thought, cutting her eyes at Evan and Wilder and spying them both wearing amused expressions. Of course they were. This just got a ton more entertaining for them.

"Oh, well, mate, you know how you Americans have been rubbing off on me," she said in her best Australian accent.

The guard nodded. "Yeah, when I was over in the UK for a bit, I picked up their accents. It's contagious, am I right?" He glanced at Evan and Wilder, who both had thick Scottish accents. It was Sophia's turn to torture them, although she should be hurrying them off on the mission.

"Yeah, isn't that right, Bill and Ted?" Sophia asked, again employing her Australian accent.

"For sure, dude." Evan sounded like a nineties movie star.

"Yes," Wilder said carefully. "That is true. I think that every time I get into my Prius or use my credit card."

Sophia glared at Wilder, not appreciating the joke as much as she should. He always teased her that all Americans drove sporty Priuses and were obsessed with using their credit cards.

"Well, we better get to work, mates," Sophia said and waved them toward the security door.

Her badge beeped when she slid it against the security device. The locked door clicked, allowing her and the guys entry. She pulled it back, preparing herself for the next part of the mission.

CHAPTER ONE HUNDRED THIRTY-FOUR

Jj-126: that was the office that belonged to Victoria Clearbeam, according to her security badge.

Unfortunately, it seemed the office wasn't near the front entrance, and they'd have to travel through a long portion of Saverus headquarters to get there, increasing the chances of them getting caught.

Sophia couldn't stand the idea they might fail before even getting started, so she pushed the insecurity out of her head.

"Look who almost got us caught with their 'head down and mouth shut' approach," Evan teased, sidling up beside her. "You've got to learn to be natural when on these missions."

"Nice American accent," Sophia muttered, looking into various labs through the glass windows as they passed. She immediately regretted it after seeing the experiments in cages—things she wouldn't be able to unsee later.

"It was a lot better than that Australian accent you tried to pull off," Evan remarked.

"I wonder if punching you in the teeth will improve your American accent," Sophia pretended to ponder.

He shook his head, mocking seriousness. "I don't see how that could. Poor reasons, Pink Princess."

"Are you guys seeing this?" Wilder asked, his tone grave.

Sophia knew he was referring to the things they saw in the labs as they passed. She nodded. "Yeah. We'll deal with it later. First we need to get to my office."

To Sophia's relief, she spotted the J offices up ahead. A tall man in a silver suit stepped out of a lab ahead of them. He was distinguished in a way Sophia had rarely seen. Handsome, no doubt, and certainly possessing a fair bit of power.

"John, what are you doing down here?" the man asked, narrowing his eyes at them.

The three halted, staring at the man. No one said a word.

John was the scientist Wilder was impersonating. She desperately hoped he remembered that much.

Evan coughed, cutting his eyes at Wilder.

"Oh, right," Wilder said abruptly. "I was just going to meet with these two for a moment."

The man marched forward, his snakeskin shoes making a loud clapping noise on the tiled floor. "Remember that you are to always address me as 'sir' or 'master.' You don't have to be painfully reminded of that again, do you?" The man twisted his head to the side, a strange expression in his dark eyes that chilled Sophia to the core.

Without knowing for sure, she felt deep inside that this man was Mika Lenna. Never before had she felt such evilness oozing off a person. His sinister nature wasn't easily dismissed. This man was purely wicked.

"Yes, sir," Wilder said, again employing his American accent.

"You don't work on the vampiri project like these two," Mika Lenna continued, pointing ahead. "You're down in animal testing and will remain there until you prove you're competent for more advanced projects."

"Yes, sir," Wilder stated again, nodding. Without hesitating, he turned on his heels and retreated in the direction of the labs with the animals they'd passed. Sophia felt incredibly sorry for him since she wouldn't want to see what was in those rooms up close.

"As for you two," Mika Lenna said, focusing on Sophia and Evan. "I want an update on the vampiri project."

Sophia didn't say anything, thinking he wasn't done talking. He was going to say, "In an hour" or "a week." When he didn't, she swallowed hard and nodded.

"Now, sir?" she asked.

"Yes, now! Do you think I employ you to sit around and take lunch breaks?"

Sophia shook her head. "Of course, sir. I just need to get my notes."

"Very well," he told her skeptically. "I expect you in my office in three minutes."

CHAPTER ONE HUNDRED THIRTY-FIVE

"Batten down the hatches," Evan said when Mika Lenna was gone and they had locked themselves in Victoria Clearbeam's office. "We've got no time now."

Sophia nodded. She went straight to work typing at the computer station and using the magitech device to break into the files. "Three minutes isn't enough."

"Well, then we are just going to have to be late," Evan stated, standing over her.

She waved him back. "Go watch the door or something. Get out of my space. That was Mika Lenna. I don't think we want to make the boss wait."

"Yeah, but if we have to give him an update, things are going to get awkward fast," Evan retorted. "I don't know anything about the vampiri project. Do you?" He laughed. "And you were worried our cover would get blown if we talked too much. How ironic."

"Shut it," Sophia warned, typing furiously to find the research they needed to fix the cyborgs. There was so much information. "On the long list of problems, we don't know where Mika Lenna's office is, so I think we are obligated to stay here anyway."

"I'm certain that guy will come looking for us in a minute or two."

Evan poked his head out the door. "Did you see how creepy he is? What was that business about a painful reminder for Wilder? Poor guy is now separated from us."

Sophia nodded. Things were going to get even more chaotic when everything came to a head. The cyborgs would be storming in, and Wilder would be elsewhere. She hoped he took off his glamour so they didn't try to kill him. Hiker had asked that they take the employees hostage, but everyone knew the cyborgs were out for blood after what had been done to them, and she couldn't blame them.

Again Evan stuck his head out the door, but this time he sucked in a breath and threw the door shut.

"What?" Sophia asked.

"He's coming…"

CHAPTER ONE HUNDRED THIRTY-SIX

"Lifeboats," Evan said in a rush. "We need lifeboats."

Sophia's heart raced.

"We need a way to save ourselves," Evan stated urgently, snapping at her. "Message Trin. Tell her to storm the place."

"No," Sophia argued. "As soon as she does, they are going to lock up the research, and we'll lose our chance again. You're going to have to stall for me. I just need another few minutes."

Evan's eyes widened with horror. "Have you seen that man? He would scare Hitler, who I've heard was awful. I've only recently been brushing up on history since I was locked in the Gullington at the time and had no idea World War II was going on. Otherwise, the Dragon Elite could have—"

"Seriously, Evan," Sophia interrupted. "Right now isn't share time. Get out there and make up a reason that I need more time."

Reluctantly, he opened the door, apparently nearly running into Mika Lenna given the exclamation he made. "Hey, sir. Victoria will be with us in a moment."

"Why?" Mika Lenna asked simply, his voice brimming with hostility.

"She's having a female moment," Sophia heard Evan explain. "You know, being hormonal? She needs some time to get herself together. Women, am I right?"

Sophia rolled her eyes. Only Evan would turn a high-octane do-or-die moment into something so ridiculous.

She was sifting through files slower than she would have liked, her nerves getting the best of her. There were so many of them on Victoria Clearbeam's computer.

Sophia kept opening windows, searching.

"Enough with the excuses," Mika Lenna yelled from the other side of the door.

Sophia flinched from the sudden rise in his voice. This was a man who needed a giant gold harp.

Her eyes darted to a folder. "Project Cyborg."

"Bingo," she whispered and starting to copy the files. Simultaneously, she pulled out her phone and typed a quick message to Trin Currante. Sophia waited until the files had completely copied before she removed the drive from the computer and sent the message to Trin.

Seconds later, Mika Lenna stormed into the office and bore down on her, his eyes narrowed. "I want answers, and I want them now!"

CHAPTER ONE HUNDRED THIRTY-SEVEN

"Hollow as I am," Trin Currante said to Hiker, having a real conversation with him about being a cyborg, "I'm still a person at my core, and I want to be seen as one."

He nodded. He was feeling a weird sympathy for her and the men around her that was unusual for him. Maybe it was the gold harp doing it, but something was making...sense. Hiker wasn't sure if he liked that. He'd always had a strong emotional compass but was never affected by the emotions of others. He needed to stay objective as the leader of the Dragon Elite. However, something was shifting in him.

"We just want to be normal again," Trin continued when he'd remained quiet. "I don't expect to ever be what I once was, but it would be nice to be seen as I used to be. To be loved as a person and not as a machine."

He didn't know what to say. Thankfully he didn't have to reply because they were interrupted by a message on Trin's phone.

Hiker didn't approve of the devices for the guys and only allowed Sophia to have one because she was from the modern world, but he was glad Sophia could communicate with Trin so quickly. It did make things easier. Otherwise, it would have been passing messages between dragons, which was fine, but this seemed a bit more direct.

Trin glanced up, vengeance in her eyes. "They have the research. Now it's our turn. Time to storm Saverus."

Wilder had a hard time keeping his face neutral as he pretended to work in the animal lab. The creatures in the cages weren't natural. Things had been done to them. Things he didn't think could be undone.

To his further disgust, the other scientists in the lab worked casually, filling up test tubes or recording information, as though it was perfectly acceptable to see mutant creatures beating at their cages, their fangs bared and their once normal eyes red with rage.

He had no way to communicate with Evan and Sophia and desperately wondered if they had been successful in getting the records. He would find out soon enough when the alarms went off, or he was caught for insubordination.

Wilder didn't know what to do and found himself idly staring at a wall. That was easier than looking at the row of cages at his back.

Several times he'd reached out to Simi to see if he could communicate indirectly with the others, but something was preventing the communication. It probably had to do with the magitech filling Saverus, or it was the security system.

All he could do was bide his time and hope he was released from this torment soon. He glanced over his shoulder, wondering if when the action started, the animals could help him somehow. He concluded that of anyone, they would want revenge on the scientists in this lab. He'd just have to remove his glamour and white coat so they didn't think he was one of them. There was no way Wilder was getting punished for something animal abusers did.

"Of course, sir," Sophia said in a rush, meeting Mika Lenna's cold, dark eyes. At his back, she spied Evan giving her an apologetic expression. He'd obviously done everything he could think of to stall the man, but it hadn't worked for long. However, it had worked well enough.

She slid her hand into her pocket, trying to hide her phone and the jump drive. Mika Lenna's sinister gaze was locked on her, not seeing anything else. It was weird to consider what she'd learned about this man. He had genetically done some strange things to himself, enhancing himself into a werewolf. Besides being intimidating and scary, Sophia didn't see how he could be a werewolf, but being locked in the small office with him, she hoped not to learn, especially without her sword.

He held his hand up to her face and snapped his fingers, a crisp, loud sound. "Update. Give it to me now!"

Sophia swallowed and nodded and attempted to smile.

"The project is well underway," she said, trying her Australian accent, which wasn't good.

"I know it's underway," he snapped. "It's close to being another complete failure. What are the pathogens saying about the current mutation?"

"Mutation," Sophia repeated, picking up a file folder on the desk and flipping through it. "Good question."

Mika Lenna ripped the folder from her hands and threw it across the office, nearly hitting Evan. "Don't look at notes. I want the report directly from you."

Catching the look in Evan's eyes, Sophia knew what he was thinking. They were both considering killing Mika right then. They probably had a good chance with both of them there. Trin had made it clear she wanted to finish this man, though, and she did deserve that.

If things got any more tense, Sophia was going to have no choice but to defend herself. She was pretty certain Mika Lenna was moments away from attacking her. She felt him needling at her thoughts, trying to get access.

"Directly from me," Sophia said, repeating his words to buy time. "The report goes as follows. All of the subjects are displaying—"

Never before was Sophia so grateful to hear sirens. She was pretty certain she smiled at the interruption.

Mika Lenna tensed and his eyes widened. He swung around, looking at the office, as though expecting invaders.

"Evacuate," he urged. "Take the tunnels. You know the drill. We are being invaded. Remember, if you're caught, whatever they do to you for not talking will be nothing compared to what I do if you share my secrets."

The leader of the Saverus Corporation stalked toward the door, moving in a blur as he shifted into the form of a werewolf—one that was unnatural and disgusting in every way.

CHAPTER ONE HUNDRED THIRTY-EIGHT

Downhill from here, Hiker thought, as he took off on Bell, flying fast over the Saverus headquarters. He was surprised to find how quickly the cyborgs sprang into action. He shouldn't have been, having seen them at the Gullington. Now they were motivated too, and hungry for revenge.

Lunis, Coral, and Simi had already been surrounding the headquarters before Sophia sent the message. They'd scouted out the underground tunnels Trin had told them about and blocked the passages from those who would use them for escaping. Mahkah and Hiker would circle overhead and keep an eye on things from the sky.

This was good for Hiker from a leadership standpoint. He didn't yet trust the gold harp in his pocket. Yes, it calmed him, but in battle, his emotions could still get the best of him. Hiker knew all too well the power flowing in his veins was both enough to save the world and damn it to hell for all time. So slight was the line between good and evil. It made him think of the dragon eggs ready to hatch at the Gullington. Some would be good. Others would be evil. The results of those hatchings would affect the world for a very long time.

Trin Currante had waited too long for this moment. Her men had too. Whatever happened next, she would accept as long as it involved making Mika Lenna pay. Yes, she wanted her life back and her human body, but if nothing else, she wanted to make the man who had taken everything feel the pain he'd caused others.

From the blimp she'd commandeered when she'd escaped Mika Lenna originally, Trin soared over the top of Saverus' headquarters, the riders on their dragons flanking them.

It should have been weird to go from enemies to allies with the Dragon Elite, but nothing seemed more natural. They represented justice, after all. She realized she should have gone to them originally and explained what had happened. She should have asked for help rather than invade the Gullington, stealing dragon eggs for her own gain.

When everything had been stolen from her, she had forgotten how to trust. Strangely, the Dragon Elite was restoring her faith in humanity, something she never thought possible.

She was the first one to disembark from the blimp, sliding down the ropes streaming over the side. With a loud thud, she landed on the roof of the warehouse and had a *déjà vu* moment from the first time she did this. It would be different this time. Mika Lenna wasn't getting away.

When the alarm in the lab sounded, Wilder was already by the door. Most of the scientists jerked their heads up in alarm.

The last few minutes had given Wilder the time to figure out what to do. He was the first out the door when the alarm sounded. He flicked his wrist at the locked cages against the wall, releasing all of the rabid animals. Then he yanked the door shut and locked all the evil scientists in with the animals they created.

What would follow, he didn't want to see. As he sped down the hallway, he heard the screams and knew that revenge was underway.

Sophia and Evan allowed themselves only a moment to breathe after Mika Lenna ran from the office morphing into the worst kind of monster she could have ever considered.

She knew what Evan was thinking on this mission. Like her, he didn't want to run into whatever Mika Lenna was becoming. They were all too glad to let Trin Currante have the kill after being in that man's presence for only a few minutes.

When the alarms were blaring and she was certain Mika Lenna was gone, she pulled off her disguise and took off down the hallway. Chaos was everywhere as scientists ran, probably in the direction of the underground tunnels.

Sophia couldn't communicate with Lunis due to the magitech in the facility, but she knew the dragons were waiting to meet the scientists, lining them up and taking them into custody. If anyone tried to flee, the dragons were all too happy to turn them into barbeque. That wasn't the normal way for the Dragon Elite, but the stakes were different with Saverus.

Running the opposite direction as everyone else, Sophia got strange looks, but probably because she was no longer wearing the glamour that looked like Victoria Clearbeam. She was just about to go the direction of the underground tunnels when she saw a face that made everything better.

"Wilder!" Sophia exclaimed, opening her arms to him.

The expression of pure horror on his face stopped her and nearly made Evan run her over.

"Run!" Wilder yelled and grabbed her arm as he passed, yanking her in the opposite direction.

CHAPTER ONE HUNDRED
THIRTY-NINE

C hased by she didn't know what, Sophia allowed Wilder to pull
her down the long corridor.

A quick glance over her shoulder told her she was probably better off not knowing deranged woodland creatures who appeared hungry for blood were pursuing them.

"What are they?" Sophia asked, employing her enhanced speed to get away from the creatures.

"I don't know," Wilder admitted, pushing Evan to speed up in front of them. "I let them out on the scientists, but some jerk opened the door, probably to escape getting eaten."

"Now your act of heroism has become a punishment," Sophia said, wheeling around a corner. At the far end of the hallway, the other scientists were bottlenecked, trying to get through a single push door. They thought they were getting away, but if things went according to plan, no one was getting out of here without a trial.

Sophia turned and held up her hand. She couldn't hurt the creatures, which were a product of animal testing, but she couldn't stand there and get eaten by them either. She threw up a barrier that locked them on the far side of the hallway. She would have felt remorse for the humans running behind the creatures also looking for this exit if she didn't know that karma had a way of coming full circle.

The rabid creatures turned once they realized there was a dead end due to an invisible barrier and gave their full attention to the scientists looking for a way out. With horrified expressions, the scientists spun and hauled ass in the opposite direction. They would try and escape through the front door—where they'd undoubtedly be met by cyborgs looking for retribution.

The scene on the ground was chaos Hiker observed from the sky as he circled on Bell. Around the entire perimeter of Saverus were cyborgs, their weaponized arms pointed at every exit and their steel fists ready for a fight.

When the first set of scientists ran from the building, they skidded to a halt at the sight, realizing there was no escape.

The cyborgs had been told to apprehend the scientists. The House of Fourteen would then take over, putting them all into custody. From Hiker's position in the sky, he saw the Warriors from the House of Fourteen striding in from a neighboring road, Liv Beaufont in the lead, flanked by her husband, Stefan Ludwig. Trudy DeVries was on the other side of him. Many would have thought that only three Warriors wouldn't be enough to do a cleanup job this big, but they'd be wrong. Hiker knew the Dragon Elite was the best, but a very close second were the Warriors for the House.

He pulled his gaze to the roof of the Saverus headquarters. Trin had been the first to land, followed quickly by many of her men. She had figured out where the underground tunnels were and the quickest way there from the roof.

A cyborg with a saw for a hand cut an opening in the metal roof, and one by one, the cyborgs disappeared. According to Trin, it would take her less than a minute to slip into the corridor right outside the tunnel. That's where she'd find Mika Lenna. That would be how he planned to escape with all his other routes blocked. It would be where Trin Currante delivered justice.

———

Having studied the last facility Mika Lenna had, Trin Currante figured out how the man had mapped things out. She was betting that he had done things the same way for this facility. So far, she'd been right. She dropped through the various levels of the warehouse, cutting through ceilings and descending farther until she was at the final one that led to the underground tunnels.

Impatiently, she waited for the cut to be made. When the circle of the ceiling dropped through, Trin allowed one of her men to check. He glanced up relief in his eyes.

"All clear besides friends," he said, hope in his one human eye.

Friends? she wondered. It was a foreign word. Trin didn't have any friends. Not even her men did she consider friends. Then she dropped through and knew what he meant—the dragonriders stood on one side of the corridor. On the other was the door that led to the underground and to Mika Lenna.

CHAPTER ONE HUNDRED FORTY

iot, please, Lunis thought from his place blocking the three routes to the underground tunnels as the scientists continued to spill into the area, looking for a way out and realizing going back the way they came wasn't an option. He was just waiting for them to rebel and give him a reason to turn them all to toast.

Unfortunately, at the sight of the three dragons blocking all of the escape routes, the scientists backed up, bewildered.

Several of the corridors to Saverus fed into this underground area where the tunnels sped off in different directions under the city and ended in random locations. Mika Lenna had believed he'd thought of everything, but he hadn't counted on the Dragon Elite.

Swishing his tail back and forth, Lunis lowered his head as a bold scientist approached him.

"Just want to pass through that tunnel behind you," the man said, offering his hand to the dragon like he was a dog who needed to smell him first before allowing him to be petted.

The guy was about to find himself without a hand if he got any closer. Remembering the warning Sophia had given him about resorting to violence last, he sneered at the man, smoke billowing from his nostrils. To his disappointment, that was enough to make the guy back up, which meant Lunis couldn't eat him for trespassing.

Hunched down in the underground space, Lunis hoped things proceeded quickly. Not only was it not the best fit in the underground area, but he was also hungry after looking at all these jerk mortals who would make better side dishes than members of society. He really didn't understand how awful people like this continued to exist, but it consoled him to know he and Sophia were putting them in their place.

All the restraint Lunis had been practicing was threatened when something unlike anything he had ever seen stepped out of the only empty corridor. The others were full of scientists pushing and shoving, trying to get out until they realized they weren't going anywhere with dragons obstructing their paths.

The monster that strode out of the hallway wasn't man nor animal. It was supposed to be a werewolf, but Lunis knew from the collective consciousness of the dragons that werewolves were beautiful creatures who were both man and wolf. This beast was neither. It was unnatural.

Whatever Mika Lenna had made himself into, it was gross with rippling muscles, red eyes, and oversized fangs. The way he moved—jerky and full of rage—put a weird fear into the dragon. Still, he held up his head and opened his mouth as Mika Lenna charged in his direction in a show of power through intimidation.

He might have lost his mind, but even Mika Lenna knew better than to push these boundaries. Although huge, Mika Lenna was a fraction of the size of Lunis and had nothing to match his fire and teeth. He stopped short of being fried and just in time as a figure as unnatural as he was stepped out of the corridor, followed by Sophia and the others.

Sophia was on guard when the cyborg known as Trin slipped through the ceiling just ahead of them in the corridor. Then she was relieved.

Everything had gone to plan for the most part. The worst of it and the hardest part was next, and it all rested on Trin's shoulders, as she'd intended.

Giving the cyborg a vote of confidence, Sophia held up her hand in the direction of the door at the end of the hallway. "He'll be through there. We have your back, Trin. If anything goes wrong, we'll step in and save you."

Trin sucked in a breath, her mechanical hair retracting and stretching. She shook her head, making a clicking sound. "I won't need your help. Let him kill me, but this fight is between him and me. I was one of his first. The first to survive. I'll be the one to end him, or I'll die trying. If I do, I expect you to kill him. I'll be watching from the afterlife, waiting to follow him to the pits of hell, where I intend to make his eternity excruciating."

Sophia could hardly fathom the things that had been done to Trin to make her so bitter, but she knew the resentment was well-warranted. She only hoped this act of revenge was enough to start to quell the fires in Trin's soul. A cure would take some time since they had just gotten the research from Saverus. Still, Sophia wanted healing for the cyborgs. She wanted it for all who had suffered at Mika Lenna's hands.

That was her final wish as she followed the cyborgs to the underground area.

CHAPTER ONE HUNDRED FORTY-ONE

"How to be dead," Trin yelled clear and loud, her mechanical voice echoing in the underground area. "Is that what you're obsessed with, Mika Lenna?"

Sophia and the guys spilled out behind the cyborg and watched her walk across the open concrete space. It was mostly dark, except for a few lights on the dark walls. Obstructing much of the open area were the nervous scientists, clinging to each other and unable to go anywhere. The corridors they'd come through were blocked by cyborgs, and the underground tunnels they had intended to take to safety were blocked by dragons.

Sophia's gaze connected with Lunis on the far side. He was like a cork in the tunnel, blocking any attempt to get through. It looked like many of the scientists were close to doing anything to squeeze by, even if it meant losing a limb or two in the process. More likely, they'd be charred until they were medium-rare.

Mika Lenna wasn't hard to spot amidst the chaos of the fearful scientists. They all backed away from the genetically altered monster as he craned his neck to one side and then the other like he was still morphing.

The suit he'd worn earlier still fit, but only in places. He was more animal than man now. As he turned in the circle of scientists, dragons, and riders to face the cyborg he created, his hand rocked forward, and he caught himself like a four-legged beast. He was a werewolf by many standards, but everything about him was wrong.

"Trin," he growled. "My biggest mistake."

"You wanted me dead more than alive," she said, striding forward, the hydraulics of her legs making hissing sounds. "You wanted to be more monster than human. Look what you've done to the world around you. You've killed it."

He shook his snout, which once looked like a man's but was growing more disfigured by the moment. He didn't seem in control of the change happening to him. It was all going wrong.

"Notice I never made another cyborg out of a woman," he spat. "They don't take to change well. They don't know how to conform. Your lot refuses to do things the right way."

Trin laughed and started to circle the man before her. "You know how to add insult to injury, but that will only ensure I crush you more decisively." She held out her metal hand and pressed her fingers shut, the force not something most would survive.

"You end here," Mika stated. "You're the reason for this invasion. For the pesky creatures."

Trin laughed and pointed a finger at the dragonriders. "Oh, no. The Dragon Elite has come to help, along with the House of Fourteen. Currently, everything of yours is being confiscated, including your scientists." She turned, looking at the faces of the employees who had taken orders from Mika Lenna without question. "All of you will go to prison for what you've done to me, to my men, to animals, to who knows who worldwide. It ends today. It ends with you." Trin pointed a metal finger at Mika. "Your death happens first, and then we fix the world you screwed up."

Without warning, the genetically altered werewolf and the cyborg he created raced toward each other, a blur of colors as they were locked on each other, instantly intertangled.

If it wasn't for the flash of metal on Trin or the rippling of Mika's muscles, Sophia wouldn't have known where the machine began and the werewolf ended. They rolled, smashing into the walls, scientists scurrying out of the way to avoid being pummeled by the fight. Many of them chose to go up the open corridors, knowing they would run into cyborgs who would take them prisoner. That was a better fate than being crushed by a werewolf and the thing he'd created.

The two yanked apart, covered in lacerations from what they'd done to each other. Sidestepping, Trin kept her eyes on Mika as he moved stealthily in the opposite direction, both looking for an opportunity to attack.

Sophia recognized the fear in his eyes and realized something. Trin being one of the first cyborgs wasn't a mistake because she was a woman. At that moment, she knew what Mika had done. He, in his greed to be like a god, made his first cyborgs too powerful. According to Trin, it was why many of them didn't survive. She had, and he knew she was more powerful than him.

The maker had met his match.

"I've pictured your death a hundred times," Trin began breathlessly. "I realize now, the quicker the better, because I will replay it a hundred times in my mind before I give it rest. It's best if I don't let you monopolize much more of my life, which will begin again today."

With that, Trin Currante's hands shot off her body on metal rods, extending out and allowing her to reach Mika without getting close.

Her hands, the real one and the metal one, grabbed the sides of Mika Lenna's head and pulled.

The next bit wasn't for Sophia's eyes. She turned away and found her face in Wilder's shoulder as the unnatural sound ripped through the air. She didn't need to know what a man's head disconnecting from his unnatural form looked like. Hearing it was more than enough.

When it was tossed to the ground and rolled to her feet, she did look down, just to know that this time, the man who had created monsters from beautiful people was finally gone.

CHAPTER ONE HUNDRED
FORTY-TWO

Black and blue all over, Trin Currante appeared much more human than Sophia had ever seen her. She was still a cyborg and would be for a bit longer. The skin on her face was cut in several places, long gashes that were oozing blood. Her hair was scorched, and her metal parts were scuffed and chipped. She looked...hopeful.

Standing outside of the Saverus headquarters, Sophia watched as Alicia looked over the files they'd recovered about the cyborg project on her tablet. She remained quiet for a long time, musing.

"This won't be easy," Alicia said matter-of-factly.

Sophia pursed her lips. "It can be done, right?"

Alicia gave her an uncertain expression. "I'll do what I can. I think I can make the cyborgs close to what they once were."

"Close?" Sophia argued, about to throw a fit.

To her surprise, it was Trin who put a hand on her shoulder. "That's good enough for now. You've done all you can. You all have." She looked at the House of Fourteen members taking scientists into custody. The cyborgs were being helped by dragonriders. Everyone had come together to defeat a man the world had already thought defeated. This time, though, things were different. Trin had seen to that.

"I promise," the magitech expert began, "that once I have a cure, or whatever it ends up being, I'll call you to the lab."

Trin nodded. "I'll be the first to take it. Not because I want it, but rather because I was the first to survive. If it's not going to work, I want it to fail on me."

Sophia blinked as emotion started to well up in her. "It will work."

The look on Alicia's face made her think she shouldn't inject false hope. "We will figure something out, regardless," Sophia amended.

Trin nodded. "Things are already better. My men are free from the demon who created them. He can no longer hurt others."

Sophia looked around as Warriors from the House of Fourteen led magicians who had been captured by Mika Lenna and were about to be experimented on back to their families. The House of Fourteen's reputation had been saved tonight. Valuable magicians had been rescued. Animals had been put out of their misery, and many wrong-doers put behind bars. It wasn't healing. That was a long way off, but it was a start, and for Sophia that was good enough.

She put her hand out to Trin and smiled. "Thanks for coming together with me to do this. I look forward to future occasions where we use our skills for justice."

Trin's face worked on smiling, although it was more scars than anything at this point. Finally it formed something that was marked by happiness. "Thank you, Sophia Beaufont, for helping to restore my faith in humanity. It's been a long time coming, and I realize now I wanted it all along, more than revenge. More than a cure. It reminds me that no matter how much of me is a machine, at my core, I'm a human."

CHAPTER ONE HUNDRED FORTY-THREE

"On and off," Sophia said, pointing to the button on the side of the phone she'd given to Evan. They were sitting on the stoop of the Castle, the sun just rising over the Expanse. Breakfast hadn't been served in the dining hall. After everything, she couldn't wait to give the guy who was a total pain in her ass the phone he'd won fair and square in a bet.

"On and off," he repeated, confused, looking at the device like it was a ten-thousand-page codex. "Oh, this will take a while."

She shook her head. "You are going to be the death of me, dude."

"Dude," he mocked her. "I'm a hundred years older than you. Give me a break for not getting your fancy-dancy technology right away."

"It's intuitive," she stated. "You'll pick it up. Wait, what am I saying? This is you. I'll give you nightly lessons. You'll need many. I'm certain of it."

"Ha-ha," he replied with no humor.

"Remember, if Hiker finds you with that, what do you say?" she questioned.

"Sophia bought it for me although I asked her not to," he answered immediately.

SARAH NOFFKE & MICHAEL ANDERLE

"Then you'll wake up with my friend Trin standing over you about to rip your head off like you're Mika Lenna," she told him with pride.

He nodded. "I meant to say, I found it, sir, at that awful Saverus place. Sophia who?"

She nodded. "Much better. Just don't have it out while you're at the Castle, or he will catch you."

A stomping sound behind the Castle door made them straighten. A moment later, none other than Hiker Wallace whipped open the door of the Castle and stood on the threshold.

The two dragonriders stood at once, trying to act natural. Evan put his elbow on Sophia's shoulder, leaning too much of his body weight on her and nearly making her topple over. Sophia found herself whistling.

Hiker's eyes were on the Expanse in the distance but he diverted his gaze to the pair. "What's wrong with you two?"

"Sophia was trying to kiss me," Evan answered quickly.

She pushed him off her. "As if."

"Well, whatever," Hiker said dismissively striding past them. "We're having a hatching."

"A what?" Sophia asked, running to catch up with the large man and his long strides.

"A hatching," he repeated, walking out to where the dragon eggs littered the grassy hills of the Gullington.

When Hiker said there was a hatching, what he meant was hatchings plural.

Sophia's mouth fell open as she took in the sight around the Expanse. Hatching was one word for it, but a great awakening was another. She couldn't believe the sight as hundreds of the dragon eggs broke open, newborn dragons poking their muzzels through their colorful shells and breaking through with their horned tails. They rolled out of their shells in brilliant shades of red, blue, green, yellow, orange, purple, white, and black.

For some reason, on that beautiful summer day, hundreds of the dragon eggs had decided to hatch at once. As they frolicked about, both evil and good dragons, Sophia knew the Gullington was going to change drastically.

They now had a huge population of dragons to care for and to train and hopefully bond to riders. Most importantly, to bring justice to a world that was worth saving.

Yes, some dragons would be evil. Some would be good. Sophia believed the good like Trin Currante and Hiker Wallace, the Dragon Elite, and Liv Beaufont and all the rest of her friends outweighed those who were evil in the world. If she'd learned anything recently, it was that good always conquered evil when forces banded together.

Standing between the leader of the Dragon Elite and her friend, Sophia looked at the Expanse as the new generation of dragons emerged. They would bring many new adventures to this world. More than anything, she hoped they fulfilled their ultimate purpose— to bring love and justice to Earth.

SARAH'S AUTHOR NOTES

MAY 18, 2020

Thank you so much for reading. Your support of the Liv Beaufont series and this one has been life changing. Thank you! Seriously! Thank you.

This was my 64th and 65th book. I should start just counting them as one, but the idea was originally to break the books up later but I don't think we'll be doing that. Anyway, my point in explaining the number is that apparently at this point, I need to do strange things with the chapters to keep things interesting for me.

My boyfriend and I originally bonded over Taylor Swift music, well after I asked him if he knew how to use a fork and told him my last name sounded like a cat throwing up. We chatted on Facebook messenger for the first few months and we'd slip in Taylor lyrics to each of the conversations. That's about the time that he told me that he starts each of his books with a Tay-Tay song title.

For this book, I picked up the challenge, but in true Sarah style, I took it a bit farther. For the first part of the book, I used Taylor song titles to start each of the chapters. That was like 60 titles. At first it was challenging to figure out how to start a chapter with "Death by a Thousand Cuts" or "Cornelia Street." And then after a while, it sort of started the chapters on it own, taking them in a fun new direction.

Although Tay is quite prolific as far as music goes, she doesn't have 130 plus titles, so I had to switch to a different band for part 2. I have an unhealthy obsession with Snow Patrol. I'm a little too proud that the lead singer, Gary Lightbody, called me out at one of their concerts. I was like, "OMG he pointed up to me in the balcony and called me 'blondie.'" Of course, he was turning down my marriage proposal, but that parts not as important. And also, Gary, you didn't even give us a chance! That's fine, I'm over it and still love the band enough that I used their song titles to start each of the chapters in the second part of the book.

Okay, so now I think I've started a tradition—like writing a book isn't hard enough that I've got to challenge myself with this new device of starting chapters. But it's really fun and you all should play along. So I need suggestions of bands I can use for song titles. They have to have a big collection and hopefully the titles aren't too crazy. Actually crazy is probably okay. I can figure out how to start a chapter with "Who Killed Bambi" or "Anarchy in the UK." Alright, so are the Sex Pistols the next band for part 1 of book 7? Rolling Stones? Aerosmith? You tell me. Put it in the review for this book or message me on Facebook or send me a telegram or carrier pigeon. Just send in your suggestions.

Other things I did with this book, is that I included many of my friends as characters. You may have read RE Vance's book, "Death of an Author." Well, when I found out that he hadn't put me in the book and killed me, I was pretty pissed. When Sarah gets pissed, people hear about it—incessantly. So then JL Hendricks and I decided that we'd put each other in our books and kill the character off. Writers are very strange people.

Ramy tried to make good on things with me by putting me as a "gnome-like" character in a short story but that one wasn't picked by the fans. Anyway, Ramy is pretty much the male version of me, I've decided. Between his constant antics and pranks and his obsession with cheese, he's like my spirit animal. So recently, he put me as a ninja in a book and that made me happy—until I learned that he gave me a gnome boyfriend. You just can't let well enough alone, can you

Ramy-Cans (that's my affectionate name for him that he doesn't really know about)?

Anyway, his thoughtful gesture earned him a place in the book as Zac Efron's bodyguard. I found out from the Scotsman that my favorite movie, the Greatest Showman, wasn't really liked by Ramy-Cans, so of course, I had to make his character obsessed with it. And then the bonus of him playing fetch with Lunis and feeding the dragon broccoli was just icing on the cheesecake.

For Jen (JL Hendricks), I wanted to make her a high-powered CEO of an Amazon like company (Hence River Corp). She's brilliant and successful and also a bit short sighted, because no one can be perfect. That wouldn't make for a fun or realistic book. I maybe let Jen down by not killing her, but I really couldn't bring myself to hurt any of my friends, even in a fictional sense.

And then as many of you know, Lee and Cat are based on my friends Crystal and Cat in France. Those chapters write themselves. So there's lots of friends in my book inspired by my real friends. I think it's safe to say that I miss my people after two months of this lockdown. Is this thing over yet?

Oh, the Amazon storyline is a bit of a homage to Doctor Who (Jodie seasons). I watched an episode on the plane to Scotland where the conglomerate is run by robots and humans and I was all over it. Not copying because my storyline is very different, but there's shades of similarities because, well, I'm a Doctor Who fanatic.

I'm pretty much obsessed with most things BBC, hence the reference to Black Books in the stories. Actually, Bernard Black is pretty much the male version of me, I've just decided. Sorry Ramy-Cans. It's just that the Irish man's sense of humor is very similar to my own. Dylan Moran, if you're reading this, can we have lunch...Oh, and do you know Gary Lightbody? He's Irish too and y'all all know each other, right?

Oh, and one last thing about Ramy-Cans. Recently, MA told you all about the virtual office place that he set up for LMBPN. I have a corner office next to Judith Anderle, which is like a dream come true. It's been a lot of fun to pop into the office and briefly chat with friends that are "mingling by the water cooler." But in true Sarah style, I had to take it a bit farther than just socializing. Like why have offices if we aren't going to really use them. David Beers sort of started it by plastering Post-It notes on my office calling asking Tiny Ninja about centaur's private parts. Actually, I unfortunately know more than I'd like about centaurs. I was once on a date with a guy who commissioned a painting of himself as a centaur and then told me that I couldn't be one because I was a girl, when I said I wanted my own painting.

At the restaurant, I all pulled up my phone and did a bunch of research, learning that female centaurs are centaurides. Then we delved into the anatomy of the beasts as he continued to tell me about this life sized painting. I've been known to do things that make no sense simply for the entertainment factor. That's why when this train wreck of a man invited me back to his place to see the painting, I totally jumped on the opportunity. It was the worst thing I'd ever seen and totally worth going back to a potential serial killer's house. In the painting, he had a mullet, a mustache and a hairy chest. When he asked me where he should put it, I pointed to the trash. This is what a bottle of whiskey and $1200 can get you, if you're so inclined. Anyway, talk about derailing the story. My point is, I know about centaurs. They have horse parts, Beers.

My other point is that we have a lot of fun in the virtual office and one day, Elaine Bateman and I decided to deface MA's office. The HR department was out that day, so we plastered his office walls with gnome porn. Really, I just told Elaine to go and make it look like MA had been searching for gnome porn by putting those search results up on one of the screens in his office. They are plastered on the walls of the virtual office. Elaine, who is the funniest person I know, then proceeded to click on the first link. "NOOOO! Just make it look like he's searching!" I yelled having seen images that I couldn't unsee.

We also put lots of lists on MA's walls of things he needed to do or brainstorming stuff. It went like this:

"Story idea: Broke Back Mountain, but with gnomes."

"To Do:

1. Rub oil on body
2. Find a gnome named Aiden
3. ???
4. Profit"

I will admit that I was giddy for MA to walk into his office the next day and see what we'd done. But then I didn't hear from him. There was no revenge attempts on my own office. Just more sticky notes from Beers telling me that I was short—first time I've heard that one. After a few days, I asked MA what he thought of his office and he was like, "You did that? I thought that was Ramy." I was highly offended that I didn't get credit for the awesomeness.

Since then, Beer's walls have been given a feminine touch with Cher and Brittany and Bett Midler stuff. Ramy, of course, has the Greatest Showman posters plastered on his walls. And every day I walk into my office, I suspect that I'll get paid back for my pranks. Apparently most people don't have time for such shenanigans. Priorities people.

Thanks to Paul for the inspiration on the Hiker and Sophia storylines. I really love getting feedback and insights from readers as they read. It's always interesting to see how they think the story is going to go. Sometimes I get to giggle and think...nope, but just you wait. And other times, I'm like, that's a brilliant idea and I'm totally using it. Anyway, Paul constantly offers me awesome input. Thanks awesome reader 12 :)

Sincerely,
Tiny Ninja

MICHAEL'S AUTHOR NOTES
JUNE 1, 2020

So, I am all of these things Tiny Ninja™ says I am, and so much more. Unless I'm not, which is often the case with Sarah.

You blame one person incorrectly and the guilty party stands up and takes umbrage. Damn!

If you ever get a chance to talk with Sarah at an event, do take it. Just member you ARE looking for a really tall halfling so unless you are about five-feet nothing, do remember to look for the tiny ninja in your path. She will absolutely remind you of everything Liv and the Beaufont sisters have ever done or said.

She is, after all, *them*.

Diary of a mad artist - The Creation of a Book Cover
These are the (often) incomplete ramblings about being an indie author and working with other (often) fun authors and the stuff they come up with.

There are many ways to get a cover for one of your books. You can do it yourself (and I have…not hugely successfully, but I have).

You can buy a pre-order and that can be fantastic. For little money (compared to a fully realized -from scratch- cover) you get to see a cover that matches what you want and it excites the little author brain to go into squeals of joy.

And you sit down and start pounding the keyboard, the keys going clickity-clack as the story comes out of you as you work away on a dopamine high all started because of a pre-built cover.

You can see yourself holding the book and a future reality has been created.

Well, until the high wears off.

Then, you print the book cover as inspiration, hoping to draw that first high again into your veins wondering if you will ever feel that way again. And yes, you really can. But possibly not with this first book cover you purchased.

Normally with pre-built covers what is missing is good typography. The fonts selected or the additional flourishes you don't realize are on the book covers you like are not on your book cover.

Somethings is a little wrong, and you don't know why.

Covers are a massive part concept, art direction, colors, point of view, action, genre tropes (an example would be six-pack abs on a romance cover that screams (to those who know) that 'there be open-door sex in this book!' If you put a bare-chested man on a book and put your sex behind closed doors you should expect to see negative reviews.

That's when you realize if you want to help your sales, you don't break the genre tropes with your book covers and should you decide that you want something without tropes, you will be making future sales more difficult.

Not impossible, and perhaps your book cover that is unique will garner an audience, just know that if you go that route, you are picking the much harder way to go up the mountain.

I should know, I've broken those rules as well.

As you do more books, you start to find that certain artists resonate with you and your readership. Fans see the cover art and associate it with your stories and another brand is born. Except, artists also work on other stories for other authors and their style is just that.

Theirs.

When you happen to see another book with a similar look and feel as your own, you know what's going on and while there is practically nothing you can do about it (except hire really expensive models most authors can't touch) you just cross your fingers and give your artists as much business as possible.

Then ~~Ramy~~ "some-author-who-shant-be-named" comes along and happens to like your style and says something like 'make it look like that.' I'm not complaining, I've certainly liked certain styles and wanted to emulate them myself so I'm throwing no stones whatsoever.

I'm merely bringing in ~~Ramy~~ somebody from Sarah's author notes and sharing the fun of working with them. And their sense of humor. And their sense of style. And their love of ... Ok, ok. His cover looked fantastic and I should know. While he might have mentioned something about getting a cover done, it wasn't until I saw it that I realized how close it would look.

And the cover DOES look good.

However, I shall be giving him shit about this for days, at least.

Although, I doubt he will be too worried, we don't speak for days at a time and I'm not even putting this little story in the author notes from one of the collaboration stories we do together. I'm putting this into a book where Sarah was miffed that he-who-shall-not-be-named ~~(Ramy)~~ received the credit for something she instigated.

Now I feel like I've appropriately remedied that situation by providing ~~him~~ Ramy a little harassment to offset the exuberance ~~he~~ Ramy must have felt. Right?

Now are you happy, Sarah?

Or did you want me to fall on my own sword rather than stab ~~Ramy~~ he-who-shall-not-be-named?

Because I'm telling you right now, that isn't happening.

;-)

Michael

ACKNOWLEDGMENTS
SARAH NOFFKE

I feel like I'm on the stage at the Oscars, accepting an award when I write my acknowledgments. I stand there, holding this award, my hands shaking and my words racing around in my mind. I'm not an actress for a reason. I'm a writer and talking to people in "real life" is hard. Not to mention a ton of people all at once.

I picture looking out at the audience and being blinded by spotlights and forgetting every word of the speech I memorized just in case I won. The speech would go like this and it's meant for all of you, not the guild. For the fans. The supporters. The people who are the reason I would ever stand on any stage, ever.

Okay, here we go. I clear my throat and smile, looking up at the camera, holding the little golden man. And then I begin:

This was never supposed to happen. I was never meant to publish a book and then another one. And then another. I was supposed to write in private and live a life that Henry David Thoreau called a life of "quiet desperation." I would always hope to share my books, but never bring myself to do it. And you would never read my words. But then, in a crazed moment of brashness, I did share my books and you all liked them. And because of that, I've never been the same. And here I am feeling grateful all just because…

That's why I'm here. Because of you. Thank you to my first readers. The ones who picked up those books that I didn't even outline and you still liked them. You messaged me and maybe you thought it was no big deal, but when your ego is new to the publishing world, it's a big deal.

I can't thank you readers enough. I've found that reading your reviews helps me to start a chapter when I'm stuck or lazy.

I really need to thank someone who has made this all possible and that's my father. I was going to quit. I can't tell you how many times I quit. But when I wasn't making it, he was the one who told me to not throw in the towel. "Give yourself a timeline," he suggested. If I didn't get to my goal by then, I'd quit. And apparently there was magic in that advice, because I'm still doing this. Dad, you're the pragmatic one, but when you believed in me enough to tell me to not quit, I knew I had to follow your advice.

And I thank all my friends who are constantly supporting me with thoughts of love and encouragement. Most don't read my books. I'm sort of self-deprecating, although I'm working on it and will be the first to tell my friends, "My books probably aren't for you." However, every now and then a friend surprises me and says, "I was up all night reading your books." It's always a total shock. But my point is, that even if they didn't read, I still have the best friends ever. Diane, you're my rock. And I love you, even though you will probably not read this.

Thank you to everyone at LMBPN. Those people are like family to me, although I'm not sure if they'll let me sleep on their couch. Well, who am I kidding? They totally will. Big thanks to Steve, Lynne, Mihaela, Kelly, Jen and the entire team. The JIT members are the best.

Huge thank you to the LMBPN Ladies group on Facebook. Micky, you're the best. And that group keeps me sane.

And a giant thank you to the betas for this series. Juergen you are my first reader and friend. Thanks for all the help. And thanks to Martin and Crystal for being some of the best people I know. What would I do without you? A huge thanks to the ARC team. Seriously, if it weren't for you all I might pass out before release day, wondering if anyone will like the book.

And with all my books, my final thank you goes to my lovely muse, Lydia. Oh sweet darling, I write these books for you, but ironically, I couldn't write them without you. You are my inspiration. My sounding board. And the reason that I want to succeed. I love you.

Thank you all! I'm sorry if I forgot anyone. Blame Michael. For no other reason than just because.

BOOKS BY SARAH NOFFKE

Sarah Noffke writes YA and NA science fiction, fantasy, paranormal and urban fantasy. In addition to being an author, she is a mother, podcaster and professor. Noffke holds a Masters of Management and teaches college business/writing courses. Most of her students have no idea that she toils away her hours crafting fictional characters. www.sarahnoffke.com

Check out other work by Sarah author here.

Ghost Squadron:

Formation #1:
   Kill the bad guys. Save the Galaxy. All in a hard day's work.
   After ten years of wandering the outer rim of the galaxy, Eddie Teach is a man without a purpose. He was one of the toughest pilots in the Federation, but now he's just a regular guy, getting into bar fights and making a difference wherever he can. It's not the same as flying a ship and saving colonies, but it'll have to do.
   That is, until General Lance Reynolds tracks Eddie down and offers him a job. There are bad people out there, plotting terrible

things, killing innocent people, and destroying entire colonies. **Someone has to stop them.**

Eddie, along with the genetically-enhanced combat pilot Julianna Fregin and her trusty E.I. named Pip, must recruit a diverse team of specialists, both human and alien. They'll need to master their new Q-Ship, one of the most powerful strike ships ever constructed. And finally, they'll have to stop a faceless enemy so powerful, it threatens to destroy the entire Federation.

All in a day's work, right?

Experience this exciting military sci-fi saga and the latest addition to the expanded Kurtherian Gambit Universe. If you're a fan of Mass Effect, Firefly, or Star Wars, you'll love this riveting new space opera.

NOTE: If cursing is a problem, then this might not be for you.

Check out the entire series here.

The Precious Galaxy Series:

Corruption #1

A new evil lurks in the darkness.

After an explosion, the crew of a battlecruiser mysteriously disappears.

Bailey and Lewis, complete strangers, find themselves suddenly onboard the damaged ship. Lewis hasn't worked a case in years, not since the final one broke his spirit and his bank account. The last thing Bailey remembers is preparing to take down a fugitive on Onyx Station.

Mysteries are harder to solve when there's no evidence left behind.

Bailey and Lewis don't know how they got onboard *Ricky Bobby* or why. However, they quickly learn that whatever was responsible for the explosion and disappearance of the crew is still on the ship.

Monsters are real and what this one can do changes everything.

The new team bands together to discover what happened and how to fight the monster lurking in the bottom of the battlecruiser.

Will they find the missing crew? Or will the monster end them all?

The Soul Stone Mage Series:

House of Enchanted #1:

The Kingdom of Virgo has lived in peace for thousands of years...until now.

The humans from Terran have always been real assholes to the witches of Virgo. Now a silent war is brewing, and the timing couldn't be worse. Princess Azure will soon be crowned queen of the Kingdom of Virgo.

In the Dark Forest a powerful potion-maker has been murdered.

Charmsgood was the only wizard who could stop a deadly virus plaguing Virgo. He also knew about the devastation the people from Terran had done to the forest.

Azure must protect her people. Mend the Dark Forest. Create alliances with savage beasts. No biggie, right?

But on coronation day everything changes. Princess Azure isn't who she thought she was and that's a big freaking problem.

Welcome to The Revelations of Oriceran. Check out the entire series here.

The Lucidites Series:

Awoken, #1:

Around the world humans are hallucinating after sleepless nights.

In a sterile, underground institute the forecasters keep reporting the same events.

And in the backwoods of Texas, a sixteen-year-old girl is about to be caught up in a fierce, ethereal battle.

Meet Roya Stark. She drowns every night in her dreams, spends her hours reading classic literature to avoid her family's ridicule, and is prone to premonitions—which are becoming more frequent. And now her dreams are filled with strangers offering to reveal what she has always wanted to know: Who is she? That's the question that haunts her, and she's about to find out. But will Roya live to regret learning the truth?

Stunned, #2
Revived, #3

The Reverians Series:

Defects, #1:
In the happy, clean community of Austin Valley, everything appears to be perfect. Seventeen-year-old Em Fuller, however, fears something is askew. Em is one of the new generation of Dream Travelers. For some reason, the gods have not seen fit to gift all of them with their expected special abilities. Em is a Defect—one of the unfortunate Dream Travelers not gifted with a psychic power. Desperate to do whatever it takes to earn her gift, she endures painful daily injections along with commands from her overbearing, loveless father. One of the few bright spots in her life is the return of a friend she had thought dead—but with his return comes the knowledge of a shocking, unforgivable truth. The society Em thought was protecting her has actually been betraying her, but she has no idea how to break away from its authority without hurting everyone she loves.

Rebels, #2
Warriors, #3

Vagabond Circus Series:

Suspended, #1:
When a stranger joins the cast of Vagabond Circus—a circus that is run by Dream Travelers and features real magic—mysterious events start happening. The once orderly grounds of the circus become riddled with hidden threats. And the ringmaster realizes not only are his circus and its magic at risk, but also his very life.

Vagabond Circus caters to the skeptics. Without skeptics, it would close its doors. This is because Vagabond Circus runs for two reasons and only two reasons: first and foremost to provide the lost and lonely Dream Travelers a place to be illustrious. And secondly, to show the nonbelievers that there's still magic in the world. If they believe, then they care, and if they care, then they don't destroy. They stop the small abuse that day-by-day breaks down humanity's spirit. If Vagabond Circus makes one skeptic believe in magic, then they halt the cycle, just a little bit. They allow a little more love into this world. That's Dr. Dave Raydon's mission. And that's why this ringmaster recruits. That's why he directs. That's why he puts on a show that makes people question their beliefs. He wants the world to believe in magic once again.

Paralyzed, #2
Released, #3

Ren Series:

Ren: The Man Behind the Monster, #1:
Born with the power to control minds, hypnotize others, and read thoughts, Ren Lewis, is certain of one thing: God made a mistake. No one should be born with so much power. A monster awoke in him the same year he received his gifts. At ten years old. A prepubescent boy with the ability to control others might merely abuse his powers, but Ren allowed it to corrupt him. And since he can have and do anything he wants, Ren should be happy. However, his journey teaches him that harboring so much power doesn't bring happiness, it steals it. Once this realization sets in, Ren makes up his mind to do the one thing that can bring his tortured soul some peace. He must kill the monster.

Note This book is NA and has strong language, violence and sexual references.

Ren: God's Little Monster, #2
Ren: The Monster Inside the Monster, #3
Ren: The Monster's Adventure, #3.5
Ren: The Monster's Death

Olento Research Series:

Alpha Wolf, #1:

Twelve men went missing.

Six months later they awake from drug-induced stupors to find themselves locked in a lab.

And on the night of a new moon, eleven of those men, possessed by new—and inhuman—powers, break out of their prison and race through the streets of Los Angeles until they disappear one by one into the night.

Olento Research wants its experiments back. Its CEO, Mika Lenna, will tear every city apart until he has his werewolves imprisoned once again. He didn't undertake a huge risk just to lose his would-be assassins.

However, the Lucidite Institute's main mission is to save the world from injustices. Now, it's Adelaide's job to find these mutated men and protect them and society, and fast. Already around the nation, wolflike men are being spotted. Attacks on innocent women are happening. And then, Adelaide realizes what her next step must be: She has to find the alpha wolf first. Only once she's located him can she stop whoever is behind this experiment to create wild beasts out of human beings.

Lone Wolf, #2

Rabid Wolf, #3

Bad Wolf, #4

CONNECT WITH THE AUTHORS

Connect with Sarah and sign up for her email list here:

http://www.sarahnoffke.com/connect/

You can catch her podcast, LA Chicks, here:

http://lachicks.libsyn.com/

Connect with Michael Anderle and sign up for his email list here:

Website: http://lmbpn.com

Email List: http://lmbpn.com/email/

Facebook:
www.facebook.com/TheKurtherianGambitBooks